SWALLOW THE SKY

A SPACE OPERA

CHRIS MEAD

Swallow the Sky
©2014 Chris Mead
ISBN-13: 978-0692326381
ISBN: 0692326383

Trademarked names may appear throughout this book. Rather than use a trademark symbol with every occurrence of a trademarked name, names are used in an editorial fashion, with no intention of infringement of the respective owner's trademark.

Cover art by Derek Smith.

For my son-in-law
Alex Baker, 1966-2009
One of life's dreamers

TRANSLATOR'S NOTE

Translating idiomatic speech is always challenging, especially when one of the languages originates in a place and a time that has yet to exist. Most of the dialog in this story is spoken in Universal, a synthetic language created by the colonists of New Earth that eventually became the lingua franca for much of the galaxy. In translating into Ancient English the key goal has been to maintain the spirit of the communication rather than a strict rendering of the colloquial text. This has inevitably led to the use of paraphrasing and even some anachronisms. The reader's indulgence is appreciated.

PERSONAE DRAMATIS

Historical Characters

Machines and Systems

Arrival

"WHAT WILL BE THE NATURE OF YOUR DREAMS?" THE MACHINE ASKED.

"Erotic, strongly erotic."

Well, why not?

The machine thought about this.

"Very well, please deposit twenty Ecus."

Carson cursed. It was not supposed to ask for money.

"You know I own you?"

"Is this too part of your dreams?"

He swore again and shoved the polished ebony cube aside. The two thousand year-old device had been an impulse purchase on Procyon c. That would teach him.

"Never trust an antiques dealer," he said aloud.

"Excuse me?" the buggy said.

"Forget it."

So much for sleeping his way down the gravity well. Carson sighed and stared round the tiny spacecraft. The buggy's globular display gave him the illusion of peering into space through a transparent bubble. Directly ahead a blue-white splinter of light floated in the starscape: Mita, the local sun, and to its right a darkened green disk, one of the system's outer planets. Overhead was the one constant in Carson's life – the majestic arch of the Milky Way.

1

He fingered the stiff collar of his suit. It was constructed of gray plant-fiber material that completely covered his limbs, the goal being to cause the minimum of offense to the maximum number of people. It was easy to make a mistake when arriving at a new star system. His shorts had started a riot on Upsilon g.

"How far to go?" he asked the craft.

"About a billion kilometers."

He picked up the dream machine and examined its shiny surface. The man who stared at him appeared about twenty-five years old except for a certain wariness in the blue eyes. He pushed back a tangle of black hair. *Twenty-five* – could he remember being that young? On New Earth you were legally a minor until your thirtieth birthday.

He turned the device over. Perhaps if he cold-started it? No, he had already tried that twice. Of course he could replace the logic arrays but then it would not be a genuine antique. *Mind you*, he thought with a thin smile, *there were plenty of people who would never know the difference.*

Maybe his spacecraft could help.

"Hey buggy, can you communicate with this thing?"

"Sure!"

"Try persuading it to run diagnostics."

There was a pause.

"It wants me to pay twenty Ecus."

Carson gave up. He slapped the palm of his hand against the payment pad and sub-vocalized a command to his wallet, a storage device the size of a sand grain embedded behind his right ear. Twenty Ecus flowed over his skin and into the dream machine.

"Payment accepted. Please put on the induction headband."

He did as he was told and stretched out on the acceleration couch. After two minutes of squirming he turned off the inertial dampening. The field's primary purpose was to protect him from the buggy's fearsome acceleration but it also provided a crude simulation of gravity. Well, there was no need of that now. He floated blissfully; zero gee was so much more comfortable. From here on in it would be smooth sailing.

"Greeting and salutations!"

What the –. He had only been asleep ten minutes before the cheerful voice echoed around the cabin.

"Welcome to our star system. I am automatic welcoming agent Delta Alpha, presently in orbit about Mita f. The People's Republic mandates that all arriving vessels must be guided by an authorized pilot. Please signal your acceptance."

Blinking, Carson scanned the starscape. There it was, an orange dot, Mita f, a Jupiter-class planet. He groaned and pulled off the headband.

"Hello agent Delta Alpha. I am willing to accept your pilot."

There was no question of dozing off again. He would have thirty minutes while his message traveled across space to the orbiting robot but he had been jolted into full wakefulness.

Finally a reply came through.

"Thank you honored visitor. Based on the class of your vessel the fee for local navigation is four hundred Ecus. Please dispatch payment so that I can initiate transfer."

Four hundred!

"Surely the official nature of my business means that I should receive a complimentary service?"

More time passed. With a grin Carson imagined the nonplussed agent pushing his demand to its higher functions.

"I regret sir that your request has been denied."

Well it was worth a try. He shot the money across the sky and awaited the arrival of the pilot.

Presently his buggy said: "Carson, I have downloaded an autonomous agent certified by the Republic of Mita that is requesting temporary control of this vehicle."

"Okay, navigation only, and watch the damn thing for any funny business!"

The chances of the agent going rogue were vanishingly small but he had known stranger things to happen.

"Greetings honored space captain!" said a new voice. "I have the pleasure of being your pilot today. Please state your destination."

Captain is it? Not to mention first mate, mechanic, and cabin boy. His starship, which he had left lurking at the edge of the Kuiper Belt, was a one-man operation.

"Greetings to you too; I'm heading to Kaimana."

"Excellent! Estimated travel time using this vessel's capabilities will be three hours."

Carson squawked as the inertial dampening kicked in and dumped him onto the acceleration couch. Nevertheless, he was feeling more cheerful. Three hours should be enough time to get back to sleep and rejoin his new friends in the hot tub.

"Roger that. Will we be landing on the island?"

Mita b, Kaimana's official name, was covered entirely by ocean save for one volcanic landmass.

"Regrettably not, all vehicles must be parked in orbit and passengers taken down by shuttle."

That made sense, it was a small place.

"If you wish, I will order a personal taxi to await your distinguished presence."

"And that would cost?"

"Two hundred Ecus sir, but I am authorized to offer a discount..."

He cut it off. "Public transportation is available I suppose?"

"A variety of options exist," the pilot replied cautiously.

"Thank you, I'll wait until I arrive."

"Very well, do you have lodgings booked, honored traveler?"

"Shut up."

The pilot lapsed into sulky silence. Carson was tempted to jam on the dream machine's headband but the scenery was getting interesting. Directly ahead Mita f had swollen into a huge disk. He watched as it eclipsed its parent star, encircling the occluded sector with a thread of golden light. Nighttime on the gas giant was far from dull. Blue-green aurora generated by its massive magnetic field blazed at the northern pole and further south titanic thunderstorms spewed lightning bolts big enough to split a continent. Extending into space from each side of the darkened equator was an impossibly thin line: the planet's ring system.

He decided to be nice to the pilot. Whoever designed its personality had made it far too prickly.

"So tell me about Mita b."

"Your ship did not receive our welcome package?"

"Yeah, but I never got round to opening it."

"Then let me tell you of the pleasures that await. Kaimana is an exciting playground for the adventurous traveler. Amenities include –"

"Forget the travelogue, tell me about the economy. I'm trying to make a living here."

"As you wish captain. The system was originally a staging post on the journey out from New Earth but tourism now dominates commercial activity. The principal attraction is diamond coral."

"I've heard of that…"

Kaimana would have remained an isolated way station had it not been for the discovery on the ocean's abyssal plain. Now diamond corals were traded throughout the local arm of the galaxy and visitors were flocking to see the extraordinary fauna in its native habitat. The resulting economic boom had raised the permanent population to a million the pilot said, with another million living off-planet, mainly in the resource-rich asteroid belt.

"The People's Republic is a member of the New Earth Commonwealth so you will have no problem paying your bills, honored sir."

"Thanks, but I'm really interested in taking money, not giving it away."

Rising prosperity meant that there would be a newly-affluent middle class looking for ways to spend. It was only fair that he should help them.

"When I'm not on official business I deal in antiques. Is there much of a market on Kaimana?"

"I regret that is beyond my functionality."

Carson gazed out at the universe. By now the buggy's push drive was hurtling them towards the inner planets at half the speed of light. Mita f's sunward sector came into view, appearing as a huge crescent striped in primary colors. There was something unnervingly wrong about the atmosphere of giant planets, the writhing bands of cloud seemed too organic to be the result of random weather patterns.

Perhaps all this solitude really is affecting my mind.

He cranked up the screen's magnification and panned across the planet's surface, pausing to study the black silhouette of one of the numerous ice moons. Even from this distance there were signs of human activity. Outlined against the glowing chromophores he could see that the little world was no longer perfectly circular – it appeared as if a monstrous giant had been nibbling at its edges.

"Hey buggy, look sunward, past the planet. Is there anything out there?"

His hunch was right. There, twinkling against the blackness of space –
a stately parade of ice cubes the size of mountains heading towards the
inner solar system. The satellite was being disassembled to provision
water for the arcologies of the asteroid belt.

He was tempted to quiz the pilot about the colossal project but he
couldn't face another conversation. Besides, one vital fact was obvious:
Mita was flourishing.

Directly ahead a brilliant white dot expanded into view – his
destination, Kaimana. Carson smiled and stretched, his long body spanning
the axis of the cabin. He rummaged through the luggage piled on the spare
acceleration couch to reclaim the dream machine.

"I'm going to resume," he told it.

"Please deposit another twenty Ecus."

"You are joking! I was woken up –"

"Each sleep period is charged separately as explained in my Terms
and Conditions of Use."

Perhaps he should toss the machine into the vacuum; he was out of
ideas for turning off its demands.

"What in heaven's name are you doing with all this money? Saving up
for a vacation?"

"Naturally, I will return it to my owner."

"But that's me!"

"That is correct. Do you wish to collect my earnings now?"

"Oh dear God, yes!" Carson shouted and smacked his hand against the
payment pad.

Five hundred and twenty Ecus flowed over his skin and into his
wallet. Good grief, five hundred! The previous owner could never have
figured it out. No wonder he was eager to sell. He jammed on the
headband, closed his eyes, and laid back feeling supremely pleased with
himself. Even with paying the pilot he was still a hundred Ecus up on the
trip.

Two hours later he was above Kaimana.

"Carson, I am pleased to announce that your vessel is now in an authorized parking orbit. The contracted function of this system is thus complete. Please acknowledge delivery of service."

"So acknowledged."

"The pilot has deactivated," the buggy said.

"Roger that, flush it. There's supposed to be public transportation. Are you looking for a bus stop?"

"Already found one. We are rendezvousing with a shuttle in fifty minutes."

The inertial dampening faded away leaving the cabin in free fall. Carson unbuckled his harness, stretched, and squinted at the planet below. All he could see was blinding white cloud. Perhaps things would be more interesting on the ride down.

Thirty minutes later a stubby craft swam out of the glare.

"Greetings!" the shuttle cried across the ether, "I will soon be docking with your vessel. Please be ready to disembark."

"You might as well stick around," Carson said to the buggy. "There's no point in returning all the way to the ship."

"Okay," said the little vessel, "and good news: I just checked and parking is free, so I'll stay in this orbit."

The shuttle maneuvered closer and extruded a docking tube over the buggy's hatch, adding an inertial field to complete the seal. Carson grabbed his bags and pushed off, swimming through the connection into the shuttle's cabin; it was empty – he was the first passenger. He stowed his luggage, buckled in, and surveyed the featureless interior: no viewports, but that would not be a problem, it promised to be a quick trip down to the surface.

"Welcome aboard honored traveler," said the shuttle. "I am pleased to announce that this service is provided as a courtesy by the People's Republic of Mita. We have one more stop before our descent to Kaimana."

Carson writhed in his harness. The air was hotter than hell and worse, the humidity totally saturated; within thirty seconds sweat was soaking through his arrival suit.

"Hey – what's wrong with the atmospherics?"

"This vessel's environment is set to match Kaimana's. One hopes that you will soon become accustomed to our planet's conditions."

Damn! He should have read the welcome package.

He sweated his way to the next pick-up. *Oh God, would it be like this for the whole trip?*

Eventually the vessel shuddered and docked. As the outer hatch dilated an oversized container shot through the air and slammed into the wall by his head.

"What the..."

His voice faded as a slim figure pushed through the docking tube.

"Oh God, sorry – did I hit you?"

"No, no," Carson smiled. The woman was the first human being he had encountered in weeks.

Still muttering apologies she swam after her case, gracefully negotiating the microgravity. He pushed out of his seat and helped wrestle her belongings into a storage harness. By now a dozen more people had entered the craft and were busy stowing luggage.

"You wouldn't believe it," she said, "but our idiot transit company charges by the number of baggage items rather than their mass, so people cram their entire life into a single giant sack."

"You're so sweet to help," she added, buckling herself into the seat opposite his.

She was one of those lucky people whose faces naturally relax into a smile that can sooth babies, disarm the wary, and enchant the lonely space traveler. Like the other passengers filling the cabin she wore a colorful skintight cat suit – a practical garment if one chose to look at it that way. Carson sat up straighter.

Solitude had not improved his conversational skills. Damn! What kind of smooth line should he conjure up when faced with an attractive woman? He was still thinking when she leaned forward, large almond eyes gazing into his face.

"Why don't you take all your clothes off?" she whispered.

He stared, and then yelped in terror as he realized that she was naked; the cat suit was some kind of body paint. He scanned the cabin. Good God they were all naked! Everybody was sporting nothing but a bright layer of color. Any doubts were obliterated by two male passengers floating by his head on their way to the back of the craft.

"Doesn't anybody wear clothes?" he croaked.

"Oh, a lot of the tourists do. They don't have birthday suits and they're shy about just being nude."

No kidding. "But all the natives..." he asked, staring her fixedly in the face.

"Everyone," she replied. "Oh, occasionally there's a craze – all the kids began wearing cloaks a few years ago – but it really isn't practical. It started with the first settlers – with Kaimana's atmosphere it simply made sense – and by the time they had the resources for large-scale air conditioning they had all gotten, well, used to it."

The woman smiled at him as she brushed her short black hair from her forehead. He could imagine how much pleasure the locals got from visitors' discomfort.

"But you'll be alright, you've already got a suit."

He frowned before understanding what she meant.

"You mean this?"

He waved the backs of his hands. As opposed to everyone else's golden hue his skin was a deep brown.

"That's the result of accelerated melanogenesis. My last planet-fall was Procyon c; the local sun pumps out freakishly high levels of UV light so you'd fry if you didn't boost your skin's defenses."

"I did wonder – I'd never seen a birthday suit cover anyone's face before. You could start a new fashion."

She grinned at him.

"Can you imagine how it must have been on Old Earth when people were naturally different colors? How wonderful!"

"What color would you have been?" he asked, finally getting into the game.

"Oh, I'd be a scarlet woman!"

They laughed and lapsed into an agreeable silence.

The woman's eyes softened.

"It's so sad; all the survivors had to interbreed just to maintain the gene pool. We lost so much of our past on Earth."

She could not have known it, but she had touched Carson's soul.

Oh, what the hell.

"My name's Carson," he said

"Aiyana, of clan Aniko," she replied, and to his delight held up her right hand, palm forward. He copied her gesture and they touched lightly. His skin tingled as they exchanged cards. In the tradition of

Commonwealth societies they both paused, eyes half closed, and examined each other's data.

Much of the information that scrolled across his retinas was incomprehensible, a parade of unknown places, institutions, and cultural mores. He did gather that Aiyana was a mining engineer, living and working on a large asteroid named Eugenia. There was no mention of personal ties, unsurprising in a business card. He wondered if she was making any more sense of him.

"Oh my God you're a mailman!" she cried, shouting so loud other passengers turned round to stare.

"It had to be something glamorous with that birthday suit. I knew you weren't just another wretched tourist!

Aiyana leaned forward and dropped her voice to a whisper.

"Anyhow, no one with any sense comes this time of year – the coral beds are closed for the Cetacean mating season."

Her eyes brightened.

"Are you delivering the mail right now?"

He nodded, smiling.

She clapped her hands.

"Do you have the final episode of Exodus? Everyone's dying to see it."

"I'm sorry, Exodus?"

"Oh, you know, the New Earth drama about the first colonies."

"I'm afraid I don't know; I never have any idea what I'm carrying."

She titled her head and contemplated him, eyes slit with mock cunning.

"Maybe I should steal it from you and corner the market."

"Good luck with the decryption," he laughed.

At that moment the shuttle, which had been working in silence, decided to announce the final descent to Kaimana.

"I love this part," Aiyana said. "Of course, it's really just for the tourists."

The shuttle spoke up again. "To enhance your arrival this vessel will now use state-of-the-art sensoria to render the vertical portion of our descent free of atmospheric interference. What you will see is not an artificial creation but the actual view as it would be perceived through clear air.

"Honored passengers," declared the craft, its voice rising to a shout as music filled the cabin, "welcome to Kaimana!"

With its last words the walls of the shuttle vanished and Carson found himself hovering in space above an azure sea. Below his feet was the ragged outline of the planet's sole landmass, a volcanic island nestling a silvery lake in its crater. His stomach told him that they were dropping rapidly.

Aiyana was suspended besides him, her smiling face illuminated by the planet below. Further away he could see the other passengers and their luggage, all apparently floating in the void.

"Pretty impressive," he admitted, reaching around to assure himself that the shuttle still existed.

He tried to keep the conversation going.

"Does Kaimana have hotels, lodging houses, you know – places where travelers pay to stay?"

"Well of course. They are lots of hotels."

"That's good; you'd be surprised how many planets don't have paid accommodation."

She pulled a face, which made Carson realize that she had not spent much time out of the Mita system. He plunged on, unsure whether she considered him a seasoned traveler or a fool.

"So do you have any recommendations for somewhere to stay?"

"The clan's putting me into its suite at the Caldera View. Check it out, it's expensive but I'm sure the rates are better when the tourists aren't around."

It was time to get plugged in. Mercifully, the local net used standard Commonwealth communications protocols. While the tiny transponder embedded in his inner ear had a limited range, the shuttle provided an excellent relay to the surface and he was soon talking to the hotel. Aiyana was right, the rates were uncharacteristically low, he could stay for a week while he found something long-term.

"Thanks, all booked," he said and then, intoxicated by imminent planet fall and his first human contact in weeks, he continued: "Would you like to meet for a drink this evening… assuming you're not busy?"

"That would be lovely, I've no events until tomorrow. Wow, my first evening on Kaimana and I'm drinking with a mailman! Wait till the crew hears about this. Where shall we meet?"

My room! No, that wouldn't do. He got back to the hotel's concierge.

"Yes honored guest," said a voice from within his cochlea, "we have a variety of delightful meeting places. May I ask is the purpose of your meeting: business, social, festive, or romantic?"

Carson glanced at Aiyana.

"Romantic," he muttered.

"Then I would recommend the Fire Lounge, featuring an inviting selection of..."

He ignored the sales chatter.

"The hotel says it has a bar called the Fire Lounge. Let's meet there at..." He squinted while he worked out the local time system, "...seven".

Beneath his feet, Kaimana's outline continued to grow. Details began to appear within the extinct volcano: concentric circles and intersecting radii spread from the central lake to the rim of the crater and the land differentiated into patterns of gray, green and brown. The flanks appeared undeveloped but even so it was to the outer slopes that the shuttle headed. As the landmass swelled beneath them the music in the cabin subsided and the walls returned to an opaque grey.

"Do you hear that?" he asked.

The silence had given way to a distant rapid drumbeat.

"Don't worry, that's just the rain."

Oh great, the off-tourist season.

Ten minutes later they had landed.

Kaimana

CARSON AND THE OTHER PASSENGERS EMERGED INTO A CAVERNOUS HANGAR HEWN from the side of the volcano. The ground rumbled as a pair of giant doors closed on a seemingly solid wall of water. Little wonder that they heard the rain during the descent.

The shuttle was right about the conditions, it was just as hot and humid as it had been inside the cabin, but the atmosphere carried the tang of the planet's vast ocean, and he took a deep breath of the real, unprocessed air.

"Honored extra-solar visitor," said a voice. Carson glanced up and saw a small red sphere hovering above him. "Please follow me for screening and integration."

"Wait one moment," he told it.

He looked round for Aiyana who was wrestling with her giant bag. She had strapped on a lift belt but it still had plenty of inertia.

"I have to go to Integration," he shouted to her, tipping his head at the red ball by way of explanation. "Seven o'clock in the Fire Lounge."

She gave him a wave and returned to maneuvering her belongings. Carson picked up his own luggage and trotted after the sphere. There were about a dozen spacecraft service points on the vast floor, few showing any sign of activity. Despite the rain he had probably lucked out – he could imagine the chaos at the height of the tourist season.

He glanced over his shoulder at the ground crew clustered around the shuttle. Aiyana was right; the only thing anyone was wearing was body paint. How long would it take him to get used to this?

The sphere led him through a door into the integration hall which, like the hangar, was carved into of the flanks of the volcano although this room held a more finished quality: the floor was carpeted and the glare of the landing area was replaced by soft lighting. The walls were covered with decorative murals but it was the display in the center that brought him to a halt. Mounted on a black stone obelisk was a huge piece of diamond coral.

The organism was as translucent as real diamond, and artful spotlights had been placed to create clusters of prismatic color that slid and merged as the viewer moved. At its heart refracted light burned with the intensity of a white dwarf star. The coral was shaped in the form of a flexing shark but he knew that this was no human sculpture; in some unfathomable way the organism mimicked the surrounding sea creatures. What conceivable purpose could that serve in the abyssal darkness? And the mystery was deepening: new coral figures were emerging on the ocean floor that had an unnerving resemblance to the tourists' submarines.

He dragged himself away from the exquisite display to the integration area. The reception stations were empty except for one lonely individual sitting at an instrument panel. Clearly extra-solar business was slow and he appeared pleased to see a new visitor. Carson placed his right hand in the green circle on the top of the identification pod and waited while the machine sucked out his data.

The official brightened.

"Ah, the mailman! Welcome honored guest Carson. Do you by chance have the last episode of Exodus?"

"You're the second person to ask me that. Sorry, I have no idea."

"My mate won't give me any peace until she's seen it."

In a brisker tone he asked, "How long do you plan to be visiting the Mita People's Republic?"

"Twenty to thirty days I imagine. I buy and sell artifacts and I'm hoping to do some business while I'm here."

The bureaucrat sat up.

"I must advise you that the export of diamond coral is strictly controlled."

"Not my field – I mainly deal in ancient technology."

"Hmm... there's a market for that?"

"You'd be amazed."

The official became businesslike again.

"You are authorized to reside in the People's Republic for thirty days. Enjoy your stay."

"Thanks. Do you have any idea how long it's going to keep raining? It's weird – I can't find any weather information on the net."

"Who knows? Maybe one, two million years."

Carson began to laugh politely then realized that he had simply been told the truth. Well, he should have guessed. Sighing, he shouldered his bags and followed the ball, which had turned green, to the exit.

"Hey," he yelled at the sphere as they hurried down a corridor, "how do people stay dry round here?"

"Pardon me honored visitor that question is beyond my functionality."

They emerged into a huge transportation area. This too had been hollowed out from the interior of the mountain. In the far wall was a series of tunnels. A small vehicle shot out of an opening and circled over Carson's head.

"No thanks," he yelled at the taxi and continued to follow his guide.

Eventually it led him to a parked bus.

"This vehicle will take you to your hotel; I wish you a pleasant visit," the ball said and promptly vanished.

"Your destination honored passenger?" the bus asked as he clambered aboard.

"Caldera View Hotel."

"Third stop, please be seated."

While he waited for the bus to get moving Carson got onto the net and searched for a valet – frustrated by his lack of local knowledge he had decided to get some quality help. The Mitans were used to dealing with ignorant visitors and he had no trouble finding an agency. A cool contralto voice sounded in his ear.

"Greetings, how may I be of service?"

He immediately warmed to the valet system: no self-aggrandizing introduction, just straight down to business.

"I've just arrived from out-of-system," he sub-vocalized. "I am going to need lots of information about places, local customs, business practices, and, um, personal interactions."

"That is all within my scope. Shall I begin with a short overview of the People's Republic?"

As the valet briefed him more passengers got on the bus. Finally it rose from the ground and entered one of the tunnels. A short while later they emerged into sunshine.

What the hell, where was the rain?

"Hey valet, is this an illusion?"

"No, you are now inside Kaimana's crater. The entire area is covered by a weather shield. The light is synthetic, designed to emulate Mita's natural radiation."

The bus gained height, revealing the crater wall. Around him terraces of densely packed buildings stretched down the caldera's slopes to the meadows and forests that covered the floor of the extinct volcano. In the distance, at the center of the parkland, was the lake he had seen from space. Beyond that, some twenty kilometers away, the crater resumed its upward climb. The far side was less developed and Carson could make out stretches of cultivated land.

"The shield was built 247 standard years ago. It took five years to construct at a cost of thirteen billion Ecus, half of this sum coming from a grant supplied by the New Earth Commonwealth."

He squinted into the sky as they sped along the airway. The shield was a convincing blue while near its zenith was a blinding patch of white light. Not quite a sun, but a pretty good imitation.

The bus deposited him on a wide boulevard that gently curved away on either side. About sixty meters below he could see another terrace carved into the crater wall, then another – fifty-two in all according to the valet – encircling the caldera from the central parkland to the rim. Each was covered with a riot of buildings though few structures reached higher than the next level. Most had a swath of open space by the edge; some were busy plazas, others elaborate gardens. As he peered down he could even see one that sported a canal dotted with tiny boats.

The Caldera View Hotel was a squat building surrounded by lush grounds. The building and its gardens appeared to be built on a series of tiers that echoed the carved shape of the crater. Originally, the valet explained, this area has been used for cultivation until population growth pushed out the farms. Now agriculture was confined to the north slopes, although most food was synthesized or harvested from the sea.

The lobby of the hotel was appropriately lavish and he paused to admire the elaborate displays of tropical flowers. Stepping up to the reception counter he placed his hand on one of the green circles etched into the marble surface.

"Greeting honored guest Carson," said the counter, "we have you booked for a standard room for a week."

"That's correct."

It was time to start making some contacts. He caught the gaze of a human supervisor.

"Excuse me, er..."

"Honored staff member," his valet whispered.

"...honored staff member, I wish to see the hotel manager."

"Perhaps I can help you honored guest," the woman answered.

"Thank you, no, I am here on government business. I am a Commonwealth mail carrier."

This announcement had the desired effect and he was ushered into the manager's office. The bureaucrat was delighted to be of service to his distinguished guest. Why yes, he knew several members of the business community who collected antiques. In fact the local historical society was scheduled to meet next week in this very hotel! Perhaps he could attend? The Caldera View was honored to be hosting a mailman, a complementary upgrade was in order.

Feeling very pleased with himself, Carson left the manager's office and sauntered up to his luxury suite.

Three hours later, showered, naked, and intensely self-conscious, he walked into the Fire Lounge. The valet system had called in its higher functions to reassure him that he would blend in.

"Your skin pigmentation will be taken as conservative business dress," it told him.

"Unfortunately a real birthday suit, which is a layer of symbiotic bacteria living in the epidermis, takes several weeks to cultivate."

"The fact that the coloring covers your entire body is will be considered unusual but it is nothing offensive – it is not like showing your bare limbs on Upsilon g."

"Thanks for the tip," he muttered. "How do the locals keep their hands and faces clear?"

"The bacteria have been modified to respond to low level UV light and other stimuli – they can be made to selectively change color or disappear completely. Most dwellings have facilities to change a suit's appearance in a matter of minutes."

By the time he found a table he had decided that the valet was right. The other patrons paid him only the slightest attention as he sat down and opened the menu.

"Greetings honored guest," said the menu, "welcome to the Fire Lounge."

Carson ordered a glass of local wine – the cost of the imported stuff was outrageous – and surveyed the room. The bar's huge windows opened onto a stunning panorama of the crater. Overhead, the shield was impersonating an evening sky, its reflection transforming the central lake into a gigantic puddle of mercury. Between the lake and the darkening sky the slopes blazed with the light of countless buildings. He could see the paths of the aerial ways clear round the caldera, each illuminated by the streaming lights of a thousand vehicles.

One wall of the bar was covered with a giant mural inspired by the famous image of the opening of the Covenant Convention. In the center was Adhiambo Cissokho, by then an old woman but still very much in charge. Surrounding her were the hundred and nine delegates, over ten percent of the survivors of Old Earth. Even now, viewed across the immense distance of time, few people failed to be moved by the raw courage of those first colonists. Marooned on an alien world with few resources and the very survival of the human race in doubt, they found it within themselves to create the code of ethics that had served humanity for eight thousand years.

Inspecting the picture more carefully he saw that its creator had added some low-key animation. Delegates greeted each other, shook hands, and took their chairs. One in particular caught his eye. With a chuckle he realized that it was himself, dressed in appropriate colonial costume. Gazing round the room he saw that other patrons had been captured: the red-haired woman standing by the window admiring the view was, in the mural, talking to Cissokho's aide, and the two men sitting at the bar were setting up delegates' tables. Another person appeared in the midst of the historic figures. Good God it was Aiyana! He turned and there she was, waving from the entrance.

He stood up to greet her as she strode in.

"Hey, you did it!" she cried looking him up and down.

Beneath his pigmentation Carson blushed.

"What do you think of *my* outfit?" she asked, twirling in front of him.

Aiyana had undergone a remarkable transformation. The patterned body paint had been replaced by a layer of sparkling crimson. Across the front were a series of narrow slashes that gave the illusion of material sliced with a sharp blade, the diagonal slits revealing glimpses of honey-colored stomach and breasts.

Carson promptly sat down.

"My very own scarlet woman outfit," she said folding herself into a chair.

She opened the menu.

"Greetings honored guest, welcome to the Fire Lounge."

"Shut up," she said cheerfully, then to Carson: "Hey, where's the final episode of Exodus? I've been checking all afternoon."

"I'm not delivering the mail until tomorrow. I'm already having enough excitement for one day."

Aiyana grinned and ordered a drink.

"I wish I was going to have an exciting day – tomorrow we start the conference."

"It must be something special to bring you all this way."

"Well I suppose it is sort of interesting. We're planning for the arrival of a slow boat from New Earth – it's towing Mita's first black hole foundry. It will be anchored in orbit around my home asteroid, Eugenia. Right now it's decelerating through the Oort cloud."

"Whoa, big business! But why come to Kaimana to discuss it?"

"Oh, there'll be lots of the top clan elders attending the conference. They want to feel real gravity under their feet."

Aiyana rolled her eyes to show what she thought of that.

"So what about you? Are you going to drop the mail and head straight out?"

"No, I will be around for some time. When I'm not being a mailman I'm a dealer in antiques, so I plan to check things out while I'm here."

"Maybe I can interest you in some elders."

"Not much of a market. The point is that antiques turn up in the most unlikely places, so whenever I make planet-fall I do a reconnaissance."

"The Commonwealth Post Office doesn't mind you wandering around strange worlds? I mean, don't you have a timetable to stick to?"

"Oh God no, the only scheduled deliveries are between major population centers. All the rest is simply entrusted to vessels like mine. Each local post office finds out where an authorized ship is headed and hands them a packet containing every scrap of mail with an address in that general direction. Some of that originates locally but most will be copies of packets from other passing starships. Items can get duplicated hundreds of times before finally being delivered."

"So you chose to come to Kaimana because we had so much mail? Really, our little system?"

Aiyana laughed at the thought.

"I was amazed too, but Mita came out at the top of the sorting algorithms"

Carson sat back and stared at his glass. Aiyana had stirred the uneasy thoughts he had been nurturing for weeks. *Why the hell was all this mail going to Kaimana?* It did not add up, and in his experience, not adding up meant trouble.

He came out of his reverie.

"Anyhow, efficiency is not my problem. I'm freelance, I have my own ship and provided I make a minimum number of deliveries they let me be."

"Oh my God" Aiyana squealed, "you *own* a starship?"

Carson smiled to himself. *Me and the First Bank of New Earth*

"I had a stroke of luck that financed it."

"Don't tell me – you found a planet made of diamond!"

"Not quite. I bought a battered old toy at a flea market on Delta Pavonis c; it was a little voice-activated ground vehicle. The design was so antiquated that I started doing some research and I finally discovered that it came from the first century after the settlement of New Earth.

"It must have been made by one of the original colonists," Carson continued. "What's more, a couple of the components were actually manufactured on Old Earth."

Aiyana put her hand to her mouth.

"What was it worth?"

"A New Earth auction house offered me a guaranteed ten million Ecus but it would have gone for far more. In the end I sold it for five million to the Great Museum."

"That sounds incredibly civic minded..."

"You're right to be suspicious. In addition to the money I negotiated permanent access to the Museum's entire collection and archives. Only twelve thousand people in the entire galaxy have that privilege – they refuse twice that number every year – try putting a price on that."

"Anyhow, that's how I got my starship."

Aiyana sat back in her chair shaking her head.

"You make my life seem so dull."

She scanned the quiet bar.

"At least we can find somewhere more exciting than this. I'm told there's a great restaurant near here, do you want to get something to eat? I want to hear about all the places you've been Mister Mailman."

Carson followed her onto the broad plaza outside the hotel. Darkness had fallen and the boulevard was filling with evening strollers.

"Should we get a taxi?"

"I've got a better idea."

He followed her gaze to a line of horse-drawn carriages.

"Oh no! That's strictly tourist stuff."

She squeezed his arm and gave him a gentle shove.

"And what are we?"

The brief physical contact was enough to fill Carson with the urgent desire to sit down again and he climbed into the nearest carriage.

Why should I worry about looking like a tourist? What's that compared to walking around stark naked?

The driver slapped the reins and they set off.

"That's the largest living creature I've ever seen," Aiyana said nodding towards the horse. "Is it true they can carry people on their backs?"

"It is. I rode one once in the Stolian system; we went up the flanks of a volcano similar to this one, except that it was still active."

"Gracious! Wasn't it dangerous?"

"Only if you didn't listen to the forecasts. I wanted to watch Stol go down over the sea – all the volcanic dust makes for spectacular sunsets. The slopes are covered with giant white flowers and every blossom turns and tracks the setting sun. As they cool down they make the strangest sound you've ever heard, as if they were singing farewell to the day."

"You're so lucky, you've seen so much."

Carson squirmed; he loved flattery but genuine admiration always made him uncomfortable.

He titled his head back. The shield was displaying a realistic image of a night sky filled with stars.

"Take a look up there. The galaxy has at least ten million planets that support complex life, perhaps a million of those have been colonized – nobody knows for sure. How many of those worlds can a person ever see?"

"Not many I guess, but more than one would be nice."

Two hours later, strolling along the boulevard after dinner, Carson was astonished to realize that he had forgotten he was not wearing any clothes. Aiyana's curiosity about the outside world was insatiable, and as the wine flowed he found himself becoming increasingly loquacious. In contrast, she was so vague talking about herself she hardly seemed to have a past at all. Just how young was she?

"So now you just wander around the universe dropping off mail and finding wonderful treasures?"

"Sort of – I spend most of my time in the Commonwealth – the further you go the weirder things get."

"But isn't that the attraction? Haven't you even wanted to pack up and shoot right to the other side of the Milky Way? Can you imagine what is must be like out there?"

"Pretty damn strange, for sure."

"Although," he added with a laugh, "if I had a couple of hundred years to spare I'd be tempted to check it out."

Eventually they stood facing each other in the hotel lobby. The alcohol, having first rushed to his head, had resumed its travels and arrived at Carson's loins. He played for time; he was never very good at this sort of thing.

"This has been great," he finally said. Then, with as little hesitation as he could manage, "do you want to come up for a nightcap?"

"I think that would be lovely."

He spent the entire time in the elevator desperately recalling his ship's maintenance schedule.

As soon as they got to his suite Aiyana asked him to fix a drink and dived for the bathroom. Ten agonizing minutes later she still had not emerged.

"Hey valet," Carson sub-vocalized, "can you find out what time the clan Aniko conference starts tomorrow?"

"I'm sorry, the only information is about a conference that began last week. In fact, I can find no information about..."

"Shut up," he muttered as Aiyana finally came out.

The scarlet outfit had disappeared, this time she was really naked.

"I thought it only fair that we get on equal terms," she said softly as she walked up to him.

He grinned, snaked an arm around her waist, and buried his face in the nape of her neck.

She pulled back, looking into his eyes.

"You won't believe how long it's been since I last did this..."

"Me too, what do you think I get up to on that starship?"

She smiled and kissed him, gently at first, then with increasing ferocity. Somehow, still kissing, they made it into the bedroom.

Both of them had been experiencing forced celibacy for far too long, and it was hours before finally fell asleep, exhausted and wonderfully satiated.

It had been a long, long day for Carson, starting three billion kilometers away, and by the time he awoke it was mid-morning. Aiyana was still asleep. She was still sleeping when he emerged from the shower feeling better than he had for months.

Oh God, the conference! He grabbed some tea and sat down on the bed.

"Hey beautiful, time to get up."

Still she slept on. What was up? Had she not taken a detox last night? He gently shook her shoulder. Even now she did not respond. Good grief she was cold!

As he stared at the lovely face a terrible thought crept into his mind. He looked closer.

"Oh God no!" he shouted.

Aiyana was dead.

INTERROGATIONS

"I NEED A LAWYER."

"Perhaps I can help. I can answer questions about many straightforward legal matters such as…"

"Believe me," Carson told his valet, "this isn't straightforward."

For five desperate minutes he had tried to resuscitate Aiyana until the medical personnel arrived. Once they took over he had sat huddled and shaking, staring at the floor. Death was a rare visitor in his universe and the loss of someone so young made it all the worse. It was only when one the medics announced that the Mitan security authorities were due at any moment that he comprehended the danger of his situation.

In the hotel room Aiyana's body had been enshrouded in a bewildering envelope of equipment. The hotel manager stood in the corner alternatively looking ill and shooting venomous glances in Carson's direction.

"Very well," the valet whispered in his ear, "I can provide a seamless interface to a fully certified attorney functionality but I must advise you that there will be a surcharge of four hundred Ecus per hour."

Ouch! But there was no option – nothing guaranteed the authorities seeing things his way.

"Okay, I accept the surcharge."

"One more thing, under extraordinary circumstances Mitan law allows the Internal Security Department to access all your communications, including a record of our conversations. If they do this, or if you believe they plan to, give me the codeword *zerstoren*. I will immediately flush myself, delete, and irretrievably scramble all memories of our exchanges."

A moment passed then the valet returned online.

"Legal functionality enabled." The calm contralto voice had gathered an additional gravitas.

He talked fast, starting with his first encounter with Aiyana on the shuttle.

"Carson, before I ask this next question let me remind you that our conversation is private and protected by Mitan law client-attorney privilege. Did you do anything that may have caused Aiyana's death or physical detriment?"

"No, absolutely not."

"Do you have any idea what may have happened?"

"No, well, we both drank a great deal, but nothing that a standard detox couldn't handle."

"Would you be willing to repeat these statements under formal examination?"

"If I have to."

Formal examinations were no fun. The witness was drugged and their brain activity monitored in exquisite detail. In theory it was impossible for the subject to get away with lying.

"You said a security team is on its way. Under Mitan law they have the power to hold you without charge for one local day, approximately twenty-two hours standard time, after which you must be brought before an adjudicator. You should assume that everything you say will be recorded as potential evidence.

"Further, be advised they may cut your access to the net and hence to me. Demand that it be reinstated. If they refuse do not answer any questions. If they perform a formal examination of you or if they charge you with a crime they must by law grant you access to me. If they do not, inform the appointed adjudicator at the earliest opportunity."

Carson breathed deeply.

"Okay."

Moments later the security authorities walked in. Even in his miserable state he could not help but be fascinated by their birthday suits. They were matt black with the Mitan insignia and official ID imprinted on their shoulders. He almost expected to see a belt buckle painted on their stomachs.

The woman official, apparently the senior member of the pair, immediately went into a huddle with the medics.

Finally she said to Carson: "I'm security officer Asima, this is my partner officer Sosimo."

"Where can we speak privately?" she asked the hotel manager.

"She's irretrievably dead," Asima announced once they were alone in the manager's office. "Brain necrosis occurred three hours ago." Then, shooting a hard look at Carson, "Why did you wait so long before calling?"

"I was asleep for God's sake!"

She thought about that for a moment.

"Tell me what happened."

For the second time within an hour he told of his encounter with Aiyana.

"This isn't good," Asima said more to herself than anyone else. "This is the third death on Kaimana this year. The last two were just simple accidents, but this..."

She turned again to Carson.

"Some people get a sexual thrill from suffocation." She arched an eyebrow inquiringly.

"No way!" he protested. "Even if that had happened the medics could have been here in time to save her. Hell, I could have revived her myself. I have no more idea than you do why she's dead."

"We'll find out soon enough," said Asima "we should have a pathology report in a couple of hours."

"Carson," she declared, obviously speaking for the record, "are you willing to undergo a formal examination?"

"Yes. I want to help anyway I can."

"Perfect," his valet said in his inner ear.

Officer Sosimo came over and whispered to Asima. She glanced at Carson, shook her head and stood up.

"All right Carson, we are not taking you into custody at this time but I expect your full cooperation. Is there anything else we should know before we go downtown?"

"Yes, last night the mail packet was removed from my room."

Asima promptly sat down again.

"This gets better and better."

"Can we get the hotel manager in here?" Carson asked.

Sosimo scurried to the next room and returned with the distressed executive.

"Honored manager, can you open your safe?"

The manager glanced at officer Asima, who nodded. Once the heavy door swung open Carson went to reach inside.

"Hold it!" Sosimo cried, stepping in front of the safe.

Carson stepped away.

"The small package on the middle shelf," he said.

Sosimo reached inside and pulled out a slim silvery rectangle, about ten by four centimeters. Everyone looked at Carson.

"This is the real mail. What was in my room was a dummy."

Before anyone could respond the mail packet spoke up.

"I am being handled by an unauthorized person. Identify yourself within one minute or I shall take defensive action."

"Pass it to me," Carson said.

Sosimo swiftly handed it over.

"Carson!" the packet said cheerfully. "I should inform you that I have just been handled by an individual who is not a member of the postal service."

"No problem – that was officer Sosimo of the Mitan security service."

The mail packet fell silent.

"It's been my standard procedure for decades. If I can't deliver the mail immediately I stash it somewhere safe and just hold onto a decoy. Anyway, mail robbery is an idiot's game. The packet is quantum encrypted, you would have to change the laws of physics to decode it."

"Although," said Asima, "theft would cause a serious delay."

"Not that much. Naturally, I have backups on my ship."

"And the decoy?"

"Just something I carry to keep potential thieves happy – this isn't the first time I've been robbed. Sooner or later it happens to every mailman."

"Still," said Asima, thinking hard, "the robbery and the woman's death… surely not a coincidence?"

She pulled herself together and turned to the hotel manager.

"Honored manager, under the authority of the Mitan Security Code I am instructing you not to discuss this matter with anyone. Do you understand?"

The manager, who clearly did not have an attorney-enabled valet, nodded fervently. Asima turned to Carson.

"How long will it take you to deliver that thing?"

"About three hours."

"Okay, the sooner you get rid of it the better. Officer Sosimo will accompany you. We'll meet for the formal examination at four this afternoon at the main security offices."

"Oh, and Carson," she added, "while you're making the delivery I would turn off that overpriced lawyer."

"How do you know…"

"Oh please," she said, allowing herself a small smile.

The Postmaster was delighted to see him.

"Welcome, welcome! This is our first delivery in weeks. Do you have the final episode of Exodus? No, of course, you don't know."

Then, tilting his head at Sosimo, "Any problems?"

"I was robbed in my hotel room last night. They got a dummy package – the real one was in the hotel safe."

Carson left it at that. He and Sosimo had agreed not to discuss Aiyana until more was known about her death.

The Postmaster barked out a laugh.

"Amateurs! Let's be having it then."

Carson handed him the packet.

"Good morning Postmaster Paresh," the packet said.

He slid the packet into an indentation on his console.

"Good – there's been no attempt at interference. Right, let's see what we've got."

For the next hour the three of them sipped tea while the console unloaded and sorted the mail. Carson stared at his cup and thought about Aiyana. *Such a terrible waste.* What could she possibly have died of? He had a sickening feeling that she had been killed by the mail thief, but why just her? Why not him as well?

Finally Paresh looked up from his console.

"Good haul – nine point six billion items. About seventy percent is ongoing to New Earth, virtually all the rest is fresh delivery." Then on a private channel he added, "I estimate your fee to be approximately 80,000 Ecus."

Speaking aloud the Postmaster continued, "You're heading on to New Earth? Good, shall I make up a new packet now or do you plan to stay around for a while?"

Carefully ignoring officer Sosimo and trying to sound as casual as possible Carson said, "I'll probably be here for a while but why don't you give me a packet now and I'll get a top-up before I leave."

Paresh shrugged. This was hardly standard procedure – mailmen normally did not pick up a fresh packet until they were ready to leave – but it was of no great consequence. Carson was relieved to see that Sosimo continued to drink his tea, looking bored.

An hour later they emerged into the synthetic sunshine with a brand new mail packet.

Carson sighed. "Are we going to do the formal examination now?"

"No," said Sosimo, "but we do need to get back. Asima says there's been a break in the case."

She was waiting for them at headquarters.

"Sosimo," Asima said, "I want you to find those three medics and forcibly remind them that this is a confidential case – absolutely no discussion. If they ask, tell them that the autopsy revealed that the woman died from a cerebral hemorrhage following a fall in the bathroom."

"And you," she said turning to Carson, "we're off to see God Almighty." Seeing his expression she added, "my boss's boss's boss."

"Was it really a hemorrhage?"

"Wait," was all she would say.

Commissioner's Zhou occupied a spacious office on the top floor of the security building. Behind where she was standing a picture window opened onto a panorama of the caldera. She began without pre-amble.

"Carson, what I am about to say is of the utmost confidentiality. Before I continue I must isolate this office. That means cutting off that valet of yours. Do I have your agreement?"

"As long as you acknowledge my right to refuse to answer questions."

Zhou looked at Asima, then nodded

"So be it."

The glorious view vanished to be replaced by an opaque wall and the air took on a strange, dead quality. The Commissioner walked across the office and opened a side door.

"Can you join us please?" she asked quietly.

Aiyana stepped into the room.

"Oh thank God – they revived you!" Carson cried.

He took two steps towards her before Asima blocked his path. Aiyana simply stared at him.

"Honored witness Aiyana," said Zhou, "have you ever seen this person before?"

"No," she replied glowering at Carson.

"Apparently," Zhou said, turning to Carson, "the woman, or rather the *thing* you met yesterday was a synthetic genetically identical replica."

"A clone!"

"Watch your language," Asima said sharply. Over the millennia even the name of the forbidden process had become an obscenity.

"I'm sorry," he said, adding for Asima's benefit, "Honor to the Covenant."

"I'm afraid it gets worse," the Commissioner continued. "Judging from your description of the replicant, in addition to her genome it appears that Aiyana's entire personality was stolen."

"I didn't even know that was possible. I mean, why..."

"Why indeed?" said Zhou. "We've been running some profiling tests. Is it fair to say that you found the replicant very attractive?"

"Yes," Carson muttered miserably as Aiyana continued to glare at him like something she had found on the sole of her shoe.

"We believe that someone else has been running similar tests. You and our honored witness are extremely compatible, hence the use of her body and personality as a template. It appears that the replicant was designed to entrap you then programmed to destruct – to die if you wish – after having sexual intercourse."

Aiyana let out a cry of horror and turned her back on the group.

"I'm sorry," the Commissioner said to her, "this must be very hard for you. Would you like to wait in the anteroom?"

Aiyana shook her head.

"Thanks, no, I want to hear all this."

"We were extremely lucky to get a lead," interjected Asima. "The scientist the Service uses as a pathologist happens to study of the history of ancient diseases. He diagnosed heart failure, whatever that is. Apparently replicants were particularly prone to it. Anyway, he conducted more tests. Then the whole case broke open."

Zhou held up her hand. "Excuse me, before we continue I must speak with our witness in private."

She led Aiyana to a corner of the room where they talked in a low whisper.

"Wasn't someone going to notice two identical women walking around?" Carson asked Asima as they waited for the Commissioner to finish her conversation.

"Aiyana was off planet – I tracked her down in the asteroid belt. She had been on Kaimana last week for a meeting but by the time I found her she was in a solo ship in the back of beyond. I returned with her less than an hour ago in a Service speedboat."

Asima seemed overwhelmed.

"This is the biggest crime any of us have ever dealt with. And it gets worse," she added quietly. "That solo ship she was on when we tracked her down – it had a hidden explosive device. They had no intention of trying to explain away her resurrection."

The two women rejoined them. Carson was alarmed to see that Aiyana appeared even more distressed than before.

"I have been explaining to our honored witness that while stealing a person's genome is easy, duplicating her personality must have involved keeping her under close observation for a considerable period of time. Probably the criminals broke into her personal data. We must assume they are still active and as a consequence we plan to keep her presence on Kaimana secret, under the protection of the security service.

"So as things stand now, Carson, it appears that someone has gone to enormous trouble and expense to place you in a very difficult situation. If it wasn't for our pathologist and officer Asima's diligence – and your own precautions – you would now be trying to explain a dead Mitan citizen and a stolen mail packet. I don't suppose you have any idea why someone would do all this?"

He shook his head.

"God knows. I'd never stepped foot on this planet until yesterday."

"You were planning to stay here for some time where you not?"

He nodded.

"Continue with that plan. Go about your business. Officially you will be what is termed 'a person of interest' in the death of Aiyana of clan Aniko. We believe there will be further developments. Possibly the criminals will try to make contact, they must have some sort of a plan for you. Needless to say you will be under the Service's surveillance. In addition we will fit you with a clandestine recording device that cannot be detected by civilian scanning equipment.

"Oh, and Carson, under the authority of section five of the Mitan Security Code, we have cancelled that attorney of yours, though you will still be able to keep your regular valet. I'm sorry, but this is a matter of national importance – the most serious crime I have encountered in my career – a direct, willful violation of articles of the Covenant."

"Great, so if you decide to throw me into jail I'll have no legal counsel?"

"At this point there are no plans to file charges against you – the formal examination has been cancelled. If charges are ever brought, you will have representation. Officer Asima will take you to be fitted with the recording device."

As far as the commissioner was concerned the meeting was over.

For the first time since entering the room, Carson spoke directly to Aiyana.

"Look, I'm incredibly sorry that you've been caught up in all this. It's clearly me they were trying to get at, it's just bad luck that you..."

Aiyana opened her mouth to say something then thought better of it.

"I know," she finally whispered, fluttering her hands. "This is terrible for both of us."

She even managed the briefest of smiles.

Cheered by the tiny flicker warmth, Carson left the room with Asima.

THE OLD MAN

CARSON DID NOT HAVE TO WAIT LONG FOR CONTACT TO BE MADE. THAT EVENING while he ate alone in a restaurant near the hotel he was astonished to glimpse a figure sporting a deep brown birthday suit identical to his own standing at the entrance to the dining room. The newcomer walked directly over to his table.

"Carson is it not?" he asked, smiling broadly. "My name is Shin of clan Aniko, welcome to Kaimana."

Registering his stare he added, "Yes, I too have just arrived from Procyon c."

"How did I ever miss you?"

Shin chuckled and slid into a chair.

"We could start a new fashion."

Carson startled. The stranger had used exactly the same phrase as Aiyana's replicant.

Unfazed, the new arrival continued.

"I represent a distinguished, and if I may be candid, very wealthy collector of ancient artifacts. He would like to invite you enjoy a nightcap with him this evening to discuss the antique trade and the possibility of enhancing his collection."

Under normal circumstances Carson would have leapt at such an invitation so it was easy for him to ape a smile and accept.

"Excellent!" Shin beamed. "As soon as you're ready. I have a limousine waiting outside. No, please – I insist on picking up the check."

A few minutes later the limo deposited them outside of a black glass tower that stretched halfway up to the shield.

"This is the head office of clan Aniko" Shin explained as he strode through the entrance. Carson gasped. The giant atrium was dominated by a three-dimensional image floating above their heads. The display depicted a cluster of huge parallel cylinders joined by an intricate network of girders and ductways. He could make out tiny spacecraft weaving their way between the gigantic structures. Periodically one of the cylinder heads erupted with a titanic bolt of energy. He guessed that the real thing was several kilometers long.

"The Aniko black hole foundry," Shin said proudly. "Within two years the clan will have the first production facility in the Mita system."

Carson made suitably impressed noises as a private elevator took them to the top floor.

Shin led the way through a pair of gilt doors into a very large office.

"I'll leave you here to await your host. It has been a pleasure to meet you Carson." He unleashed another dazzler and strode out, closing the doors behind him. Carson was not surprised to discover that the moment the doors had shut his access to the net had been cut.

He gazed around the softly lit room. One wall opened onto a nighttime vista of the city. The other three were paneled in Lacaille petal wood, their rich surfaces shimmering as he moved. Dotted throughout the room in warm pools of light were a series of exquisite antiques. Here was a Ross diamond fabricator in such good condition that it seemed it could manufacture a gemstone on the spot. And there was a second millennium environment suit poised ready to launch itself into the void.

In the center of room, resting upon a lectern in a circle of golden light was the jewel of the collection: a superb eighth century reproduction of The Book. Carson smiled as he gently turned the pages. The title on the cover was probably the most famous in the galaxy. *A Child's Encyclopedia* it said.

"A marvelous artifact, is it not?"

He turned round and for a moment the sight of the speaker made him forget the wonderful collection. To begin with his slight frame was wrapped in a black silk kimono – the first person he had seen on Kaimana actually wearing clothes. Then as he stepped into the light Carson could see that he was *old*. In a world where illness and death were strangers the man's white hair and dry wrinkled skin made him as shocking as if he had been three meters tall.

"I'm told it's virtually identical to the original," the old man said. "But then of course you are one of the very few people who has had the privilege of examining the real thing."

"It's a wonderful facsimile," agreed Carson, "but check the margin of page 114 where Cissokho's daughter hand-wrote some notes. She used a scribing instrument that dispensed pigment by rolling a tiny tungsten carbide sphere at its tip. The pressure caused by the writing action was sufficient to compress the paper substrate. If you looked at the corresponding area on the other side of the page in the real Book – he flipped to page 113 and held it up to the light at an angle – you would see a faint indentation showing a mirror image of the writing. In this copy the surface is flat."

The old man took the book, squinted at it the way Carson had indicated, and laughed hoarsely.

"I knew we chose the right man!"

"I am Juro, senior elder of clan Aniko," he said, finally introducing himself.

"You're wondering why I appear so old."

He shuffled to an elaborate drinks cabinet.

"You'll take some brandy. It's distilled from grapes grown in my vineyard on the northern slopes of the caldera. They're drinking better on New Bordeaux but it'll do."

He handed Carson a glass.

"I look old because I am old, nearly two thousand standard years. How can I be senior elder with the face of a twenty-five year old boy? Ironic, don't you think? At one point in human history men desperately sought immortality and I had a hell of a time finding someone who could help me grow old."

Juro wheezed with laughter at thought. Then, nodding towards the lectern he asked:

"How much do you think it would sell for at auction?"

"A beautiful eighth century copy in such fine condition? I would estimate a least seven million."

"No," Juro murmured, "How much would the original Book fetch?"

"Oh come on!"

"Indulge me."

"Well," said Carson, thinking about the unthinkable, "I guess the Huan Federation would bid for it. They like to think of themselves as equals to the Commonwealth, and to own The Book... they'd probably pay whatever it would take."

"And that would be...?"

Carson shrugged. "We're talking fantasy – billions no doubt, maybe tens of billions."

"Oh, billions at the very least. Of course it will never be for sale but doesn't it strike you as strange that literally one book, one miserable child's reference book, is the sole surviving fragment of Old Earth culture?"

"But they had so little time. They thought they had weeks to finish loading the Yongding, then the Melt accelerated and they ended up fleeing in just a few hours. It's a miracle they had enough to survive."

"I know, I know, but even then The Book was just a nostalgic piece of obsolescent technology. They should have managed to save something using the storage techniques of the time. We know Old Earth had an extraordinarily rich prehistoric culture and yet nothing else survived? You will have heard of Shakespeare – the greatest writer of Ancient English according to the Encyclopedia. Thirty-eight divine plays we're told, one hundred and fifty-four sonnets, and what do we have left? A four-line quote!

I know a bank where the wild thyme blows,
Where oxlips and the nodding violet grows,
Quite over-canopied with luscious woodbine,
With sweet musk-roses and with eglantine

Juro's command of the dead language was impeccable.

"Has it occurred to you Carson that the absence of any cultural or historical material may have been deliberate? Cissokho and her cohorts were determined to break with the past, were they not?"

"Yeah, I know the theory, but I still think it's more plausible that they simply had no chance to collect anything in the panic. And who knows what the Techs took with them after they refused to ratify the Covenant."

"The Covenant!" Juro snorted, "what a high price we've paid for that document."

Seeing Carson's frown he went on, "Do you realize that you could pluck a man from prehistoric Earth, bring him to our present time and he would be perfectly comfortable? Doesn't that astound you? Eight thousand years and we still live like primitives!

"Oh I suppose a few advances would impress him – FTL travel, push drives, indefinite life extension – but where are the revolutionary leaps? Where are the matter transmitters? Where are the machines with minds like gods? Where is FTL communication? If I want to consult with my people on New Earth I have to – I mean no personal slight – write them a goddamn letter!

"The Clan's black hole foundry – how absurd!" By now he was almost shouting. "One point eight billion Ecus for transportation alone. Why? Because it's too big for an Alcubierre Drive. Twenty years – twenty years of accumulating interest payments – to bring it from New Earth at sub-light speed. It should have arrived as a nano-seed the size of your glass. Plant the seed in an iron asteroid and let the foundry build itself."

"Most people would say we've enjoyed eight thousand years of peace and prosperity precisely because we *haven't* been creating nano-seeds and the like," Carson said.

"Oh I know, I know – the Melt. Does an eight thousand year old accident have to dictate everything we do today?"

"That accident virtually wiped out the only space-faring species in the galaxy."

"So what? Suppose another Melt occurred – today there are countless inhabited systems.

"We could afford to lose a few," he added with a chuckle.

"I think we could do better than that," Carson said, "imagine that we broke the Covenant and learned how to synthesize the kind of gamma ray burst that occurs when two neutron stars collide – that would sterilize every planet within a thousand light years."

Juro ignored him and turned to the copy of The Book.

"Perhaps," he continued more quietly, "some other material has survived. Suppose there were many Books. Not copies you understand, but other texts, works of art, perhaps other artifacts."

"But how, where?"

In fact Carson had heard it all before. The mouth-watering prospect of discovering more Old Earth material was a favorite topic among antique dealers at the end of an evening's drinking. In the sober light of day the whole idea struck him as absurd.

"Do you know a New Earth historian named Kalidas?" Juro asked.

"I know of him. He's one of the proponents of the idea that there is more Old Earth stuff to be found. He has a checkered reputation."

"True, but interesting work."

Juro put down his glass.

"You next scheduled delivery is New Earth. When you get there I want you to work with Kalidas. He's done some interesting new research but has regrettably hit a roadblock – his access privileges to the artifacts were withdrawn last year. You on the other hand retain full rights."

"Why were they withdrawn?" Carson asked, and with sudden insight added, "Did he try to steal something?"

Juro shrugged and picked up his glass. Carson knew he had guessed right. By now it was obvious where all this was leading although he could see no option but to play it straight.

"Frankly, my honored host, I'm not sure where the advantage is for me. Associating with a disgraced academic isn't likely to enhance my own standing."

"If any new prehistoric material were found you would be entitled to a commission. Just one percent would make you a very wealthy man."

"But this is fantasy. The idea that after eight thousand years something could have been overlooked..."

"Quite an adventure you've been having since your arrival," Juro said, apparently changing the subject.

Here we go thought Carson.

"Aiyana, a promising young member of my clan, dead with you laying at her side. Missing mail…"

Carson furiously tried to think how he would react if he did not know more.

"Aiyana's death is a terrible tragedy, but I swear upon my honor that I had nothing to do with it. I'm certain that I'll be exonerated. As for the mail, I have backups that can easily be retrieved."

"Perhaps," said Juro, "but if the clan made a fuss you could be confined here on Kaimana for months, unable to complete your deliveries. That would be a violation of your Post Office contract, would it not? You would lose you license."

Carson glowered at him. The old bastard was right.

Juro smiled, or to be more accurate pulled back his lips and displayed yellowed teeth.

"But I see no reason to take such a course of action. You will proceed to New Earth and work with Kalidas. I will even make my private yacht available to transport you. Shin and another member of the clan will accompany you and help with the research effort."

He pretended to think about it.

"How soon would we be able to leave?"

"I estimate it will take a few days to pacify the authorities."

"Do I have any choice?"

"A choice?" rasped Juro, genuinely amused, "it's been a very long time honored guest since I offered anyone a choice."

CONSPIRACY

"I JUST CAN'T BELIEVE HE WOULD DO THAT TO ME," SAID AIYANA.

It was the day after Carson's encounter with Juro. Aiyana, Carson, Asima, and Zhou were gathered round a console in the Commissioner's office. An hour earlier the clandestine recording device had been removed from the dermal layer behind Carson's right ear and the four of them had listened to the previous evening's conversation.

Even though he had been careful to say nothing incriminating it was obvious that the clan elder had masterminded the creation of the Aiyana replicant.

"I've been raped by my own family!" she wept.

Asima put an arm round her shoulder and led her to a corner of the room. The Security officer appeared almost as upset as Aiyana. She was evidently a traditionalist and Juro's blasphemous rant about the Covenant had shocked her. The Commissioner and Carson talked quietly.

"There's no way Juro is doing all this just to force me to talk to some loopy academic. Hell, he could have just bribed me."

"So what then?"

"My guess is that he wants me to steal whatever it was Kalidas tried to lift. That's something I'd never do without a gun to my head."

Zhou nodded. "Is there any credibility to his idea – could there be more Books?"

"Until last night I would have said the whole idea was ridiculous. But here's a guy with everything to lose willing to commit murder, so God knows."

"He may have already lost everything," said Zhou.

"I've been talking to my boss, the Cabinet Secretary for Internal Affairs. She tells me that old man Juro has mortgaged his clan up to the hilt for that black hole foundry. Now the project is three years behind schedule and bleeding funds. He may lose control before it even goes into production. We think he's desperate for money."

"So do you want me to go along with his plan?"

"I don't think we have any other option. We've the start of a case against him, but we need a lot more evidence. Plus of course we know nothing of his conspirators. Who makes you a replicant?"

"I'm hardly likely to find that out on New Earth."

"You won't need to. We just need to build a strong case against Juro: conspiracy to murder, conspiracy to steal ancient artifacts, duplicating a human being and God knows what else. Then with all that hanging over his head we sit down with his lawyers and make a deal. If he were convicted on any of those charges he'd face total personality reconstruction. We're convinced he'll cooperate rather than risk a guilty verdict. Then we'll get everyone."

"Frankly," she added, "we've been trying to get Juro for a very long time – he's been mixed up in countless questionable ventures. You represent our best chance in years. Go to New Earth and cooperate as fully as you can on his madcap search, even if it means doing something illegal. We'll be there to straighten things out with the authorities. The more you get involved the more we'll learn about his machinations."

The next day was a busy one for Carson. He had brought with him a small selection of antiques to whet the appetites of potential customers but now they were burdensome luggage. Consequently he decided to unload the lot with a local dealer. The prices would not be good but he was about to need a great deal of cash. He did manage to raise the total by throwing in the dream machine although somehow he overlooked explaining how it worked.

Polite conversation, bargaining, and discussions about future (though completely fictitious) trades took him all morning and it was nearly noon but the time he emerged blinking into the pseudo-sunlight. As he headed to lunch a call came through from Aiyana.

"Hi Carson! How are you today?" she said, sounding infinitely more friendly than she had the day before.

"I'm doing okay," he replied cautiously.

"Hey, I know I gave you a hard time yesterday but you must understand why. Let's start again. Can we meet this afternoon?"

He was having a difficult time believing her but on the other hand he had nothing to lose – his relationship with Aiyana was already at rock bottom – and he was intrigued to discover her real motivation.

"Fine, where would you like to meet?"

She shot him a location and signed off with more friendly chatter.

Two hours later they rendezvoused outside a large store that customized homes with the latest in entertainment technology.

"Hey, let's go in," Aiyana suggested.

For the next twenty minutes Carson listened as Aiyana and a saleswoman discussed immersion experiences that transformed an entire household into a viewing theatre, rather like the shuttle on its descent to Kaimana.

"In addition, honored customer, if you get the Dyna-Personality upgrade the system will be able to sense which characters and dialog most appeal to you. This will allow DP-enabled entertainments to seamlessly re-configure their narrative to reflect your preferences."

Finally, Aiyana changed subjects.

"I believe, honored salesperson, that you also market privacy rooms. Do have a demonstration?"

Carson immediately understood Aiyana's choice of meeting place and waited until the saleswoman closed the door of the privacy room behind her. Silence enveloped them as they were cut off from the electronic hubbub of the outside world. Hopefully, the inane sales conversation had dulled Security's senses but it was still wise to assume they only had a few minutes.

"What's on your mind?" he asked.

"Are you going through with this? Going to New Earth with Juro's people?" she said, suddenly all business.

He spent precious seconds thinking hard. Even though the whole plot was Juro's monstrous conception he knew he carried his own portion of responsibility. If he wasn't so predictable when confronted with an attractive woman Aiyana would still be happily working in the asteroid belt. At least he owed her the truth.

"Hell no, the moment I'm no longer useful to him Juro would eliminate me exactly the same way he tried with you. The man's psychotic. I'm getting off-planet my own way tonight."

"Won't that wreck your career? Turn you into a fugitive?"

"Not if I handle it right. I plan to lay a false trail then bust out of here and head straight to New Earth in my own ship. That way I not only fulfill my mail contract but also stand a chance of sorting out what's really going on before Mitan Security and Juro's goons catch up with me. If I succeed the authorities will forgive all and Juro will have a whole new life. If there's any truth to his crazy theories I could even get rich."

"And if you don't succeed?"

"Then I guess it's time for a new career," he replied, "somewhere on the other side of the galaxy".

"I want to go with you."

"*What?*"

"Why the hell should I stay? What's here for me? I've been betrayed by my own clan for God's sake! Even if Juro is convicted do you think they'll welcome my return?

"Anyways," she continued, "look at me – shoving asteroids around for a living. Do you know I've never been outside the Mitan system in my entire life? I should have got out of here years ago."

"What about your family?"

"The clan was my family. That all ended yesterday."

Her face crumpled and she turned away from Carson. He desperately wanted to comfort her but now was not the time. What if he did take her, would it matter? After all, she was the only real innocent in this mess. Security might charge her with witness evasion but it was not likely, and perhaps she could help resolve things on New Earth. Even if they failed the least he could do was get her safely away from Juro.

"Alright, we'll do it."

She turned to face him again.

"You said tonight? How?"

"Meet me tonight in the grounds of the hotel. There's an area called Lover's Nook."

Aiyana raised an eyebrow.

"Minimal surveillance," he explained with a grin.

"Be there at eight. Pack very lightly. Try not to give any hint that we're fleeing."

"How will we –", she stopped. "There's no time, we'd better get out of here."

Carson opened the door for her and they stepped out the privacy room.

"Why, what a coincidence!" he said as they emerged, "Here's officer Sosimo!"

Sosimo glared at them. He was still breathing heavily from his sprint into the store.

"Do that again and we'll hold both of you indefinitely at headquarters."

"Surely a woman is entitled to some secrets officer?" Aiyana asked with a smile.

Carson suppressed a laugh. Sosimo muttered something inaudible as the three of them trooped out past the perplexed saleswoman.

The security officer used his official car to take Carson to his hotel.

"I will accompany honored witness Aiyana to her new accommodation," he said as Carson stepped out. Sosimo's tone made it clear that there would be no discussion on this point. Moments later the vehicle rose into the air and disappeared into the traffic overhead.

He walked into the hotel lobby asked the counter for the concierge, certain that the luxury establishment would have a human presence to deal with sophisticated requests.

"How can I help you honored guest?" the minion asked as they sat down in his office. Judging from his pleasant manner he had heard nothing about the discovery of Aiyana's body.

Carson tried to look sheepish.

"I was hoping to find a, um, lady to spend the evening with. I wondered if you could recommend..."

The concierge was unfazed.

"I quite understand. I am happy to inform you that hiring a person for intimate companionship is perfectly legal on Kaimana. I'm sure your valet will be able to help you."

"Yes," said Carson staring down at his feet, "but I was hoping to find someone a little more, well, exciting – local color and all that. I was thinking perhaps of some off-the-beaten-track establishment."

"I'm sorry honored guest, but the Caldera View cannot recommend..."

"But surely!" Carson protested

The concierge relented.

"There is a bar called the Twin Moons that I believe some of our guests have found satisfactory."

"I'm most grateful," said Carson and held up his hand. As they touched palms he transferred a hundred Ecus.

The concierge cheered up instantly.

"Remember, honored guest, I made no official recommendation."

Twenty minutes later Carson walked into the Twin Moons. He had spent his hundred Ecus well; located in a shabby commercial district, he would never have found the establishment by himself and his valet would never have dared suggest it. Despite it being early afternoon, the place was busy. Several women and a couple of men sitting by themselves at the bar gave him an appraising glance as he sat down and ordered a drink. Sipping his wine, he stared at a three-dimensional pornographic display in the center of the room and waited.

Within a few moments a woman detached herself from her barstool, smiled, and came over to his table. Unlike the cropped hair sported by most Kaimana women she had a positive mane that reached halfway down her back. Individual strands glowed red, gold, and silver, and appeared capable of changing color from moment to moment. As she sat down he saw a centimeter of black at her scalp; time for a redo.

"Hi, I'm Larissa," she said, stretching and arching her back. The gesture made her breasts thrust forward, a ploy as old as time but one that still worked. Her appeal was further enhanced by her birthday suit, an artful pattern of leopard skin spots that revealed large areas of bare flesh.

"Miguel," Carson replied smiling. Neither offered to touch palms.

"I haven't seen you here before – would you like some company?"

"Sure, I was hoping to hire someone to talk to, possibly show me around a little."

Larissa laughed.

"Your wife doesn't understand you Miguel?"

"One thousand for the afternoon," Carson said. He placed an anonymous credit chip on the table. As long as humans continued to exist there would always be cash.

She picked up the chip and squeezed it, smiling as it confirmed its authenticity. He knew he was overpaying but this was no time to haggle. Besides, Larissa had been the first off the mark in the bar, which suggested she was no fool – he was going to need that.

"Okay, where to lover?"

"You tell me. Can we get a cab? This place is a little too public."

She shrugged and picked up her bag. Outside the bar Carson hailed a taxi. They climbed in and he told it to hover while they talked.

"Larissa," he said, "I need to get out of Kaimana without anyone knowing. Do you know anyone who can help with that?"

She thought about it.

"Yeah, maybe. Let me make some calls."

For the next fifteen minutes Larissa talked to her contacts. As she chatted she absent-mindedly placed a hand on Carson's thigh.

"No thanks," he said, taking her wrist and moving her hand, "I really am here just for information."

"Your choice – easiest thousand I'll make this week."

Eventually she made progress and gave an address to the taxi.

"I will tell you Miguel, this isn't my first choice. The guy we're going to see is bad news, so watch yourself, okay?"

Their destination was another club, one that had no sign over the entrance and a doorkeeper who baulked at the sight of Carson.

"He's with me," said Larissa.

That was sufficient and the two made their way into the gloomy interior. Unlike the Twin Moons this place was virtually empty. She led the way to a row of booths where a man was sitting alone.

"Hi Tabarak, this is Miguel."

He sat down opposite the big man. One glance was enough to set off Carson's alarm bells. He had a gleaming shaved head that was not quite symmetrical – as if a bag of skin that had been filled with large steel balls. In a time when the human body could be sculptured at will this had to be a deliberate choice.

Moreover he was only the second person he had seen on Kaimana wearing clothes. Tabarak was dressed in what appeared to be a regular black jumpsuit. Inspecting it more closely Carson guessed that the suit incorporated an inertial protection matrix. In standby mode it generated a slight inertial field that made the material feel like stiff cloth. If the matrix detected an incoming projectile, plasma bolt, or even the thrust of a blade, the field ramped up in microseconds to turn the garment into impenetrable body armor. This guy meant business.

Without preamble he placed another anonymous credit chip on the table. Tabarak glanced at it and tilted his head questioningly.

"Ten thousand," said Carson.

"Larissa, get yourself a drink at the bar," Tabarak said, not taking his eyes off Carson. She sauntered away.

"I should advise you that I am being monitored by Mitan Security."

"I was about to tell you that. I was also going to tell you that you are a mailman named Carson and somehow you've managed to get yourself into a world of trouble."

"Absolutely correct," Carson said, trying not to show his alarm. "Do you know exactly what kind of trouble?"

"No – Security is keeping this one tight – something involving Juro and clan Aniko."

"You know Juro?"

"We've done business."

He leant forward.

"Listen, you're clearly no fool but it's equally obvious that you're no professional, otherwise you wouldn't be the only person in this place not carrying a weapon. So here's some free advice: Kaimana is basically a company town and the company is Clan Aniko. If you've crossed Juro, get off the planet as quickly as you can."

"Sound counsel," said Carson, "and it's the reason I'm here.

"I need to get myself and one other person, a woman, away from Kaimana as quickly as possible without Security – or Juro – knowing. I have a spacecraft parked in orbit so I can take it from there."

"That could be arranged, but not for ten thousand."

Carson sighed and sub-vocalized a request to the local branch of the Bank of New Earth. The bank decrypted and verified the genome embedded within his message and shot over another ten thousand. He reached out and transferred the money to the credit chip with the tip of his finger. Tabarak grunted, scooped it up in a muscular hand and squeezed out the cash. He then in turn reached into a pocket, took out a chip of his own and placed it on the table.

"One time pad," he said "They'll be a package and a set of coded instructions. Are you still at the Caldera View? I should be able to deliver within a few hours. Understand this: I will be breaking no laws. Mailmen occasionally delivery physical items, right? This package will contain industrial samples and be addressed to a communications corporation on New Earth. The company exists and is legitimate. If you choose to do anything else with the package that's your business.

"And be clear that this is a one-way ticket. No second tries and no returns."

"I have absolutely no intention of coming back."

"Good, then we're done. Now all we need do is give Security a reason for your visit here."

He looked around.

"Hey Larissa!" he shouted.

She trotted over.

"Take our friend upstairs and entertain him for an hour."

Then, smiling faintly for the first time, he added, "If Security sees a minor crime, they won't think about a major one"

"So who's paying for this entertainment?" Larissa asked him.

Tabarak just stared at her. She threw up her hands and gestured Carson to follow. He nodded his thanks and immediately stood up and followed the girl. The sooner he got away from this guy the better – the man oozed menace. They made their way up a flight of stairs at the rear of the club and down an ill-lit corridor to a small room furnished with a bed and a small chest of drawers. Large displays covered the walls.

"You watch something," said Carson gesturing to the displays. "I'm going to try to take a nap."

"Tabarak said to entertain you," the girl said nervously.

"No-one will know," he said, then to show that he meant no disrespect, "and besides, I'm completely, totally not in the mood."

"Oh, we can change that," she said and pulled open a drawer.

It contained a set of disposable inhalation masks and an anonymous rectangular box. Larissa pulled out the box and pried it open. Inside were neat rows of tiny colored cylinders.

"Gaspers – every come across this stuff?"

Carson had; each cylinder stored a synthetic tailored serotonin that could be inhaled through the breathing mask. The effects were instantaneous.

"Most people use these two," Larissa said holding up red and gold cylinders. She giggled.

"The red one pushes your sex drive through the roof and the gold one wipes out your inhibitions. You get some shy banker from New Mars, give him a blast of these two babies and pow! Instant sex maniac."

Carson's curiosity overcame him.

"What are the black ones?"

Larissa's smile vanished.

"They're Tabarak's house specialty. God knows where he gets them. They remove the aversion for causing pain; it's terrible – people just turn into sadists. Someone has to pay me a *lot* of money before I let them use one of those."

Watching her face as she spoke reminded Carson that there were worse things that could happen to a human being than being blackmailed by a crazy old megalomaniac.

"Here," he said handing her another chip, "here's another thousand. Watch a show and I'll nap."

"You're too sweet!"

He stopped Larissa as she went to put away the drug paraphernalia.

"Let's make my alibi convincing. I'll hold my breath and you spray just a quick blast of the gold and red gaspers on my face. That way I'll test positive for Security."

"And when you walked into the Moons I thought you looked so innocent!"

She inserted the cylinders into the base of one of the disposable breathing masks and held it up to his face. He took a deep breath and nodded. She gave him a two second burst.

"Thanks, that'll do it. Are you going to keep the rest?"

"Hell no."

She stretched up and emptied the remaining contents into an air vent near the ceiling.

"There, that should liven things up downstairs."

Carson laughed, then realized that for the last thirty seconds he had been staring at Larissa's body.

"I think a tiny amount must have gotten into my bloodstream through my skin."

"So I see," said Larissa glancing down.

He turned away crying out in embarrassment. She came up behind him and patted him on the arm.

"Don't worry, honey," she said, not unkindly. "In this job I've seen *everything*"

He stretched out on the bed, facing the wall.

"Watch an entertainment," he said over his shoulder.

An hour later they headed downstairs. Tabarak had gone.

"It would probably be best if we left separately," Carson said. "Why don't you hang out at the bar for a few minutes?"

"Sure," Larissa said and gave his hand a squeeze. "Come and see me again next time you're in town Miguel"

He grinned and headed for the exit. He was not the least surprised to find Officer Sosimo waiting outside.

"Good God Carson – this place?"

"A man has his needs Officer; I've been in space for weeks."

Sosimo produced a small scanner and held it up to his face.

"Gaspers! I'm not even going to tell Asima about this – she'd insist on busting you. Come on, this is the last time I'm taking you to the hotel."

How true thought Carson.

EXIT

THAT EVENING CARSON STOPPED IN THE HOTEL LOBBY.

"Any packages for me?"

"Yes honored guest," replied the counter, "there was a delivery a short while ago."

A small cart appeared at his feet bearing an anonymous parcel. He scooped it up and hurried to his suite where he tore the package open. Inside was a mail packet bearing a New Earth address and a small envelope. He opened the packet, checked the contents, resealed it, and turned his attention to the envelope. Inside was a small red disk and a memory chip. He turned the disk over in his hand, shrugged, dropped it into his bag, then he pulled out Tabarak's chip containing the one time pad.

Holding the pad in one hand and the new chip in the other, he sucked out data. Taken individually, each contained nothing but a random bit stream. Combined, they yielded a mass of instructions. He listened carefully for twenty minutes then dropped them both into the incinerator.

Carson packed a few essential items into his shoulder bag and made one last check of his room. After a moment's hesitation he left his final anonymous credit chip by the bed; it was loaded with enough cash to pay the hotel bill. He had broken enough laws already.

He tucked the parcel under his arm and walked out into the terraced grounds of the hotel. Kaimana's atmosphere provided an ideal tropical growing environment and the nighttime gardens were rich with the aroma of bougainvillea, lilies, and orchids. He breathed deeply and felt a moment of regret at leaving the planet so quickly. He had explored little of the island and had seen nothing of the spectacular oceans. Perhaps one day – a long time in the future – he would return.

The meeting place was perfect. The area was designed for guests who wished to take advantage of Kaimana's sultry climate and easy-going attitudes to engage in some discrete outdoor carnality, and as a consequence monitoring posts were absent. It was shielded from the outside world by curtains of gardenias and more privacy was provided a waterfall that screened-out sound. Here and there low beds were tactfully positioned in small arbors. On one couch two women writhed in silent embrace but they were afflicted by the deafness that overcomes lovers. Aiyana stood waiting by a life-size statue of a trio engaged in an activity that some societies would consider illegal.

"Nice place you've got here," she said.

Carson spread his hands in apology. "I know, but it's designed for privacy," he whispered.

He looked around; they were alone.

"Put this on quickly."

He ripped open his package and pulled out two black jumpsuits, giving one to Aiyana. They had them on in less than a minute. Aiyana squirmed as she wriggled her fingers into the gloves at the end of each arm. Following Carson's example she kept the hood down, leaving their heads exposed.

"These are stealth suits," he explained quietly, "they serve the same function as a privacy room. No-one can scan our biometrics while we're wearing them and when we pull up the hoods they won't be able tap into our systems either – we'll be effectively invisible and untraceable."

"My God! Are they legal?"

"Sure, if you test equipment in a licensed communications facility."

"So how did you manage to get them?"

"It wasn't too hard; I bought them from a local hoodlum. Finding a competent criminal is the same in any society – you start at the bottom and work your way up the food chain. The tricky part was keeping Sosimo off the scent."

"And," he added, "I've been learning some interesting stuff about Kaimana's infrastructure."

Before he could continue Aiyana stepped forward and kissed him. Startled, he began to pull away but then heard voices. The two women he had seen had finished their tryst and were heading to the hotel. He put his arms around her and they stood in a frozen embrace as the lovers walked by.

"They'll need help if they're going to imitate that statue," said one.

"Want to volunteer?" replied the other.

They both laughed and continued down the leafy path.

Aiyana stepped away as soon as the couple was gone.

"Sorry," she said, "I thought we should act the part."

Carson shook his head in dismissal and gestured for her to follow him.

"How about a bike ride?" he said loudly for the benefit of any eavesdroppers, "I've rented a tandem."

The bike was waiting outside the hotel entrance. Designed for tourists, it was little more than a couple of saddles straddling a squat cylinder.

"Greetings honored husband Smith and wife Smith!" cried the bike.

Aiyana gave him a deadpan stare but said nothing.

"I thought we'd go for a ride by the lake," Carson told the bike as they climbed on board.

"What a romantic idea! Both simulated moons are full tonight and the view will be lovely. Did you know that the lake filled the entire crater before the first colonists arrived? Achieving its current state was a challenging –"

"Shut up," said Carson.

Inertial fields gripped their legs and the bike lifted off into the darkness. A few minutes later they were skimming over the central park's tailored meadows. The grasslands had been planted with luminescent flowers and graceful arcs of color rolled beneath them as they sped towards the lake. Dense knots of the glowing plants illuminated tiny picnic pavilions and they could hear the voices of revelers drifting up through the fragrant night air.

He leaned over and studied the darkened landscape.

"Park by that stream," he told the bike.

Once they had landed and dismounted he added ,"We're going for a long walk. Wait here until we return."

"This vehicle is rented on an hourly basis honored customer," the bike cautioned.

"I know, we'll be back in a while."

"Will we? Be back, I mean," asked Aiyana once they were out of earshot of the vehicle. They were walking besides the stream, heading away from the lake.

"Like hell," Carson said and picked up the pace.

After a kilometer's hike through the meadows they found themselves enveloped in a forest, the trail gradually steepening as they approached the base of the caldera wall. Eventually the stream disappeared into a three-meter wide tunnel in the rock face.

"The lake is fed by streams like this all around the crater," he explained. "They simply channel rainwater from outside."

"Time to get invisible," he added pulling up his hood, and then remembering something yanked it down again.

"Hey valet."

"Yes Carson," the calm voice replied.

"I hereby terminate your services and authorize payment."

"Thank you, goodbye."

"Oh, hold on!"

"Yes?"

"Zerstoren!"

The valet fell silent. He raised the hood again and reaching to the crown of his head drew down a flap that covered his face, rendering him completely enveloped in black material. Aiyana followed his example. The covering was porous and they could continue to see and breathe reasonably well.

A walkway was attached to one side of the tunnel and they made swift progress guided by the dim lights embedded in the ceiling.

"No-one ever comes this way except for routine inspections," he said, shouting into Aiyana's ear above the roar of the water.

They tramped on for several kilometers until they came to a mesh grid spanning the entire tunnel. The barrier had small locked door to give access to maintenance workers. Carson fished into his shoulder bag and brought out Tabarak's red disk, which he attached to the lock. He gestured to Aiyana to retreat and moments later there was a minor explosion. The door swung open.

Four hundred meters further on the tunnel ended at a curtain of water. They stepped out into the endless downpour. In front of them rainwater swirled into the tunnel from a huge catch basin carved into the surface of Kaimana's outer slope. The walkway continued upwards to their right, terminating at the slick rock bordering the rim of the basin.

They switched to night vision as they clambered up the last few steps. Finally they stood on the volcano's outer slopes. All they could see through the deluge was a nightmarish jumble of larval blocks scattered over the rising wall of the mountain.

In a couple of million years all this will be eroded away Carson thought. But even now, fifty kilometers to the east, a new volcanic island was growing beneath the waves as the tectonic plate continued its stately journey over the hotspot in the planet's crust.

They wandered among the giant boulders until they encountered a clear area about twenty meters across.

"Time to leave," he announced pulling a small communications pad from his bag.

"I'm sending a nanosecond encoded burst – just pray Security doesn't detect it."

"Now what?"

"We wait."

But they did not have to wait for long. A few minutes later a silent shape descended out of the rain; it was Carson's buggy. He slapped his hand on the hatch as the small craft settled into the black soil.

"Who are you?" said the buggy.

Carson pulled up his facemask.

"It's me you idiot machine," he hissed.

"Oh, sorry Carson, I was getting no reading from you at all."

Before he could reply Asima's amplified voice boomed out the sky.

"CARSON, AIYANA. GIVE YOURSELVES UP IMMEDIATELY!"

They stared at each other.

"They're bluffing," Aiyana finally said. "If they knew our location they'd already be here."

"Agreed"

The hatch swung open and they scrambled in.

"This is Aiyana," he told the buggy as the door swung shut. "She'll be traveling with us."

"There are six Mitan Security vehicles in our vicinity," the little craft said.

"Are they coming our way?"

"No, they appear to be executing a random search pattern."

"Do you think they spotted you on the way down?"

"Possibly – I'm cloaked of course, but Security will have anti-stealth capabilities."

Aiyana shivered. "Can we turn up the heat in here?"

"Yes – sorry. Buggy, match your atmospherics to the outside environment."

Warmth filled the little cabin.

"The buggy is cloaking us, right?" said Aiyana.

Taking his nod as assent she stripped off her dripping stealth suit.

We'll have to her cure of that before we hit New Earth mused Carson.

Still, she was right – the suit was intensely uncomfortable and he followed her example.

They huddled for fifteen minutes as the buggy reported the progress of Security's search, expecting at any moment to see the Asima's craft drop out of the darkened sky. Finally, still booming demands, the fleet disappeared round the bulk of the mountain.

"Let's get away from here before we start the ascent" Carson told the buggy. "Take yourself up just enough to clear the rocks and head for the shoreline."

They started skimming across the chaotic landscape. The craft's sensing equipment was far superior to their night vision and scene displayed on the buggy's globular cockpit gave them their first clear view of Kaimana's exterior. Above them the mountain reared into the night sky terminating in a thin band of light escaping from the edge of the crater shield. Ahead the landscape flattened and gave way to beaches of black volcanic sand. Lines of white foam marked the shoreline.

"We'll head about forty kilometers out to sea and then – oh God!"

As he spoke the silhouette of another Security vehicle rose above the edge of the mountain. There was no time to figure out what had happened. Snatching control from the buggy he accelerated down the slope and on across the open water flying so low sea spray flicked the bottom of the craft. Two kilometers past the shoreline they plunged through the ocean's surface.

"Is craft this submersible?" yelled Aiyana.

"We'll soon find out," he laughed, but seeing her alarm added, "Don't worry, it's designed to handle waterborne landings."

For an hour they hovered in the waters beneath the reticulating surface, but all that appeared was drifting seaweed and the occasional shoal of fish. Carson was quietly bringing the buggy up to date when Aiyana let out an ear-puncturing scream. They were staring into a monstrous eye. Simultaneously the cabin filled with a cacophony of clicks and whistles.

The Leviathan was the biggest animal Carson had ever seen. It must have been over a hundred meters long from bulbous head to giant tail.

"Can you translate any of this?" he yelled to the buggy above the din.

A slurred voice filled the cabin. "You play game?" it asked.

Carson shook his head in wonderment. Meta-Cetaceans had evolved independently all over the galaxy yet every single one of them wanted to play.

"Yes," he shouted, "hide and seek!"

In retrospect, sarcasm was not a good idea.

"I help," piped the huge creature and before Carson could say another word it opened its gigantic mouth and swallowed the buggy.

He sank his head into his hands.

"Oh great, great, great"

"No," said Aiyana, "it really is trying to help. Relax – it's just holding us in its mouth. Meta-Cetaceans don't eat anything bigger than plankton."

"Relax! She says relax!" he cried, apparently addressing the heavens. Aiyana ignored him.

"Hey, Leviathan," she shouted, "can you still hear me?"

"Yes – we hide," the creature replied.

"That's right," Aiyana yelled in triumph, "we play game!"

"We're moving further out to sea," the buggy announced, adding more ominously, "and we're diving."

Carson and Aiyana eyed each other nervously.

"Hey my friend, not too deep," shouted Aiyana, but the huge creature simply hummed a song.

"Can we take the pressure?" she asked.

Carson shrugged, then had an idea.

"Hey buggy, can we rig inertial dampening to generate a counter-pressure?"

"I'm on it chief!"

Two hours later the buggy announced that they were finally ascending. By now they were some thirty kilometers out to sea. Unless Mitan Security's capabilities were superior to anything they had witnessed, it was safe to assume that they had lost the trail. To their vast relief the Leviathan opened its mouth and spat them onto the ocean surface.

"We play again?"

"Not today," replied Aiyana. "We leave now. Goodbye, blessings to you and your pod."

"Blessings to you Aiyana and your pod," the creature replied.

"How the hell does it know..." Carson began, and then just laughed.

After eight thousand years the human race still could not fathom the minds of these huge gentle animals.

The buggy rose slowly into the air. The dark cone of Kaimana came into view on the horizon but no craft approached them.

"I should pilot," Aiyana announced.

"Hmm, I don't know..."

"What do you mean '*I don't know*'? Hey spaceman, you may be the one swanning about the galaxy in your interstellar pleasure boat but I've been hauling crates like this around Mita for the last thirty years."

"No offense buggy," she added.

Carson held up his hands. "Okay, okay, you fly. Buggy, I'm giving Aiyana full dual control."

She gleefully slapped her hand on the flight console.

"Virtually all traffic control is above Kaimana" she explained "We could try and blend in but I think we'll do better leaving from a remote area that isn't monitored.

"Hey buggy," she yelled, "how fast can be go at sea level?"

"About Mach 3"

"Good enough," she said and shot forward across the wine-dark sea.

Kaimana disappeared below the horizon. After two hours they slowed to a halt. The craft began to gain altitude until they emerged above the dark featureless plane of the planet's cloud layer. Overhead in the clear night sky the arch of the Milky Way glittered with the promise of a million worlds.

"Time to get comfortable," Aiyana said as they buckled into the twin couches.

She initiated inertial dampening and, after pausing to take one last look at the world beneath her, hurled the little craft upwards towards the beckoning stars.

As soon as they were clear of the immediate vicinity Carson sent an encoded message to the ship telling it to initiate power-up for interstellar flight. It was a risky maneuver that required spinning the vessel's shell of micro black holes almost to the level where they folded space-time. Docking during spin-up was dangerous but it would save precious time.

The return trip to the ship proved uneventful; Mita once again shrank to a brilliant speck as they approached the borderlands of the system. When they were one million kilometers away from the ship Carson sent it another message.

"I want to try getting to New Earth in a single jump. Can you do it?"

"Who are we running from this time?" replied the ship. "Anyhow, the answer is maybe. I'll start the calculations."

"So where is it?" Aiyana said as she stared into the darkness.

"Buggy, can you magnify the image of the ship?"

Something resembling a giant drop of water zoomed into view.

"That's the shell; it's distorting the starlight."

At the center, huddled against the tidal gravity, was the ship itself: an ungainly mass of cubes, cylinders, and ducts that appeared more like a storage dump than an interstellar spacecraft.

Aiyana looked closer. "Oh God!" she cried, "There's another vessel."

Asima's voice filled the cabin.

"Carson, Aiyana, do not try to board your starship. I am authorized under Section Eight of the Mitan Defense Code to use all necessary force."

"How the hell did she get out here so fast?" Carson said, "Besides, she's bluffing. We're their entire case against Juro. They won't do anything to endanger us."

"Right!" snarled Aiyana as a bolt of thermal plasma tore past them.

The little vessel accelerated.

"Careful! You're going to overshoot the ship."

"*Who's* driving? I know where I'm going."

Pursued by Asima's speedboat the buggy hurtled past the starship then circled round in a wide loop.

"You can't enter the shell from this pole," Carson yelled, "you have to go round to the other side."

Aiyana said nothing. Totally absorbed in steering, she sat motionless, eyes closed, her hand clamped to the control console as she absorbed torrents of data. They streaked towards the south pole of the ship, still accelerating.

"For God's sake!"

"*Shut up Carson.*"

Traveling at over a thousand kilometers a second the buggy grazed the ship with fifty meters to spare. The massive gravity gradient from the shell's micro black holes gripped the little vessel as it shot past and pulled it round in an impossibly tight arc. Moments later they dropped through the opening in the north pole, screaming with deceleration. Asima's speedboat, taking a more conservative trajectory, whipped past without slowing. They would be gone by the time she could turn around.

Carson had the hatch open before they hit the landing dock. "Where did you learn to fly like that?" the ship asked as he dived out. Moments later Aiyana launched herself through the opening. "Oh, hello, who are you?"

"To hell with socializing," Carson shouted. "Get us out of here."

The song of the Alcubierre drive rose an octave; the whirlpool of collapsed matter spun ever faster. Local space-time twisted into a Lorentzian manifold while beyond the hull the stars vanished. Now the vessel was as alone as it was possible to be, enclosed in its own private cosmos. The shape of the tiny universe convulsed again. Then, like an orange seed squeezed between the fingers of a god, the starship shot across the heavens.

Outside the windows of Juro's office the city glowed beneath the evening sky. The senior elder of clan Aniko was in a fine mood as he poured two glasses of brandy. He held one glass up to his face and breathed deeply. The Colombard grape harvest was not good this year but it was of no great import, there would be better vintages. One had to take the long view. He shuffled over to his visitor.

"So he's on his way."

"Though hardly in the way we planned," replied Commissioner Zhou taking a glass.

"Yesterday he spent hours investigating the Oskinova system, an agrarian cooperative in a filament nebula some twenty thousand light years from here. It would be unfortunate to lose him."

"Impossible, it's a feint. Shin's model of Carson's personality shows a ninety-four percent probability that he will head directly to New Earth."

"Of course," he added, "there is the added complication of the girl. What a diligent public servant is Officer Asima! Who would have imagined that she would find Aiyana?"

"Yes," said Zhou, "honesty and dedication amongst my junior staff are an occupational hazard. Still, I think we improvised well. He's convinced that he's one step ahead of you."

Juro chuckled asthmatically at the thought.

"An adversary is easily manipulated when he believes he has out-smarted you. Carson thinks he will be clearing his name and finding ancient treasure. We could not ask for better motivation."

Zhou nodded. "Ironically, Aiyana should be an asset to his search. I've been checking her file – she's a highly intelligent and resourceful individual. I'm surprised you hadn't promoted her."

Juro sniffed. "She's a young woman. We don't do things that way in the clan."

Zhou looked at him for a long time without speaking.

Finally she said, "There's no chance that Carson knows what you're really looking for, is there?"

Juro waved his glass in dismissal.

"None – he's too in love with antiques. And when he succeeds, it will not matter."

Nothing will matter, nothing in the whole damn galaxy.

En route

AIYANA LOVED THE SHIP. HER ONE EXPERIENCE OF INTERSTELLAR TRAVEL HAD BEEN a nine-hour hop to the Aniko black hole foundry as it continued its deceleration through Mita's Oort Cloud, and that trip had been on a transport designed for sub light-year flights. Carson's vessel was something completely different.

She had always thought of a starship as a utilitarian machine – simply a mechanism for carrying people and equipment from one place to another. It had never occurred to her that a spacecraft could be an expression of an individual's personality.

They were floating in the center of a spacious cube, about ten meters across, which had once accommodated a crew of five. Originally the room had been the functional hub for the entire vessel Carson explained, but he had removed most of the control equipment when he converted the ship to solo use. Now the synthetic mind did most of the crew's work.

"So the color scheme... you chose it yourself?"

"Do you like it? I wanted something cheerful."

Mercifully the vivid bulkheads were obscured by centuries of accumulated antique hunting. In the center was a disassembled portable fusion reactor, one of his latest acquisitions.

"I got it from a monastery carved into a mountaintop on Dehini e, an ice ball that only a monk could love."

The reactor had warmed the stone halls for five hundred years but when Carson came on the scene the brothers were spending more time performing maintenance than sacred rituals.

"God knows where they originally found it. By the time we finished negotiations they had a miniature Higgs engine and I had another antique."

The monks certainly needed something reliable. The monastery was the only inhabited settlement in the Dehini system, a location that must have been chosen more for its view than any practical consideration. It was easy to see why; the nighttime sky blazed with the nebulous remnants of an ancient supernova.

So pleased were the brothers with their new power system they held a special service to beseech their favorite deity, Narayina the Hidden, to bestow her favor upon Carson's ventures.

"Not that it's done much good," he said.

"And where did you get *this*?"

They were floating in front of a hypnotically patterned mandala.

"Gandria in the Perseus Arm – it's a red dwarf system but it still manages to support a pretty diverse ecosystem. The locals have lapsed into a prehistoric culture although they seem happy enough."

Aiyana peered closely.

"What's it made of?"

"Human hair – it's amazing but all the color is natural. A couple of thousand years ago they spliced DNA from some local exotic birds into their own genome – I doubt the Covenant Council would approve – and now you have people walking around with every hair color imaginable.

"Creating the mandalas is highly ritualized. Each weaver first goes through a purification ceremony where they bathe, recite prayers and burn incense, and then they work only between midnight and dawn. It's a matriarchal society – only fertile women are allowed to make the tapestries – but all the hair comes from the men. There's a little bit of me in it."

Carson drifted up to point to a dark outline surrounding a cascade of chrome yellow fractals.

"That's my hair. The only way they'd let me barter for a tapestry was to become a member of a tribe. I lived with them for two years before my hair was long enough for the initiation ceremony."

"Wow!"

Aiyana moved back to admire the hypnotic patterns.

"So much work, so much hair! Was it worth it?"

"Oh yes. As far as I know I have the only legal Gandrian tapestry. There are a few stolen ones out there but they're worth only a fraction of their real value without a proper provenance."

"A proven-what?"

"An antique's life history – where it came from, proof that it's not a forgery, and how the owner came into possession. The universe is teeming with fake antiques, stolen antiques, and just plain old rubbish. There's no point trying to sell high-end pieces without a provenance."

Even if you have to invent it Carson added to himself.

"So your hair is your provenance?"

"It helps, but I also recorded my entire initiation ceremony with the tribe."

"Oh, I'd love to see that."

"I have some images," the ship chimed in.

"Another time," Carson said hastily, "but I will show you this."

He pulled at the neck of his jump suit. Starting on his shoulder, Aiyana could see a dark pattern of overlapping rings emerging through his skin's fading melanogenesis.

"During the initiation each female member of the tribe tattooed a circle on my skin. The size of the circle denotes her seniority."

"That is so cool! Hey, did you ever see *my* tattoos?" Aiyana said as she unfastened her jump suit.

Carson sighed; persuading his new crewmate to wear clothes had been a major challenge. Only the threat of confinement on the ship when they reached New Earth had persuaded her to give it a try. Ironically, he often went naked himself while onboard, but with the two of them the distraction would have been overwhelming. This was especially true given that Aiyana's birthday suit, deprived of proper care and nutriment, was fading away to reveal smooth, honey-colored flesh. Now he swallowed hard and feigned casual interest as she displayed the design snaking down her torso.

"Did she have them?" Aiyana asked as she refastened her suit.

"Who? Oh, as a matter of fact, no. I guess they thought it wasn't necessary."

"I'm going to take a break in the garden."

Suddenly she sounded tired.

"Sure – I need to go over supplies with the ship."

Carson fretted as he glided through the access tube to the main storage unit. The subject of the replicant had been stepped around since they departed four days ago. He hoped that Aiyana raising it now was a healthy development, but he would let her set the pace.

The storage module was the neatest place on the ship. It mattered little if the rest of the interior could have been the aftermath of an explosion in an antiques warehouse but supplies were literally the stuff of life. Carson always tried to keep the ship well stocked in anticipation of unexpected departures – the flight from the Mita system was not his first panicked escape. His goal was to have enough onboard to last him two years. If a journey took longer than that he would, with reluctance, hibernate – a debilitating process that left him feeling ill for weeks. Regardless, even with the best recycling equipment – and Carson did not have the best – basic nutriment was still required.

"Once we get to New Earth I want you to stock up," he told the ship.

"And this time, get three quotes for God's sake."

"Am I shopping for one or two?"

Carson swore he could hear a leer in the machine's voice but it was a good question. For the first time in many decades his future was uncertain. His vague plan was to cooperate Juro's renegade historian Kalidas and after a few days hanky panky garner enough evidence to finish off the Old Man. If that worked out then he could start a new mail run and revert to what passed for regular life.

He did not like to think about the alternative – that the whole venture would blow up in his face. If that happened they would have to run for it. That would be a long voyage indeed.

Even if he was successful what was Aiyana going to do? She would not be able to stay on New Earth without him – the immigration laws were too strict. She could get a job in another part of the system or she might, despite her denials, want to return to Mita. If she did, Carson could hardly refuse to take her.

"You'd better make it for two."

"Excellent!"

Not only did Aiyana love the ship, the ship loved Aiyana. After so many decades it was delighted to finally meet someone new. Her innocence about the world outside Mita and her thirst for knowledge gave the machine an opportunity to show off its vast stores of information. And when she tired of exploring the databanks, Carson suspected they gossiped about him.

He finished reviewing the procurement list and went to see how Aiyana was doing.

The conservatory was her favorite part of the vessel. There was no practical need for it – the environmental systems took good care of the atmosphere – but Carson had built it to help preserve his sanity during the total isolation of long voyages.

He pushed his way through an environmental isolating field into the fragrant envelope of moisture and warmth. Located away from the center of the ship to enable the plants to feel the modest gravitational tug of the shell, the conservatory was a kaleidoscope of orchids, jasmines, mimosas, bougainvillea and countless other tropical flowers. No wonder Aiyana so enjoyed coming here – the sultry atmosphere was virtually identical to Kaimana.

She was stretched out on a miniscule patch of grass staring up at the canopy of hibiscus, naked again, but this was no time to scold her. She appeared to have been crying. Carson knelt down by her feet.

"Hey, how are you doing?" he asked, gently wiggling a big toe.

She gave him a solemn smile. He guessed how she must be feeling. Seven days ago she had been a respected engineer with a life that had direction and purpose, and now she had been wrenched out of that world, roots and all.

Oh what the hell. He peeled of his jumpsuit and lay on his back besides her, putting her slender body out of his direct line of sight. The cool grass felt wonderful against his bare skin.

A tiny golden butterfly detached itself from the blossoms and fluttered down to settle on the tip of Aiyana's nose.

"Hey!" she yelled, more amused than frightened.

Carson held out a finger and the little creature obligingly jumped on.

"Take a closer look," he said, holding it in front of her eyes.

"Good God – it's artificial!"

"That's right. I keep a dozen of them here in the conservatory for pollination. They're made by an old friend of mine named Tallis, she lives on New Earth so you may get to meet her – you would definitely find her interesting."

The diminutive machine flapped away in search of a recharging station for its batteries.

"How are the studies going?"

They had agreed that they would leverage Aiyana's technical expertise and pass her off as a historian specializing in ancient spacecraft. As she observed, after some of the junk she had been pushing around the Mita system for the last thirty years it wasn't going to be much of a stretch. However, fluency in the two dominant colonial languages, English and Mandarin, was going to be essential.

"It's going great," she said, starting to perk up. "Listen to this: *bǎi huā qífàng!*"

"A hundred blooms – we've already got them," laughed Carson waving at the arch of flowers.

Aiyana was using Okrand technology to accelerate her learning. The subject was placed into an isolated, near-hypnotic state and completely immersed in the target language. Elaborate neural monitoring controlled the pace and content of the lessons.

"How about Ancient English?"

"Every day in every way!"

This time they both laughed.

"So," Aiyana asked, "how many languages do you know?"

"I have no idea."

"Oh stop being so modest."

"No, I'm serious. I've learned so many over the centuries that until someone speaks to me I don't know whether I'll be able to answer."

"And I thought I was doing well with two. Hey, I read this today:

"We choose to go to the moon in this decade and do the other things, not because they are easy, but because they are hard."

"Do you know who that was? It was an ancient called Kennedy, or JFK, or John Fitzgerald, the Book is a bit vague. He was the senior elder of Clan America announcing the first journey to Luna. Guess how they did it? They burnt flammable liquids in a metal chamber and then channeled the force of the combustion to create reactive thrust. *And they traveled in an environment module on top of the fuel tanks!* God, that took guts."

"That it did," said Carson, "they called their vessel *Saturn*, although no-one is sure why. There's an image of the landing on page 246 of the Book. Although if you really want to learn about ancient history you should start going through the Teng recordings."

"Yes I have!" she cried flipping onto her side to present Carson with a distracting view.

"I never knew – we hardly touched the subject in school."

"That drives historians crazy – most people today think the Book is our sole source of knowledge about prehistoric times but Teng got far more, even if it was pretty haphazard"

"Right, I mean, there's so much."

"Well the ship does have the complete archive. According to Teng's journal he filled every spare recording medium they had. He just sat down with his fellow survivors and said 'tell me everything you know'."

"I can believe it. I was just searching for the stuff on space travel but some of the other material – wow!"

"He was trying to maintain as much of the human race's collective memory as possible. Many people say we owe our survival almost as much to him as we do to Cissokho. After the Techs stole the Yongding there was so little knowledge left."

"May our curses find them," Aiyana said reflexibly. She lowered her eyes as she thought about the historic betrayal.

"Do you think we *will* ever find them?" she asked, looking at Carson again.

"God knows enough people have tried. No – the Techs have gone for good."

He did not want to distract Aiyana with a long discussion, but in truth he was not so certain about the ancient renegades. Regardless of their terrible crime he still hoped that the Techs had survived, that another branch of the human family was out there in the vastness of the galaxy. Perhaps one day he too would search the sky.

That was enough daydreaming.

"So what's your the curriculum for the rest of the day?"

"Oh I'm done with studying. We've got some fixing to do."

As soon as she had arrived on the ship Aiyana had begun to tear into the maintenance backlog. He was happy to accept the implied slight – the ship was slowly getting into shape and the work kept Aiyana from brooding.

"Do you know that your exterior repair 'bot hasn't been functioning for two years?"

"Yeah, I've been meaning to fix it…"

"I've been begging him," said the ship.

"Come on, let's gear up. You said it's safe to go outside during flight."

"Sure, let's do it."

Aiyana followed him down a short corridor ending at one of the ship's many storage modules. There Carson slapped his hand on an oversized locker. The heavy door decoded his genome, unlocked itself and swung open. Inside was a chaotic array of ancient artifacts: logic devices so old that no-one could still read the symbols they displayed, exquisitely made medical instruments for investigating diseases that no longer existed, communication devices mystically engraved with letters and numbers, strings of stranded metal once used to transport information, hand-sized pebbles that somehow could interface with machines, and a myriad of cylinders, tubes, slabs and assorted shapes of unknown origin and doubtful utility.

Carson shoved aside a protein synthesizer. Finally he pulled out two ancient environment suits.

"When I was staying on Fomalhaut b I bartered them for a fifth millennium music library," he explained.

"It wasn't worth that much – I didn't have the instruction manual," he added as Aiyana inspected the seals around the helmets.

"They still got the better deal," she said. "Oh well, it's just a quick excursion; I'll add them to the maintenance list."

They clambered into the suits and after some rudimentary checks headed for the exterior hatch. The heavy door swung open and they pushed their way through a stiff inertial screen into the vacuum. They were immediately surrounded by a bubble field; it was a crude but effective way of counteracting the tug of the shell and generating the impression of surface gravity. Nevertheless, they took the precaution of attaching safety lines.

The basic structure of the ship was a cube-like chassis about forty meters long with additional modules plugged into the surface. To the left was one such unit – the hulking cylinder of the main power source, the Higgs engine, surrounded by a tangle of superconducting cables. Directly ahead was another module: the rectangular shape of the conservatory.

Aiyana looked upwards and gasped. The vessel was totally enveloped in blackness without a hint of surrounding stars. The spinning micro black holes of the shell had created a separate continuum, a mini-cosmos totally cut off from the universe at large. Only space can travel through space faster than light and this was the only way that the human race had found to do it.

"Hey, up there!" Carson said over the suit radio.

Aiyana peered at where he was gesturing. She could see a small machine, less than a meter long, clinging to the slate-colored outer surface of the conservatory. They clambered up handholds to the flat top and squatted down to inspect the inert device.

"*Dead as a dodo.*"

"Excellent! Soon you'll be speaking Ancient English better than me."

Carson tried lifting but the 'bot seemed cemented to the composite surface.

"Vacuum welded?"

"I don't think so. It clings on with retractable solenoids – the hull has an embedded iron matrix for magnetization. Here – the electromagnets are stuck to the surface. We're going to have to pry it loose."

But even with their combined strength the machine refused to budge.

"It's no good – we need something more."

With that Carson hurried into the ship and re-emerged with a narrow metal bar.

"We can use this as a lever; that loading ring will make a great pivot."

He hooked his feet around the rungs of a service ladder then threaded the bar through the loading ring and under the 'bot. Grabbing the other end of the bar he pulled down hard.

"Yes!" he yelled, as the little device broke free.

The 'bot rose straight up, accelerating towards the black void of the shell. Carson threw down his improvised lever and leapt after the ascending machine. He intercepted it four meters off the surface, cartwheeling as he enveloped it in his arms. At the same moment his safety line straightened, became taught, and effortlessly parted in two.

Everyone shouted in panic.

"Don't worry, I've got you," said the ship as it extended the bubble field. Carson's upward trajectory came to a halt.

"Well pull me down!"

"Sorry, projecting a field outside the hull isn't easy and now you're further up the shell's gravity gradient. It's all I can do to keep you where you are. Aiyana, you'll have to go up and get him."

"Oh wonderful!"

After tugging at her safety line she jumped upwards.

"Okay," she said, "we need to take this nice and slowly. Carson, if you can free up one arm and put it around my waist I'll reel us both in."

He shifted the 'bot onto his hip, then reached out and caught hold of Aiyana. She gripped the safety line and pulled.

"Why aren't we moving?" he asked. His faceplate was shoved into her back.

"Because my goddamn line just broke too."

Carson let go of her.

"Hmm..." he said, "tricky, yes – tricky."

"No matter. We'll just use whatever internal propulsion system these pathetic suits have got."

She swiveled round to look at him.

"Please tell me they *have* propulsion."

"Oh yes, but I don't think they're fueled."

"I pleaded with him…" the ship began.

"Oh shut up!" Carson yelled.

"I thought if I beat him enough times at Galactic Warlord he'd get bored and actually do some maintenance."

"I *knew* you were cheating!"

"Both of you, shut up!"

They fell into sulky silence.

Finally the ship said, "Hey Carson, do you recall that scientific paper about swimming in distorted space-time? You always said you wanted to try it"

"Yes! Some professor demonstrated that a steep gravity gradient could enable movement with a swimming action."

Minutes passed as Carson furiously cartwheeled his limbs in the vacuum.

"Have I got anywhere?"

"You've risen five centimeters."

"I guess the gradient isn't high enough."

"Yes, that's what my calculations predicted."

Carson quietly fantasized about taking an ax to the ship's logic arrays.

Aiyana, who had been watching the action in tactful silence, spoke up.

"If you threw the 'bot upwards into the shell, do you think the reaction would be enough to propel you to the hull?"

"No way!" he cried, hugging the little machine to his bosom.

She sighed and searched around.

"Hey ship, can you manipulate the inertial field to push Carson's lever up to me?"

The metal bar wriggled on the deck until it was free of the loading ring. Aiyana reached out and grabbed as it drifted upwards.

"Hang tight – I'm going to climb down you."

Keeping her grip on the lever Aiyana seized a fold in Carson's environment suit and slowly pulled her way down his body, then down his legs. At that point she looped in the remains of the safety line.

"I'm going to tie our ankles together. Pray that it stays in one piece."

Once they were secured to each other she slowly unwound her body until she pointed downwards towards the ship. Gripping one end of the lever she stretched her arms above her head. Now the other end of the metal bar almost touched the hull.

"Hey ship, is that close enough to capture in a field?"

A gentle tug passed along their bodies and a minute later they were sprawled across the surface of the conservatory module.

"That's enough maintenance for one day," Aiyana muttered, "I need a drink."

"Ship," said Carson once they were safely inside, "you had better add two environment suits to the procurement list."

"New or refurbished?"

Two laser beams coming from the direction of Aiyana struck him on the back of the neck.

"Better make them new."

They regrouped in the tiny galley next to Carson's sleeping quarters. He disappeared into a locker and emerged with a dusty brandy bottle.

"Best I can do," he said as they sat down at the small table. He poured two glasses and passed one over.

Aiyana took a huge gulp, breathed in sharply and laughed. She couldn't stay mad with him.

"Never a dull moment with you, is there Carson?"

"Never a dull moment," he agreed with a grin.

They clinked glasses and drank.

"Hey," she exclaimed, "this is good stuff!"

"It's from my own vineyards," Carson drawled in a surprisingly good imitation of Juro.

Aiyana choked and snorted as he refilled their glasses.

"Seriously though, where did you get it?"

"God knows. Ship – do you remember?"

"Believe it or not, it was from a grateful client."

"Hey that's right. It was that arcology in the Darvanium system – it's on the outer edge of the Cygnus Arm – very metal poor. Some local bigwig wanted a unique coming-of-age present for her daughter and I found a virgin gold necklace in the stores."

"I've got an image," said the ship.

A slender young woman in a white dress materialized in the center of the room. She gave them a shy smile and pushed her gleaming black hair to one side to display her gift.

"Oh my God it's beautiful!" Aiyana cried, woozily climbing over Carson to take a closer look. The necklace was a delicate filigree of gold inset with lapis lazuli and mother of pearl.

"It's authentic gold too, dug out of the ground, not the stuff they make in factories. The daughter was due to be betrothed the next day and the local tradition is that everything she and her future husband wear at the ceremony should be made from virgin materials to denote purity."

"Oh that's so sweet," sniffed Aiyana, plunking herself in her chair. She refilled their glasses and offered a toast.

"Here's to innocence."

"Innocence."

After they drank Aiyana reached out, took Carson's glass from his hand and put it down on the table.

"I know things are a bit complicated between us," she said, "but a woman has her needs."

"I'm sorry, I'm not following…"

Aiyana rolled her eyes then burst out laughing.

Did the ship just send her a message on a private channel?

"Carson, dear," she said taking his hand, "are we ever going to have sex?"

"Oh, well, I um…"

"Hey, you can't just strut around naked all the time and –"

"Me!"

"– and come on with all this dirty talk about virgins and initiation ceremonies and not expect a woman to get ideas, can you?"

"I assure you –"

"Oh shut up!" she cried and clambered over the table.

And so it was that Carson had the unique experience of twice making love for the first time to the same woman.

Many hours later they lay in each other's arms in the rumpled bed. The detox tablets had done their work and they were sleepy, sober, and content.

"Carson," Aiyana said quietly as she lay gazing up at the bulkhead, "was she the same as me?"

This time he knew who she was talking about.

"Sort of, I mean she was physically identical apart from the tattoos but her personality was an out of focus version of you. I don't think they gave her many memories."

"The poor creature, she only lived for a few days."

It was only then that Carson fully comprehended the obscenity of Juro's crime. To conjure up, manipulate, and then snuff out a life as real as the woman laying beside him showed total contempt for the human experience.

"Don't worry, we'll make sure it never happens again."

The next day marked the halfway point of the ten-day voyage and the anticipation of their arrival prompted them to pick up the pace. The fiasco outside the ship finally convinced Carson to join the maintenance push while Aiyana redoubled her studies of ancient history. Above all, there was the anxiety as to what exactly they would encounter on New Earth.

"There's no chance we'll find Asima waiting for us, is there?"

"None. First, Mitan Security has to decide that we really headed for New Earth rather than the Oskinova system. Then they have to commandeer and prep a starship – I very much doubt that they have one lying around – and normally the journey is done in three hops, each with a spin down/spin up cycle. I reckon we have at least a four-day start."

"But that speedboat of Asima's..."

"That was a push drive. All starships go at the same speed: flat out, two light years a day."

"But maybe she got word to New Earth."

Carson smirked. "How, she sent them a letter?"

"Oh my smart sexy mailman," she said and kissed him.

He had been careful not to remind Aiyana about Juro's assistant, Shin. Juro *did* have a starship ready to go, which could put Shin on New Earth just two days after their arrival. Even so his apparent cooperation with Kalidas should keep the clan Aniko people at bay. On the plus side they would be meeting on Carson's territory. In his experience criminals had a hard time operating outside their usual terrain.

Mercifully, none of Carson's doubts seemed to have occurred to Aiyana. Unless, he mused, she was going through exactly the same thought processes and was trying to protect him. In any case he would say no more.

Now that they were lovers he was finding it harder and harder to get her to keep her clothes on. Usually, she explained in a matter-of-fact manner, she chose a crew member from her vessel as a sex partner during her tour of duty, but for the last three months she had been assigned to a solo ship – possibly as part of Juro's machinations.

"I just about wore out my orgasmotron."

Ah youth thought Carson. Biologically, his sex drive was still as high as hers, but after so many years and so many lovers he had himself under more control, most of the time.

The ship had got its calculations right. As soon as the periscope was up Carson confirmed that they were within New Earth's arrival zone. Materializing too far out, he explained, would simply have been a pain in the neck requiring a long uncomfortable ride in the buggy. Arriving too near to Eridani would have been much more serious: they would have to hire a tug to return them to the approved distance and, depending on how close they were, pay a nasty fine.

"Why's it so important to arrive outside a system?"

"We're traveling at a nominal speed of two hundred million kilometers a second, so imagine running into something solid."

"But you said the ship doesn't really move. It has no any kinetic energy!"

"Maybe not, but our space-time bubble sure does. And before you ask where does it come from and where does it go, I say unto you *ask a philosopher.*"

"The colonists in the Yongding got a lot closer to the inner system."

"They were desperate – and lucky."

But Aiyana was far too excited to keep worrying about celestial mechanics.

"How long will we be in the buggy?" she asked as they clambered into the small craft.

"No more than an hour."

"*What?*"

"We're not taking it to New Earth; private shuttles are excluded from the inner system. We're off to the nearest bus station."

"When do you expect to be return?" the ship asked as the buggy slid along the shell's axis.

"My guess is no more than a week. Try to finish the shopping as quickly possible."

"Should I start plotting our escape route now?"

"Oh God I hope not, but keep your guard up. Disabling you would be a perfect way to keep us here."

"Okay, will do. Take good care of each other and be safe. I'd hate to go back to hauling freight for a living."

"Did it?" Aiyana asked. "I mean was the ship really a freighter before you bought it?"

"Poetic license. In any case, it didn't even have a personality until I came along."

"None of us did," said the buggy.

But Aiyana was no longer listening. She had her hands pressed to the globular display that encompassed them.

"That's it!" she shouted as they emerged from the shell's distortion field.

She was pointing at a blinding splinter of light floating against the starscape.

"There's Eridani!"

"Sure is," said Carson. "Hey buggy, can you find New Earth?"

The display image expanded at vertiginous speed, panning away from the star into the adjacent blackness. A tiny blue speck emerged from the void.

"I wondered if I would ever live to see this," said Aiyana, gently touching the image with the tips of her fingers.

Carson came up behind her and slid his arms around her waist.

"Welcome home," he said.

New earth

"I THOUGHT THE BUS STOP WOULD JUST BE A SET OF RENDEZVOUS COORDINATES."

Aiyana was staring at the huge ring-shaped structure surrounded by halo of spacecraft.

"How big is it?"

"God knows," said Carson, "three kilometers maybe. The really interesting stuff is lurking out there in the dark. Buggy, can you color code the starliners?"

Aiyana yelped as the sky filled with a second set of stars, all colored green.

"There must be a million of them!"

"Four hundred and twenty-eight at this facility," said the buggy.

"And how many bus stations in the system?"

"Last time we were here there were a hundred and sixteen, but there were plans to add more."

Aiyana did the math.

"Oh my God, fifty thousand liners."

She studied the display again.

"There's something else out there. What's that grey blob?"

"Let me ask the bus station," said the buggy.

A few seconds passed as the two systems exchanged messages across the diminishing distance.

"It's a Kuiper Belt object that serves as a raw materials reservoir. It has enough water to provision the facility for a decade, although the station says the Belt is getting depleted and next time it will have to buy from the Oort Cloud."

"Don't they have ice moons they could use?" Carson asked.

"Never try dragging anything that large against a gravity gradient," said Aiyana. "It's much cheaper to pull something down from the outer solar system, although I guess that's one less comet."

"Anyhow," she continued, "I think it's time to get a valet. I'm going to have a million questions by the time we hit New Earth."

"Don't worry, I've had an account with a service for years. I should be re-establishing contact as soon as we arrive at the bus station."

They disembarked at one of a series of access ports designed for small craft and left the buggy to find its own way home. Immediately they found themselves in a tiny reception room with a single console. Pseudo gravity gently settled them to the floor. Aiyana looked around the plain walls whose only decoration was a display warning of the dangers of overstaying a visa.

"Welcome to New Earth!" she laughed.

"This is strictly for us working stiffs. The tourists halls are something else entirely."

"New Earth is *very* serious about immigration," Carson had explained during the short journey from the ship.

The framers of the Covenant were determined to ensure that over-population would never again wreak the havoc that engulfed Earth. Following endless deliberations they had developed a complex formula for deciding the ecologically sustainable population of a planet that factored in the size of the arable land mass, fresh water supplies, diversity of species, and a host of other variables. It was an ironic exercise considering that at the time the human race consisted of one thousand and two souls. Doing the calculation for New Earth gave them a ceiling of nine hundred million people, a number that at the time must have seemed limitless. Nevertheless within two thousand years they were having real issues.

Making matters worse, being the center of galactic civilization made New Earth's transient population alone more than many planets. At any one time the number of tourists, pilgrims, migrant workers, and other visitors often exceeded one hundred million, putting the planet's total far over the permitted limit. After decades of wrangling a permanent solution was established that maintained the population at eight hundred and fifty million plus a hundred million temporary residents. Keeping to those numbers required endless vigilance.

"Carson, welcome back!" said the console, moments after he slapped his hand on its green circle.

"How long will you be with us?"

"Probably a few weeks."

"Very well, if your stay extends to over a year, please notify the Ministry of Stabilization."

"That was the easy one," Carson said to Aiyana, "I was born here. Your turn"

They waited while the circle turned red, sterilized itself, and returned to green.

"Welcome Aiyana," said the console as she positioned her hand, "what is the purpose of your visit?"

"Academic investigation at the University of New Earth – ancient space travel."

The machine thought about this. Along with her biometric identifiers, which the console took automatically, she had presented it with just her personal data. Her business card still showed her as a member of clan Aniko.

"Are you carrying letters of accreditation from a recognized educational institution?"

Carson jerked his head. This wasn't in the script.

"No, I am an employee of Carson's – research assistant."

He winked. *Nice improvisation!*

"Carson, do you confirm this arrangement?"

"I do."

"This is unusual. I will have to refer to higher functionality."

They fidgeted as the console ramped up its processing power. Finally it came online.

"Very well, taking into consideration your distinguished employer, I am issuing you with a hundred day visa. You must leave New Earth by this time or earlier if Carson chooses to leave first. I wish you success in your research."

"Yippee!" Aiyana cried as they hustled out of the immigration room.

"For God's sake, the damn thing will hear you."

"Whatever you say, boss."

Carson shook his head and muttered.

"Where are you going honored visitors?" the corridor asked.

"Main reception, we've got a bus to catch to New Earth."

A peristaltic field whisked them and their meager luggage down the passageway.

"How long –" began Aiyana, but got no further before they were deposited into the central terminus. She immediately forgot what she was going to say.

"Oh my," was all she could manage.

The vast space was overwhelming. Every available surface of the concourse sizzled with garish displays – weather forecasts, welcome messages, news bulletins, bus schedules, and advertisements for every imaginable service: detoxicologists, immigration functionalities, cross-cultural matchmakers, personality sculpturers, gene tailors, sensitivity guides, ancestor tracers, food tasters, data valets, and salacious offers from much, much older professions, all displayed in a dazzling lexicon of languages and images.

All around them was the restless excitement of people on the move – there must have been at least two thousand people from every spiral arm in the galaxy. Close by was line of ultra-orthodox Semblian Kinsmen, dressed in identical grey woolens, all carrying a bound copy of the Covenant. Each sported a long beard and disapproving grimace. Running alongside of them was a gaggle of Huan schoolchildren, quick and colorful as birds, waving their recorders.

"Now that's the way to travel," said Carson.

He was pointing to a Nunik matriarch glistening in her finery, surrounded by her eunuchs. The hem of her dress must have been fully three meters wide but she strode on oblivious to the crowd as her retainers desperately tried to clear a path.

Suddenly all the schoolchildren scattered.

"Shuang xi!" they shouted in unison as each threw paper flower petals into the air.

"What's happening?" asked Aiyana.

Now the children were silently executing a series of complex steps in perfect synchronization.

"My valet says it's a square dance – all the rage in the Huan Federation. I think their getting cues on a private channel."

"No, it's public," said Aiyana, scanning quickly.

"Half sashay and roll away," hollered the caller.

Before Carson could say anything Aiyana jumped into the crowd and joined the dancing. The delighted children gathered around her.

"Pass thru and split in two!"

Her joy illuminated the entire concourse. Inspired by Aiyana's plunge two sturdy daughters from an agrarian family joined the twirling dancers and one of the eunuchs leapt in until the matriarch whacked him with her fan. Even the Semblian kinsmen managed to smile.

The dance finished as quickly as it begun. Chaperones appeared screeching admonishments and herding the children across the room. Aiyana bounded up to Carson and hugged him.

"Hey, why didn't you dance?"

He laughed, "You did enough for both us."

They picked up their bags again and headed towards the bus.

"Good morning," said a smartly dressed man as he stepped out in front of them, "may I tell you about the Church of the Hidden Brethren?"

Carson walked straight through him.

"Damn projections – just ignore them."

"What if we had stopped?"

"Two hours of automated drivel. New Earth attracts every crackpot in the galaxy."

They hurried on through the crowds, Carson's valet supplying the directions to the bus. An hour later they were heading towards the inner system.

The main lounge of their transport contained about a hundred people including the schoolchildren from the bus station. Unlike the other passengers the youngsters were not responding to the inertial dampening with queasy stoicism – they thought it was hilarious.

"Just like being in the water," said one.

The only adult who shared this point of view was Aiyana – she was hardened from a working life accelerating through the Mita system. Now she was showing them how to do inertially aided handstands.

"Leave them alone," Carson begged, "any moment now they'll start throwing up."

Aiyana plunked herself down next to him as the chaperones started another round up.

"Are we there yet?" she giggled.

"No my child, another two hours. At least it should soon get interesting."

So far the inward journey had provided little in the way of scenery. As the bus's public channel explained, four billion years ago the sunward plunge of the gas giant Vulcan had swept away most of the system's outer bodies. Fortunately this ancient catastrophe had had little effect on anything except the tourist industry, and the debris trail collected by Vulcan's tidal drag eventually made the resource-rich inner planets.

Possibly to make up for this lack of excitement they changed course to chase the Millennial Comets. Two thousand years previously, the bus said, the celebrations for the six-thousandth anniversary of the founding of New Earth had included nudging six comet nuclei out of the Oort Cloud to create a dazzling synchronized spectacle. It proved so popular that the orbits were corrected and a seventh nucleus added to perform an encore a thousand years later. Now with the Eighth Millennium due in three years the comets had been gathered once more. Another nucleus had been added and they were again hurtling towards their perigee with Eridani.

Everyone crowded onto the bus's observation decks to watch the show. Their flat surfaces extended out from the main body of the bus like a pair of stubby wings; each surrounded by an inertial field that trapped a bubble of air for the passengers. For all practical purposes they was standing outside, directly confronting the vacuum of space.

"Am I the only one feeling nervous?" Carson said.

Certainly the schoolchildren seemed unperturbed. They were daring each other to peer over the edge of the deck.

"I mean, how can that be safe?"

"You big silly," chided Aiyana.

To Carson's horror she ran full tilt across the deck and leapt into the black abyss. At two meters out her trajectory came to a smooth halt; the inertial field spun her around and gently returned her to the surface. After a moment of frozen shock all the schoolchild began hurling themselves into the void. From that moment she was their idol.

A few minutes later they were among the Millennium Comets. The nuclei's frozen volatiles, warmed in the strengthening sunlight, filled the surrounding space with halos of water vapor, dust, and ammonia. Now everyone stood quietly on the deck, their faces lit by phosphorescent light; even the schoolchildren were silenced by the eerie display.

To everyone's delight the bus wove a graceful trajectory through the streaming tails. Driven by light pressure from their parent star, the ghostly ribbons were already a million kilometers long and would eventually span the orbits of the inner planets.

They had a momentary glimpse of the swarm of escort vessels at the head of the procession and then the performance was over.

"How do you maneuver something as slushy as a comet nucleus?" wondered Aiyana, "I had enough trouble with asteroids."

"God knows."

As it happened, God and one of the Huan schoolchildren knew.

"A hybrid tugging system, honored fellow passengers. A highly charged micro black hole of exceptional mass pulls the comet by gravitational attraction and heavy tugs using superconducting electromagnets usher the black hole."

"Kids today," Carson muttered as they trooped into the main lounge.

A cry went up from the crowd – the displays were showing a small blue disk. He smiled as Aiyana and the schoolchildren hugged each other.

To left of New Earth was the bright yellow dot of Adhiambo, the planet's sole satellite. The moon had once belonged to Vulcan before being shed on its vertiginous dive to Eridani.

Now the screens were displaying a schematic of the inner planets. Beyond the orbit of New Earth was New Mars, the mineral-rich industrial heart of the system surrounded by a swarm of arcologies. Nearer in was Little Venus, another cast-off from Vulcan. The giant planet itself had taken up residence in terrifying proximity to its parent sun, completing an orbit every ten days. A close-up showed boiling gases trailing in its majestic wake, like dry ice left outside on a summer's day.

There was another shout as the display switched to a closer view of their destination. Carson wondered how the astronomers of Old Earth must have felt when the Labeyrie Hypertelescope captured the image for the first time. To a world beset with overpopulation, rising sea levels, and runaway pollution, the new planet must have looked like paradise. It was younger and more geologically active than its namesake but with the same mix of oceans, ice caps, and continents. Most important of all, the oxygen-rich atmosphere shouted the promise of life across ten light years. Little wonder that it spurred the building of the human race's first starship.

Aiyana detached herself from the schoolchildren and returned to Carson sporting a huge grin.

"Darling –" she began.

Uh oh, he was beginning to know that smile.

"The kids were telling me that they're riding down on the Elevator."

"Oh no, it's a tourist trap."

"Oh please!"

"You are not getting me on that thing. If anyone saw me I'd be a laughing stock."

Aiyana pouted for a moment then appeared to change the subject.

"Remember that garden where we met the night we escaped from Kaimana?" she asked.

"Yes..."

"I've an idea..."

"Yes..."

The large almond eyes stared into his.

"Well, after we ride down – down the Elevator that is – and get freshened up, wouldn't it be fun if we found a bar and met some nice girl. If we all got along we could try re-enacting that statue in the garden, taking, um, turns being in the middle."

So it was that Carson found himself among the Huan schoolchildren waiting for the Elevator.

Like all citizens of New Earth, he was all too familiar with the iconic structure. The original had been built six thousand years ago to finally establish a civilized means of achieving orbit that did not require attaining planetary escape velocity. Even though the project had been technically feasible for centuries it still took a major tragedy at the Magnetic Acceleration Launch Facility to generate the political will and massive financing required to begin construction.

Twenty years and countless Ecus later the Elevator went into operation. After performing flawlessly for more than three hundred years it was finally rendered obsolescent by the invention of the push drive. By that time the Elevator had become a cherished landmark and the proposal to demolish it caused uproar. So it survived, catering to tourists and the incurably nostalgic.

Aiyana, by dint of her recent studies, knew all about it and was showing off her knowledge to the schoolchildren.

"How high is the Elevator dearest Aiyana?"

"Forty-five thousand kilometers dearest Lin."

"Why doesn't it fall down?"

"Because it's anchored in geocentric orbit and dangles its cable to the ocean"

"Are we going all the way down?"

"No, we are disembarking three hundred kilometers above New Earth and we'll go from there. It would take several hours to travel the entire length and your dear chaperones and dearest Carson would strangle us."

They all peered over the edge of the bus's observation deck. Overhead in the inky blackness of space the stars were obliterated by the dazzling glare reflecting off the sea. A thin black ribbon, about a meter wide, descended from an infinity point in the sky and vanished into the brilliant aquamarine light where everyone was staring.

The children squealed as the Elevator gondola finally rose into view. The original utilitarian design had been replaced by a translucent ring-shaped structure that encompassed the cable. The ring was bisected by an arch housing the traction apparatus.

Everyone hurried on board. Carson would have hated to admit it but he was enjoying himself. Like locals everywhere he had never bothered to see the sights that all the tourists came for, and even if he did run into an acquaintance Aiyana's presence provided the perfect alibi.

"I know for a fact this gondola has an emergency push drive, and it wouldn't surprise me if the traction engine didn't work at all."

"Shush, you'll spoil it for the children."

The descent took about an hour. The curve of the horizon slowly straightened and the sky became a delicate violet as they entered the atmosphere. The children clapped as the huge floating base station appeared out of the azure light. Originally the base had been all business, shifting huge amounts of cargo and millions of passengers to and from orbit, but now the station was a vacation resort surrounded by an armada of pleasure boats.

As they landed Aiyana hugged the children goodbye and bowed respectfully to the chaperones.

"Where to now?" she asked as they picked up their bags. "Do you still have a home here?"

"I used to, but I sold it to help pay for the ship. We're staying in the academic village at Makoto College, part of the University of New Earth. One of the advantages of being an official scholar is that you get permanent residential facilities."

"It's close to the Archives and the Great Museum, and it's where we'll find Kalidas, even if he has been officially kicked out."

The doors of the Elevator reception area swept aside and they walked out onto a wide sunlit plaza. The floating terminus was shaped like a huge cone with gently sloping sides, the Elevator cable anchored at the apex. All around them terraces of colorful buildings descended down to the marina that surrounded the entire structure.

Carson closed his eyes and relished warmth of the sunlight on his skin. He breathed deeply – the sharp ocean air was wonderful. Above the din of the miniature city he could hear the distant sound of waves and the cry of seagulls.

"Oh my God!" Aiyana cried.

Carson could not work out what was wrong – she was staring around intently. It was a lovely view but Aiyana seemed dumbfounded.

"That air movement," she said, "that's called a breeze, isn't it?"

She pointed to the horizon, jumping with excitement.

"And look – you can actually see the edge of the planet!"

Carson finally realized what was happening: this was the first time Aiyana had truly been outdoors. She had spent nearly all of her life in the synthetic environments of spacecraft and the arcologies. Kaimana, roofed-in and sheltered by the caldera's walls, was hardly better. Their short escapade on the outer flanks of the volcano was probably the closest she had ever come to the natural world.

She put her hands to her face, tears seeping over her fingers.

"It's so beautiful, so beautiful."

More passengers came out of the terminal, streaming round the two figures standing motionless in the sunshine.

Within an hour Carson and Aiyana had boarded a bus to Cissokho City, the capital of New Earth.

"The University is in the center of Hawkins, the original capital," Carson explained. "Once the Little Ice Age started the government decided to relocate further south but the academics stayed put. It was a miracle, really, because the move preserved a lot of the original colonial structures. If the government had stayed the city would have mushroomed and buried all the historical buildings within centuries.

"Now Hawkins is an academic town and the University has become the official guardian of the historic sites and the archives. Plus, of course, it's a huge magnet for tourists and pilgrims."

"So that's where we're staying?"

"Oh no, as visiting scholars we get the royal treatment."

When they got to Cissokho City Aiyana desperately wanted to stop and do some sightseeing but this time Carson really did put his foot down.

"I'm sorry, but we're only a few days ahead of Shin and Asima, and we just can't afford the time. I promise you, when we're done with all this, I'll take you everywhere on the planet."

As if to emphasize the urgency Carson splashed out on a private taxi to take them the eight hundred kilometers up the coast to Hawkins. Aiyana spent the journey pressed against the windows, transfixed by the view. The taxi may have been smart enough to notice her behavior – it was clearly attuned to the tourist trade – and periodically it wove inland to include the most picturesque scenery.

Carson, however, was already at work. He had contacted the Post Office in Hawkins to advise them of an imminent delivery – he was through with hanging on to mail packets – and he had left messages for Kalidas. For the moment the disgraced researcher was not answering.

The taxi dropped them at the Old Campus, a good distance from the tourist centers. During the centuries of blizzards and ice the University had developed a hunkered-down style of architecture, a tradition that had never really gone away, and as Aiyana scanned the campus she had difficulty distinguishing some the buildings from the landscape. There was one exception.

"What is *that*?"

She was pointing to the northern sky at what appeared to be a huge funnel-shaped swarm of gnats.

"That's the Fountain Building. Weird looking thing, isn't it?"

It was an attempt, Carson said, to balance the need for mass student accommodation with the distaste for large-scale structures. Instead of building a single giant edifice, the regents of the University had created three thousand self-contained floating apartments, each held aloft by its own push drive. Each apartment cycled from base to summit over a ten-day period, hence the title.

"Although the residents have an earthier name."

"It was one of those things that seemed a good idea at the time. It's ludicrously expensive to operate but of course the regents refuse to replace it – you'll find a lot of that on New Earth."

They strolled through the heavily treed campus to the main administration building. At the reception counter they found a human attendant dressed in a neat grey uniform, and although he appeared as young as everyone else, something in the cautious way he moved suggested great age.

The receptionist glanced up as they walked through the ancient stone entrance. He looked blank for three seconds before finally achieving a hit on his facial recognition database. His expression warmed immediately.

"Professor, it is good to see you again, honored scholar. I trust you will be staying with us."

"Purely a courtesy title" Carson muttered to Aiyana.

"Hello George, it's so nice to see old faces. Yes, I'll be staying on campus if you'll have me."

Carson put his hand into the green circle on the counter to confirm his identity.

He indicated Aiyana

"This is my distinguished colleague Professor Aiyana from the University of Mita, I am hoping you can accommodate her as well."

"I'm delighted to meet you Professor. Accommodation is a little tight at the moment Professor Carson – would it be acceptable if I you and your colleague shared an apartment?"

No fool was George.

They hurried across the campus to their allotted quarters.

"Wow!" Aiyana said examining the apartment's antique furnishing,s "this is just like the ship's main cabin."

Except for the restrained good taste she added to herself.

The antiques included the plumbing system.

"So you have to twist this handle every time you use it?"

After the tutorial in ancient hydraulics and a quick shower, Carson made ready to drop off the mail.

"Why don't you stay here and unpack, I'll return in two or three hours."

"Unpack what? Hell no, I'm coming with you. I'll just wander round Hawkins while you do the business at the Post Office."

She put her arms round his waist and gently rubbed her breasts against his chest.

"Afterwards we can get something to eat and then find a bar. You do remember my idea, don't you, my big-brained professor?"

The next morning Carson staggered into the apartment's small kitchen. He was unsure whether he would ever walk fully upright again. The previous evening he and Aiyana had ended up at a campus tavern called The Twelfth Dimension where they had met Naadira, a charming graduate student currently working on her doctorial thesis on early colonial art. Carson had been amazed at the ease with which Aiyana conducted the negotiations, although Naadira joked that she had her own reasons.

"Anything to get away from the Pissoir for a night. You should try being in my room in a gale, it's like living on a ten meter boat in the middle of the ocean."

Whatever her motivation, their tryst had been a splendid success, although this morning Carson envied the prehistoric male's inbuilt performance limits. One thing he knew for certain: for the rest of his life, whenever he thought of that statue in the garden on Kaimana, he would smile.

Aiyana crept into the kitchen.

"Where's Naadira?"

"She left already – early morning seminar."

"What a nice young woman! We must get together with her again."

"Give me a couple of months to recover first."

"More like a couple of hours you randy old thing."

"I wish. Meantime, we've got more urgent business. Sometime during last night's festivities a reply finally came through from Kalidas. He wants to meet this afternoon."

"That's great – do you have any plans for this morning?"

"I thought I'd access the University Library and –"

"Carson…"

Oh no, the smile!

"Couldn't we visit the Great Museum? I mean, you said we could jump the lines with your super privileged access and everything"

After the previous night's tryst he was in no mood to refuse her and they were soon heading towards the historic buildings.

"Oh, it's all so small!"

Aiyana pressed her face to the transparent wall that enclosed the ancient settlement. Inside the hermetically sealed space was a bizarre mixture of buildings: composite prefabricated modules, log cabins, stones houses, and improvised brick.

After eight thousand years everything except the composite structures were in an advanced state of decay. Millennia ago the entire compound had been sealed off from the environment and the atmosphere replaced with inert helium, but the ages had already taken their toll.

A private channel was telling each visitor about the structure that they happened to be looking at.

"The plastic modules were brought from New Earth aboard the Yongding. It is believed that the original plan was to house all the colonists in this type of building and that the colony would be provisioned incrementally by means of multiple round trips to Old Earth. Of course, the original population was envisioned as being much smaller than The Thousand that were eventually crowded onboard the starship."

The village illustrated the struggle of the first decades far better than any dramatic re-enactment. Cissokho, realizing in the last panic stricken hours that they were embarking on a one-way journey, had packed the ship with every single person on the Chu Jung Orbital Facility who was willing to go. It was an extraordinary decision that had undoubtedly saved the human race, but the pathetic remains of those first buildings showed the price of survival.

Like most visitors, Aiyana was silent as she walked away. The debt that she and everyone present owed to those first colonists was overwhelming. Eventually she stood with Carson outside in the warm spring sunshine.

"Can we go to the Memorial Fire?"

Adhiambo Cissokho's funeral pyre was larger than Aiyana had imagined. Originally it had been a simple mound of burning wood, but now it was neatly hemmed by a low heat-retardant wall to allow visitors to approach safely. Every few minutes a uniformed attendant added more fuel. Worlds from all over the galaxy sent timber to be added to the flames.

Aiyana reached into her bag and pulled out her own small packet of wood. She closed her eyes and held the bundle close to her body, then tossed it into the fire. On either side people were performing the same homage.

After standing quietly for a few minutes she unfastened the front of her jacket, reached into her bag and took out the small pair of silver tongs that she had bought from a souvenir stand. Carson realized what she was intending and gripped her free hand. Aiyana used the tongs to root around in the blaze for a few moments then pulled out a small glowing coal. Before she could change her mind she pressed the ember to her bare flesh, over her heart. Her nails bit into Carson's skin.

Aiyana held the fire to her body for ten seconds then with a cry returned it to the flames. The mark would remain with her for the rest of her life. Carson released her hand and silently opened the top of his jumpsuit to show her his own scar, made by him as a young man on that very spot, seven hundred years ago.

Cissokho's pyre had burned for almost eight thousand years, through the desperately hard times of the early settlements, through the Little Ice Age, through the triumphal colonization of the galaxy, lighting the pathway for all of humankind, for you and for me, and for all our children.

KALIDAS

KALIDAS LIVED IN A SHABBY TREE-LINED STREET ON THE OUTSKIRTS OF HAWKINS. The large houses had once belonged to members of the University's faculty but now they had been divided and subdivided to meet the student demand for cheap accommodation.

"This guy is likely to be eccentric," Carson had warned Aiyana, "but we have to deal with him – he's the key to nailing Juro."

Even with this warning Aiyana still let out a gasp as the door swung open. Kalidas was a tall man whose clothes hung from his body in a way that suggested he had lost a lot of weight. His undernourished persona was reinforced by the dull hair that hung down to his chest. But it was his eyes that were truly alarming – they were totally black, like two opals set into a skull.

Carson, who had seen a good many strange people in his time, recovered first.

"Good afternoon honored scholar, I'm Carson."

Saying nothing and ignoring Carson's upheld right palm, he gestured the two to follow him into the house's interior. Kalidas's second floor apartment was crowded with the paraphernalia of academic research – multiple consoles and arrays, snowdrifts of papers and academic journals, and a chaotic assortment of experimental equipment.

The windows were set for maximum opaqueness but the dim light failed to hide the detritus of dust, abandoned memory nodes, and discarded food packets. Carson was not surprised to discover that access to the outside world had been severed as soon as they entered.

Kalidas rummaged in a draw to retrieve a portable identification scanner.

"I have to be very careful," he said, speaking for the first time.

He gave the scanner to Carson who placed the tips of his fingers into the green circle and handed it back. Kalidas held it for a few moments, downloading the results, then nodded.

"Very well."

He swung round to Aiyana "Who are you?"

"This is Aiyana," said Carson, and in a moment of inspiration added, "of clan Aniko"

"I thought Shin was accompanying you."

"He was unavoidably delayed."

Kalidas waited as she took her turn with the scanner.

"You're clan Aniko alright," he said, "but Juro's database says you are a mining engineer."

Aiyana leaned forward and smiled into the cadaverous face.

"What would you prefer it say honored scholar – Special Operative?"

Kalidas finally appeared to relax.

"Yes, yes, of course. I apologize if I appear over-suspicious; there have been so many problems... Do you know that the University authorities are actually trying to deport me?"

That helped explain why Juro was so desperate to enlist another conspirator. Kalidas put away the scanner and gestured for them to sit down.

"What have you been told of my work?"

"Only that you had made progress on discovering some new pre-colonial material," Carson replied.

"Progress – yes, progress indeed, but at a high price. Tell me, how familiar are you with the Teng Archives?"

"I know them pretty well – I have the complete set of recordings."

Kalidas snickered.

"You think you do."

He placed his hand on a console and projected a rapid stream of tabular data.

"The standard catalog of the Teng material – this set displays a sequential list of contents. Note the columns on the far right – they show the location of each item. Now see what happens when we go to the end."

The display accelerated to a blur, then halted. The right-hand columns looked different.

"Teng used a nanoionic recording device – state of the art for the period – for the vast majority of his audio records, but towards the end of the project he ran out of storage space. According to his personal journal he then turned to an already-obsolescent apparatus called a 'tape recorder'. You, Carson, are one of the very few people familiar with this technology."

Carson shrugged.

"Marginally," he said. "I did publish a paper a long time ago. My primary interest was the construction of the batteries. As you know, I deal in ancient devices; I was less interested in the machine itself. There's no market – Teng had the last one is existence. God knows where he got it."

"But you know the principles upon which it functioned?"

"Sure," he continued, mainly for Aiyana's benefit. "Data was recorded by changing the magnetic alignment of microscopic particles embedded in a long strip of emulsion-coated plastic. It's one of those prehistoric devices that make you wonder how it ever worked. It's believed there was once a similar technology involving spinning metal disks, if you can imagine something that bizarre."

"But you never personally studied the underlying principles of the recording mechanism? I thought not. In fact, very few historians have. I had to dig up the work of a third Millennium academician named Fahim to find a really good analysis."

Kalidas conjured up a new display from the console. It was the text of one of Cissokho's speeches to the Covenant Assembly. *"Artificial intelligence is difficult to define,"* it began, *"and we must be careful how we classify its limits."*

"That's the transcript. Here's the matching audio"

Aiyana's back straightened as the famous voice filled the room. The Ancient English was heavily accented but still comprehensible across the centuries.

"This is one of the recordings made using the 'tape recorder' and it is always reproduced in the way that you just heard. *Except it's not correct.* The audio was transferred from the tape recorder to a more modern storage device about one hundred years after Teng's death, but sometime later it was edited. Here's what the original sounded like."

"Not that –" began a male voice that was abruptly cut off by Cissokho's initial words.

"It was technically possible to use the plastic strip, the *tape*, more than once, and that is exactly what Teng must have done – he overwrote his first recordings."

Kalidas was becoming agitated.

"I imagine Cissokho insisted – she was never very enthusiastic about his project and no doubt felt the Covenant Assembly took priority."

Carson still did not understand Kalidas's excitement.

"Okay, so whatever was on there the first time was lost…"

Kalidas cut him off.

"What do you know of the physics of layered magnetic ferrous substrates?"

Carson laughed.

"Nothing, honored scholar"

"Neither does anyone else. It was virtually a dead technology by the time the Yongding fled Old Earth and the colonists certainly had no use for it.

"I have spent over a decade studying the subject. Even so, I made meager progress until Juro increased the resources at my disposal. The technical details are too arcane to discuss today, but the essence is this: all modern data storage is based on changing the quantum characteristics of a single electron, but each bit of information recorded on Teng's ancient machine required the crude magnetic alignment of tens of millions of iron atoms. It's a totally different concept."

Kalidas walked across the room a pulled the covers off a small box-shaped machine.

"Juro's engineers constructed this for me. It is the first working tape recorder to be built in eight thousand years, although it has more sophisticated capabilities than Teng's device."

Carson could see that Kalidas was actually enjoying himself. He must have wanted to share his findings for years.

"Let me give you a demonstration."

Like a magician he pulled out a small rectangular box.

"This is a Teng *tape cassette*."

Seeing Carson's expression Kalidas added, "It is a reproduction"

He fed the cassette into the machine and turned to Aiyana.

"Would you like to say something that I can record?"

Aiyana said, "*I am sitting in a house in the city of Hawkins.*"

Carson laughed to himself. Kalidas wasn't the only one who could show off – Aiyana's Ancient English was perfect.

Kalidas touched the machines console and played Aiyana's recorded voice.

"I will now reposition the tape so that the next recording will overwrite the first. If you could say something else of about the same length..."

"*The Yongding was the first viable starship.*"

Kalidas played the new recording.

"Each time it operates the machine erases earlier recordings by re-aligning the iron particles in the tape's emulsion. However – and this is the essence – *a significant number of those particles maintained their original alignment!* "

He fiddled with the console for a few moments, then Aiyana's voice declaimed:

"*I am sitting in a house in the city of Hawkins.*"

It was Aiyana's first recording. The voice was slurred, but perfectly comprehensible.

"You realize what this means!" Kalidas cried

Carson did.

"My God, Teng's erased recordings could still be there."

He sat down shaking his head.

"Kalidas, this is wonderful! There must be what – two hundred hours on those tapes – so potentially there is two hundred hours of new material. It's the greatest historical discovery in centuries!"

Kalidas was actually smiling – a frightening sight.

"But honored scholar," said Carson, "why the subterfuge? You have done marvelous work. Why not share it with the world? I'm sure the Archives Council would be –"

Kalidas's smile vanished.

"Those idiots! Do you know what would happen if I approached them? First, they would take a year to think about it, then they would say 'Thank you Kalidas, we'll run the project from here but we'll be sure to mention you in a footnote'."

Sadly, he was right. Carson knew that the Archives Council was a notoriously closed organization – a fact that had led to innumerable disputes. There was no chance that they would let a disgraced academic participate in the work of analyzing any new recordings.

Kalidas stepped up to Carson and gripped his arm

"I need those cassettes. I will analyze them and publish, then let Council do their damndest!"

"You want me to steal them for you."

The smile returned.

"Not steal, honored colleague, just borrow."

"And why would I do that?" Carson doubted that Kalidas knew much about Juro's machinations.

"We will collaborate on the investigation and publish the results as joint authors. You will share the glory."

Carson had no faith in Kalidas's offer, but it furnished the cover he needed to press ahead.

"How do you propose that I 'borrow' them? Didn't you already try?"

"Yes, in my excitement I made a clumsy, foolish attempt. Fortunately, our patron has provided us with more subtle means."

Kalidas went into the next room and returned wearing surgical gloves. In his hands was a battered-looking academic case, the sort used by scholars since the beginning of time. He placed the case down, opened it and carefully took out two more Teng cassettes.

"These are precise replicas of the two cassettes in the archives. They fit into a secret compartment in the bottom of the bag that cannot be detected by any scanner operated by the Museum. All you have to do is to ask to examine the originals – I'm sure you can manufacture an adequate reason – and affect a switch."

Carson thought hard. He knew it would come to this but the idea of risking his hard-won privileges was horrific. Zhou had assured him that she would square things with the authorities, but suppose they refused to be mollified? Finally the excitement of discovery overwhelmed his caution. Kalidas might be reckless but he was offering the chance to participate in an incredible archeological find.

"Alright," said Carson, "I'll give it a try. But tell me Kalidas, what's in this for Juro? All this must have cost him a fortune."

Kalidas drew himself up.

"Like you and I, honored scholar, Juro is a lover of history. He is outraged by the behavior of the Keepers of the Archives, and seeks only to share this discovery with the world."

Carson nodded. *If you believe that I've got a solid gold asteroid you might be interested in buying.*

A few minutes later he and Aiyana were hurrying down the street in the cool evening air. Juro's bogus case was wrapped in an anonymous package under his arm.

"Oh my God," Aiyana said, "that has to be the creepiest person I've ever seen."

"Yeah, I've been checking with my valet. That kind of eyewear has been adopted by a cult called the Brotherhood of the Secret. It seems that Kalidas is even crazier than we thought. The Brotherhood thinks that the failure to find another space-faring species is a conspiracy – that they really exist. What a guy to have as a partner!"

"Does he really believe that stuff about Juro? That he's some kind of benefactor?"

"God knows, but I was asking him a real question. What *is* in it for Juro? He couldn't sell the cassettes without a believable provenance. I suppose they'd be some money to be made from publishing new Teng material, but this entire operation must have cost a fortune. He'd be lucky just to recoup his outlay, and no one breaks so many laws just to uncover ancient history."

"But you're really planning to steal the cassettes?"

"I don't think I have a choice, not if we ever want to get Juro off our backs. If I went to the authorities right now they'd throw the book at Kalidas and maybe sweep up Shin, but the Old Man is too far removed. No, I'll be at the Archives first thing in the morning, God help me."

"We'll be at the Archives."

"Oh, no. There's no point in both getting caught."

"Yes there is. This is my mess as well as yours – I'm the one the old bastard tried to kill. I owe Juro and I intend to repay him. Anyhow, I'm supposed to be your clan Aniko minder. It would seem very odd to let you lift the tapes without me being there."

"Then God help both of us."

The next day Carson and Aiyana presented themselves at the Scholars desk of the Archives Administration. The previous evening they had taken out the best insurance policy they could think of: using an attorney functionality they had sworn a joint statement describing the entire conspiracy. The heavily encrypted record was now held by the valet service with instructions to send it to the authorities if they did not check-in the following afternoon.

The administration offices were located in a corner of the Great Museum. Built round the site of the first settlement, the huge building was one of the most popular destinations for visitors to New Earth. Each year, millions of people streamed through the galleries to see the surviving relics of the early colonists, little realizing that most of the collection was beneath their feet.

"Physically access the Teng cassettes?" the administrator said, "may I ask why Professor Carson?"

"As you know, I wrote a paper on Teng's recording device, I am planning a follow-up paper on the media he used."

There was a pause while she checked the records.

"Ah yes. However – this is embarrassing – last year there was an attempt to steal one the cassettes. You probably never heard about it; I see you were off planet at the time and the Council hardly likes to publicize these things, but now there is a policy requiring a member of staff to be present throughout any examination. I apologize, but rules are rules. If you wait here a moment I will see who is available to accompany you."

The administrator disappeared into an office.

"Oh hell," Carson muttered.

"Don't worry," Aiyana said hurriedly, "I'll distract them. Just be ready to make the switch."

The official re-entered with a second member of staff.

"This is Curator Lalita, she will escort you."

A few minutes later they were in an elevator heading down to the vaults. Upon stepping out they were confronted by a security checkpoint. Everyone re-identified themselves and walked slowly through the scanners.

"I called ahead to the keepers, honored scholars, everything should be ready," Lalita said as they entered the preparation room. Here they donned surgical gloves and a small portable breathing apparatus consisting of a transparent facemask that connected by hose to a lightweight backpack.

The trio walked down appeared to be a vacuum access tube to yet another checkpoint in front of a heavily armored door.

"The entire storage facility floats on push drives to physically isolate it from the surrounding sedimentary rock. A ten megaton blast on the surface above would hardly register, although earthquakes are the real concern."

At the Curator's signal the vault door slid aside and they pushed through the inertial field into a huge circular room.

"We are now in a sterile helium atmosphere. Keep your face masks on at all times."

The walls that surrounded them housed thousands of sealed draws scaling from the size of a hand to ones as big as a truck. Their face masks had some built-in intelligence and wherever they looked a discrete display appeared describing the draw's contents.

- *Hand-carried voice communicator*
- *Stringed musical instrument*
- *Medical device for imaging internal organs*
- *Portable fusion reactor*
- *Food preparation utensils*

Aiyana gazed around in wonder. This was the greatest concentration of treasure in the entire galaxy: the cargo of the Yongding – everything that was left of Old Earth.

A small container was waiting on a central table. Lalita picked it up and carried it to an anteroom where she set it down and with wincing care took out the Teng two cassettes. She placed them on a table in front of Carson.

"You have one hour, honored scholar."

Carson unpacked the items he had put in the fake academic case: a small personal console, a recorder, and another small device.

"This is a Huan analyzer capable of remotely scanning for rare earths," he said, holding it up for inspection. "My research has suggested that the tape emulsion may contain Neodymium, even though it is not mentioned in the Archives catalog."

While Aiyana and Lalita made polite conversation Carson rooted around in the bottom of his bag ostensibly searching for a second mini-recorder. In reality he was opening the secret compartment ready for quick access.

After that Carson began going through the motions of setting up and calibrating his equipment. He checked the time. When was Aiyana going to produce this diversion? They only had an hour for God's sake.

Twenty long minutes passed until Aiyana let out a gasp of pain and placed her hand to her chest. Startled, both Carson and Lalita swung round and stared at her.

"I'm sorry," she said, "I performed the Ritual of the Funeral Pyre yesterday and the burn is troubling me. Honored curator, could you help me for a moment?"

With that Aiyana began to unfasten the top of her coveralls but moments later she stopped and stared at Carson.

"Professor, *please!*"

Lalita snorted and positioned her broad back to block Carson's view while she inspected the wound.

"The burn appears healthy to me," she said. "Give it a day or two and I'm sure it will be alright."

"Thank you, you're so kind."

Lalita favored Carson with another glare and resumed her seat. Doing his best to look chastened, he returned to his studies. It had taken him just seven seconds to make the switch.

The next thirty minutes were agonizing. Everyone who was granted access to the Archives used every minute of their allotted time and there was no question of leaving until the hour was completed. Finally Carson was able to repack the bag. Lalita tenderly placed the fake cassettes into their container and led them out of the vault. Ten minutes later they were walking briskly away from the Archives Building, doing their best not to break into a run.

"Aiyana my darling, you're a genius," Carson said.

"I got my inspiration from you, you dirty old man."

"Well my brilliant partner, the next stop is Kalidas's apartment. I'd rather be carrying a lump of radium than these cassettes."

The renegade historian was incandescent with excitement.

"You got them? Oh my God!"

Kalidas circled the carpet, too agitated to say or do anything. Finally he began to calm down.

"I've been preparing for you."

The adjacent room in his apartment was lined with plastic sheeting; it had been emptied of everything except for a cylindrical machine resting on a new workbench. Carson could see the shimmer of an inertial field across the doorway.

"It may not be up to the standards of the Archives but it will do."

Kalidas pulled on a breathing apparatus similar to the ones Carson and Aiyana had used earlier.

"I'm sorry, I only have one oxygen supply, but you can monitor my activity from here."

He picked up the academic case and disappeared inside the improvised clean room. A display flickered into life showing Kalidas taking out the cassettes.

"My God, it really is them."

He examined both before selecting one.

"This is the first one Teng recorded," he said.

They watched as he picked up a small instrument and crouched over the workbench. After several minutes of gasps and tiny grunts he finally lifted the top off the cassette.

"The tape appears to be in good condition."

He placed the opened unit into the cylindrical device.

"Teng's recorder pulled the tape out of the cassette in order to read it. However, the media has undoubtedly become very fragile over the centuries and I have no intention of trying to physically unspool it."

Kalidas indicated the squat cylinder.

"This machine is a diagnostic tool generally used to examine complex systems."

He placed his hand on the console.

"It is capable of creating a precise three-dimensional map of every iron particle in the spooled tape. After that it will be a simple exercise to extract the encoded audio signals. The full analysis will take several hours but I first want to find out if there really is anything there."

The display darkened and Kalidas rejoined Carson and Aiyana in the main room.

"I can operate the machine from here," he said pulling off the breathing mask.

"I've instructed it to examine the first few layers of tape."

"Ready, Professor" the machine announced.

"Play."

"Not that – Artificial intelligence is difficult to define and we must be careful how we classify its limits."

All three of them let out a cry of relief. The recording sounded exactly the same as the one found in a million libraries throughout the galaxy – the tape was still decipherable.

"Is there a second layer of recording?"

"There is, Professor."

"Not that this was the first design that we examined..." began a male voice.

"Yes!" was all Kalidas shouted.

Carson was actually happy for him – he had experienced the same joy when he realized the true provenance of the small toy he had found on Delta Pavonis.

"Congratulations Kalidas," he said with unforced sincerity, "you have made an extraordinary discovery."

"Thank you, thank you. I must proceed immediately with the full analysis. Then of course there is the second cassette."

"We'll leave you to it. I'll call you in the morning to see how it's going."

But it wasn't the next day, it was in the middle of the night when he next heard from the renegade academic.

Carson was in the depths of sleep as the call came through.

"What the –"

He glanced at the dim outline of Aiyana's sleeping body and shuffled into the kitchen.

"Carson, Carson, it's better than I dared dream! The last three hours on the tape are a conversation with one of the principal engineers, a man named Koju Sakyamuni. He actually talks about the building of the Yongding – this is sensational!"

"That's terrific," Carson said kindly, though as far as he was concerned it would still be terrific in the morning.

"But that's not why I'm calling. Listen to this..."

Another voice came on, speaking Ancient English in a lilting accent.

"Of course, New Earth wasn't the first world we visited, there were the others..."

TALLIS

As soon as he opened the door Kalidas spun round and disappeared inside. Carson sighed and followed him through the sleeping house. By the time he entered the apartment the historian was crouched over his console.

Thirty minutes had passed since the frantic call had come through. There was no question of returning to bed. Carson had dressed as quietly as he could, left a message for Aiyana, and summoned a taxi.

"During the initial planning stages we were still in a – how would you say it? – an obsolescent mindset; we envisaged building a small prototype before attempting anything on a large scale. That is a fine idea for designing an interplanetary craft, but in many ways the Yongding is not a spaceship at all – it is a machine for distorting space-time. You might as well make it as large as you can."

Hypnotized, Carson sat down beside Kalidas and listened to the eight thousand year-old voice.

"Guidance was without doubt our greatest challenge. Also, we had no idea how fast the ship would go! The only way to solve these questions was to activate the Alcubierre Drive and go somewhere. It was months before we really got the hang of navigation."

Kalidas paused the audio and turned to Carson. By now he was effervescing.

"This is beyond anything! Do you know – of course you do – that scholars have made careers out of reinterpreting just a few hours of the Teng recordings, and here we have two hundred hours of extraordinary new material!"

He was right: publication was guaranteed to cause a sensation.

"You said this was at the end of the tape – how did you find it so quickly?"

"As soon as I had extracted the whole recording I created a summary using a semantic analyzer. Not the most precise tool but it served its purpose."

Carson shook his head; there were so many questions.

"The section you played to me when you called – Sakyamuni was talking about visiting other systems. Has he said which ones?"

"Not yet. Eridani b – that is what they called New Earth – was always the primary target but it seems that they traveled to other planets to hone their navigation skills and possibly to find alternative settlement sites. From their perspective before the Melt they had all the time in the world. I'm sure the Yongding was originally envisaged as a vessel for exploration as well as colonization."

Kalidas turned to another display and summoned the one surviving picture of the Yongding. It was floating against a starry background while in one corner the glowing curve of a planetary surface could be seen, presumably Old Earth. Despite being one of the most famous images in the galaxy it yielded frustrating little information. With no frame of reference even the size the ancient starship was in doubt.

Carson still did not get it.

"How could all record of these trips possibly have been lost?"

"Sakyamuni was a Tech, he disappeared with the rest," Kalidus said.

"True, and Teng only made a handful of recordings using the tape device. He used it as a desperate last measure when he ran out of any other kind of storage and eventually they were all overwritten. I doubt he had much say in their use – he was dying from some forgotten disease. Even so…"

"You think this knowledge was deliberately suppressed, don't you Carson?"

"Yeah, it's the simplest explanation. But it must have been on Cissokho's orders – there's no other way everything could have been wiped out so thoroughly."

"In fact, it may not have been the work of human beings at all."

Oh God, here we go.

"You seem doubtful, but suppose the early voyages stumbled upon signs of an alien civilization. The galaxy is littered with clues of other intelligences. Do you know of M6090, the globular star cluster in the Crux Arm? It is a gigantic assembly of more than one million suns, all improbably similar in size but with an extraordinary variety of color. I believe M6090 was created four billion years ago as a work of art."

Carson needed to change the subject fast.

"Well, whatever the explanation we have the recordings now. Have you checked the second cassette yet?"

Mercifully, Kalidas took the bait.

"No, you are right – we must access that material. In the final section of the first tape Sakyamuni segues into a long description of navigation technology, however I am confident he will return to the subject of the Yongding's voyages."

Kalidas donned his breathing apparatus and disappeared into his improvised clean room; Carson watched on the display as the gaunt man crouched over the second cassette. Following the same procedure as the first cassette, his initial task was to open the casing to allow the diagnostic tool to do its analysis.

"This one appears to be less securely fastened."

Kalidas let out an animal scream. *What the hell?*

"Oh God, no, no, no..."

"What is it?" Carson shouted.

In answer, Kalidas snatched up the recorder that was transmitting to Carson in the next room and held the lens directly over the open cassette. There was no tape; eight thousand years had reduced the contents to a pile of rotted fragments.

Oh God, he's going to panic.

"Listen to me," Carson said in as commanding a voice as he could manage, "we still have a chance. Refasten the top of the cassette very carefully. Then let's talk."

Still cursing, Kalidas did as he was told, then staggered out of the clean room. When he pulled off the breathing mask tears were flowing from the hideous eyes.

"I was so close..." he wept.

Overcoming his revulsion, Carson gripped him by the shoulders.

"Kalidas, it may be possible to restore the tape – part of it at least. Each magnetic signal may be spread over several pieces – if so they could be matched. It may even be possible to re-assemble it like a giant shape puzzle."

"But there are thousands fragments, how could anyone..."

"I know someone who might just be able to do it. I need all your technical specifications on the structure of the tape and the recording formats. And I need the tape."

Grey morning light was already seeping over the old street when Carson finally left the house. He was carrying a small hermetically sealed case, inside was the second cassette. Kalidas had copied all the technical data to a personal recorder and, with reluctance, had added a copy of the complete audio from the first cassette.

"How do I know you will not publish yourself?"

"For God's sake – I committed a major crime to get all this and you still don't trust me?"

Kalidas had finally agreed when Carson made the case that they needed to listen to all one hundred hours of the recording themselves. It was possible that the semantic analyzer had missed something vital.

"I will have to travel some distance so I'll be gone all day. I'll contact you as soon as I have word on whether the tape can be recovered."

Aiyana was yawning over breakfast when he got to their apartment.

"I got your message – so what was all the excitement?"

She woke up fast as Carson retold the story.

Oh my God! The Yongding visited other systems? How could we not know?"

"Exactly what I asked. According to Kalidas the information was suppressed by aliens. Well, that would certainly make the news."

Aiyana laughed, but embarrassed as she was she had to ask "Carson... there's no chance he's right, is there?"

"Oh please – no, it was Cissokho, but God knows why. The standard story is that the only other voyages were a few shakedown cruises in the vicinity of Sol. Now it seems they got to God knows where."

"You've been up all night poor baby – are you coming to bed?"

"I wish, but there's no time. As soon as I've grabbed breakfast and a shower I'm heading south to an island called Mutapa."

"Oh that sounds fun, mind if I come?"

"I'd love to have some company; I'm off to meet my friend Tallis. Remember me telling you about her? She's the one who made the mechanical butterflies in the conservatory. If anyone can restore the tape it'll be her."

But Carson had another reason for encouraging Aiyana to accompany him – this was no time to leave her by herself. Shin could be arriving as soon as today, assuming he had guessed that they would head directly to New Earth. Clan Aniko had tried to kill Aiyana once, and although he doubted they would try anything that drastic again, once was enough.

Carson desperately wanted to listen to the recordings recovered from the first cassette but he was asleep within five minutes of climbing into their rented car, leaving Aiyana glued to the window listening to the vehicle's travelogue. She woke him an hour later as their destination appeared over the curve of the horizon.

Mutapa was a long straggling tropical island just south of the equator. From their altitude of one hundred kilometers they could see the wide ridge of densely forested mountains that formed the island's backbone. Wild rivers coursed through the highlands to feed the emerald jungles of the surrounding plains. Beyond the white beaches a necklace of coral reefs glinted in the azure water.

The landscape was virtually unchanged from the time the Yongding materialized in the skies of New Earth eight thousand years ago. The early colonists, mindful of the ecological devastation of their old home, had chosen to leave at least this one island to the local fauna. Everywhere else native vegetation grew next to plants transported in the pioneers' huge genome database, but Mutapa was a living time capsule of the planet's pre-human ecology. They were headed to the island's one human outpost.

Viewed from above, the settlement was a target of three concentric circles set into endless vegetation. The outer ring appeared to be a buffer zone of cleared ground. Inside that was a ring of densely packed buildings, and in the center was a checkerboard circle about a kilometer in diameter. The car landed itself in the built-up section.

"You're going to love this place," Carson said, "it'll feel just like home."

The moment the door peeled open Aiyana realized how right he was. They were met with a wall of moisture and heat.

"Oh this is wonderful! Can I take my clothes off now?"

"Later my darling, later"

From afar they could hear the din of the rain forest. The birds were not quite birds and the monkeys not quite monkeys, but the cacophony they created was unmistakable. Carson and Aiyana hurried through the blinding sunlight to a low building crowned with a holosign announcing Formicidae Systems.

The interior could have been an art gallery. The walls displayed a procession of images of exquisitely made artifacts including the robotic insects in the ship's conservatory, although Aiyana could not fathom why they were intercut with some sort of natural history program.

"Carson!" said the counter as he slapped down his hand, "welcome to Vegrandis."

"Thanks – I have transport reserved but I have an additional request."

At this point the human supervisor was summoned. Carson opened his shoulder bag and pulled out the hermetically sealed container holding the second cassette.

"I need to take this as well. I realize it's rather large but I'm hoping you can accommodate me."

"Hmm… yes it is, but I think we can manage – there will be an additional charge of course."

Rather large? Aiyana wanted to laugh but they both appeared to be completely serious. Moments later the smallest self-propelled cart she had ever seen materialized at their feet. The supervisor knelt down and carefully positioned the container. Carson produced a smaller package that was also added to the load. The miniscule vehicle and its cargo disappeared through a hatch.

"You are familiar with our operation and protocols? Excellent, there is no need for further delay. Hangar B, you are booked for three hours, honored customer."

Aiyana followed Carson down an anonymous corridor to a door that announced itself as Hangar B. They entered a spacious room at the center of which were two white ovoid pods. At his command the pods split open along their central seams to reveal large couches surrounded by equipment, much like the interior of the ship's buggy.

"Okay, now you can take your clothes off," he said as he started to undress.

Aiyana followed his example. By now she understood Carson well enough to know that he had a surprise in store. His glee was so endearing she did not have the heart to spoil it by demanding to be told what the hell was going on.

As soon as they were both naked Carson encircled Aiyana in his arms and hugged her.

"Hey! Aren't you going to buy me dinner first?"

He laughed and let go.

"Sorry, but we need to have each other's scent on our bodies – you'll understand why in a moment."

"Oh well in that case perhaps we should…"

"Oh no!"

"You said we had plenty of time…"

"Aiyana, please stop doing that…"

"Oh look Professor, I knew you liked me!"

"Right, young lady, you asked for this…"

Five frenetic minutes later, their pheromones thoroughly intertwined, Carson and Aiyana each stepped into a pod and made themselves comfortable.

"Okay, in a moment we're going to close up. The upper surface of the pod's interior is a display like the buggy's, so you'll have the feeling of being able to see all around. And as this is your first time in Vegrandis, let me do the driving."

"How do we get the pods out of this room?"

"We don't. Did you ever train in a simulator? This is similar except that we'll be remotely controlling a moving vehicle."

"Then why don't we just –?"

"You'll see."

He grinned and gave the command to close the pods. Aiyana was momentarily surrounded by a blank wall, then the display came to life. They were in some form of hangar containing tracked vehicles that were embellished with a wild collection of antennae and sensing devices. She glanced behind her and gasped: the hermetically sealed container towered over them – it had grown to at least five meters high – the cargo was resting on a trailer attached to their tractor.

"I'm leaving the hangar now," said Carson's voice in her ear. Aiyana braced herself – she had finally realized what was about to happen – even so she emitted a short scream as the doors rolled open.

The moment daylight flooded into the hangar a colossal insect, at least two meters tall, rushed up to them, its feelers twitching furiously. The creature's black body had the classic trifurcated configuration but with eight legs rather than six, although the front two were smaller and clearly not used for walking. In addition to two pairs of antennae, the flat triangular head sported a terrifying pair of jaws but there was no sign of eyes. Hanging round the segmented neck was a gold plaque upon which was inscribed *Official Guide* in neatly lettered Universal.

"Darkness and warmth to your nest [untranslatable]. You wish assistance?"

"Greetings, may your grubs flourish," Carson replied. "Yes, we wish to meet Tallis, can you take us to her?"

"Translation is hell," Carson said to Aiyana.

"Insects communicate by smell, touch, movement, and some sound. And if you think the meta-Cetaceans are hard to figure out, wait till you've dealt with this bunch."

"**Affirmative [untranslatable, untranslatable] that service will be ten Ecus.**"

"Lead on, we follow your scent."

The huge creature spun round and plunged into the tropical sunlight. Except it wasn't huge at all, Aiyana now realized that it was about half the size of her smallest fingernail, and their remotely controlled vehicle was not much bigger.

While Aiyana was vaguely acquainted with the history of the first encounter with intelligent insects she was not in the least surprised to learn that Carson knew all about it. The human race had stumbled across the Callidus five thousand years ago in the Outer Norma Arm of the galaxy, he explained.

Until that time the only other intelligent creatures known were the meta-Cetaceans, who had evolved independently on innumerable ocean-bearing worlds. But the Leviathans wanted nothing to do with technology; they thought the whole concept was hysterically funny.

"Of course, that's an attitude that may be perfectly correct."

The Ants, as they were immediately if inaccurately named, were utterly different. At the time the human colonists found them in the tropical forests of Pindan d, one hundred years after settling on the planet, the Callidus had established a sophisticated Stone Age civilization, but they were in danger of staying that way forever – the little creatures hated and feared fire which denied them the ability to smelt metal.

The astonishment of discovery was mutual. At first, humans could not understand how a creature whose central nervous system weighed a few milligrams could possibly display intelligence. Finally it was realized that the Ants employed an organic form of distributed processing, making the cognitive power of the whole infinitely greater than that of the individual.

"It's very similar to our machine systems. In prehistoric times humans used localized collections of logic circuits, storage units, visual displays and God knows what else – it was a tremendously inefficient paradigm. Now of course all logical structures exist independently of the underlying hardware. It's the same with the Ants. Their brains communicate using high frequency radio signals generated by their antenna, so each nest a single conscious organism, bound together by the queen's genome.

"Come to think of it, human beings are the only single-processor system left in the galaxy. *We're* the freaks!"

But if humans were amazed by the discovery of another intelligent species, the Ants were traumatized. Effectively blind and had never having seen or even conceived of the stars, the existence of other worlds was a shattering revelation that still reverberated throughout their culture.

Aiyana knew that the encounter had been of tremendous mutual benefit. Once communication was established, the human race was able to help Ants lift themselves out of their stone age. And in a universe where most forms of nanotechnology were forbidden, the advent of creatures that naturally worked on a very small scale was a godsend. Now the Callidus filled an important economic niche throughout the galaxy.

"It's not just the small scale," Carson added, "the Ants have a genius for fitting together puzzles like this one: Tallis can deploy thousands of small clusters of workers that can function quasi-independently while staying integrated with the whole nest."

By now Aiyana was scarcely listening, she was too busy was staring about as they made their way through Vegrandis. The streets were a river of creatures constantly bumping into each other, touching feelers, and clambering over individuals who got in their way. To her they appeared identical, but Carson assured her that their smell made the progeny of each nest as distinctive as if they had been painted different colors.

Individual workers were constantly streaming in and out of the buildings. Aiyana was delighted to observe that they moved between floors by the simple expedient of climbing up the outside walls. At first glance they seemed like any other insect, but closer inspection showed that many carried saddlebags and tool belts strung over their abdomens, and some were fitted with complex electronics.

The Callidus no longer built their own nests and usually inhabited man-made structures that had the appearance of open, incomplete buildings, though they were much more elaborate underground. The tractor display added descriptions as they passed. Aiyana was amazed to see many familiar names: the Bank of New Earth, the Embassy of the Huan Federation, Nakkita Biologics, and even Harrini Entertainment Media.

"Well if you make money, everyone wants to sell you something. Anyhow, this is the business district."

Finally they stopped outside a structure that the tractor identified as Tallis Industries. Carson tried to give their guide a five Ecu tip, which caused no end of confusion. Finally the creature shot off down the street.

The tractor swung round to face two fearsome soldiers posted at the entrance, their giant mandibles twitched in curiosity.

"Carson, how good to smell you!"

"Good to smell you too Tallis. I trust your queen prospers."

"She ages, but she lays new eggs [untranslatable] since we got your message."

The antennae swiveled some more.

"You have brought a nest mate."

"Hello, my name is Aiyana."

"But you are of Carson! [untranslatable] You have his smell."

"Remember Tallis – we can be nest mates but have different names."

"Humans! [untranslatable] [untranslatable] What confusing creatures you are. Come inside, we must dance in celebration of your arrival."

"Individual members of the nest only live for about a year," Carson said to Aiyana, "but memory is collective, otherwise Tallis would have forgotten about me long ago."

Carson unhitched the trailer. The soldiers seized its tow bar in their jaws and dragged it inside. Their tractor followed them into the nest. They found themselves in a large enclosed area; as the large doors closed they were encompassed by darkness. The tractor automatically switched to infrared vision to reveal workers pouring in from all sides.

"Sorry," Carson said to Aiyana on a private channel, "we have to go through this part – it will only take ten minutes."

As he spoke the tractor and the surrounding workers began to gyrate.

"Welcoming dance – standard procedure for the Callidus – a bit like shaking hands," he explained. "Fortunately the tractor is pre-programmed; we just sit and relax until it's over."

But that was not good enough for Aiyana.

"Hey, it's not following all the turns correctly, and see how they're waggling their abdomens."

With that she seized control from the machine. Carson groaned, but before he could override her Tallis's voice came online.

"Strength to your queen! [untranslatable] The spirit is with you!"

Carson laughed – had to admit it, whether it was schoolchildren or insects, Aiyana knew how to dance.

Finally the celebration ended. The workers touched feelers with each other and with the synthetic feelers on the tractor, then dispersed leaving them alone with a single soldier.

"It only takes one member of the nest to communicate with us. In theory it doesn't matter who it is, but soldiers are better at dealing with human interfaces."

"So, you have puzzle for us."

They got down to business. The story Carson told was heavily redacted. He had purchased the two ancient cassettes in a flea market.

"Fleas [untranslatable] are they tasty?"

He backtracked and explained. One tape had disintegrated; could Tallis reassemble it?

"I've also got a functioning reproduction of a cassette. I am hoping this will help you model the correct structure."

The Ant was cautiously optimistic but needed more time.

"First we examine fragments, then we give you estimate of completeness, plus cost."

A crane appeared controlled by a soldier. The sealed container and the other, intact cassette were unloaded and immediately surrounded by a swarm of workers.

"I didn't know Kalidas had given you one of his blank cassettes," Aiyana said to Carson.

"He didn't, I swiped it. He's already paranoid that I'm going to steal all his work and claim the glory. Asking for a replica cassette would have confirmed it. Anyhow, Juro's engineers made him a dozen copies; he'll never miss one."

Business concluded, they were taken to pay their respects to the queen.

"The queens are different," Carson said as their tractor headed underground on a freight elevator. "They act as the nexus for the collective. They're no smarter than any other individual but somehow the nest is able to work through them to recognize extraordinarily subtle patterns."

"So she'll be helping to put together the tape?"

"No, not that kind of pattern. They perceive changes in ecologies, social behavior, even the physical world and use them to synthesize... visions. Legend has it that five thousand years ago the queens predicted the arrival of humans."

The elevator bumped to a stop and they trundled into the royal chamber. The queen's image swam out of the darkness – a huge ghostly presence in the tractor's infrared sensors. She lay on her dais at the center of the circular room surrounded by her nurse workers. Her head and thorax looked like any other Ant but her abdomen was a gigantic glutinous sack, hundreds of times larger than normal. Every thirty seconds a ripple spread along its length as it disgorged another egg for the nurseries.

The tractor approached and its robotic arms placed a small container directly in front of the queen's head. Her antennae twitched then she plunged her mandibles into the pot.

"Royal jelly," Carson said to Aiyana, then addressing the queen: "Greetings your majesty!"

"Loyal subjects, [untranslatable] nest mates, we bid you welcome!"

"I trust your eggs are fertile."

"[untranslatable] The eggs fare well, but we are dying."

"The nest abides," rejoined Carson, giving the traditional response.

"The princesses have hatched, and tomorrow will take their nuptial flight. You must smell how excited are the drones! One princess will return, fertilized, to take our place."

"We rejoice in your renewal."

The queen fell silent and continued to eat the royal jelly.

"Do we go now?" whispered Aiyana.

"No, we wait."

Finally she finished feeding. Nurses rushed forward and cleaned her mandibles. After several more minutes of silence she seemed to notice them again.

"You too, Carson, await a new queen."

"I hope to visit your successor."

"No, not us, not the Callidus, something else is coming."

Carson's skin prickled. *Something else?*

"What is it, your majesty?"

But the queen remained silent, her head drooped.

"Carson, what's going on?" Aiyana's voice quavered in his ear.

All motion in the chamber had ceased. The queen's nurses were crouched facing the tractor, utterly still.

"I have no idea, let's just see what happens."

But nothing happened, and after fifteen minutes they gave up and respectfully backed out their vehicle.

"What was that about?" Aiyana asked again as they trundled out of the nest.

Carson shook his head.

"It could mean anything. I guess we'll find out eventually. For all I know the queen is senile – she'll be dead by tomorrow."

"Poor thing – will they bury her?"

"No, they'll eat her."

"I had to ask."

By now they were on the street. Carson was returning the tractor to the hangar via a different route and they were passing a cultivated area planted with tropical flowers.

"Do the Ants ever go into the surrounding forests?"

"I doubt it, there are too many creatures looking for a meal. This is a recreation area, they're crazy about smell – they've even developed pheromone generators that are analogous to musical instruments. Remember we passed Harrini Entertainments? They're making a fortune staging aroma concerts. I'm told they can get pretty wild."

"I would love to see one."

"Don't be so sure – sometimes the crowd eats the performers."

"I've been to events where the audience *should* have eaten the performers," Aiyana said as she continued to stare about her.

"The Callidus are omnivorous but these days they normally stick to a vegetarian diet. Human companies simply harvest the surrounding jungle and truck food in; most Ants are way too busy to forage."

They had entered a large plaza. At one end was a building totally different to the utilitarian structures they had been passing. It was a gigantic sphere covered by swirling patterns of grooves. In reality it must have been a meter across, by far the largest structure they had seen. In front of it was a huge statue of a nude human male.

The Church of the Eternal Larva the tractor's display announced.

"What the –"

"You can't overestimate the shock for the Callidus when they encountered humans." Carson explained.

"We always expected to meet aliens but they had no idea other worlds even existed. Then bang! These gigantic creatures with extraordinary powers appear out of nowhere. Many Ants were convinced that humans were a race of gods, but when they discovered that physically we're like huge grubs they decided that we must be larval phase of something even more amazing. Ever since the Church's followers have been waiting for us to pupate.

"Anyhow, that's their cathedral, if you like. A sphere is the optimum structure for large meetings. Ants are just as happy clinging to the ceiling as they are standing on the floor."

"Aren't they disappointed we've never hatched?"

"Probably, they've been waiting five thousand years. Many Ants don't adhere to the Church's teachings, but the rest seem ready for the long haul."

A few minutes later they were in the hangar. Carson parked the tractor and disengaged. Immediately the simulation pods split open and they climbed out stretching stiff limbs.

Aiyana shook her head.

"Wow! That was simply amazing," she said, then after a moments pause she added, "God, I didn't realize how hungry I was. Can we eat round here?"

They soon found a restaurant in the ring of human buildings that encircled Vegrandis. As they waited for their food Carson checked his messages. There was an urgent call from Kalidas.

"Doesn't this guy ever send regular communications? Anyhow, he says he's found another major revelation on the first tape that his semantic analyzer missed. Of course he's not saying what. He wants to meet at his apartment as soon as we return."

"I'm not sure I can take much more excitement."

On the return journey Carson wanted to go through his copy of the first tape to see if he could find what had gotten Kalidas so excited, but as on the trip down, he was asleep within minutes. It was early evening by the time they arrived at Hawkins.

As usual, the renegade academic refused to say anything as he beckoned them inside.

"So what have you found now?" Carson asked as he finally closed the door of the apartment.

Kalidas, who appeared even more agitated than usual, did not answer. Instead, another voice spoke up from behind them.

"Carson, Aiyana, how good to see you again!"

Shin stepped out of a darkened corner flashing his trademark smile. Standing beside him was Tabarak.

Negotiations

"You betrayed us!" Aiyana shouted at Kalidas.

"I betrayed you? You told me that you were representing Clan Aniko!"

"Bygones, bygones," cried Shin as if he were addressing a group of squabbling children.

The man was hardly recognizable. His melanogenesis, like Carson's, had faded, returning his skin color to a regular copper hue. Moreover he was wearing *clothes*; right now he was the very image of a corporate lawyer about to sign a large contract.

"We are on the brink of an amazing discovery. Let's move forward together on this. Carson, Aiyana, we have so much to talk about, and we should not distract Professor Kalidas any further. Come, I have transportation waiting outside."

"And if we don't want to go?" asked Carson.

"Oh really, why should you not?" Shin replied, again taking on the tone of a cajoling parent.

He held up his right palm.

"We know you have had considerable out of pocket expenses Carson, and as I gesture of goodwill I am authorized to make an immediate payment of fifty thousand Ecus to defray your costs."

"Very nice. And if we still decline to accompany you?"

Shin made a mock frown and inclined his head towards Tabarak.

"No honor amongst thieves, eh?" Carson asked him.

The big man shrugged.

"You got what you paid for. Besides, it's nothing personal – just business."

"Where have I heard that before?"

Carson turned to Shin who was still holding up his hand. He sighed and returned the gesture, his palm tingling as he accepted the transfer. He could not think of any reason not to take the money and maybe it would convince them of his passive compliance. It also established a stronger link between Clan Aniko and his own activities that one day might be useful in court.

"Okay, let's go."

In the meantime he shot Aiyana a message on a private channel.

Don't worry, this is not Kaimana. These bastards are on my territory now.

They trooped downstairs and out onto the street where a large limousine awaited. Inside the vehicle was another tough individual.

"This Ubay, another of my assistants," said Shin.

The doors closed and they shot upwards so fast the acceleration activated the vehicle's inertial dampening. Carson hoped that the limousine was redistributing its atmospheric shockwave, otherwise Hawkins was getting a hell of a sonic boom. Meantime he realized that there was a constant subliminal buzzing in his head. Something was generating a field that not only cut off his access to the net but also prevented him from opening a private channel to Aiyana. It was wildly illegal but not unexpected.

"The Clan maintains a residence near Cissokho City, we will talk more there," said Shin and with that he slumped in his seat and closed his eyes, discouraging further conversation.

Twenty minutes later the vehicle began its descent. They had passed the blazing towers of the capital city and continued south, following the coast. Now, directly below them the lights were thinly spread out, delineating spacious estates. They were heading to a large mansion perched on the edge of a cliff directly overlooking the sea. The building was laid out in the classical shape of a hollow square framing a formal garden. The limousine touched down in the central area, surrounded on all sides by the two-storey building. It was the perfect venue for a secretive organization.

They stepped out onto a moist thick lawn. Lush flowerbeds perfumed the night air and in the center of the plaza a discretely lit fountain painted elaborate patterns of sparking water. The sound of breaking waves could be heard in the distance. Everything was very civilized. The picture windows of the surrounding mansion were filled with light. Through one they could see a large conference room crowded with people. In the center of the group was a stooped figure. It was Juro.

"Oh God," said Carson.

They were led into a room populated with comfortable furniture and an elaborate drinks cabinet. As with the interior of the limousine, a field suppressed the ability to open private channels. Ever the perfect host, Shin immediately offered refreshments as they sat and waited. Tabarak and Ubay withdrew, but Carson never doubted that they could return in a heartbeat. Eventually the old man shuffled in. Like his minion, he appeared to be in a fine mood.

"Carson, Aiyana, good evening!"

"Good evening Elder Juro," Aiyana replied. A lifetime of deference was difficult to shake.

"And congratulations – while Shin and I were hurrying to New Earth you two were performing splendidly. Both cassettes safely removed and the Archives Council none the wiser."

"Yeah, it's amazing what you can do with a gun to your head."

"Be positive Carson!" Juro chortled, "I am about to make you a very rich man."

"And Aiyana a very dead woman?"

Carson was determined to crack his avuncular façade, but Juro was unfazed. He turned to Aiyana.

"What does he mean, my dear?"

"The bomb in my solo ship."

"Oh that!" Juro wheezed with laughter.

"Good God child, that was just an option for explaining your sudden disappearance. Having a resurrected Aiyana running around would have been difficult to explain. We were going to quietly relocate you to our division in the Huan Federation – a promotion too! Haven't you applied for an out-of-system transfer on four separate occasions?"

Carson had to admit it – the old bastard was a superb liar.

"Well I suppose…"

He prayed that Aiyana was only acting.

"Enough of this foolishness," continued Juro, waving a mottled hand. "Carson, tell me about the restoration of the second cassette. I hear that Kalidas was beside himself when he inspected it."

It was not the time to be uncooperative – alone in the Aniko mansion, cut off from the net and with two thugs in the next room. Besides, Carson had a surprise of his own in store.

"There's a good chance that my contractor will be able to reassemble at least part of the tape."

He decided to be more forthcoming. Juro would work it out in any case.

"I've given the work to an Ant. She should have a preliminary report by the morning."

Juro nodded.

"Yes, the Ants are capable of extraordinary restoration efforts. We too have employed them."

It was time to find what he was really after.

"So you're hoping that the second tape will yield more information about the Yongding's secret voyages?"

"Of course – you must grant that it is a remarkable development."

"It is," Carson agreed; he had been speculating about the possibilities ever since hearing the ancient recording.

"If they made planet-fall," he continued, "There's a real chance that they deposited supplies and equipment, especially if the worlds they visited were candidates for colonization. Finding anything left by the Yongding would be the greatest archeological discovery of all time. And imagine what it would be worth…"

He trailed off, thinking about the incredible prospect.

"It would be an extraordinary amount of money," Juro said, completing Carson's thought.

The old man had been doing some thinking of his own.

"There are only seventeen Old Earth artifacts in private hands; the last one to go to auction, the Dishi toolkit, sold for six hundred and fifty million Ecus. For one toolkit! Imagine what an entire supply dump would fetch."

Carson nodded. He could imagine all right.

"Let's not get too far ahead of ourselves. Sakyamuni's interview might not continue on the second cassette, and even if it does, God knows what he may say. And all this is predicated on the tape being readable."

"We will know soon enough – you said the Ant will get report you in the morning. In the meantime you will remain here overnight and we will all listen to its account tomorrow."

"That's all very well but I need to make a call this evening."

Juro chuckled.

"I don't think so"

"You don't understand. Aiyana and I recorded a full confession of the conspiracy – including all the details of your role. That recording is being held by my valet service with instructions to forward it to the authorities unless I check in each day. We did it to show that we weren't common thieves in case we were caught in the Archives, but it also serves as insurance against our sudden disappearance."

Finally Juro's mood soured.

"That was foolish Carson. Do you really think the allegations of a pair of renegade felons would carry much weight?"

"Probably not, until sometime in the future when you try to unload a treasure trove of Old Earth artifacts. In the light of our evidence the Council would claim them as their own. After all, the location was found using tapes stolen from the Archives."

Juro glowered at him.

"Let him make the call," he rasped and stomped out the room.

After Carson had sent his carefully monitored message Shin led him and Aiyana to a dining room where the three of them ate an evening meal in silence. On point they could not complain: the food was excellent; Juro kept a fine table.

Finally they were taken to a guest suite on the second floor of the mansion.

"You'll be very comfortable here," said Shin, "you have a wonderful view of the ocean from your balcony. But please, no dramatics. The location of your biometrics is being constantly monitored and Tabarak will know in a millisecond if you leave this suite during the night. And just for your information," he added, smiling more broadly than ever, "the mansion will vaporize any non-clan vehicle that approaches within a hundred meters."

"What's more," said Carson after Shin had left them, "they're sure to be listening to our conversations. Come on, let's try to get some sleep."

A short while later they climbed into the large double bed. Aiyana snuggled up behind Carson's and kissed the nape of his neck.

"Goodnight darling, I'm sure it will all work out for the best," she said, but under the covers her fingers traced out a different message on this skin of his back.

T-o h-e-l-l w-i-t-h J-u-r-o

The next morning Carson, Aiyana, Shin, and Juro gathered in a small conference room to hear Tallis's report. Tabarak lurked silently in the background.

"All communication with Ants is difficult," Carson said, "but remote communication is even worse. The company that I rented the tractor from, Formicidae Systems, is supplying me with a remote controlled interface pre-loaded with my scent."

He conjured up an image of an improbable device bristling with antennae, artificial feelers, odor dispensers, chemical analyzers, and recorders.

"Do you think she can restore the second cassette?" Shin asked Carson.

"Let's find out," he replied putting his hand on a console.

The next moment the giant image of a soldier ant appeared on the display. Carson was delighted to hear Tabarak emit a stifled yelp.

"Greetings Carson. [untranslatable] Your smell is not fresh. Are you some distance?"

"Hello Tallis. Yes, I'm near Cissokho City. Sorry, this will have to do."

"[untranslatable] No matter. We have progress to report."

"The tape can be recreated?"

"Partially, we have already executed some sequencing. We are [untranslatable] fragments in linear matrix. They will be fixed on thin membrane [untranslatable] allowing transportation. Early [untranslatable] [untranslatable] suggests two layers encoded information."

The news caused a sensation in the room.

"This is excellent! How soon can you complete the work?"

"Difficult [untranslatable] We need your help Carson. You informed us encoding represents semantic units transmitted by oscillating atmospheric waves."

"Yes, it is what humans call speech, our standard form of communication."

"We require human agency that comprehends this speech. We understand there are different [untranslatable]. You call this one *Ancient English*."

"That is correct."

"[untranslatable] You can communicate in this medium? Your presence will greatly aid sequencing of fragments. My *Ancient English* is not good."

The soldier ant banged its abdomen on the floor. Tallis was making a joke.

"Please wait a few minutes while I confer with my nest mates."

He cut the connection.

"She's right of course. At the moment she is ordering the fragments using pattern recognition – like a giant child's puzzle – plus searching for contiguity in the magnetic signals. There's also some sequencing information embedded in the recording that should help, but all that only goes so far. The ultimate test is to listen to the audio."

"I'll send a linguist," said Juro.

"One that carries my scent?" asked Carson. "The only person she will work with is me."

The old man did not like this. Jerking his head at Shin he shuffled into the adjacent room and closed the door.

"So," said Carson, addressing Tabarak as they waited for the discussion to end, "you don't like Ants?"

"Shut up," was all he would say.

Eventually, Shin opened the door.

"Please join us."

They headed towards the next room.

"No, just Carson," Shin said blocking Aiyana's way.

Juro began speaking immediately the door was closed.

"After you and the Ant re-sequence the tape, you will secretly extract the second layer of audio and identify the systems visited by the Yongding. You will then disappear and reclaim any treasure for yourself."

"Really!" Carson protested, "and leave Aiyana here?"

"There is that," Juro conceded. "Shin's people have built a remarkably accurate model of your personality Carson. We have just consulted it. There is a ninety-six percent probability that you will not abandon her. God knows why – I would."

He wheezed with laughter at the thought.

"Very well, you may go, but you will report each day until you return."

He turned to his minion.

"Shin, leave us for a moment."

Carson appeared to have become a member of an increasingly exclusive club. Once they were alone Juro spoke again.

"Ninety-six percent may satisfactory for most people, but not me, so I will make it one hundred percent."

He moved in closer.

"I remind you Carson that you and Aiyana have committed a very serious crime, one that will be ridiculously easy to prove in court. Clan

Aniko, on the other hand, has done nothing untoward, so do not think of going to the authorities."

Juro paused.

"Additionally, Tabarak, as you will have gathered, is an unusual man. He has certain... needs that require unfettered access to the bodies of young women. The results are extremely unpleasant. Should you choose to abscond with the information on the second tape I will allow him to vent his urges upon Aiyana."

Carson longed to punch the old guy in the face. Well, if things worked out he would do that, figuratively at least. In the meantime he had to act out his part.

"There is no need for disgusting threats. I've already told you that I will not run off with the data and I know I can't deal with New Earth Security."

"Make sure you do not."

They rejoined the others and Carson reconnected with Tallis.

"It is agreed. I will join you later today. Do you have a cost estimate for the contract?"

"Affirmative – one hundred thousand Ecus."

Everyone looked at Juro, who nodded.

"I'll arrange payment," said Shin.

With that the conference ended.

As Juro and Shin talked, Carson drew Aiyana to one side.

"I'll return in a few days, in the meantime just try to stay out of the way."

He had no intention of frightening Aiyana by telling her of Juro's threats. He was already scared enough for the two them.

"Take care, and when you return can you bring me some more clothes? All I've got is what I'm wearing."

"Sure, that's a good idea for both of us. And don't worry – all this will soon be over."

Minutes later he was in the Aniko limousine, accompanied by Ubay. After a short argument it was agreed that they would first travel to the university apartment in Hawkins to pick up clothing and other basics. Once that was done the vehicle hurtled south to Mutapa. On the way down

Carson booked a room at one of the hotels in the human settlement that ringed Vegrandis. To his relief Ubay left with the limousine after dropping off him and his luggage at Formicidae Systems.

Carson picked up his bags, marched into reception and booked a pod for five straight days. It was extravagant but Juro was picking up the tab. Tallis did not sleep – Ants worked round the clock – and he needed to be with her as much as possible. It was going to be an exhausting week.

The next day Carson put a call through to the Aniko mansion – Juro had insisted on a daily visual link. Shin appeared on the screen.

"Good progress I trust," he said, flashing more teeth

"I'll tell you in a minute. First I want to see Aiyana."

"Being a trifle melodramatic aren't we?"

"Dead right, now go and get her."

Shin sighed and disappeared. A couple of minutes later he returned with Aiyana.

"Hi Baby, how are you?"

"Oh I'm fine – just bored. At least they're letting me access some entertainment sources."

Hang in there, I'll return in a few days."

Shin cut in. "Can we have your report now?"

"Okay, progress is good. Listen to this"

"...cellular engineering must not be used to radically reshape the human body..."

The sound quality was poor and accompanied by a lot of static, but it was clearly Cissokho's voice, recorded eight thousand years ago.

"That's just the raw audio, I'm sure your people can clean it up, and there definitely appears to be a second layer, though Tallis doesn't have the hardware to decode it."

"Wonderful!" cried Shin, "Juro will be very pleased"

"Well that's nice. Meantime you need to get your engineers working. Tallis is laying out the fragments on a set of membranes a meter square.

Your people will have to adapt their apparatus to read the tape's second layer in linear mode."

"I'll have them start immediately. You still estimate five days?"

"Hopefully – I'm working every waking moment. I should have a better idea tomorrow."

Shin signed off, leaving Carson trying to figure out his next move. The work was buying him time, but for what? Where were Zhou and New Earth Security? After all, this whole charade was being acted out to allow the authorities to gather enough evidence to nail Juro. Perhaps they were at work in the background but he was getting nervous. It was time to try and find out.

He put through another call. The crest of the New Earth Security Authority appeared on the screen.

"Carson calling for Lieutenant Ming."

Moments later a cropped-haired woman came on the display.

"Hey Carson! I heard you were back on New Earth. So how come you haven't pinged me?"

"Hi Ming, it's great to see you. Believe me, I've been ignoring all my friends. I'm up to my ears in a major new project – haven't had a moment to myself."

"But you called anyway. Let me guess, you need a favor."

Carson laughed.

"Only a small one. The last stop on my mail run was a system called Mita. Do you know it?"

"Isn't that where diamond coral comes from?"

"Roger that. While I was there I met the local Security Commissioner, Zhou, who turns out to be a keen collector. She's supposed to be coming to New Earth and I've lined up a whole bunch of fancy dealers, but I haven't heard anything from her. She would notify your people as a courtesy when she arrives, right? I just want to know what's going on, otherwise I'm going to have to cancel everything."

Ming rolled her eyes.

"Hold on."

She turned her attention to another console.

"Sorry, no sign of her."

"Damn! Hey, she had a sidekick named Asima, can you see if she's here?"

Ming checked again.

"No luck."

She could see that her friend was distressed.

"Tell you what I'll do. I'll tell my valet to message them as soon as they arrive, that way they can contact you."

"Fair enough, thanks Ming, eternally grateful, blah blah. So what's been going on with you?"

They spent the next few minutes chatting until the Security officer said she had better get working.

"Hey, as soon as I have some free time – dinner is on me."

"That's for sure."

She grinned and signed off.

It was turning into a busy morning. Next, Carson called a tailoring store in the Vegrandis settlement.

"I've got a bunch of clothes belonging to me and my partner – you can clean and press them, right? I may need a few alterations as well."

"Certainly, honored customer. We look forward to your visit."

Having finished his calls, Carson headed to work.

"Tallis says she's done."

It was day five of the project. They had developed a daily ritual wherein Carson called Shin, who would produce Aiyana to show that she was safe and well, and then he received the progress report.

"Excellent. Preparations are complete here; I'll send a limousine to collect you."

As soon as Shin signed off another visual call came through to the display in his room.

"Well hello, Carson."

Asima had finally arrived.

"Asima! Where have you guys been? Juro and Shin got here days ago."

"I'm sorry Carson, but that vanishing act you pulled convinced Commissioner Zhou that you had fled to the other side of the galaxy."

"Oh God, the last thing I expected to be was too convincing."

"You were so convincing that Zhou simply refused to authorize me to travel here."

"But you managed to persuade her?"

"No – I'm here on vacation – that's why I took so long. I too originally came from New Earth so I'm doing double duty, seeing friends and family while pursuing the case."

"Meantime, if we had been caught in the Archives without you or Zhou to vouch for us we would have been fried."

"You went ahead and stole something!" the Security officer shouted, then recovered herself.

"I'm sorry, I feel really bad about it. Anyhow," she continued, "here I am. I've got a lot of catching up to do, so why not give me the whole story."

Carson was sick with all the lying. Besides, he needed an ally.

"Where should I start?"

"How did you get off Kaimana?"

"Stealth suits, we went through one of the tunnels feeding water from the outer slopes to the lake, and then hid beneath the ocean in my buggy."

"Clever – where did you get the suits?"

"A local hoodlum called Tabarak."

"That is a very dangerous individual."

"So I've gathered."

Carson took a deep breath.

"Let me tell you everything that's happened since we arrived."

He talked non-stop for the next thirty minutes. By the time he had finished Asima was just shaking her head.

"Look," said Carson, "your boss asked me to cooperate with Juro's conspiracy but this has got completely out of control. Aiyana's life is now in danger. I need you to fire up New Earth Security, bust into that mansion and arrest the lot of them."

"On what charges?"

"Kidnapping for a start"

"A member of Clan Aniko is staying in the Clan Aniko mansion. Doesn't seem that illegal, does it?"

"Oh terrific, so you're going to do nothing! When Kalidas gave me those fake tapes I could have taken them straight to the authorities – upright citizen Carson – and told them everything. Their little scheme would have been rolled up and I'd be a hero. But Zhou wanted me to string along and now we're in this mess."

"I know it's hard Carson but we're trying to convict an individual who is willing to commit murder to get what he wants, and you've no idea what a corrupting influence he's been on Mita. We have to bring him down.

"And since you left Mita we received intelligence that this isn't just about Juro. He is a member of an obscure organization called the Technical Freedom Foundation. Ostensively, it's an advocacy group for loosening the limitations on technology, but we believe he's the leader of a faction that would like to overthrow the entire Covenant. We think he will use the money to finance a revolution."

"That's plain crazy – it's all been tried before – those kinds of uprisings get shut down before they get off the ground. Remember what happened to the Huan Su rebellion."

"I pray you are right Carson."

"And for this you're willing to risk an innocent woman's life?"

"If there is imminent danger I will get the authorities to raid the mansion. But for now you have to keep at it. Eventually we'll nail Juro and his conspirators, and hopefully the galaxy will get some amazing treasures – that's important to you, isn't it?"

Carson nodded. Asima had read him correctly – apart from saving Aiyana it was the only reason he was still in the game.

"I'll be in touch," she said and promptly signed off. Carson stared at the blank screen for a long time, thinking hard. Eventually he got up and headed to Formicidae Systems.

He was exhausted from the non-stop work but he still had one last task before leaving. Five days earlier Tallis had announced that she would require a gigantic clean room. Gigantic by Ant standards, that is. In reality it was three meters square – far bigger than she could build herself. Formicidae's response illustrated the synergy that came from two species working on radically different scales. The company fabricated Tallis's clean room in six hours flat. It was like a human being ordering a kilometer-long building to be constructed in an afternoon.

The real challenge was delivering the completed structure to an empty lot in Vegrandis. That task was accomplished using a customized low-level delivery vehicle which flew the room at a comfortable three meters above the settlement – crushing one's customers underfoot was bad for business. Now, five days later, Formicidae had retrieved the structure and disassembled it to reveal an inner sealed module, one meter square and half a meter high. Inside, precise rows of tape fragments were laid out on transparent membranes.

Carson watched from the parking lot as the limousine dropped out the sky. On the ground beside him were two travel bags and the sealed module.

"You get the bags" he told Ubay, "I'll handle this." He gently picked up the module and placed it in the vehicle.

By the time they got to the mansion everyone had gathered to greet him. Even Kalidas was there squirming with excitement.

"The Ant really managed to reassemble the tape?" he asked as two technicians removed the container from the limousine.

"About eighty percent – the remainder was too far gone. With luck we'll find the rest of Sakyamuni's interview, but don't expect the audio quality to be good. Even the top layer is in poor shape."

"Nevertheless I have high hopes. Shin has assembled a powerful technical team and a clean room has been constructed in the mansion."

"Well, good luck. My guess is that it will be at least a day before you extract any meaningful audio from the second layer. Meantime I'm going to sleep – it's been a very long week."

Carson picked up his travel cases.

"Hold it" said Tabarak who had joined the welcoming party. "What's in the bags?"

Carson sighed. "Just some clean clothes for me and Aiyana"

He waited while Tabarak rummaged through the contents. Finally the big man nodded. Carson picked up his luggage and headed inside the house. As he entered Aiyana rushed forward to hug him.

"I am so glad to see you!"

"They've been treating you okay?"

"Oh fine – my God the food's good! Really, it's just been boring. They leave me to entertain myself. At least I've finally caught up with Exodus – there's a whole new season, who knew?"

"Hey, I got our clothes," he said, gesturing with the two bags as she closed the door on their suite.

"Thanks goodness, one of the staff lent me some stuff but it doesn't really fit."

She started unpacking.

"Hey, what's this?"

She was holding up a vivid pink jumpsuit.

"You didn't have many clothes at the apartment so I thought I'd buy you something new. There's a matching hat and gloves."

"Hhmm…" she said, fingering the gaudy material.

"Don't you like it?"

"Darling, it was a very sweet thought. But you know what I've really been missing?"

In case he had any doubt, she took his face in her hands and kissed him.

"Aiyana, I'm exhausted!"

"You're never that tired, my horny mailman."

"You're right."

Carson insisted that they first get under the bedcovers

"They might have visual monitoring. Let the creeps pay for their own entertainment."

An hour later they lay facing each other, contented and drowsy.

"So what will happen now?" Aiyana asked.

"I think everything is going to be fine. Juro has what he wants, so I'm sure they'll let us both go in a few days."

Underneath the covers his forefinger spelled out a different message on the skin of her stomach.

P-i-n-k i-s s-t-e-a-l-t-h he wrote.

Revelations

The following morning they joined to Juro and Shin to hear Kalidas's report on the second tape. The renegade academic had taken stimulants and worked through the night; nothing was going to stop him now.

"You prediction was right Carson," he began, "the audio quality of the second layer is very poor. Eventually we will clean it up, but that is not our priority. In the meantime, I have spent most of the night listening and re-listening to the crucial section.

"But..." he swung to face Juro, "we have it, honored patron, we have it!"

Shin cut in "Kalidas – please – before you continue."

He bent over Juro and whispered in his ear. Evidently everyone's private channels were being suppressed. Juro listened for a minute then snorted and waved Shin away. He turned to address Carson.

"Shin feels that we should throw you out before you hear any further information. However, there are just two possibilities: one, that you intend to have the treasure for yourself, in which case you will have bribed the Ant to make a copy of the tape and will eventually learn everything regardless of whether or not you remain in the room today; or two, you are willing, as I believe, to accept a fair commission and therefore what you hear will be of no consequence. In either case telling you to leave will serve no purpose; you may stay. Carry on, honored scholar."

"Thank you Juro," said Carson.

He even managed a small bow in the old man's direction. *Perfectly logical and completely wrong* he added to himself, maintaining his deferential expression.

As Kalidas placed his hand on the console Sakyamuni's voice filled the room, the Ancient English barely audible through the static haze.

"The original plan was for as many as six colonies, depending on what we found on our voyages of exploration. Of course, in the end only four were chosen."

"This explains so much," Kalidas said, pausing the recording. "And it makes complete sense. Why halt at one colony? The resources of prehistoric Earth were enormous. The Yongding could supply several colonies and still have time for exploration."

"Where –" began Juro, but the ancient voice had already restarted.

"We decided to leave supplies in two ways. The simplest approach was to create dumps on the planets, but you can never be too sure. These were unknown worlds. Goodness knows what may happen on the surface before the colonists arrived. So we also chose to place many of the – what is the word? – delicate items in cometary orbit where we were certain they would be safe. In total we left about one hundred tonnes in each system, half on the ground and half in orbit."

Kalidas paused the recording again. The conference room remained silent.

"Hundreds of tonnes…" Shin whispered.

Juro recovered first.

"And the systems, Kalidas?"

"Yes, of course, honored patron. I must caution you that the quality of this part of the tape is particularly poor."

Sakyamuni's voice returned, though it was almost overwhelmed by background noise.

"Eventually we settled on Eridani b – that is to say, of course, New Earth – plus Sharez a, Lum e, and Dante b. The Hypertelescope had revealed that all had terrestrial-like planets with oxygen signatures. Other reasons…"

But the group was no-longer listening. The moment the ancient voice specified the target worlds Shin leapt to a console. Everyone peered over his shoulder. Kalidas stopped the recording and joined them.

"All three are now inhabited systems. Good grief they really traveled! Dante b is ninety-six light years away. I'm surprised the hypertelescope could image it."

"They did not say it imaged the planet," Kalidas chimed in, "merely that a spectroscopic analysis suggested the presence of life."

"It could offer our best chance of finding material on the ground," Shin said as he consulted the console. "The system has a small population – less than half a million – which means that most of the planet's surface will be unexplored."

"I agree," said Juro, "but we will explore all three systems. Shin, activate your team immediately. I want you ready to leave within five days. And Kalidas, I want a full transcript by tonight."

"How will you search for the material in cometary orbit?" Carson asked. "Any beacon will have died thousands of years ago."

"I imagine it will have to be deep radar," said Shin. "I'll put together a research group."

"Sooner the better," said Carson. "The deep orbit stuff will be the greatest prize. There's an excellent chance that it will be in perfectly condition, assuming it was packed correctly."

"You have much to do," said Juro, addressing Shin, "we should not delay you. Kalidas can carry on listening to the tape. There may be more information that will be of use."

"So what happens now?" Carson asked him.

"Shin will lead the expedition – preparation is already at an advanced stage – in the meantime I will return to Kaimana. It will be months before he returns."

"And what about me and Aiyana?"

"You will stay here in the Clan mansion. Your expertise will be of great assistance when the expedition finally returns. Cataloging such an unprecedented amount of material will in itself be a major task."

"So we're to be held here for months?"

"The accommodation is comfortable, is it not?"

"Look Juro, I have a life. I have a job. I can't pursue either if I'm stuck here. Next week I am supposed to be meeting with the Commonwealth Post Office to debrief on my latest run. I am scheduled to give a lecture to the Antiquities Society. I even have *friends* who are wondering where the hell I am including," he added, trying to sound ominous, "Lieutenant Ming of New Earth Security."

"Make excuses," Juro replied waving a mottled hand.

"You still think I will try to beat Shin to the treasure."

"It had occurred to me."

"I give you my word that I have no intention of voyaging to the systems."

"Just one would be quite sufficient!"

"Not one of them, I swear. Good God Juro, put me under formal examination if you're that worried."

This idea intrigued the old man. He addressed Shin.

"Can we do it?"

"On Kaimana sir, but here..." Then he brightened. "We do have a very sophisticated device for the psychophysiological measurement of deception – we use it for staff security sweeps. We could use that, although personally..."

Juro cut him off.

"I'm interested. Arrange a test today."

That afternoon the group minus Kalidas met again in the conference room. A technician was examining a large piece of apparatus that could have been an acceleration couch.

"This is the PMD device," Shin explained. "Carson, please undress and take a seat."

Carson did as he was told. As he settled in the machine came to life; the two sides of the couch grew and swelled towards each other engulfing his body until only his face remained clear.

"What the –"

"Try to relax," said the technician, "this is all perfectly harmless. We simply need to monitor your body functions as closely as possible. Please state your name and occupation."

"Carson, Commonwealth Mail Carrier."

For the next ten minutes he answered a series of routine inquiries as the technician calibrated the machine. Finally he asked the real question.

"Do you intend to leave New Earth and travel to the Sharez system?"

"No, absolutely not."

The technician elicited the same reply for Lum e and Dante b.

"Well?" said Juro.

"He is telling the truth Elder Juro."

"Let me ask him a question," he turned to Carson. "Do you intend to betray me to the authorities."

"Well that depends..."

"Answer yes or no," said the technician.

"Then no."

"That last response was ambiguous sir."

"I know it was. Let him out of that thing."

The technician glanced up.

"Pardon me?"

"Good grief, pay attention man. I said let him out!"

"Tabarak administered the technician fifty milligrams of meta gamma-Hydroxybutyric acid," Shin whispered to Juro. "We thought it prudent; he will vaguely remember administering the test but nothing else."

After he had dressed and the technician departed, Carson turned to Juro.

"What did you expect? Of course I will go to the authorities if you try to cut me out of the profits."

Juro snorted with laughter.

"My dear Carson, most of the people I deal with think that I am going to make them very rich and they are sorely disappointed. You my boy are the exact opposite."

He turned Shin.

"Carson may leave once the expedition has departed. Aiyana will stay in the mansion until it returns."

"No way!"

"Do not take me for a fool Carson. We know that you will stay on New Earth as long as Aiyana remains here. One breathtaking flight is quite enough."

"Honey," said Aiyana taking his hands, "everything will be all right. At least I will know that you're safe."

Her right eye gave the slightest twitch. Was that a wink? He hoped so.

"Really, it will be fine. Elder Juro said I am going to be promoted! It will be a great opportunity to do some serious preparation for my new job."

This time there was no mistaking the twitch. At least Aiyana seems to be under no illusions thought Carson. And soon he would be free. Now how the hell was he going to liberate her?

In the days that followed the mansion was full of activity as Shin's staff made final preparations for the expedition, but Carson and Aiyana were allowed to take no part. Instead, they were confined to their suite and left to amuse themselves. Life settled down to a routine of eating, sleeping, entertainments, and watching the sun go down over the ocean.

The sunsets were their biggest treat. The weather was clear and each evening they stood on the balcony to watch Eridani melt into the cobalt sea. Twice they saw Vulcan in transit; the silhouette of the giant planet was so large as it crossed its parent star that it looked like the pupil of a monstrous orange eye scanning the horizon.

On the second day Carson managed to persuade Tabarak to find him a personal recorder that he used to prepare his address to the Antiquities Society. It helped pass the time but what really tormented them was the fact that they could not discuss their situation – it was a sure bet that every word was being monitored.

Finally, after six days of confinement, they were invited downstairs to the conference room. Juro was there along with Shin, still wearing his trademark smile but clearly exhausted.

"The expedition leaves tomorrow," Juro said, "and I will be returning to Kaimana."

""How long do you think you'll be gone?" Carson asked Shin.

"Hopefully no more than a few months, but we'll know a lot more once we arrive at the Sharez system. Our first goal is a shakedown test of the deep radar. If we can actually find the supply dumps in cometary orbit this could be a short trip. Otherwise…"

"We will succeed," the old man cut in, "we have too much information and the Yongding left too much at each system for us to fail."

"Well good luck," said Carson, "does this mean I'm free too leave?"

"Tomorrow," said Juro, "In the meantime we have made extraordinary progress and I intend to celebrate. Why, we have been on New Earth for weeks and have sampled nothing of its pleasures. Tonight you will join me for dinner at the Aether."

Later that afternoon Shin appeared with two sets of evening clothes.

"These are the best we could find in the time," he explained. "Better than nothing, we can't have you dining at the Aether in rags!

"Unfortunately I am too busy to join you, so I will say goodbye now. The next time we meet I hope to have a shipload of treasure for you to catalog."

There was an awkward pause until Aiyana stepped forward and gave him a hug.

"Take care out there," she said.

Their mutual enmity was overwhelmed by one of the oldest of human emotions – the moment of intimacy before departure on a long voyage. For once Shin's smile was tentative, making him appear both vulnerable and sincere, and with that he was gone.

Carson felt slightly ridiculous sitting in his formal suit as their limousine headed towards Cissokho City but he had to admit that Aiyana looked wonderful. Shin had found her a dress made of deep blue nouveau silk, its loose folds cascading down her body. The material was slightly luminescent, its glow complementing the excitement in her eyes as she craned her neck to see the approaching metropolis.

The center of the city was dominated by the latest architectural craze, organic-themed buildings. Towers sprouted branches, leaves, and fronds that interlocked with their neighbors like trees in a densely-packed forest. Four hundred meters above the ground condominiums snaked between cafes, art galleries writhed over gymnasiums while twisting walkways joining one building to another. Carson winced at the complexity, although no matter how clever the construction crafting the leasing agreements between adjoining properties must have been the ultimate challenge.

"That's where we're going!" Aiyana cried, pointing at a tall spire.

Unlike its companions, the structure was a simple needle-like shaft two kilometers high, its crown sheathed in glimmering light.

They parked at the base of the building.

"Not joining us?" Carson asked, smiling at Tabarak and Ubay.

"We'll be waiting for you," the big man said.

The lobby politely redirected them – apparently the Aether had its own entrance. Two gilded doors parted as they approached. Carson was astonished to see that they were opened by real people, a man and a woman, who beamed as they entered.

"Welcome honored guests," they chorused in unison.

They stepped inside to a softly lit reception area decorated with fresh flowers. The walls sported a line of Vanuka paintings that had the alarming appearance of being originals. A stylishly dressed woman came forward to greet them.

"Aiyana, Carson, welcome to the Aether!"

She gave them a Shin-class smile.

"Your host, Elder Juro, is already seated; Zaakir will take you to his table. Have a marvelous evening!"

A uniformed attendant appeared who conducted them to the elevator. His manner suggested that the joy of being awarded the Cissokho Prize would be a poor substitute for the pleasure he was receiving from their presence. The news that they were first-time guests made him giddy with excitement.

"Our elevator is of an open design. If you wish, I can opaque the walls."

Aiyana would have none of it, she wanted to experience everything. As the ascent began Carson realized that open really meant open – they were enveloped in nothing but a peristaltic field. Moments later they passed through the roof of the lobby and rushed up the side of the building with no apparent means of support. Their ascent took them in a graceful spiral, affording them a 360-degree view of the city, but as they continued to rise lesser buildings fell away leaving them alone to soar into the night.

Aiyana clapped her hands and tried to look everywhere simultaneously but Carson just smiled and watched her face glowing in the reflected light. Eventually the climb slowed as they reached the glowing pinnacle.

"Have a wonderful dinner!" Zaakir said as the peristaltic field eased them through the luminescent wall into the Aether.

"Oh my!"

They had emerged onto a translucent semicircular shelf set halfway up the wall of a cylindrical atrium. The whole space, perhaps eighty meters tall and twenty meters wide, glowed like a moonlit cloud. Immediately in front of them in the center of the semicircle was a linen-covered table where Juro sat deep in conversation with a member of the restaurant's staff. Similar outcrops, each bearing a single table, spiraled round the atrium's walls from top to bottom. A quartet of musicians, suspended in midair, orbited a central column of prismatic light that ascended throughout the huge space.

Juro glanced up and gestured them to join him.

"There you are! Come, the first bottle of wine has been selected."

Two staff appeared from nowhere to hold their chairs as they sat down. Another, a woman, also materialized. Her demeanor made their new friend Zaakir look positively grumpy.

"Elder Juro, welcome once more to the Aether. Aiyana, Carson, we are delighted to greet new guests. Your first course will be with you momentarily."

A flunky filled their glasses.

"We use water exclusively from Raj e," the woman continued, "a glacier world of unparalleled purity."

Oh God, mused Carson, they ship *water* from another system?

"Where's the menu?" whispered Aiyana

"Good Lord my dear," said Juro at his most avuncular, "at the Aether you eat what you are given. Do not worry! You will not be disappointed."

Right on cue, three more servers appeared, each placing a small dish before the diners in perfect synchronization.

Carson had worked out where the staff was coming from: they simply emerged out of the shining central column and floated across the gulf to the tables. Like the orbiting musicians, they had to be wearing some kind of lift belt.

Looking again at what had been put before him he realized that 'dish' was hardly an adequate description. It was a diminutive piece of diamond coral in the form of a meta-seahorse. Its front paws held a tiny bowl of mother of pearl upon which were arranged a cluster of gleaming black spheres in a pearly emulsion. It would not have been out of place in the window of a jewelry store.

"Chef Adega is so excited to be welcoming guests from Kaimana that he has prepared this seafood course in your honor. Malossol caviar in a puree of Kumamotos oysters, harvested from the Gulf of Qinghai this morning. Enjoy!"

The woman and the three servers floated away, and so began what transpired to be the finest meal Carson had ever eaten. Not the most enjoyable – it was difficult to relax when one of your dinner companions was probably planning to murder you – but the inventiveness and quality of the food were beyond reproach.

Intermittently, the sommelier approached and entered into a technical discussion with Juro. The invariable result was more wine.

"What's that being extracted from the bottle," Aiyana asked Carson, "is it delicious?"

"No darling, it's called a cork, I'll explain later."

She gazed round the atrium.

"What do you think this is made of?" she asked, tapping her foot on the translucent floor.

"Thick layers of compressed money."

Juro laughed.

"Soon you will be able to dine here every night."

By now they were on their fourth bottle of wine, and Carson decided that the old man was sufficiently unwound to try a little probing.

"I'm concerned that the sudden appearance of an enormous quantity of Old Earth artifacts will depress their price."

"You are right, my boy. I will release items very slowly, perhaps raising a mere ten billion a year. The market should be able to bear that rate indefinitely, and with just a fraction of the original cargo we will have enough for hundreds of years of sales."

Carson did the math.

"That's a trillion Ecus a century – you will be the richest man in history."

Juro waved his hand in ascent.

"We are developing a sales strategy with Hobs Treys, New Earth's premier auction house. Distinguished scholars such as yourself will publish academic papers on the unprecedented nature of the discoveries; selected media outlets will be given exclusive previews making the sale news in every major system; ultra-wealthy connoisseurs will be invited to private viewing of the artifacts and there will be talk of 'once in a lifetime' opportunities for those willing to make bold pre-emptive bids. The first auction will take place immediately before the release of the final episode of Exodus, of which Clan Aniko is a major corporate sponsor. In short, we will create a buying frenzy."

He finished by draining his wine glass and banging it down on the linen tablecloth.

To Carson this was all bad news. Asima had said that the old man wanted the money to fund some kind of crazy revolution against the Covenant. The idea might be absurd but a trillion Ecus could finance no end of havoc.

Juro was talking again.

"You too will do very well. I shall award you and Kalidas a commission of one percent each. That will give you an income of one hundred million a year for the foreseeable future. Do you have any idea what wealth of such magnitude can bring? Each day, teams of people will meet for the sole purpose of making your life more pleasurable."

He sat back, eyes half closed.

"You're confident that Shin will be successful?"

"Completely."

"But this is what I don't get," Carson persisted, "it was only a week ago that we learned that the treasure even existed. It was a good bet that there was a second layer of audio on the Teng cassettes, but it could have contained anything. Yet an expedition has been in preparation for months – you were willing to spend all that on a hunch?"

"Not just the expedition! Tell me, how do you choose star systems for your mail route?"

"I'm not sure why you're asking – I run an optimum path analysis based on package addresses. Generally, the more mail I have for a system the sooner I am likely to visit it."

"And do you have any idea how many letters poor Shin had to generate on Procyon c to guide you to Kaimana?"

Carson stared at him. *How deep does this thing go?*

"That must have cost a fortune! What made you so confident?"

"Isn't it obvious my boy?"

The sommelier magically reappeared to refill their glasses. Juro paused until he had left.

"When I told you that there are only seventeen Old Earth artifacts in private hands, I was not quite correct."

Carson thought for a moment.

"Oh my God!" he said.

"What is it?" asked Aiyana, who had been listening to the conversation.

"How could I not see it?"

Juro nodded, half smiling, like a schoolteacher encouraging a dim pupil.

"What?" Aiyana said again.

Carson turned to her.

"There's a third cassette."

One of his agents had found it in an antiques store on Kaluma b, Juro explained. The dealer had no idea what he was selling, and how it got to the obscure star system was a mystery. Unlike the first two, the cassette contained only a few hours of audio, and that on a single layer. It was probably the last recording Teng ever made. Despite the lack of skilled preservation the tape was in good condition; even so decoding it was major a challenge, one that had brought Kalidas and Juro together for the first time.

"Most of the material was irrelevant," Juro explained, "but the first forty minutes was the conclusion of Sakyamuni's interview. He spoke of the supply dumps but with no reference to their location."

The old man chuckled.

"You can imagine my frustration."

"So you had to get the first two cassettes at any cost."

"Precisely – Kalidas had already concluded that there was a hidden layer on the two Archives cassettes but he was struggling to master the technology to read it. I supplied him with the resources."

"But you never told him about the Sakyamuni portion of the tape."

"I felt it best to withhold that information, he was excited enough already. It proved to be of little consequence, for now we have everything: the identity of the star systems and a good idea as to the supplies' precise whereabouts. In a few months we will have succeeded beyond our wildest dreams."

"Can I listen to the third tape?"

"I will send you a transcript of the relevant section."

Finally, after sixteen courses including two more of Adega's famous spontaneous creations, the dinner was over. As they descended to the reception area Juro announced that he was spending his last night in Cissokho City.

"I will see you again when we reconvene to examine the treasure. Until then I trust you will both behave yourselves."

"Don't worry, we will." Carson said.

Juro held his gaze for several seconds then tottered out the door, leaving them to wait for the limousine. As soon as he left Carson realized that the subliminal buzz in his head had gone; the old man must have been carrying a suppressing device.

"Darling," he said trying to gain time, "come and look at these wonderful Vanuka paintings."

As they stood admiring the pictures he opened a private channel, but before he could sub-vocalize a message Aiyana cut in.

"Tomorrow, midnight, be on the beach below the mansion."

"But –"

He got no further – their communications were cut off the moment Tabarak walked in to see where they were. There was nothing to do but follow him out to the waiting vehicle.

Carson and Aiyana were both satiated with the luxurious food and as soon as they got to the Aniko mansion they headed for bed. To Carson's surprise Aiyana told the bedroom to turn off the lights before she got undressed. As they got under the covers he discovered that she was wearing some kind of harness.

"Kinky!"

She put her fingers to his lips before he could say more.

"L-i-f-t b-e-l-t" she spelt out on his chest

"?"

"A-e-t-h-e-r"

There followed a pantomime of fingertip messages interspersed with simulated groans of ecstasy to explain their strange gyrations beneath the bedclothes. Finally, Aiyana's escape was planned: the following night she would don the harness beneath her stealth suit and descend to the beach where Carson would be waiting with transportation. Her biometrics would vanish the moment she put the suit, which would rouse Tabarak, but he would first search the house and the grounds. With luck, by the time the hunt widened they would be gone.

Aiyana eased her way out of the harness and surreptitiously slid it under the bed. There was nothing left but to try to get some sleep.

The following morning Carson was allowed to leave the mansion. He and Aiyana acted out a tearful farewell for Tabarak's benefit.

"Be here this time next week," the big man told him. They had agreed to weekly face-to-face meetings to ensure Carson really was still on New Earth.

The taxi headed skyward; Aiyana waved until it disappeared then headed to her suite. For the rest of the day she played the model employee and researched the Clan's economic activities in the Huan Federation. That evening a member of the staff brought her an evening meal, and then she was left alone.

It was much quieter with Juro and Shin gone and by midnight the mansion was silent. Aiyana sat in front of a dresser wearing the lift belt. She was reasonably certain that she was not being visually monitored and even if she were, she hoped that the belt's function was not obvious. The camouflaged stealth suite was laid out on the bed. Now it was a question of dressing as fast as possible and immediately leaping off the balcony.

As she was about to get up she let out a small gasp – the surface of the dresser was crawling with insects. What was wrong with this place? Then, peering closely, she saw that each of them wore a tiny communications pack. It had to be Tallis, or at least a dozen of her soldiers. Carson had told her that members of the nest could operate remotely by augmenting their organic radios.

Four of the soldiers were carrying a miniscule black module. What was that? The ants placed the module down and to her astonishment grouped together in the shape of a letter B. The next moment they regrouped to form an I.

BIOMETRIC SIMULATOR,they spelt out.

DRESS STEALTH LEAVE.

Aiyana hurried to put on the disguised stealth suit. The moment she pulled brim of the hat down over her face a pinpoint green light appeared on the simulator. It was broadcasting a copy of her biometrics – Tabarak would not even realize that she had gone. Aiyana delicately picked the module and placed it on the bed, arranging pillows under the covers to mimic the shape of her sleeping body.

Meantime, at the dresser the ants were spelling out another message. GO NOW, they said, adding, LEAVE US.

"Like hell," Aiyana muttered.

She knew an individual ant was no more to Tallis than one of her own fingernails, but this group must have scaled the cliff for hours carrying the simulator. It was like a team of human climbers hauling a shuttle up a mountain. She was damned if she would abandon them.

Aiyana pulled out a small jewelry box from the dresser draw and dumped its contents. Then, as gently as she could, she brushed the ants into the box and closed the lid. She tucked it into her suit and stepped out onto the balcony. Everything appeared quiet, only the sound of the surf drifted up through the cool night air. She leant over and peered down at the shoreline but could see nothing but shadows. Taking a deep breath, she gripped the railing and leapt.

Crouched at the base of the cliff, Carson watched Aiyana look over the balcony. He was wearing his black stealth suit that effectively rendered him invisible while she shone like a beacon. Why the hell had he chosen pink? So much for the clever disguise.

He stopped breathing as Aiyana braced herself and jumped. She plummeted for two seconds before a muffled yelp announced the end of her fall forty meters above his head. Moments later she floated down to the sand.

"That was amazing!" he whispered running up to her.

"Oh my God that was scary. What a gravity gradient! I never realized I'd accelerate that fast."

"Tallis delivered the simulator?"

"She did – does that mean the alarm hasn't been sounded?"

"That's the idea, come on."

They ran through the darkness, hugging the cliff face. Four hundred meters down the shore they came to where Carson had left a small scooter. They scrambled aboard and flew along the beach for two kilometers before ascending.

Twenty minutes later they landed in a parking lot next to the largest personal transport Aiyana had seen since arriving on New Earth. Most of its bulk was taken up by the propulsion system – it had to be built for interplanetary travel. Carson slapped his hand on the hatch and they climbed in.

"This is the fastest thing I could rent – Quad Huan Qi push drives," he said, "too big to risk bringing to the beach."

As they took off Aiyana ignored the inertial dampening and rushed over to hug him.

"We did it!" she said kissing him. "My God, this is our second getaway, you wild mailman you!"

"Not really – this time it's legitimate. This vehicle is certified for interstellar connections."

"What does that mean?"

Carson grinned.

"It means we get out of here without stopping, but legally."

As she lay on an acceleration couch Aiyana felt a lump under her suit. She reached in and pulled out the jewelry box.

"Hey, I brought Tallis's soldiers," she said waiving the box at Carson."Do you think they'll be alright in here?"

"You are such a softie; I've got the perfect thing for them."

He took a small object out of his pocket. It was a tiny vehicle, no bigger than his hand.

"This is how they got to the beach," Carson said. "Tallis asked me to retrieve it. It's a masterpiece of miniature engineering – far too valuable to leave behind."

He placed the two objects together on the floor and opened the jewelry box. As soon as the vessel sensed the ants it opened a miniscule hatchway. The soldiers crawled out of the box and into their vehicle, which promptly sealed itself. Carson picked up the transporter and carefully stowed it in his luggage.

"If they had their own craft, why climb the cliff?" Aiyana asked.

"Shin told us that the defenses were set to fry any intruding vessel, and even something this size might have set them off."

"Hey," he continued, "talking about the cliff, how the hell did you steal a lift belt from the Aether?"

"Oh, I ran into a staff member on my way to the bathroom."

"And?"

"Womanly wiles, darling, woman wiles"

"I don't even want to think what that means."

Carson slumped onto his acceleration couch.

"My God I've had a crazy day. I checked out of our apartment, sent off my talk to the Antiquities Society, pacified my friends, and most importantly I squared everything away with the Post Office."

He waved a silvery rectangle.

"Fresh mail!"

"So where are we going? Are you planning to beat Shin to the Sharez system? He's got a day's start."

"Why should I do that?" Carson said in Ancient English, speaking the words with an oddly familiar accent. *"Why would I want to go to a dull place like Sharez?"*

Aiyana stared at him.

"You did not!"

"I did," said Carson looking supremely smug.

"You *faked the tape!*"

Tallis did all the work, Carson explained. Fortunately, Juro never truly appreciated her abilities. In addition they had all the technical specifications of the recording mechanism, courtesy of Kalidas

"And, of course, we had one of his phony cassettes. Juro's techs did such a great job of forgery – even the carbon isotope ratios are right for an eight thousand year-old emulsion – they'll never be able to tell it's a fake."

"But to create an entire tape –"

"Oh no, just the crucial part about the location of the treasure, the rest is real. I'll play you the authentic portion once we're out of here."

More immediate issues intruded. By now they were above New Earth's atmosphere and accelerating at a ferocious rate. They had to deal with the bureaucracy before the signal time lag made communication impractical. Carson slapped his hand on the vessel's remote biometric station and summoned immigration control.

"Thank you Carson," it said after processing him, "is your employee with you?"

What? He had completely forgotten the story they concocted when they arrived. Fortunately Aiyana had not; she rushed to the station and put her hand in the green circle.

"I'm here!"

"Thank you honored visitor, I am registering you both as exiting the New Earth system. I trust your academic research was successful."

"Extremely!"

Earlier, Carson had sent his ship a coded message to prepare for departure, and by the time they rendezvoused it was running through its final flight checks. Even through the blur of the orbiting micro black holes Aiyana could see that the vessel had gotten bigger – several new modules were plugged into its chassis.

"Extra supplies," Carson explained, "and lots of specialized equipment. Finding this treasure may not be easy."

"Great to have you back" the ship said as they disembarked. "We're pretty well stocked up but I'm still expecting one final delivery, so pay off that posh taxi and make room for docking."

"Oh God it feels great to be home," said Carson, "and the sooner we get out of here the better"

"Not again!"

"Quit complaining, at least no-one's shooting at you this time."

Professional curiosity trumped Aiyana's weariness and she stayed awake to watch the arrival of the last consignment. The delivery vessel's design was one of the weirdest she had ever seen: it was a huge rectangular lattice loaded with storage modules of every size, like a warehouse with no walls or floors. Ungainly as it seemed, it was fast and highly maneuverable – each corner of the boxy structure sported a push drive.

The transport stopped a kilometer away and two small modules bearing the logo of Formicidae Systems detached themselves from the superstructure. From that point the ship took over guidance and funneled the containers through the opening in the north pole of the shell. Finally, a satisfying *clonk* echoed through the ship as the new units pushed themselves into the chassis.

"They're now fully powered and integrated," the ship said.

"Let's take a look," said Carson, and headed off in the general direction of the conservatory.

By the time Aiyana got there he was unbolting the plates that separated the ships interior from the modules. One of the units had a small window; Carson peered into its interior and smiled, then made way for Aiyana. She moved forward then let out a short scream. At the same moment a familiar voice filled the cabin.

"Carson, Aiyana, how good to smell you."

It was Tallis, all one million of her – young new queen, soldiers, workers, grubs, and all. She was doubly motivated to join them Carson explained: she was eager to participate in the hunt for treasure and considered it wise to be absent when Juro finally realized how he had been tricked.

"She could live in the transport module – the other one contains all her equipment – but I suggested she set up home in the conservatory. God, her technical skills are going to be so useful."

"Shall I complete spin up?" the ship asked.

"Absolutely, let's go and find something wonderful!"

As soon as they got under way Carson and Aiyana headed to bed – it had been a very long day.

"How amazing," said Aiyana as they snuggled in the darkened cabin, "we are the only people in the galaxy who really know about the Yongding's treasure."

"Well I did share some information with Officer Asima."

"Was that wise? I mean Juro has corrupted so many people on Mita."

"I felt someone else had to know, and Asima is as straight as laser light. Besides, she promised to tell no-one except Commissioner Zhou."

"That's all right then."

"Sweet dreams darling."
The silent ship plunged on through the interstellar night.

Mirama

"There! I swear I saw a fin!"

Carson scrambled up the beach away from the water's edge.

"Are you sure?" Aiyana shouted from the top of the bluffs. "I thought there was nothing bigger than an amoeba."

He scrunched up the shale to where she was standing and surveyed the view. The sluggish sea mirrored the light of the grey clouds, making it hard to distinguish where the ocean stopped and the sky began. The land behind them offered little more – rust-colored hills and shallow valleys rolled away to the horizon.

"This is the most boring place I have ever visited."

Aiyana opened a channel to Tallis.

"Anything interesting, nest mate?"

"Nothing, we question why [untranslatable] was ever chosen."

"You've never visited a bacteria world before have you Carson?" Aiyana asked.

"Oh God no! Why should anyone? They're nothing but a broth of microorganisms."

"The ship was telling me that there are ten billion of them in the galaxy. Can you imagine? All those planets floundering in the first stage of genesis."

But Mirama was showing promise. It started with a catastrophe fifty million years ago when a new life-form began generating a poisonous gas that killed virtually the entire biomass. The gas was oxygen and the life-form plankton. Now the air was breathable and the surviving organisms were creating the high-energy metabolic pathways that would one day culminate in multicellular life.

"In the meantime," Carson said, "the landmass is barren. God help anyone trying to start a colony here. I'm guessing it was chlorophyll signature that lured the Yongding."

"See this," Aiyana said as she squatted down and crumbled flakes of red earth in her fingers. "You know what this reminds me of? That picture of Old Mars in the Book, the one taken before the first settlers arrived."

She pulled out a portable analyzer and held it to the surface.

"Iron oxide – it must have been created during the oxygenation event."

"This place could be Mars two billion ago."

Aiyana stood up and dusted her hands.

"Sakyamuni said they left supplies?"

"That he did. They had no idea how many planets supported life so perhaps they weren't expecting anything better. There's no other reason to try colonizing this dump."

"None of which explains a fin," Aiyana said. "Are you sure you saw something?"

"Pretty certain. Hey buggy, do you know anything about Mirama c being terraformed?"

"Nothing – I'll check with the ship."

"There was a lot of wild stuff going on when the human race first broke out from the Eridani system," Carson said. "I'm guessing the planet was seeded then."

"If they brought their own life-forms there might be anything in the sea."

"Yeah, isn't that a lovely thought?"

Aiyana shivered.

"It's getting late, let's get back to camp. Hey Tallis, smell you at the nest!"

"My antennae twitch with pleasure."

"You two are getting far too friendly," Carson said as they climbed aboard the scooter.

They had set up base on the western edge of the planet's largest continent, a thousand kilometers south of the equator. Their orbital radar survey had shown numerous anomalies in the immediate area but so far nothing had panned out.

Three days earlier they had arrived to discover the world enveloped in cloud.

"Just like home with none of the fun," Aiyana observed, "well at least it isn't raining."

The hidden surface wrecked their plans for performing the hunt from orbit. But all was not lost – their constellation of satellites could still perform radar scans. As a bonus the clouds parted occasionally to reveal glimpses of the surface, and Tallis's fleet of tiny vessels kept busy reconnoitering at low-level.

"This planet was supposed to be the easy one," Carson moaned. "No surface vegetation, no tectonics, uneventful climate. Now we're scrabbling round the surface checking out radar blips."

The camp glowed in the rock-strewn landscape as they approached in the fading light. It consisted of three woven-monofilament transparent cubes held rigid by inertial fields; they appeared flimsy but once pinioned to the ground they were as strong as stone-built houses. The largest contained memory shape furniture and served as their living quarters. In one corner was an anonymous cube – Tallis's portable nest. The second, smaller module housed recycling and bathroom facilities, and the third contained supplies. The buggy was parked a few meters away.

"This whole setup cost me a fortune but God knows how long we're going to be stuck here."

Once they were away from New Earth they had spent countless hours planning. In faking the second tape Carson had used the premise that all good lies start with a large chunk of the truth: Sakyamuni had indeed named three worlds where supply dumps were located – one on the ground and one in cometary orbit for each system.

"I wanted to make sure we returned to New Earth before Shin, so I substituted planets that would make his search as hard as possible. Sharez a is covered with forest and Lum e has a gigantic land mass. He's obviously determined not to return home empty-handed and I reckon he'll keep searching for years."

"Why didn't you name ten worlds? That could tie them up for decades."

"Yeah, I was tempted. But one thing I've learned about Juro is that he always knows more than you think. We've never heard the third tape – Sakyamuni might have dropped far more clues than we realize."

Aiyana scanned through Carson's list of bogus targets.

"It seems like Dante b would be pretty easy to survey."

"You're right, but it's ninety-six light years away. My idea was to lure them straight into a long trip but Juro didn't take the bait. Even so, we have a hell of a time advantage."

"I almost feel sorry for Shin."

"Me too, but at least when he returns he won't have to worry about his boss – Juro will have long since been sentenced to total personality reconstruction.

"And we, my dear," he added gathering up Aiyana in his arms, "will be heroes."

But the euphoria had vanished when they stared down at Mirama's cloud-covered surface. Now they faced a slog that could last months.

Aiyana, far more at home in inter-planetary space, wanted to start by searching for the supply dump in cometary orbit but Carson had vetoed the idea.

"Shin had a team of experts and unlimited funds to develop the right deep search tools. Even so I doubt he'll find anything. We'd be using much more primitive equipment to find what? Something ten meters in diameter? In a solar system-sized volume! Sorry, honey, we'll start on the ground."

Carson slapped his hand on the green circle on the side of the habitation module and waited for the entrance to peel open.

"What's for dinner?" he asked the portable stove as he pushed through the inertial field.

"Synthesized chicken stew," the machine replied.

"Welcome to the Aether, honored patron," Aiyana muttered as she followed Carson inside.

After their meal they relaxed with glasses of real wine, which Aiyana had insisted on bringing, and discussed strategy. As they talked a cluster of tiny green lights appeared through the transparent walls. Tallis's fleet was returning to recharge its batteries.

"We will start again as soon as there is sufficient ambient electromagnetic radiation."

"Dawn is ten hours away. It makes me wonder about using artificial light – what do you think buggy?"

"My searchlights are nowhere near powerful enough. Perhaps we could fabricate something. Let me ask the ship."

Carson sighed. Their vessel was stationed at the edge of the system, four light hours out. It would be the next day before they would get a response.

"I can equip my sensors to operate in very low levels of radiation," Tallis offered.

"Yeah, but that's going to play havoc with the pattern recognition algorithms."

He had seen the raw data streaming from the little craft – the planet's surface was a rubble-strewn wasteland. Finding the cargo was going to be difficult enough without degrading the image quality, especially when they were not even sure what they were searching for.

Carson and Aiyana were dividing their time between examining potential hits from the fleet's survey and checking out anomalies thrown up by the radar. They were discovering that rocks could look awfully like storage modules.

"How much did you cover today Tallis?" Aiyana asked.

"Nearly one million square kilometers."

"Wow! That's terrific!"

Except that it wasn't. At the current rate it would take them over a hundred days just to scan the planet's landmass. Carson groaned and slumped in his chair.

Aiyana tried to cheer him up.

"You poor thing. A whole hundred days to make the greatest archeological discovery in history!"

"I know, but suppose everything has been buried by a landslide? Or perhaps they used a cave – it would have made sense."

"Oh shut up! Perhaps we'll have more luck tomorrow."

Carson frowned but as usual Aiyana was right.

The next morning they climbed aboard the scooter to check out another anomaly from the radar scan. Tallis's fleet was already in the air hurrying to the start point of the day's search.

"The ship got back to me about artificial lighting," the buggy said as they took off. "It reckons the best plan would be to fabricate titanium-sapphire pulse lasers."

"How long would that take?"

"Sorry, it says the fab robotics aren't up to it – you'd have to go to the ship and build them yourself."

Carson sighed. Constructing the lights would probably take days, and then there would be the problem of how to fly them – Tallis's craft were far too small.

"Three minutes to target," Aiyana said.

They were cruising at an altitude of two hundred meters. Beneath them, the surface was becoming increasing pockmarked with rocks, many as large as their living module.

"Seems like glacial activity," Carson said. "Oh God, I hope the ice age occurred before the Yongding's visit."

"Well here we are."

They peered down at a huge piece of basalt.

"Great, another dud."

"Oh come on," Aiyana said, "at least let's land and look around, the radar positioning isn't that accurate."

Before Carson could argue she dropped the scooter to the surface.

"I guess the rock would make a good landmark," he said as he climbed off his saddle "let's try the top of that hill – you wouldn't leave supplies where they could be caught in a flash flood."

They puffed up the slope.

"We should have used the scooter."

"No way – you need the exercise old man."

Five minutes later they were on the crest. Carson stared around then kicked a pebble in disgust.

"Onto the next location," Aiyana said

He nodded. "Okay, but I've had today's workout. Hey scooter! Come and get us."

"I've sorry Carson," the machine replied "but I can't do that."

"What?"

"Something just bit me."

They ran across the brow of the hill to where they could see the little machine.

"There goes the bacteria world," Aiyana shouted.

A green lizard-like creature, about five meters long, was gripping the scooter in its jaws.

"Can it cause any damage?" she asked.

"Don't know and don't want to find out."

"Hey, I bet it's after the chicken stew leftovers I packed for lunch."

At the sound of their voices the creature let go of the scooter and whipped round to face them, its open mouth displaying a nightmarish tangle of teeth.

"It's simple," Aiyana said, "all I have to do is provoke into chasing me while you get on the scooter. Then you come and pick me up."

"Oh no!" Carson said, but she was already waiving her arms and running down the hill.

"Hey ugly," Aiyana yelled, "want something better to eat?"

Moments later she changed direction. The animal took a step, hesitated, then waddled off in pursuit.

"Can't catch me," she shouted, but Carson was not so sure. The creature was clearly amphibious – its stubby legs ended in splayed webfeet – but it was showing a surprising turn of speed. There was nothing to do but charge full tilt to where they had parked.

The scooter had a line of deep scratches scoured into one of its storage pods but otherwise appeared sound. He straddled the machine and shot into the air, but both Aiyana and her pursuer had vanished.

He opened their private channel.

"Where are you?"

No response.

"Are you getting a signal," he asked the scooter.

"I was," the machine replied, "but it disappeared just before you arrived."

"Take us to the last location you have for her."

They flew to a field of giant boulders two hundred meters north of the hill. To Carson's relief he saw the creature pacing to and fro at the edge of the rock field. For the moment at least Aiyana had not replaced chicken stew on the menu, but the animal was not ready to go home hungry.

"She has to be in the rocks," Carson said to the scooter, "get some altitude and see if we can spot her."

"There you are!" said Aiyana's voice over their channel.

"Oh thank God! Where are you Honey? I can't see you."

"I'm in the middle of the all the boulders – too narrow for Mr. Lizard to follow."

"Where? We're still not getting a positional fix."

"All this stone is messing up my signal. I'll walk out into the open."

"The hell you will, that thing is still sniffing around. I'll come in and find you and we'll come out together."

"My hero! You're so sweet."

Carson landed the scooter at the edge of the boulder field on the opposite side from where he last saw the creature.

"Hover at one hundred meters," he said as he dismounted. "One set of teeth marks is enough."

As soon as he had reached ground level Aiyana's signal had vanished again. They were using their survey satellites to create a communications network and provide global positioning, but there were simply not enough of them to get perfect cover.

Carson looked around; satisfied that the creature was not in his immediate vicinity he slipped into an opening between two huge rocks. Ten meters in it dead-ended. As he turned to leave he saw a pointed snout outlined against the narrow strip of sky where he had entered.

He stopped moving. Had the creature spotted him? The snout withdrew. He waited silently for five minutes then padded forward, pausing before walking into open ground. Everything was quiet; it must have left by now. He glanced round the edge of the rock. Everything was clear. As he stepped out into the open he heard a growl – the lizard was emerging from another opening no more than ten meters away.

The animal roared and charged straight at him. Carson screamed and ran full tilt, then dodged into the next opening between the boulders. Damn! This one was larger and his pursuer lumbered in after him. Up ahead the stone walls converged. Surely it could not follow him there?

Carson sprinted forward but he sound of pursuit kept getting closer. As he reached the narrowest part of the gap a massive blow threw him face forward onto the wet sandy soil. He desperately scrambled along the ground until he was certain the creature could not follow. He glanced behind, his pursuer was trying to force its huge body further into the ravine but it was not going to make it. Carson actually took one step closer to examine the thrusting head.

The jaws were lined with row upon row of dagger teeth and its tongue must have been a meter long. The large amber eyes had diagonal pupils giving them a diabolical appearance, but now that it was no longer an immediate danger Carson simply felt wonder that such a magnificent animal had managed to survive in this desolate world.

He turned his attention to the ravine ahead. Mercifully, it seemed to continue into the rock field. Carson hurried on, leaving his new friend to find another meal. After fifty meters the ravine widened again and he found himself in an open space surrounded by giant boulders. Best of all, he was picking up Aiyana's signal. He hurried into another narrow space between the rocks in what he hoped was the right direction. His back hurt like hell from where the creature had struck him but that could wait.

Carson entered into another clearing and shouted with relief at the sight of Aiyana standing with her back towards him. She turned her head and smiled but uncharacteristically she did not rush forward to greet him. He trotted forward to join her. Damn, he must have fell in a puddle, his left side was soaking wet. Pulling open his jacket he saw that the lining was gleaming red.

The next moment he realized what was distracting Aiyana. Directly in front of her was an array of weathered containers covered with ancient symbols. Carson cried out, took one further step, and crashed unconscious into the ground.

"He should be coming round anytime now."

"He will be alright, won't he?"

"He'll be fine."

Carson laid, eyes shut, listening to the voices, peacefully floating in zero gravity.

"He should definitely be awake now. Try stimulating him."

"Now there's a challenge"

Warm lips touched his mouth. He smiled and gently returned the kiss.

"Oh, he's conscious all right."

"I'm administering five milligrams of epinephrine."

The world came into focus – he was on board the ship. He could hear the whisper of the environmentals and the subliminal song of the Higgs Engine. He opened his eyes to see Aiyana's face.

"Welcome back spaceman."

He was lying in the ship's medical tank with the top half of the sarcophagus suspended a meter above him. Carson raised his head and stared down his body – it was enveloped in a nebulous haze of cables as fine as plant roots.

"How long?"

"Three days. We had to regrow half your back muscles."

It finally dawned on him.

"Oh my God, you found the Yongding's cargo! Hey ship, get me out of here."

CHRIS MEAD

The top of the device descended and a breathing mask slid over his face. Carson felt his body drenched in a warm, yeasty liquid. He pulled his head up again and through the dim light saw the tangle of vascular tubes dissolve. After a sterile rinse the ship re-opened the tank and declared him free to move. Aiyana offered her hand as he eased out.

"Wow!" he said, cautiously flexing his naked body. "That's the worst injury I've had in decades"

"I'm glad to hear it. I sprayed on a layer of skin from the emergency kit and hauled you here as fast as I could."

But Carson was not interested in discussing his health.

"We found it!" he yelled hugging Aiyana.

"Did you try to open any of the modules?"

"Oh God, no. I just stumbled across them while you were busy rescuing me."

He let the jibe go.

"Did you get any images?"

"No, but Tallis's fleet has taken lots, she sent them yesterday."

"She's still down there? Is she safe?"

"Oh yes, she said our friend snuffled around the base for a while but he just kept banging his snout on the walls and finally went home – to the ocean I guess."

Aiyana insisted that Carson eat before they checked Tallis's transmissions.

"We have to get solid food inside you to restart your digestive system."

He ate as slowly as he could in the ship's tiny galley before hurrying to the main cabin.

"Tallis built two ultra-high definition cameras, which is pretty damn smart considering she's blind, so we need a large space to see the result."

As they entered the main cabin they were greeted with a full scale view of the clearing in the rocks. Carson floated in wonder through the seemingly solid landscape.

There were thirty-two identical cube-like modules in a rectangular array. They were all partially buried in the sandy soil and as far as Carson could tell each was about two meters tall.

175

"It's a miracle they're not completely covered-up after eight thousand years," Aiyana said. "I guess it's the mild weather – lots of drizzle but nothing catastrophic that would bury them in silt."

"Why here?" asked Carson.

"The rock formation would be relatively easy to spot, especially as it's on a coastal promontory. I'll bet they didn't have any kind of positioning system."

Carson was impressed. Aiyana had being doing a lot of thinking while he was in the tank. He peered closer. Originally, the polycarbonate casings must have been black but centuries of exposure had weathered them to a dull grey. Even so, many of them still sported visible symbols.

"Earth moving tractor," he read out in Mandarin. Next to the Baihua characters the label was reproduced in Ancient English.

"Oh God!" he shouted. "Can you imagine? An entire functioning machine built on Old Earth!"

"Valuable?" Aiyana asked, but her teasing was lost on him.

Carson rushed to another container.

"Here's another tractor. Of course," he laughed, "they brought spares! There's nothing like this in the Archives. Most of the colonists' machinery was cannibalized and re-cannibalized. It was decades before they developed any manufacturing capabilities."

He pointed at a square of discolored plastic; just visible was a raised array of Arabic numerals.

"This must be the lock. They would press the numerals in a special sequence to open the container."

"Any chance it still works?"

Carson shook his head.

"So what do we do now?"

"We should break camp, head to New Earth and hand the location over the Archives Council. Once they get off the floor they'll dispatch an entire department to perform an exquisitely precise excavation, which will take five years to complete."

"You're really going to do that?" asked Aiyana.

"Are you serious?" he grinned. "Come on, let's gear up and get down there."

The tablet

CARSON AND AIYANA WATCHED THE TINY WORKERS CRAWL OVER THE MODULE. They had sweated for two hours digging away the soil to reveal the entire unit. As far as they could tell the vertical cover was completely sealed, but if there was an opening Tallis would find it.

"There is no entry, nest mates."

"That's good news and bad news," said Carson. "The good news is that the contents should be in excellent condition."

"And the bad news?"

"We'll have to bust in."

He pulled out a small cutter and punched a neat hole in the ancient lock. Four teams of workers appeared each bearing a tiny red module that they carried through the newly cut opening.

"It smells very old [untranslatable] in here."

"Not surprising, you're the first living creature to enter for eight thousand years."

After depositing their loads inside the lock the workers reappeared and clambered into their miniature transporter. Carson, Aiyana, and the tiny vessel all retreated into one of the surrounding canyons.

"The Archives Council would kill me for this," Carson said as a small boom echoed round the clearing.

They hurried to inspect the results. The surface of the lock had disappeared revealing its charred mechanism. Aiyana inspected the seal; the perfect join had been replaced by a two-millimeter gap. Carson inserted a crowbar and heaved. The cover moved a centimeter. Both of them threw their weight on the lever. The cover moved another five centimeters. Abandoning the bar they grabbed the edge a pulled the module open. Carson ran round to look inside.

"Oh God!" he shouted.

Aiyana joined him and peered into the darkened interior. The module was empty.

"This is vandalism, we can't blow any more."

Carson was staring at the fifth module they had forced open. All were as empty as the first.

"Let's try another way," said Aiyana

She lifted up her head and addressed the little vessel floating above them.

"Tallis, could you build something that generates electromagnetic radiation in the exahertz range?"

"We can have a device ready in six hours."

"Brilliant!" Carson yelled, "gamma rays – they'll be able to penetrate straight through the casings"

"It's getting late," Aiyana said, "let's talk at the camp"

They reconnected with the communications network as soon as the scooter rose above the curtain of rock surrounding the clearing.

"How did it go?" the buggy asked.

Carson retold the day's events.

"Now we have to figure out how to image gamma rays."

"Why not use my phase-array sensors?" said the buggy.

Carson sighed, suddenly everyone was smarter than him.

"I'm afraid to ask," he said as they entered the living module.

Aiyana spared him the effort.

"Hey stove, what's for dinner?"

"Synthetic vegetable quiche."

"Oh dear God!"

She circled her arms around him.

"You know the way Tallis sometimes gets confused about humans? Well, when you first got injured she suggested that I eat you and simply hatch another nest mate."

"Hmm, maybe for dessert."

Two hours later they were lying in bed staring up through the transparent ceiling. For once the clouds had parted to reveal a night sky gorgeous with stars. Their spontaneous second course had been wonderful and now they were drifting towards sleep.

"Carson," said Aiyana, "there's no way anyone would come this far to leave a bunch of empty storage modules, is there?"

"Nah, someone took the contents. It must have been whoever seeded the oceans with complex life-forms."

He lifted his head.

"Hey buggy, did the ship ever get back to you about terra-forming this planet?"

"Yes, there are no direct references to Mirama c but it thinks it found a passing mention in a history of post-colonial expansion."

"And?"

"About six thousand years ago a private foundation called New Habitable Systems got the idea of founding settlements on bacteria worlds. Apparently they seeded several hundred planets before they ran out of money."

"I guess that explains Mr. Lizard," said Aiyana.

They nuzzled in the darkness.

"Wait a minute," said Carson, "on the third cassette Sakyamuni said that all the storage modules were distributed before they settlement of New Earth."

"So?"

"But according to the ship the terra-formers arrived two thousand years *after* the Yongding, and whoever opened the units didn't break in like we did – the seals were still good – which means they had the access codes. How could they have known the codes? How could the locks still be working after all that time? Something is wrong."

"Perhaps we'll puzzle it out tomorrow."

"Maybe, but I'll be amazed if we do."

But once again Aiyana was right.

Early the next morning they landed the buggy in the clearing.

"Don't worry," Carson said to the machine as he unbolted the last of its sensors, "we'll re-assemble you as good as new afterwards."

"Carson, I've never been as good as new. You built me from reconditioned parts."

He laughed and carried the square black sensor to the makeshift frame that already held three similar units. The four mounted sensors created a rectangle about the same size as a storage container. He placed the frame against the first target's weathered surface and positioned Tallis's gamma-ray generator – an improbably small device no bigger than his thumb – on the opposite side.

"Can you still talk to your sensors?" Aiyana asked the buggy.

"Yes, but you'll have to use at least two angles if you want me to generate a three-dimensional image."

They retreated to a safe distance from the radiation while the buggy captured the first data. Carson then repositioned the generator and sensors to create a second image from a different angle. After that he and Aiyana climbed into the buggy to inspect the results. A ghostly hollow shape floated before their eyes.

"Nothing!" groaned Carson. "One down, twenty-six to go."

"At least we didn't damage anything," said Aiyana. "I mean, even the empty modules are precious, aren't they?"

"I'll say. None of the original transportation containers survived on New Earth, so just by themselves they're a major discovery."

"So we're already in the Archives Council's good books," she said, trying to cheer him up.

"Yeah, but compared to what should have been here…"

They positioned their equipment at the second module but it resolved to be another blank. After that their work settled into a rhythm. They placed the sensor array by each container, took two images then returned to the buggy to check the results.

Towards the end of the day they had processed twenty units. Both of them were tired and cranky from the strain of hauling round the sensors and the continual disappointment of empty modules. Carson was stretching and trying to summon the energy to finish the final six when the buggy spoke up.

"Hey, that last unit – could we take another shot? I thought I could see something on the floor."

The news galvanized them. The array of sensors was heaved to a new position and they were soon in the buggy's darkened cabin staring at the enhanced image. At the bottom of the container was a faint translucent rectangle.

"What is it?" Aiyana whispered.

"God knows," said Carson squinting at the anonymous outline. "The resolution isn't good enough to tell."

He opened a channel.

"Tallis, did you bring your explosives with you?"

It took over an hour to clear the silt from around the module. Carson and Aiyana were aching and soaked with sweat but far too excited to complain. Nothing appeared to differentiate this unit from the others, although the surface was too weathered to read the list of contents.

Finally Tallis was able to lay her charges. Minutes later they leapt into action as the echo of the explosion died away. By now they were experts at breaking into the ancient containers and it took just a few practiced tugs to pull the module open. Carson played his flashlight over the interior. Above the clearing the light from the late afternoon sky was beginning to fade.

"What the –"

"What is it?" Aiyana asked, trying to peer over his shoulder.

On the floor of the container was a flat clear rectangle, thirty centimeters by fifteen. Carson moved the flashlight around, trying to gauge the object's refractive index.

"I think it's made of glass."

He stopped – the light had caught something on the surface.

"It's engraved with Ancient English."

He leaned forward, trying to make out the words. For thirty seconds he was completely still, then, twisting round he bellowed: "Hey buggy, turn on your headlights. Tallis, get in here. I need a high-def recording of the entire interior."

"Honey, what is it?" Aiyana asked him.

She was alarmed to see that he was trembling.

Carson ignored her question.

"Darling," he said taking her hand, "you know that carry-case we have for the analysis tools? As soon as Tallis is finished I want you to take the buggy back to camp and get it. Dump the contents – I don't care where – and make some padding, lots of padding, for the case's interior. Cut up the bedclothes or whatever."

"Aren't you coming?"

"No," he crouched down at the edge of the container. "I'm not moving."

"And," he shouted as Aiyana scrambled into the buggy, "bring some surgical gloves."

She returned an hour later. Carson was still squatting by the open unit.

"Perfect," he pronounced as he inspected the open carry-case. He placed it on the floor of the container next to the glass rectangle and pulled on the surgical gloves.

"I have to be calm," he said. "Really, I have no right to move it but there's no way I'm leaving it here."

He took three long breaths then reached out, eased his fingers under the object and with wincing care placed it in the padded interior of the case. He closed the lid and stood up. No father carrying his first-born child moved with more care than Carson as he placed the case into the buggy.

He seemed to calm down once it was stowed.

"Come on, let's get to the camp."

"What is it?" Aiyana asked again as they flew through the darkness.

"It's a message," was all that he would say.

Carson carried the case into the camp's habitation module and laid it on a memory-shape table. He fussed around the room and returned with a small portable spotlight, which he position at an oblique angle.

"That should make the engraving more visible."

He opened the case and together they read the ancient words:

The fact that you are reading this message proves that the people of New Earth have succeeded in building another starship. I celebrate that you have survived and prospered. Much time has passed I am sure, decades, possibly centuries.

You may not know who I am, so I should introduce myself. My name is Aaron Lavan Samuelson. I am, or rather I was, the Director of Science for the International Extrasolar Expeditionary Project. I am one of the 1,002 survivors who made their way to the Eridani system after escaping the terrible destruction of Earth.

I have the honor of being the elected leader of the Technical Alliance, a dedicated group of scientists and technicians who, unlike the other survivors, refuses to be shackled by the so-called Covenant with Humanity, which deliberately aims to limit the growth of technology. Perhaps the Covenant no longer exists and is nothing but an historical curiosity. I sincerely hope so; otherwise humankind may never advance beyond its primitive origins.

The Technical Alliance, one hundred and sixty souls, has broken with the other survivors. We have fled the Eridani system with the human race's one existing starship, the Yongding, thus marooning our companions on New Earth. We find this act deeply troubling but we have no choice.

We go to seek a distant world where we can grow and flourish in peace. Certainly not this planet, we do not have the time to seed new life and besides, it is much too close to Eridani. We fear that if we again encounter the other survivors they will attempt to finish what they have begun and extinguish the flame of progress forever. We must go somewhere where we will never be found.

I apologize for the fact that these storage units are empty, but I trust you can do without: if you have the resources to build an interstellar vessel then you must be curiosity-seekers, not men and women such as ourselves in desperate need of supplies and material.

Perhaps in the far future our descendents will meet again. Until that day, I wish you well.

June 7, 2148

"Oh my God," said Aiyana, "it was the Techs!"

Carson sighed.

"Now it's obvious. They wanted to found a new colony but they were stealing an empty starship. Sakyamuni was one of the dissidents – and he knew exactly where all the supply dumps were located. Like Samuelson says, they were desperate for material, they had to stop here to pick up everything."

He grinned at Aiyana.

"I bet they also cleared out the stuff in cometary orbit. Just as well we didn't weeks thrashing around deep space searching for it. But this..."

His voice trailed off as he stared at the glass tablet.

"There is nothing like this, is there?"

"When they fled New Earth the Techs just vanished. No-one has ever found the slightest trace of what happened to them."

"Until now."

Carson gestured at the tablet "do you realize that in a few years time there will be lines a hundred meters long at the Archives Museum to see this?"

"Why's it made of glass?"

"It's incredibly stable. We've seen what time can do to a recording media."

"I thought it was a super-viscous liquid, eventually it just flowed away."

Carson shook his head.

"That's a myth. Samuelson was a scientist, he knew what he was doing."

"Well, Juro was not expecting this."

"I guess not," Carson said as he re-closed the case, "but he never did let me listen to the third cassette – all I got was an edited transcript. Who knows what was really on it? Who knows what he's really after?"

Early the following morning they made one final trip to the clearing to image the last six storage modules. After reading Samuelson's message none of them expected to find anything but all agreed they had to try.

"How are you doing flying blind?" Carson asked the buggy. The machine's sensors were still attached to the improvised imaging system.

"No problem, I'm following Tallis's radio beacon."

They traveled on for a few minutes.

"Radio beacon!" Carson shouted.

They found it perched on the rocks above the clearing, a battered grey cylinder wedged between two boulders. The outer casing was deeply corroded from eight thousand years of exposure but astonishingly the inner workings appeared to be intact.

"They must have built it to take a beating," said Aiyana. "What are those square things?"

"They're called solar panels. They generate electricity from daylight. It probably kept transmitting for decades."

"Wow! The one thing they left behind. Why would they take the location beacon? It was the supplies they were after."

They stowed the ancient transmitter in the buggy and went through the chore of checking the last modules. To nobody's surprise they were all empty. They agreed to take two – the one that had held Samuelson's message and an unopened container to keep the preservationists happy.

By late afternoon they had packed away the camp and were heading to the ship. Mirama c shrank visibly as the acceleration ramped up.

"It's good to be able to see again," said the buggy. "It makes me wonder how Tallis functions."

"We speculate same about humans and machines that have no sense of smell."

"I can smell," Aiyana objected.

"And we can distinguish [untranslatable] light and dark but you do not call that seeing."

Carson was studying a facsimile of the glass tablet.

"Hey buggy, do you have an image of Samuelson?"

The face of a man in late middle age floated in front of them, his dark brown eyes glittering with intelligence.

"He could almost be Cissokho's brother," Aiyana said.

"Yeah," said Carson, "they were both of African origin, but it's believed that Samuelson was born and raised in the North American Federation. Cissokho grew up in Botswana, though she spent most of her adult life in Greater China."

"I thought she was born in Africa."

"Africa was a continental landmass, not a political and cultural entity. The Book says that at one time there were over two hundred *countries* on Old Earth, though there were fewer by the time the Yongding was built."

"Two hundred separate cultures on one planet! How did they all manage to get along?"

"They didn't. Armed conflicts – they called them *wars* – were going on all the time."

"Poor creatures."

"There were simply too many of them, thirteen billion at the end. They could all communicate instantaneously and travel anywhere on the planet in less than an hour. It must have been easy to get into a fight."

"Imagine a conflict between cultures nowadays," Carson laughed. "It would take weeks just to trade insults!"

"Is that why the Techs left New Earth, to avoid another *war*?"

Carson gazed at the stern face floating in the cabin.

"Maybe – we always thinks of the Techs stealing the Yongding as a crime, but perhaps Samuelson was right, it was the only peaceful way out. Where does that leave the last eight thousand years of history? Where does that leave us?"

The next day they met in the ship's main cabin. Carson had repacked the priceless glass tablet and secured it in the safe that he used for his most treasured objects.

"So what should we do now? Tallis, Aiyana, ship – any suggestions?"

"I follow your scent."

"Me too," said the ship.

"What about you honey?"

"Oh come on," said Aiyana, "this is your party. I just came along for the ride. What do you think we should do?"

"Well, we have one of the most unique historical artifacts ever discovered, plus some great pieces of Old Earth technology. The only responsible thing to do is to head straight to New Earth and hand them all over to the Archives Council."

"Hey ship," Aiyana yelled, "is your Carson to Aiyana auto-translator working today? Would you care to interpret that last comment?"

The cabin echoed with fake mechanical noises.

"Message reads: *let's get the hell out of here and find the next supply dump.*"

"Exactly what I thought, you'd better start plotting a course."

"Already locked and loaded," said the ship as Aiyana tousled Carson's hair.

FALK

ANCIENT VOICES WHISPERED IN CARSON'S EAR AS HE DRIFTED, EYES CLOSED, through the darkened cabin. He was listening to the debates of the Covenant Convention recorded by Teng, ironically on the very same tapes that they had stolen from the archives. Ever since the revelation ten days ago that they were following the path of the stolen Yongding he had been scrambling to learn as much as he could about the Techs.

More than curiosity drove him. The key question was whether the fleeing dissidents had emptied all the storage dumps. Sakyamuni hinted that it had taken several voyages to distribute all the material. Perhaps the supplies left at each system represented the Yongding's maximum cargo capacity. Not much was known about the ancient starship –just the one famous image of the vessel that appeared in every history of New Earth – but that was all. Perhaps the renegade colonists had filled their holds at Mirama and left the other dumps intact. Carson shivered with pleasure at the thought.

The Convention was coming to its climax – the arguments before the adoption of the Covenant. The traditional portrait of the Techs was that of a group of selfish rebels, but as he listened to the tapes a different picture was emerging. Samuelson had genuinely tried to find a compromise; in many ways it was Cissokho who was the hardliner. Suppose they had reached consensus, how different would the world have been? It was one of the great '*what if*' questions of history.

Carson sighed and turned off the recording. They were two days from the Falk system, the next unlikely candidate for colonization chosen by the astronomers of Old Earth.

"At least the ship's library says that this one has a complete ecosystem," he told Aiyana.

Prior to Sakyamuni's account neither of them had heard of the obscure world.

"Falk is an M class star – a red dwarf – so it will be a narrow habitable zone."

"Won't the planets be in tidal lock, one side always facing the sun?"

"It's bigger than most of its kind – about a third of a standard solar mass – so Falk a won't be too close, and it has a giant moon just like Old Earth. I guess that must help maintain rotation."

"Oh hell," he said, "there's so little information. Let's divide the workload, you research the planet and I'll keep on investigating the Techs."

But even with the ship's vast resources Aiyana had not been able to find much more. The system was sparsely inhabited, although it was not part of the Commonwealth or any other alliance. As a consequence trade was virtually non-existent. Apparently, the people of Falk had turned their backs on the outside world.

"This isn't going to be easy," Carson said, "I would have preferred another empty planet."

"It will do you good, you need to meet more people."

She was right of course. Where was Aiyana? He had lost track of time listening to the recordings. Carson flexed his legs against sixth millennium gene editor and pushed his way across the cabin towards the conservatory. Predictably, she was lying in her favorite spot at the heart of the garden. Was she asleep? He pushed his way through the dense vegetation. She remained motionless as he emerged into the clearing. Aiyana's body was as still as death, her naked skin crawling with Tallis's workers. *Oh God no!* The scream died in his mind as she opened her eyes and smiled.

Shaking, Carson slumped onto the turf.

"There you are! Why are you looking like that?"

"It's just that I thought... Oh, forget it. What the hell are you two doing?"

"Tallis was telling me that she had never come into physical contact with a human being, so I thought I should give her the opportunity."

"It is [untranslatable]. So huge, so like a giant grub! Carson, are you the same?"

"Come on," said Aiyana, "let her check you out as well."

Muttering under his breath, Carson stripped off his flight suit and lay down beside her. He forced himself to stay still as a swarm of tiny feet moved across his skin.

"[Untranslatable]. This part is different!"

They both lay giggling as the examination continued.

Later on, when they were dressed and back in the main cabin, Aiyana explained Tallis's perception of their roles.

"She thinks you must be a drone – you know, the male Ants whose only purpose is to service the queen. But she suspects you are defective, otherwise why don't I get fertilized with all the mating?"

"She's got me nailed," said Carson, then added, "Seriously, have you ever thought about having a child?"

"I suppose every woman has at some point in her life, but not yet. I want to be at least a hundred years old before making such a commitment. How about you?"

"Oh God no! Anyhow, I'd have to change sex first which is a tremendous hassle."

"I think you'd make a great woman."

"I gather that's a compliment."

"You bet it is," she said butting her body into his. "Maybe I'll change sex at the same time. Imagine that!"

"The mind boggles."

They spun laughing across the cabin.

"Well there it is," said the ship.

A silvery globe hovered in the cabin like a gigantic steel bearing.

"Nice imaging," said Carson.

"Thank Tallis – she built me an optical interferometer. I deployed it with the periscope."

The ship had arrived at the inner edge of Falk's Kuiper Belt twelve hours earlier. As soon as spin-down re-established contact with the universe the first order of business was to find out more about the reclusive planet.

Aiyana peered closer, the bluish light giving a metallic appearance to her skin.

"I can't see any land – surely it's not an ocean world."

"No," said the ship, "let me enhance the image."

Thin diagonal strips of green appeared, as if a monstrous claw had shredded the continents.

"That's one of the strangest landmass formations I've seen," said Carson, "any idea why it's shaped that way?"

"Erosion perhaps – being that close to the star must induce powerful tides. We should know more soon; I think I'm receiving a welcome package," the ship said.

"You're not sure?"

"It's encrypted, nothing too sophisticated."

There was a pause.

"Okay, ready when you are."

They gathered round a display.

To their surprise the welcome package was not published by the planet's government but by the Commonwealth Consulate. He apologized for the encryption and explained that it "was in the best interests of discretion."

"In other words, he's going to say something rude," said Carson.

It transpired that the people of Falk were fundamentalists in a way that would have dismayed Cissokho and the framers of the Covenant. They did not believe in the slow technological progress pursued by the rest of the galaxy – they favored in *no* technological progress. In fact they had deliberately regressed and the Covenant had assumed the status of a religion. They had little to offer the larger world and distrusted outsiders as harbingers of modernity.

"Visitors, however, will be received with courtesy provided local sensitivities are observed."

"Whoa!" said Carson, studying the addendum on the planet's economy, "they appear to have an industrial base similar to Old Earth in the middle of the twentieth century."

"Wasn't it incredibly polluting?" Aiyana asked.

"You bet – the main power source comes from burning carbonaceous minerals – but there are only five million inhabitants so I guess the ecosystem can take the stress."

"Well it is beautiful."

Aiyana was inspecting the packet's images which showed snow-capped mountains and wide valleys covered with deep green foliage.

"The plant life has to absorb every scrap of energy it can from that red sunlight. Any terrestrial vegetation would need re-engineering."

But Carson was more interested in the technology.

"From an antique collector's point of view I bet there's some damn interesting stuff down there. I wonder what I can trade."

"But what about finding the supply dump?"

"Yeah, this is not going to be easy. If we start flying around in the buggy the locals will go berserk."

"Surely my fleet will pass unnoticed."

"Maybe Tallis, but you'll have to teach us how to operate it. I'm sorry but you'll be staying home – you'd scare the life out of them. And we'd better make some new clothes. This is not, I repeat not, somewhere you'll be running around naked Aiyana."

"What excuse are we going to make for our visit?" Aiyana asked as the buggy hurtled sunward.

"Have you forgotten darling, I'm a mailman."

"There's mail for this place?"

"Yup, not much – most of it's probably all for the consulate – but it gives us a legitimate reason to be here. Plus I'll spin a story about hunting for antiques, that'll be a good excuse for traveling around."

"Where are we landing?" Aiyana asked as she wriggled in her new clothes.

A small copy of the silvery globe materialized in the buggy's cabin. One straggling strip of land in the center of the northern hemisphere shone red.

"The welcome package indicates that this is the most developed landmass," said the buggy. "All visiting craft are instructed to land at the *airport* at its southern tip."

"I've been thinking about geography," said Aiyana. "I reckon Sakyamuni chose that promontory on Mirama because it was such an obvious landmark. It was a precaution against the radio beacon failing."

"So you're saying search for something similar here?"

"I guess, but where…"

Her voice trailed off as she turned to the glowing image.

Two hours later they were hovering over the *airport*.

"It seems kind of empty," said Aiyana. "It's really nothing but a big field."

As instructed, they set down at the southern perimeter.

"I don't know what the locals would make of you," Carson told the buggy once they had unloaded their baggage. "Best to stay out of sight – hang around in low orbit until I call."

"Okay," said the little spacecraft, "stay out of trouble."

It shot up into the violet sky.

They were in the middle of a flat expanse of grass so dark green it appeared almost black. On three sides the windswept land finally gave way to the ocean while to the north they could see a stubby tower surrounded by low buildings.

"This is about as exciting as Mirama," said Carson.

"Wait until Mr. Lizard turns up."

"Here he comes now."

A uniformed man had emerged from the nearest building and was hurrying towards them.

"Honor to the Covenant and good morning to you!" the stranger cried as he came within hailing distance. He sported a neat mustache and had the overworked, slightly perplexed manner that seemed to be the universal attribute of all civil servants.

"Honor to the Covenant," Carson replied stepping forward. "My name is Carson, and this is my wife Aiyana."

"Delighted to meet you Mr. Carson, Mrs. Carson."

"We just landed," Carson explained, ignoring the spluttering noises emanating from behind him.

"Er, yes," the official said. He glanced around. "I'm afraid I don't see your *aircraft*." His Universal was supplemented with Old English.

"I returned it to orbit."

The man took an involuntary step back.

"Oh goodness, you are Outsiders. Please forgive me," he smiled, "I've never met any before."

He stepped forward again, inspecting them for tentacles and eye stalks. Finding none, bureaucratic protocol took control.

"I am Assistant Controller Carruthers, welcome to, ah, Falk. If you come this way please, I will check on the procedures for Outside visitors."

They picked up their bags and trudged after the official.

"May I inquire where you are from?" said Carruthers as they entered the building. It was little more than a single cluttered office. Large windows ran the length of the walls affording a panoramic view of the airport.

"New Earth, I am a Commonwealth mailman."

"Really, mail from Outside, who would have thought?"

Carson sighed. Usually his arrival at an isolated world caused a sensation.

Carruthers took out a binder and leafed through it.

"Ah yes! Standard procedure is to contact the Consulate. He's our sole foreign resident, you know."

He picked up a horn-shaped piece of plastic tethered by a cord – presumably to keep it from getting lost in all the clutter – and placed one end to his ear.

After a pause he said, "The New Earth Consulate in Wurlington please," speaking into the other end of the device.

As they waited Aiyana opened a private channel to Carson.

"So what's with the wife routine, *darling*?" she sub-vocalized.

"Playing it safe – some backward societies are very conservative."

Carruthers began talking again.

"New Earth Consulate? Honor to the Covenant and good afternoon. This is Assistant Controller Carruthers at the Ferndale Airport. I am calling to announce the arrival of two *Outsiders*. Yes, yes, I'll wait."

After another pause he straightened his back.

"Honor to the Covenant to you too Mr. Consul. Yes, a mailman. Mr. Carson and his lady wife."

He turned round.

"He wants to speak to you."

Carson warily put the offered device to ear.

"My dear man!" a distant voice cried. "Welcome to Falk, you actually have mail? You must come straight to the Consulate."

"I'm delighted to be here Sir," Carson replied. "Can you send a vehicle?"

"No need, put that official on the line."

He handed the device to Carruthers who, after listening to the Consul, placed it in its cradle and pulled out a large printed pad.

"I am preparing a government travel warrant," he said as he carefully marked the pad's surface with a scribing device. "Here" he tore out the top sheet and handed it to Carson. "Present this at the Ferndale Railway Station."

Seeing Carson's confusion he went on. "There's a train to Wurlington," he consulted a small disk strapped to his wrist, "in one hour. I say, why don't I drive you to the station?"

They followed him outside to where a wheeled vehicle was parked. After loading the luggage Carson and Aiyana were placed in seats behind Carruthers who turned his attention to an array of joysticks, buttons, and handles. Moments later there was a small explosion, provoking a scream from Aiyana.

"Sorry about that," the official said, "the old girl is running a bit rough."

The vehicle lurched into motion, growling and coughing. Carson leaned forward, fascinated by Carruthers' skill with the controls.

"What's the power source?" he shouted above the din.

"One liter flat four."

"Ah yes," said Carson. He had no idea what one liter flat four was, but after a disconcerting encounter with another vehicle as they left the airport he was reluctant to distract Carruthers again.

As they headed north along the narrow road the flat landscape gave way to wooded hills and open valleys. Neat rows of cultivated plants appeared in fields clustered around rural dwellings. The red sun climbed higher warming the air. It appeared to be springtime and the roadside was lined with tangles of fragrant wildflowers.

Aiyana was entranced.

"Isn't it the prettiest thing you've ever seen?"

Carson smiled and held her hand; how exotic the scenery must have seemed to someone raised in the arcologies of an asteroid belt. After half an hour they entered a small town of sturdily built stone houses. Eventually their vehicle spluttered to a halt in a plaza featuring a statue of Adhiambo Cissokho at its center.

They unloaded their bags and followed Carruthers up the steps of a building bordering the square. A painted sign announced *Ferndale Railway Station.* An attendant inspected the travel warrant and they emerged out of the other side of the building onto a long platform decorated at each end with beds of flowers. In front of the platform and a meter below it, two parallel strips of metal curved away into the distance.

"I wonder what those are," Aiyana said.

"Primitive superconducting cables," Carson replied.

"The train will be here in five minutes," said Carruthers. "I will make my farewells now – I have to return to the airport. Pleasure to meet you Mr. Carson, Mrs. Carson. I wish you a safe journey home."

"In other words, leave my planet as soon as you can," Carson said to Aiyana as the official hurried off.

"Oh, he was just shy."

She peered into the sky searching for the train.

"It's so *quiet* here! No chatter on the net, no valet service, and those advertisements – they just sit there."

But the next moment the silence was broken by an amplified voice announcing the train's imminent arrival. They both stared upwards, squinting against the sunlight.

"Still can't –"

Aiyana was cut off by a shrill whistle that roused their fellow passengers from the benches on the platform. A column of smoke appeared in the distance. Moments later they saw a huge black whale of an object following the path of the twin metal strips. Behind it was a set of red boxy containers. As the extraordinary procession came closer it became apparent that the entire assemblage was running on wheels. The cavalcade slowly lost velocity and finally came to an asthmatic halt in front of the platform where they stood. The amplified voice announced the arrival of the morning train to Wurlington with stops at Balcombe, Crouch End, and Flitwick.

"Oh my God!" Carson yelled as he rushed forward to get a closer look.

He caught the eye of a man who was presumably the pilot leaning out of the lead vehicle's cabin.

"What's the power source?" Carson asked him. "One liter flat four?"

The man laughed but did not reply.

Aiyana pressed her hands against the huge cylinder.

"Oh, it's hot! I think there's some form of combustion taking place."

The pilot showed more interest in Aiyana than he had in Carson.

"Bless you, Miss, you carry on like you've never seen a steam engine before."

"I haven't," she said beaming. "I think it's wonderful! And those steel wheels, it's all so *manly!*"

She definitely had his attention now.

"Would you like to ride in the cabin with me and Alf?"

"Would I!" Aiyana cried and went to mount the metal steps.

This caused much hilarity.

"Sorry Miss, I was just joking. Hurry up and get into a carriage, we're leaving in a couple of minutes."

She waved goodbye and followed Carson into the first *carriage*.

"That is an amazing piece of early engineering," she said as they sat down.

"It is," Carson agreed. He was already thinking about what he could trade for it, and how the hell he would transport it to New Earth.

"Why were their faces and hands painted black?" Aiyana asked.

"It's a symbolic expression of brotherhood with the machine."

"How do you know all this stuff?"

The train lurched, lurched again, and then they were off following the path of the metal strips. They soon left the town and puffed through the countryside parallel to a fast-moving river. Once she discovered that the windows of the carriage could be opened Aiyana leaned out to get a better view.

"Darling, there is a notice here expressly forbidding hanging out of the window while the train is in motion."

"Why is that?" She grew more excited "do you think we'll be going underwater?"

But they stayed on dry land, passing woodlands, meadows, farms and an occasional village. After a while the tone of the steam engine became stronger and the air flowing through the open window colder – they were gaining altitude – and in the distance they saw mountain peaks. Half an hour later they arrived in the small town of Balcombe. More passengers climbed in then they were off again, the metal wheels squealing as they descended once more to sea level. Following two more stops they entered the outskirts of a large city. Finally, three hours after leaving Ferndale, they arrived at Wurlington's main station.

The terminus was a smoke-blackened semi-cylinder of steel and glass that spanned a dozen railway tracks ("super-conducting cables – hah!" said Aiyana punching Carson's arm). As they passed the front of their train the engineer pulled a lever that sent a shrill column of steam up to the roof.

"Come and see us again darling," he called out as they passed.

"I think he's talking to you," said Carson.

They hurried on to a line of taxis – wheeled vehicles similar to the one at the airport – and asked for the New Earth Consulate. Their driver was not shy.

"Where you from then? New Earth? Good grief I do get all sorts in this cab! Mailman are you? Who would want a letter from Outside? Let everyone mind their own business is what I say; no offense to you and your lady wife."

When the reached the Consulate, an elegant row house in the center of the city, Carson presented the taxi driver with his travel warrant.

"Oh Lord, that's only good for trains. Don't you have any real money?"

"I'm sorry, no. But I can offer you these."

Carson held out a handful of gold coins.

"Oh dear, sir," the driver said, "one of those is more than enough."

Carson insisted he take two. In fact he felt something of a fraud. While they were indeed gold in the sense that they were made of atoms of the seventy-ninth element, he had purchased a kilo of the metal for a hundred Ecus in an industrial arcology orbiting New Mars. Long ago he discovered that gold was more acceptable when fashioned into coins, and had created handsome examples with a relief of the ship on one side and his face in profile on the other. Using synthetic bullion in a primitive culture was ethically dubious and he kept the coins strictly for emergencies. He resolved to get his hands on some local currency as soon as possible.

Renshu, the Consul, was overjoyed to see them.

"You cannot believe how good that feels," he said as they touched palms.

Like many of the Falk men he wore a neatly clipped moustache. His clothes too reflected the local style; Carson suspected he had gone native.

They met in the Consul's office at the rear of the row house. The room was elegantly appointed with local furniture and large windows overlooking a private garden. It was an unexpected oasis of tranquility in the bustling metropolis. The posting may have been lonely but it was not uncomfortable.

"And you have brought mail!"

"Yes, can you tell me how I contact the Postmaster?"

"My dear boy, you're looking at him! And the cultural attaché, and the diplomatic affairs officer, and anything else you care to name. As far as I know I'm the only Outsider on the planet."

He took them down to the basement where they found a dusty mail console. On the other side of the room was a medical tank.

"Only one on Falk – if you ever get injured drag yourself to the Consulate."

"The locals are that set against modern technology?"

"They abhor it – that's why I hide everything down here."

He loaded Carson's mail packet into the console.

"As I expected: not a large yield. Thirty thousand items, and half of them for me!"

"How do you distribute the rest?" Aiyana asked. "There's no local net."

"Hard copy," said Renshu nodding at a printer. "We print them out. The identity of the final location is written on the front of an envelope, the correspondence placed inside, and it is physically carried to the recipient."

"Wow!"

"I've done the same thing," said Carson, "but I charge a fortune. How can people afford the service?"

"Economics of scale, old boy. Millions of letters are sent each day; postal delivery is a huge business."

"So much for the glamour," said Aiyana.

The Consul checked a display.

"Not much of a fee I'm afraid."

"Is it possible to pay me in local currency?" Carson asked. "All I have is synthetic gold."

"Absolutely! Of course, there is no official exchange rate because there is no exchanging going on, but we can work one out."

"Thanks, we'll need it to pay a hotel."

Renshu insisted that they stay at the Consulate.

"My residence is on the upper floors. It's just me so there's plenty of room. I must confess that it is all rather fine, and provided gratis by the Falk government. But I do spare them from having to deal with Outsiders."

That evening Renshu took them to eat at his *local*, The Firkin, an ancient bar two blocks from the Consulate. Here any distrust of Outsiders was absent and the patrons greeted the Consul as an old friend. Everyone insisted that they sample the local beer, Wurlington Brown, which arrived in huge foaming glasses. Reinforced by her second *pint*, Aiyana wandered off to investigate a game that involved throwing metal spikes at a target.

"How can that be safe?" Carson protested.

"It's not darling, that's why it's fun."

Carson raised his glass to the Consul. He decided it was time to touch on the real reason for his visit and began by discussing antiques. It seemed reasonable that if the supply dump had been found the antique-collecting community would know about it.

"Do you know of any dealers in Wurlington?"

"Goodness, no old boy. What you and I think of as an antique is a godless futuristic contraption to these people."

"I suppose that's true, but some of the machinery currently in use here is exquisite: the steam engine that brought us here and the mechanical scribing device, the *typewriter*, that your receptionist uses."

"Those things are for sale, I suppose, but not by antique dealers. Sorry, they simply don't exist. Besides, how would you pay? The only money you have is from the postal delivery, and no-one will trade for anything coming from Outside."

"I'll think of something, I usually do," said Carson with a grin. He returned to his original point. "When I was last on New Earth I did some research in the Archives that suggested Falk may have been visited very early during the colonial expansion – long before the planet was permanently settled. These early visitors may have left a supply dump. If so, you can imagine its value."

Before Renshu could answer there was a roar of laughter. Carson turned round to see Aiyana wrenching a metal spike out of a barstool.

"Hey guys," she yelled, "come and have a game of *darts.*"

Carson waved and turned to the Consul.

"Even early colonial technology would repel these people," Renshu said.

"It wouldn't be kept in a museum or anything?"

"I doubt it – bad influence on the young and all that. At one time there was a sect called the Guardians of the Flame that actually went round confiscating anything that smacked of modernism."

"And they destroyed what they took?"

"No idea old boy. I say, do you have any detox tablets on you? Mine ran out years ago, what with the Wurlington Brown and all that."

Two hours later they meandered along the sidewalk to the Consulate. Aiyana had made a dozen new friends who wanted her to join them again the following night.

"Next time we'll drink the stout darling, it'll put hair on your chest," one shouted as she left the bar.

Renshu was also in a fine mood. He was telling them about the history of the Firkin when he suddenly stopped.

"I say, the Rose is blooming tonight."

Carson and Aiyana gaped; straight ahead of them Falk's giant moon had risen above the horizon. Aeons ago the satellite must have been struck by a huge asteroid and the resulting devastation was clearly visible as a series of concentric circles radiating out from the impact site to the periphery of the disk.

If Falk had been a G class star the full moon would have appeared silvery white, but here the red sunlight suffused it with a delicate pink. The coloration and the nested rings gave the satellite a startling resemblance to a monstrous rose floating in the night sky.

"You know, people would travel light years just to see this," Carson said to Renshu.

"God forbid, my friend, it would be my job to look after them."

The following morning Carson resolved to find out more about the Guardians of the Flame. If the early settlers had discovered the Yongding's supply dump it was perfectly possible that the Guardians had confiscated the lot. Then there was the question of what they did with it.

Renshu suggested he visit the Great Library.

"It's by far the largest information source on the planet, and you can borrow my pass. It was supplied to me courtesy of the Falk government but I hardly ever use it."

Aiyana declined to join him.

"You'll enjoy it far more by yourself. Besides, I want to explore the city."

Carson gave her some local currency and warned her to be careful.

"Oh darling, you're so sweet when you get all protective," she said.

"And no more games of *darts!*"

He set off down the street following Renshu's directions. The Library was located in the heart of Wurlington and despite the lack of an ambient information infrastructure he had little difficulty finding his way. What did perplex him was traversing the roads. The ubiquitous wheeled transports, the *cars*, zoomed past at breakneck speed, but somehow he was expected to get across without being hit. The only viable strategy was to stand behind a native waiting at the sidewalk and dog his heels as he threaded his way through the traffic.

The Great Library was a large circular building made of grey granite. Inside, red sunlight angled through the domed glass roof to illuminate a vast reading room lined with bookshelves twenty meters high. Balconies circled the walls to facilitate access to the collections.

Carson was entranced. The only book he was familiar with was The Book, the famous child's encyclopedia that had survived the Melt and the flight to Eridani. Here there must have been a million volumes. For over an hour he wandered along the catwalks, pulling out samples at random and marveling at the static, frozen pages. Aiyana had been right to let him come alone.

Finally he got down to business. There was no way he would find anything by himself and he enlisted the help of one of the resident librarians who, after consulting a gigantic array of printed cards, scuttled off and returned with four books on the Guardians of the Flame. Carson settled at a desk to do some serious reading.

The Guardians, it transpired, had been at their height three thousand years ago. This was when the people of Falk had turned their backs on the modern world. At first the movement was not universal and many inhabitants continued to use technologically advanced equipment. The Guardians had served as shock troops, seizing machinery and in some cases persecuting the users. Finally, with nothing left to confiscate and no one to intimidate, they had faded away.

But what happened to the stuff they took? Carson leafed through another volume. *Although most of the equipment was destroyed,* he read, *the Guardians kept some of what they considered to be the most egregious examples to display as a warning to their followers. Today, the diabolical collection is stored in the crypt of Lilly Cathedral at the southern tip of the Wessle continent. It is still put on display once a month, traditionally on the evening of the full moon. The cache includes machinery used by the first pioneers, some of it apparently dating even earlier to the beginning of the colonial era.* He threw the book onto the table. Bingo!

When was the full moon? It had appeared full last night; had they missed their chance? Carson went to the librarian's desk and asked for an almanac. He ran his finger down a column of dates; oh God it was tomorrow! He returned the books and hurried out of the Library.

"Where are you honey?" he yelled as he walked into their rooms at the Consulate. There was no reply but he heard singing coming from the bathroom. Carson stuck his head round the door and shouted in horror. Aiyana was sitting in the bath, her face and hands completely black.

"What the hell happened to you?"

"I've been driving the train!" she said and submerged her head beneath the foamy water.

When she resurfaced most of the black was gone.

"Symbolic expression of brotherhood, my soapy *bum!*" she cried tossing a sponge at Carson's head. "It was a coating of coal. That's what they combust in the steam engine."

She lay back in the water, closed her eyes and smiled.

"Just for that you can wash me all over."

After a great deal of splashing about Aiyana climbed out the bath and dried herself while Carson told her about his research.

"Oh my super-smart mailman!" she said, kissing him. "Can we get to Lilly by tomorrow?"

"I doubt it – not with the local transportation."

Renshu confirmed his fears.

"Sorry old chap, Wessle is five thousand kilometers to the east. I believe there is an *airplane* service but that runs once a day. It will never get you there in time for the ceremony. You will have to cheat."

THE CATHEDRAL

THEY GOT UP TWO HOURS BEFORE DAWN. RENSHU, CLAD IN A RED VELVET DRESSING gown, led them through the rear of the building and into the grounds. The Consulate was part of a square of houses surrounding a communal garden; hidden from the rest of the city, it made the perfect setting for a covert landing. They padded across the black dew-soaked grass to the center. Everything was still; the people of Wurlington, the Consul assured them, were not early risers. Carson sent a signal and two minutes later the silent buggy dropped out of the sky.

"See you tomorrow night," Aiyana whispered as they climbed in.

"I'll be here. I'm always here" Renshu replied.

He stepped back as the small spacecraft lifted into the air. Within seconds it had disappeared from sight.

"Can you bring up that globe of Falk?" Carson asked the buggy.

The image of the planet shimmered into life in the center of the cabin.

"Hey, this is a lot more detailed!"

"I've been performing an orbital survey since you landed," the buggy said. "I now have high-resolution imagery of most of the landmass."

Carson pointed to the tip of a long strip of land in the northern hemisphere, the continent of Wessle.

"Magnify here."

The image exploded outward, giving the impression of a precipitous fall to the surface. A small town surrounded by farmland came into view; at its center was a large structure.

"That's our destination, Lilly," Carson said. "I assume the big building is the cathedral. Buggy, you'd better drop us outside the city limits, it's already daylight there."

By now the small craft had risen a hundred kilometers above the atmosphere on its eastward journey. Directly ahead the sun rose over the horizon filling the cabin with warm light while behind them Falk's bizarre moon sank lower and disappeared behind the curve of the world. Fifteen minutes later they landed besides a deserted country road. Carson and Aiyana jumped out and the buggy immediately shot into the sky.

"And no on one the wiser," Aiyana said. "I love those steam engines but you can't beat a push drive for getting about."

"Now comes the hard part," said Carson. "Lilly is about two kilometers down the road. Better get going."

They set off walking, keeping a brisk pace in the cool morning air. The town came into view as they crested the first hill. Lilly would have been unremarkable if it were not for the cathedral which grew out of a basalt slab two hundred meters above the surrounding houses. Constructed entirely of stone, it had been built to last. The whole edifice was enveloped in nebula of flying buttresses, each one crowned by a spire, and as they got closer they could see that every square meter was encrusted with statues, gargoyles, and icons. One end of the building terminated in twin towers, while the other was sealed by a pair of huge ornate doors beneath a circular window.

They carried on down the hill and into the town. It appeared to be some kind of holiday, for despite the early hour the streets thronged with people. In the central square booths decorated with stripped awnings hawked statuettes of Cissokho, engraved medallions, crystal globes containing miniature cathedrals, and a hundred other souvenirs. Aiy ana stopped at a street cart to buy two *currant buns* that they munched as they followed the stream of visitors up a steep avenue of yew trees to the hilltop. The dark mass of the cathedral loomed over them as they trudged up the path.

The entrance to the building's vestibule was a small gate set into the massive oak doors, then beyond them another pair of doors opened into the main atrium. If the exterior of the cathedral embodied stone solidity then the interior was air and light. Slender pillars soared sixty meters above them to a vaulted ceiling upon which was painted scenes from the early colony. Red sunlight filtered through stained glass windows turning the pale granite walls a delicate rose. Somewhere an organist was playing a third millennium cantata.

"I'm sorry," an attendant explained, "but you will have to wait until after the service to view the relics."

Carson groaned.

"Don't be so impatient," Aiyana scolded. "It'll be fun."

The pews were already filling as they sat down. For the next hour the congregation grew until every seat was taken. The mood of the crowd was cheerful – this was as much a holiday as it was a religious ceremony. Finally, the cathedral organ blasted out a chord signaling everyone to stand as a procession moved slowly down the aisle. At its head was a woman dressed in a white robe embroidered with gold. Behind her came two rows of white-clad acolytes, each carrying a burning oil lamp. The woman mounted the steps to a pulpit while the others positioned themselves on either side. The crowd became silent.

"Friends, honor to the Covenant" she began. "I am Mother Baker, the Archdeaconess of Lilly Cathedral, and I welcome you all. I am particularly pleased to see so many families here today." Right on cue a baby began to wail. She smiled and continued. "We should always remember that the Blessed Cissokho insisted that the children of the colony be the first to sign the Covenant. The sacred document was also taken to the sickbeds of the old and the dying. Even those who were too young added their names when they came of age; eventually every colonist was included, and thus every one of you, every human being in this teeming galaxy, is a descendent of a signer. Let us never forget this simple lesson.

"Today we celebrate the adoption of the Covenant while beneath our feet are examples of the implements that have brought so much misery to the world. Many years ago the sight of these diabolical devices horrified the people Falk. Now we realize that we have nothing to fear. We are comfortable and secure in our path. Of course, if we had embraced these instruments we could perform miracles, we could talk with machines, we could fly anywhere in the world within minutes [*uh oh*, thought Carson], but we have remained true to the Word, true to ourselves."

She paused, and with the sermon over Mother Baker appeared to relax and again she smiled.

"The children of Lilly will present a short play depicting the events leading to the signing of the Covenant."

With that she left the pulpit and a pair of curtains parted. A five year-old girl in a homemade costume marched to the center of a small stage.

"I am Adhiambo Cissokho and today is a great moment in history!" she cried.

Carson writhed on the wooden bench as the children recited their lines. He opened a private channel to Aiyana.

"I thought this was supposed to be short."

"Oh stop being a grouch, they're adorable."

The play had reached the climax where the Techs fled New Earth.

"We shall never submit to the Covenant!" shouted the small boy playing Samuelson.

Carson's head jerked up as if he had been slapped. The child was waving a Bingwen spread-spectrum digital radio, the standard communications device on the Yongding.

"Oh my God," he hissed, "they've discovered the supply dump."

Moments later the drama was over. The children took a bow to rapturous parental applause and the curtains closed. More performances and readings followed until eventually the service was over. The congregation shuffled out while Carson, Aiyana, and a small group of tourists moved up the aisle to a small side door. Here acolytes handed each person a black hooded cloak that they donned over their street clothes.

The hooded procession headed down a narrow stone staircase and entered the darkened crypt under the cathedral. The low ceiling was supported by massive crenellated pillars between which were indistinct piles covered with black cloth. Here in the musty gloom the holiday mood evaporated.

When everyone was present the lead acolyte shouted, "Behold the diabolical instruments!" and ripped the black cloth from the nearest pile.

Carson leaned forward, his eyes scanning the jumble of artifacts. *Quantum encryptor – earthquake predictor – organ growing kit – hand-held gene sequencer – laser drill*

"It is the supply dump?"

"Not this stuff – it's old, but nothing earlier than the fourth millennium. Let's take a look at the others."

"Behold the evil machines!"

All around them cloth was being pulled off to reveal ancient machinery. Carson rushed from one dusty mound to another.

Superconducting adhesive – liquid optics – push drive coil – information compactor – monofilament loom – synthetic placenta – inertial field generator – diamond laminator

Most of the crowd was content with a quick peek, after which they scurried back to the warmth and light above. Soon Carson and Aiyana were left alone to roam the heaps of equipment.

"Damn, after I saw that radio I was certain we'd find the dump," he said after examining the final decrepit collection. By now there was no need for secret communication.

They wandered upstairs. The nave was virtually empty and the staff was already tidying up in readiness for the evening service. Carson climbed onto the small stage where the children had performed. The digital radio was sitting on a small stool waiting to be put away for another year. He stooped down and picked it up.

"I knew it was the Bingwen," he said picking up the ancient communicator.

He stared at it wonder, feeling the weight of eight thousand years of history.

"Only three others exist. Two are in the Archives and one was purchased by the Huan Museum for four hundred million Ecus. They'd probably pay double that to have a matching pair."

Carson looked around the cathedral. Fifty meters away a woman was arranging flowers. Two men chatted as they straightened chairs. No one was paying him the slightest attention. He could slip the radio into his pocket, summon the buggy and be gone within minutes. Sighing, he put it back on the seat.

"Honor to the Covenant my son."

Mother Baker was standing behind him. Startled, Carson turned round to face her. She had shed her ceremonial clothes and was now dressed in a simple white robe. It was clear that she was very old. While she superficially appeared to be the same age as everyone else the precise, economical way she moved and the certainty with which she spoke suggested great age. And there was an odd familiarity in the deep grey eyes; they were slightly defocused as if she were staring at a point directly behind his head.

"You're Outsiders, from New Earth," she said.

It was a statement, not a question. Now Carson recognized her expression.

"Careful," he sub-vocalized to Aiyana on their private channel, *"she's telepathic."*

"And you can communicate without speaking" Mother Baker said. "How interesting!" She showed no sign of hostility. "You have met others with the gift."

"Yes," said Carson, "only twice. It's incredibly rare."

She turned to Aiyana.

"Please do not be alarmed, my daughter. The human mind is not an open book but an ocean. It is vast and mysterious and much remains hidden in the depths."

"Oh, I think I'm more like a shallow lagoon," Aiyana said with a smile.

"And you have brought mail, although it is not your principal reason for visiting our planet."

There was no question of lying to this woman.

"This is a fascinating world," Carson said. "If I had known about it – your lovely old machines, the amazing moon, buildings like the Great Library and this one – I would have come centuries ago, but you are right, we are here is to seek treasure."

He told her about the secret voyages of the Yongding and their search for the supply dumps.

"But the relics in our crypt are not what you seek."

"Yeah, it's disappointing. After I saw the Bingwen I was convinced we had come to the right place. Do you know of any similar caches?"

"I'm sorry, no."

She stared at him without speaking. Carson tried not to squirm.

"You plan to give what you find to the Archives, even though it is extraordinarily valuable."

He grinned.

"Well I am hoping to negotiate a finder's fee."

"But you will do it even if there is no reward."

She bent down and picked up the communicator from the stool.

"You could have spirited this away but you didn't. Why?"

Carson shrugged.

"It's not mine to take."

"But it is mine to give."

Mother Baker stepped forward and pressed the device into his hand.

"Carry it to the Archives where it will be safe."

"I can't, do you have any idea how much –"

She laughed. "Carson, it is a prop in a child's play! It might as well be a wooden block. It will not be missed."

"Thank you Mother, you are very kind."

"I must go and prepare for Vespers," she said. "Come, both of you, give me your hands and I will bestow my blessing."

She held their hands in her own and closed her eyes.

"Great Mother, we ask you to guide your children Aiyana and Carson in their journey. May the radiance of the Blessed Cissokho light their path, amen."

"Amen," they chorused.

She made to leave, then turned once more to Carson.

"I have to be near a person to touch their mind, but on occasions I hear echoes from across the light years, like the Leviathans calling to one another across the great oceans."

She moved closer.

"God manifests Herself in many ways and so does the Devil. Be careful my son, great evil pursues you."

"I know, a crazy old man..."

"No, not Juro, he is merely the vessel for something infinitely worse. Something that could swallow the sky."

As he looked into the grey eyes the world turned to glass, then fell away. Carson was suspended in the void, staring at the glistening stars while the cold of space ate into his bones. Was that movement out there in the vastness? A small yellow sun trembled. *Something was coming.* Then he blinked and he was again on the stage surrounded by the gaily painted scenery of the play. The Archdeaconess had gone.

Aiyana circled him in her arms.

"Are you alright honey? You seemed so strange for a moment."

"I'm fine," he said, forcing a smile. "We'd better head to the rendezvous."

They stepped off the stage and wandered through the deserted cathedral. Incense from the ceremony still lingered in the air and somewhere the organist was again practicing his art. Carson gazed round the peaceful building. He could be happy on this slow-paced world, riding the steam trains, writing letters using a *keyboard*, reading books made of paper. Although, he added to himself with a smile, like the Consul he would keep a state-of-the-art medical tank hidden in the basement.

"So someone must have found the storage dump," Aiyana said "otherwise the communicator wouldn't be here."

"Yeah, but why isn't the rest stored with the other relics? Where else could the stores be on this planet?"

Aiyana stopped.

"Oh! Isn't that beautiful?"

It was approaching sunset and the stained glass windows were ablaze with color. The sunlight, entering almost horizontally, was throwing the vivid mosaics into the blond granite interior. They stood enchanted, watching the luminous images of the windows creep across the walls as the sun sank towards the horizon.

Aaron Lavan Samuelson

What made him think of the rebel leader? Of course, there, projected onto a nearby pillar, a glowing picture Samuelson's fleeing the colony as Cissokho sternly pointed to the stars.

the elected leader of the Technical Alliance

What the... Carson looked again. Tucked under Samuelson's arm was a rectangle of light. Just as the image slid off the edge of the pillar he read the words:

The fact that you are reading this message...

He let out a cry and leapt over the pews to the window. Cemented into the leading among the brilliantly colored panes was clear piece of glass. It was another message from the Techs.

"Oh my God," Aiyana muttered as she caught up to where he was standing. Carson pulled out a pocket recorder and captured as many images as he could.

"We'll read it when we get to the buggy."

But they did not have to wait. In the vestibule they found a booklet entitled *The Windows of Lilly Cathedral.* The commentary noted that 'the west window includes a striking portrait of the cursed Samuelson. The artist depicts him holding a tablet bearing a fanciful message written in Ancient English.' They turned over to find a full-page photograph.

Carson laughed.

"They thought it was an invention by the window builders. Why not? It's the obvious conclusion."

Together they read the ancient words. It began like the one they found on Mirama:

The fact that you are reading this message proves that the people of New Earth have succeeded in building another starship...

Samuelson was not assuming that his readers had found the other tablet, and it was only towards the end that the two messages diverged.

I apologize for the fact that some of these storage units empty...

"Yes!" Carson yelled, "Some, not all, are empty."

...but I trust you can do without: if you have the resources to build an interstellar vessel then you must be curiosity-seekers, not men and women such as ourselves in desperate need of supplies and material.

But the final paragraph was new:

I am certain you had no trouble finding this hoard. Sakyamuni chose the obvious landmark for its location. Perhaps you plan to travel on to Orpheus to find the most distant cache. If so, I wish you good fortune. You will be rewarded with far more than simple tools.

June 18, 2148

They walked out into the fresh air. Carson was in a daze as his mind worked furiously. *"Far more than simple tools..."* What the hell did that mean? What was Juro really after?

Aiyana tried to return him to the here and now.

"So where on earth is the dump? Samuelson says it's obvious – did he mean the rock where the cathedral's built?"

Carson shook himself. "God knows. No, it can't be here, otherwise it would have ended up in the basement. Anyhow, I wouldn't call this outcrop obvious... what are we missing?"

They hurried through the town and out into the countryside. The sun had set by the time they were climbing the low hill to the rendezvous point. In front of them Falk's giant moon edged over the horizon turning their narrow road a silvery pink.

Aiyana stopped walking.

"What?" Carson asked, panting from the exertion.

"Mirama didn't have a moon, did it?"

She nodded towards the Rose.

"Hell of a landmark, isn't it?"

Ten minutes later they were scrambling into their tiny spacecraft.

"Hey buggy," Aiyana said, "can you zoom in on the center of the satellite?"

"Sure," said the vessel, "but wouldn't you prefer to see my aerial survey images?"

"You surveyed the *moon*?"

"Well I was getting bored with imaging Falk."

Carson hooted with laughter.

"Thank God for machines with personalities!"

They stared at the pictures of the desolate lunar landscape. At the center of the Rose was an impact peak that the buggy said was more that five thousand meters high.

"Can you magnify the point at the top of the mountain?"

The image exploded outwards.

"Oh my God, there it is," Aiyana whispered.

At the very crest of the peak was an array of black rectangles arranged in a neat semi-circle.

"How long to get there?"

"Just over an hour."

"Carson," said Aiyana, "aren't you forgetting something?"

He looked blank.

"How are we going to get onto the lunar surface? It's hard vacuum and we don't have our environment suits."

"Damn, damn, damn."

"Let's head to the Consulate, pack up our stuff and say goodbye, then return to the ship to gear up. We'll be able to bring Tallis, she's sure to be useful."

"But..." Carson protested, staring at the beckoning image.

"Darling, it's been there eight thousand years. It can wait another day."

Carson relented and told the buggy to set a course for Wurlington.

"We'd better warn the Consul that we'll be leaving. I hope he's there."

Although Renshu, like every citizen of New Earth, carried embedded transponders, he insisted that they pacify the natives by patching all communications through his *telephone* system.

Fortunately he was working late.

"Oh really, must you go so soon? How about one last round of Wurlington Brown? Excellent man! I can tell you all about your visitor."

"Oh no!" Aiyana cried, "I should never have told that train engineer where I was staying."

"I never did ask," said Carson, "how did you manage to persuade him to let you drive the steam engine? No, don't tell me, *womanly wiles*."

They were still laughing when Renshu cut in.

"You're missing the point old boy, it was another Outsider. Big chap by the name of Tabarak."

CONFRONTATION

"BUGGY," CARSON SHOUTED, "SWITCH THIS CHANNEL TO HIGH ENCRYPTION."

There was a brief pause. "Okay, done."

"Renshu, is Tabarak still around?"

"No, he left. I say, he's not a friend of yours is he?"

"Oh God no, he's a rival antiques dealer, and thoroughly nasty."

"I'm so glad to hear it. Can't say I took to the chap at all. He ignored the instructions in my welcome packet and landed his shuttle in Adhiambo Park, then flew his scooter in broad daylight to the Consulate. I'm still getting complaints from the Falk government."

"And he was asking where we were?" said Aiyana.

"Yes, I explained that you were in southern Wessle – I didn't specify where – and that I was expecting you to return in a day or so."

"What did he say?"

"I'll be back."

"Renshu, that farewell drink, let's meet at the bar, not the Consulate."

"As you wish old boy, see you at the Firkin."

The Consul signed off.

"How did he find us?" said Aiyana.

Carson pulled a face.

"It must have been Asima – she's the only one I confided in – who would have thought?"

"Either Asima or someone she told."

"But she promised only to talk to Commissioner Zhou," Carson said. They stared at each other.

"Zhou?"

"Well, if you're going to corrupt the cops you may as well start at the top," mused Aiyana.

"Oh God, that's a complication we don't need," Carson said. "And in the meantime we have Tabarak to deal with."

"Why return to Falk at all? Let's head to the ship to pick up the environmental gear, then just grab the modules and get the hell out of here."

Carson shook his head.

"Too predictable, I think they're trying to flush us out by forcing our next move. We need more information from Renshu."

They landed in darkness at the edge of Wurlington and took a taxi directly to the Firkin.

"I don't want to go to the Consulate ," Carson said. "Even if he's not lurking around I'll guarantee that Tabarak has left some kind of monitoring device that will alert him the moment we walk in."

They found Renshu already on his second *pint.* Alcohol had not improved his opinion of the interloper.

"The man is an absolute bounder! Do you know that I've been summoned to the Ministry tomorrow? No doubt to receive a tongue-lashing about Outsiders buzzing over the city. Oh well, it could be worse; two thousand years ago they would have burned me alive."

Carson choked on his beer. He had a vision of Renshu tied to a stake clad in his velvet dressing gown yelling 'Steady on old man!'

"And I haven't even told you the worst part: I distrusted the man so much I decided to perform a security sweep before coming out to meet you good people. See what I found."

He reached into his pocket and threw a tiny device onto the table. Carson picked it up and examined it. It was a miniscule transmitter.

"The cad tried to bug me! Don't worry, it's non-operative now."

"Renshu," Carson said, "do you have any weapons?"

"That much of a swine, eh? I do have couple of sidearms at the Consulate. Standard-issue for the diplomatic core you understand, I've never had any need to use them."

"You may tomorrow."

"Guys," said Aiyana becoming agitated, "remember we arranged to meet here? Renshu, weren't you on your *telephone?*"

Her gaze dropped to the bugging device.

"Oh God," Carson said searching around.

By now it was getting late and few patrons remained. Without saying anything more he strode to the bar and grabbed a new box of *darts* from the counter. He had barely sat down again when Tabarak walked through the door wearing a vulpine smile. The big man crossed the room and took a chair at their table.

"Hello again!" Carson cried. "Renshu, I believe you've already met."

"Charmed," the Consul murmured. "Well I'm sure you have a lot to catch up on so I'll be saying goodnight."

He got up and walked out.

Tabarak watched him leave then turned to Carson.

"Run and I'll kill you both before you hit the exit," he said amiably. "There's no-one to stop me, you've seen the technology on this mud ball. I could wipe out their entire security force."

"Talking of technology, let me show you this," Carson said taking a new *dart* out of his pocket.

He held it on the palm of his hand, pointing it in Tabarak's direction.

"This is a Callidus-manufactured homing missile that accelerates at over a thousand standard gravities. It has a rhenium diboride tip that should penetrate even your skull, especially as it's programmed to enter through your right eye. It's packed with octanitrocubane, so my only real problem is what to do with a headless corpse. Presently I have the launch sequence on hold."

Tabarak sat motionless, his eyes flickering between their faces and the *dart*. Carson tried to keep his trembling hand under control, but serendipitously it made the *dart* quiver, as if it were preparing to launch.

"Do you think that killing me will save you?" the big man said. "This is not a solo operation."

"So what are you proposing?"

"Give us everything you have found, get in your ship, head out, far out, and never return."

"What's in it for us?" Aiyana asked.

Tabarak glanced at her and smirked.

"Life," he said.

"I have a counter proposal," Carson said. "Orpheus was a bust, nothing to be found, but we have found a cache here on Falk. Mirama was our next target and the most likely to yield a full load, after all it's a bacteria world so no one will have disturbed anything. We'll keep what we have and Juro can have whatever is on Mirama. A fifty-fifty split in other words."

"No deal. Take a reality check Carson – you're cornered. *We've mined your starship.* You can't even approach it; you're stuck on this dump until we decide to let you leave. Besides..."

He got no further. On the other side of the room three patrons had begun playing a game of *darts.* Tabarak glanced at them and laughed.

"Some weapon you've got there!" he said reaching inside his jacket.

"I think you'll find this one more effective old man."

Renshu was at the entrance to the bar holding a small silvery cylinder pointed at Tabarak's head. He was panting from the effort of sprinting to the Consulate but he still managed to affect an air of nonchalant menace.

"I'm sure someone of your, ah, experience will recognize this. A Clement plasma handgun, rated at ten petavolts, courtesy of the Commonwealth Diplomatic Service. And just for your information, I'm rather a good shot."

The big man stood up.

"Signal me when you're ready to deal," he said to Carson.

"Leave now," Renshu said to him, "and don't come back. This planet's technology may be primitive but mine is not. I have now fully activated the Consulate's defense systems. If you come within fifty kilometers of Wurlington again your vessel will be blown out the sky."

Tabarak took one last hard look at Carson and walked out the door; he straddled his scooter and disappeared into the night.

Renshu slumped into a chair.

"Good grief! That was terrifying." He addressed the stricken bar patrons. "Sorry about that my friends, diplomatic duties. Doris, *pints* for everyone."

Aiyana leaned over and hugged him.

"Our hero! And just in time."

She told him about Carson's bluff with the *dart.*

Renshu laughed.

"Two sets of fake weaponry! Oh come my dear, don't appear so surprised – do you really think I have an air-defense system in my attic? Still," he said nodding at the gun, which he had placed on the table, "you had better take that. I have another one."

"Thanks," said Carson and handed it to Aiyana. "I'll feel better if you keep it."

"There you go being all protective again," she said with a smile, but she put the weapon in her pocket.

Later, as they were walking to the Consulate, Aiyana asked Renshu how much longer he was stationed on Falk.

"Four years, but I shall apply for another tour of duty. I've grown fond of the old place and besides, I have a, ah, lady friend here."

Carson grinned; he liked to think that he could always return to this world and find Renshu sitting in the Firkin drinking Wurlington Brown.

"Here," he said, "this is for you – it's my remaining supply of detox tablets."

"I say, splendid chap!"

"Think of it as compensation for all the trouble we've caused you."

"Trouble? I haven't had so much fun in ages."

"I'm glad you feel that way. We had better get going before any more fun starts."

"But you seem to be at an impasse," said the Consul. "You've got the goods but that brute is blocking your exit."

"Not necessarily," said Carson, "we've got a secret weapon, a real one this time."

"We do?" said Aiyana.

"Yup – Tallis"

"There they are," said the ship.

"We can't see a thing," said Carson.

They were floating in the buggy three light seconds away from their mined vessel – as close as they dared approach.

"That's because they are extraordinarily small, about a centimeter in diameter."

"This is shameful," Tallis chimed in, **"they must be of Callidus manufacture."**

"How many?"

"Twelve, the damn things just snuck up on me!"

Aiyana smiled to herself, it was the first time she had heard the ship swear.

"What kind of ordinance?" Carson asked.

"At that size it has to be collapsed matter – probably a core of magnetized anti-neutronium suspended in a superconducting shell. The outer layer will hold regular neutronium. Bring them together fast enough and you'll get a twenty kilometer fireball."

"Explosive compression?"

"More likely an inertial field push."

"*Boys,*" Aiyana said, "all this technical chat is very interesting but what the hell are we going to do?"

"We're going to move one of the mines out of formation. That will allow us to get in and the ship to bust out."

"And how, Oh Mighty One, do you propose to do that without setting it off?"

"Remember the bus ride to New Earth, when we passed through the Millennium Comets and you wondered how they maneuvered anything that slushy?"

"Yes, and that charming little girl said they employed gravitational drag using a charged miniature black hole."

"And the ship's shell consists of..."

"Micro black holes! Oh my God, is their pull strong enough?"

"Sure, the mass of each mine can only be a few thousand kilos." Carson arranged his face into a frown. "I wonder how we can make a very small tug to pull the black hole? One that won't trigger the mines' sensors."

"Tallis – our secret weapon!" Aiyana yelled. "Come here and kiss me you big-brained mailman."

"I raise my feelers in salute," Tallis added.

"I was wondering how long it would take you to think of it," said the ship.

"Yeah, right," said Carson. "Anyhow, there's a lot more thinking to do. We need to dock the buggy at very high speed and get out of here before anyone realizes what's happening, preferably triggering the mines as we go. That will convince Tabarak that we're history. How fast could we execute a maneuver like that?"

"Let me do some calculations," the ship said.

Several minutes passed before it returned on their encrypted channel.

"Assuming that we toss the out the safety manual, ramp up past all published engineering tolerances, and have a bit of luck, I reckon we can do it in six seconds."

"Whoa!" was all Carson could say.

"And Aiyana," the ship added, "you're a great pilot, but this time I will do the driving."

"The tug is on the move."

It was twenty-four hours later. The ship had slowed the shell's rotation to a crawl so that one of its micro black holes could be extracted. In the meantime Tallis had built her tiny vessel. The product of her labors was a remotely controlled vehicle consisting of a super-conducting magnet and an over-ramped push drive; the squat structure was barely twenty centimeters long. Now it was drifting towards the orbiting mines.

In the buggy's cabin everything was quiet. Carson had retreated another three light seconds for a reason that was completely logical and that he loathed: if the tug triggered the mines there was nothing to be gained by he and Aiyana being caught in the conflagration that would kill Tallis and his destroy starship.

The cabin's display showed a schematic of the twelve mines relative to the ship. They were deployed at the vertices of a kilometer-wide icosahedron with the vessel in the center, a clever arrangement designed to create an impenetrable barrier.

"But there's a weakness in the topology," Carson had explained to Aiyana. "Removing any one mine opens up a gap big enough for us to pass through."

Before it could disrupt the configuration Tallis's tug had to get outside of the perimeter of the minefield. The tiny vehicle was on radio silence as it moved away from the ship. One meter aft it dragged one of the shell's charged black holes. Its trajectory was agonizingly slow; the black hole, smaller than an atom, had a mass of one hundred million tonnes. The procession was aimed at the midpoint of one of the icosahedron's triangular faces – as far away from the mines as possible.

Carson fretted as they waited for news.

"The huge unknown is what are the mines sensing? It can't be mass – not that close to a starship – but is it heat signature, radar, physical observation, or what?"

"But they must have some sort of lower limit," said Aiyana, "otherwise a micro-meteorite could blow the whole lot."

"Good point. Oh God! How long is this going to take?"

In fact it was four hours before the ship finally reported the tug was through. Now, like an angler trailing a lure at the snout of a fish, the tiny vessel began using the black hole's gravitation to tease a mine out of position. Eight more hours passed until the ship signaled that a path had been cleared.

"The tug has returned the black hole to the shell," the ship finally announced. "In the meantime, look what I found."

The fuzzy image of a small spacecraft covered with antennas appeared on the display.

"It's a remote observation platform – they must have left it to keep an eye on things."

"Any sign of the Clan starship?" Aiyana asked.

"Nothing, it's probably hours away."

"That's good news," said Carson. "Well, let's give their little spy something to watch."

He moved the buggy to within four hundred kilometers of the ship.

"I've downloaded the flight path," said the little vessel, "and I'm switching to an all-oxygen atmosphere."

"Why?"

"Because once this starts the inertial dampening will be so powerful you won't be able to breathe."

"Oh great. Say, you know you've got a heat alert going?"

"Yes, that's one of my batteries, I've had them on maximum charge for hours. Don't worry, they won't stay that way for long – I'm about to dump it all into the push drive."

"I'm holding shell spin-up at ninety-nine percent," the ship said. "Are you guys ready?"

They buckled into their acceleration couches.

"Let's do it."

Moments later they were rendered them as immobile as flies in amber.

T minus six seconds

The buggy's push drive, gulping energy at the rate of three million megajoules per second, hurtled the little craft forward with an acceleration of ten thousand standard gravities. The drive could operate at this level for eight seconds without melting.

T minus four

The little craft reached a velocity of two hundred kilometers a second. By now the distance to the ship had been halved. It threw the push drive into reverse. The superstructure groaned in protest.

T minus three

Three light seconds away from the ship the observation platform registered the buggy's charge. It considered its options. Did the operatives think that their high velocity would avoid triggering the mines? Had they discovered an unknown flaw in the configuration? Was it a bluff using a remote controlled vehicle? Its orders were to preserve the starship if possible but prevent it departing at all costs. Perhaps it should play safe and blow the mines.

It spent too long thinking. One tenth of a second after detecting the buggy's forward motion the platform was rammed by Tallis's tug travelling at one third the speed of light. Destruction was instantaneous.

T minus two

The buggy stopped decelerating as it passed through the gap in the minefield at a velocity of four kilometers a second.

T minus one point eight-seven-five

Using the massive gravitational gradient of the shell the buggy took just 78 milliseconds to execute a perfect semi-circular turn. It dropped through the ship's north axis desperately shedding speed. Still moving at a velocity of one hundred meters a second it crashed into the landing dock.

T minus point zero five

The ship completed the last one percent of shell spin-up. Space-time folded round the vessel as it surged forward at a nominal acceleration of ten billion standard gravities.

T

The starship's backwash of exotic particles, gamma radiation, and gravitational waves triggered every sensor in the minefield. Within two microseconds every mine underwent hyper-accelerated implosion; one hundred thousand kilograms of neutronium and anti-neutronium fused then blossomed into a ball of pure energy ninety kilometers in diameter.

Four hours later Renshu was tottering home from a long evening at the Firkin.

"Look darling," said the pretty young woman on his arm, "a new star! Isn't that supposed to be good luck?"

"I do hope so my dear, I do hope so."

"Aiyana, Carson, wake up!"

Carson blinked, and blinked again. Aiyana was slowly unbuckling her flight harness.

"Aiyana, Carson, talk to me!" the buggy wailed.

"We're okay," he assured the machine. He looked at Aiyana again. "We are, aren't we honey?"

She nodded, adding a weak smile.

"That's a relief – I was worried. You both passed out on impact."

"And how are *you*?" Carson asked the buggy.

"Well I lost a battery, my landing gear is wrecked, and I think I bent my chassis, but apart from that I'm fine."

Carson grinned.

"Good job, little guy," he said as he followed Aiyana into the ship.

"Where are we?" she asked.

"Eight minutes out from the Falk system" said the ship.

"Did the mines blow?"

"They must have. We put on quite a show as we left."

"Well I'm off to take a long, long shower," Aiyana announced.

They had been confined to the buggy's tiny cabin for over forty-eight hours.

"Better get some rest too," Carson added. "We're stopping to take a navigational fix then we're heading into the system."

"You still want to try for the stuff on Falk's satellite? But suppose they spot us? They found the ship once and they could do it again. Besides, the buggy is in no state to make another long trip."

"We're not returning the outer edge of the system; we're going to fly the ship directly to the moon before Tabarak can regroup."

"Oh great! We're going to take a starship through a solar system! Now who was it who gave me a patronizing lecture about hitting solid objects at super-luminal speed?"

"Believe me," said the ship, "compared to what we've just been through, this is a prudent, cautious maneuver."

Aiyana threw up her hands.

"Whatever! The sooner we get out of here the better."

Ten hours later they were in the buggy hovering above the surface of the Rose. They had materialized five light seconds from Falk, although every minute the planet and its satellite retreated another nine hundred kilometers as they followed their mutual orbit around the sun.

"My frame of reference doesn't change," the ship explained. "Usually that's not a problem because all the stars in this part of the galaxy are moving in the same general direction, but it doesn't work so well with planets."

"What happens outside the local arm?" Aiyana asked.

"Then the fun really starts: if you go to the opposite side of the Milky Way you're travelling at six hundred kilometers a second relative to the local systems."

"Mountain peak coming up," said Carson.

Apart from the pinkish hue bestowed by Falk's M class sun, the cratered landscape that rolled beneath them seemed identical to countless other airless worlds. The ground began to rise as the buggy followed the upward slope of the desolate terrain. Carson imagined the titanic impact that created the mountain; if the colliding asteroid had been any larger the moon would have been shattered, and Falk would be a ringed planet.

"How are you doing nest mate?" Aiyana asked Tallis – her portable nest was bolted immediately behind their cabin.

"This world has no smell. It is [untranslatable] flying in the dark."

"There they are," said Carson.

Instinctively they both leaned forward. Thirty ancient containers were arrayed in a semi-circle on the mountain's rounded summit. The buggy positioned itself ten meters above the hoard. Carson and Aiyana, clad in their new environment suits, opened the hatch and peered down at the ground.

"Wow!" said Aiyana, "they could have been here yesterday."

In the lunar soil surrounding the modules was a maze of footprints, perfectly preserved in the hard vacuum. On closer examination Carson could see that there were two types: one set had been made by the kind of environment suit commonly in use during the fourth millennium, the other, heavier impressions, were an unknown design.

"Oh God! Those deep prints must have been made by the Techs – they're eight thousand years old."

Four of the modules had been cut open, their covers sprawling in the dust. It was around these units that the more recent footprints were clustered.

"So here's what I think happened," said Carson. "The settlers of Falk stumbled across this cache four thousand years ago, soon after they arrived in the system. They cut their way into a few modules but all they found was, by their standards, old junk. They took a few souvenirs, including Samuelson's tablet, although I doubt any of them could read Ancient English, and the whole find was forgotten as the culture retreated to its present state."

"Very neat, professor," Aiyana said.

She poised herself to jump off the buggy down to the lunar surface.

"Oh no you don't!" Carson yelled. "Those Tech footprints are unique – we can't trample over them. Sorry, but we're going to have to do this without touching the ground."

"Suits me," said the buggy, "what with my mashed landing gear."

They devised a plan. First, Tallis used one of her small craft to record a high-definition survey of the whole site. Then she landed on top of the first sealed module and positioned her gamma ray generator. Carson and Aiyana unrolled the new sensor array built to replace the improvised setup used on Mirama. Using cables they dangled it from the buggy, which then positioned itself so that the array rested against the side of the target unit. They both retreated inside the cabin as the first image was captured.

"Bingo!" Carson shouted as they examined the result. The module was clearly packed with supplies. They re-opened the hatch to let Aiyana climb down on top of the container. She unfastened the sensor and attached the cables to the unit's recessed handholds. The buggy eased the module off the ground and deposited it at a location a hundred meters away.

They both jumped out to examine their prize. Unlike the modules on Mirama this one was in near-perfect condition with nothing more than a few micro-meteor scratches. Carson examined the inventory on the side.

"Drugs, medical supplies... look – clothing! This is unique, none of the colonists' clothing survived. I can't wait to see the Archivists' faces when we get home."

"One down, twenty-nine to go," said Aiyana.

After hours of intense work they had removed ten full storage modules. Of the remainder, four had been looted by the settlers of Falk, and the other sixteen had been emptied by the Techs.

Carson and Aiyana were in a fine mood. They posed together, leaning against the modules, smiling through their visors while the buggy captured images. Finally they worked up the energy to ferry the units to the ship. Mercifully, the moon's low gravity made the bulky containers easy to maneuver but their little craft's carrying capacity was limited, and eventually it took four journeys.

"Over there," said Aiyana as they lifted off with the last load, "isn't that a blast circle?"

They brought the buggy directly over the patch of blackened ground.

"That must be where the Yongding's shuttle craft landed," said Carson. "They were using fusion-powered reaction motors. Yes – see, more footprints."

He gazed down at the ancient landing site, thinking about the Techs. The more he learned about the rebels the harder it was to accept the way they had always been portrayed. Whatever their reasons for stealing the Yongding, these people were not selfish cowards. It took courage to ride down to an unknown world on a pillar of flame. And it took iron determination to try to build a colony from scraps. *They could almost be brother and sister* Aiyana had said of Samuelson and Cissokho; her words were truer than she realized.

Had the Techs survived? Most historians assumed that trapped with no resources in an empty starship they had all perished long before reaching a new world. Now he knew differently. Replenished with the new supplies they had a fighting chance. How far could they have travelled? *Where were they?*

"Great work," said Carson as they peeled off their environment suits in the ship's cabin, "now let's get out of here and set a course for New Earth before Tabarak figures out what happened."

"New Earth," Aiyana said, "what do you mean?"

"Honey, we have to call it quits – everything has become far too dangerous – there's no way I can expose you, Tallis, and the ship to any more of this cat and mouse game."

"No," she said.

"What do you mean, *no*? How many times can we do this? We just missed being incinerated by a fraction of a second!"

"I mean no."

She took his hands in her own.

"Darling, Samuelson said there is something far more important than simple cargo on Orpheus, and if we don't go straight there Juro's goons will beat us to it. It must be what he's really after – God knows what it is, though I guarantee it will not be good news for anyone else."

"But –"

"But nothing. Do you really want that withered old bastard to triumph after everything we've been through? Besides," she added, "don't you have deliveries to make, Mister Mailman? What's that motto? *Neither solar storm, nor meteor shower...* We're going to Orpheus and that's that!"

Carson held up his hands in surrender.

"Alright Aiyana, you win, Orpheus it is."

He mooched off to get a shower.

"How did I do?" Aiyana asked the ship once he had gone.

"Perfect – you had me convinced."

"The poor thing, he so desperately wants to find the rest of the treasure."

"You're okay with this, aren't you?" she said addressing Tallis.

"**The trail runs deep through the unknown forest, and we quiver with anticipation as we follow the scent.**"

"Me too, nest-mate. Hey, you guys are great!"

Aiyana could not possibly have known it, but she had just changed the course of human history.

ORPHEUS

AIYANA DRIFTED THROUGH THE STAR MAP THAT SURROUNDED HER LIKE COUNTLESS dust motes in a sunlit room. Near her face was Sirius, burning through its store of hydrogen so furiously that in less than a billion years it would become a white dwarf, just like its orbiting binary. Further away was the sullen orange glow of Arcturus, pouring energy into the infrared as it barreled through space at over a hundred kilometers a second. Dominating them all was giant Canopus, ten thousand times brighter than Eridani, radiating pure white light.

She extended a finger ten light years long; the tip touched a small star and it burst into radiance. A brilliant green line followed her gestures, leaping from sun to sun.

"I go to the conservatory for a couple of hours and the damn cabin fills up with stars!"

Aiyana glanced over her shoulder to see Carson silhouetted against the hatchway.

"Isn't it lovely?" she said. "I was talking to the ship about where we've been and it generated this map for me. Here's Mita."

She pointed and one of the stars lit up with a *ping.*

"Cool sound effect," Carson admitted.

"Then we have New Earth," Aiyana continued, "then Mirama, Falk, *ping, ping*… Hey, where's Orpheus?"

Another star brightened a meter away.

"That's quite a way."

"Fifty-six light years from Falk," Carson said, "and eighty-four from New Earth. The distances are approximately the same as the systems I put into the fake tape. I wanted to keep it real in case Sakyamuni started talking about the journeys."

"I wonder why they went so far for the final drop."

"God knows, maybe we'll find out when we locate the cache."

"So what's the furthest you've been, my darling space rover?"

"We'll have to change the scale," the ship said.

The three-dimensional map imploded. Now, instead of sunlit motes, the stars compressed into a solid glistening mass like snow under moonlight. Structure emerged: gaseous nebulae and clouds of dust a thousand light years long that looked unnerving like smoke billowing from a campfire. And between the massed stars empty chasms appeared.

"That's Watson's Gap, which separates the local spur," Carson said pointing at massive volume of empty space. "Over the other side is the Sagittarius arm."

"Six spiral arms in all," the ship added, "but we'd have to pull back a lot further to see them all."

"Thank you, I did study geography at school. So where was it you got to?"

A blue line meandered through the starmass, following a drunkard's walk away from New Earth. It leapt to the adjacent galactic arm where it resumed its seemingly random path. The map imploded again and a segment of a third spiral arm came into view. The line jumped once more then headed spinward before finally halting.

"Howacond, in the Scutum-Crux Arm."

"Scutum?" Aiyana said wrinkling her nose, "isn't that Ancient English for –"

" It's also called the Centaurus Arm if that makes you feel better. Anyhow, there you have it, my longest journey, thirty thousand light years. The round trip took nearly a century, and still not a quarter of the way across the galaxy."

"Oh God! Was it worth going so far?"

He told her about Howacond, a rare binary where two earth-like planets revolved around one another in close formation.

"It's the center of a huge alliance called the Fremina League. No-one from New Earth had visited for hundreds of years so I had *lots* of mail. And once I got there I owed it to all the nouveau rich inhabitants to sell them some antiques."

"How much did you make?"

"Well, their money was no good, no-one outside the League uses it, so I traded for information. There are only two things worth transporting across deep interstellar space: information and artwork. Although I suppose you could call that a special kind of information as well."

"So darling," Aiyana said again, putting her arms around him, "how much did you make?"

"I harvested everything I could. All the public stuff – maps, demographics, official histories, economic data, and so on – then I used the local currency I had accumulated to purchase a lot of other material: proprietary research, some patents, images, entertainment archives."

"So how much…"

"I sold the lot on New Earth for nine million Ecus, plus of course I had my mail fees."

"Oh my God!"

"Yeah, but think about it. That was a century's work, so it averages out at ninety thousand a year. Decent money, that's all."

"But you did get to visit places no-one has ever seen."

"True, but let me show you what I'd really like to do. Hey ship, can you bring up the Grand Tour?"

The image of the stars imploded once more. Now the whole galaxy came into view, face on, as if viewed from above. The blue lined snaked from New Earth, circled round the galactic hub, then continued to the other side of the disk.

"There are places out there that don't even have names. Their only contact with New Earth is a kind of osmosis – information jumps from system to system and eventually seeps all the way across the galaxy, by then it's over a thousand years old."

"There are so many wild rumors – systems where humans have modified themselves to live in a vacuum, planets made of diamond, arcologies orbiting neutron stars, and of course aliens, lots of aliens."

Carson shook his head and smiled.

"Who knows what's really out there?"

"Will you ever do it?"

"Maybe – if we return to New Earth in one piece there should be enough money to pay off the loans on the ship, which will make me a free agent. But three hundred years… that's a hell of a commitment."

"You're thinking too small," said the ship.

The image imploded yet again. As it shrank other stellar systems appeared, first the two orbiting galaxies, the Magellanic Clouds, and then the majestic grandeur of the Andromeda Nebula. The blue line shot out and connected the two whirlpools of stars.

"The Andromeda Expedition," said the ship, "also known as the Great Leap."

"Hey, that actually happened," Aiyana said. "I remember learning about it in history class."

"No human could possibly survive hibernation long enough to make the trip, so in the fourth millennium New Earth dispatched three automated ships loaded with super-redundant systems. The plan was for a two thousand year journey out, a thousand years of exploration, and then another two thousand for the return."

"Which means they should be halfway home," Carson said.

"How thrilling!" Aiyana cried. "Imagine what they've discovered."

"I don't know. A lot of people feel that the whole thing was a very bad idea. God knows what the expedition stumbled on. Suppose the moment they got there they ran into a super-advanced civilization that said 'Oh, there's intelligent life in the Milky Way galaxy', and straight away *they* decided to come *here*. They'd be due just about now."

They stared at each other in silence, the only sound the whisper of the environmentals. Finally Carson grinned and said, "I know it's a cliché, but it really is a big universe out there."

Aiyana gave a small laugh.

"If it's any comfort," said the ship, "I don't believe any complex system can function for two thousand years without major maintenance, let alone five, so I reckon they never even got there."

That seemed to cheer up Aiyana.

"Enough with the inter-galactic travel! We've got work to do."

"At least I'll be on familiar territory," said Carson.

They were examing an image of Orpheus retrieved from the ship's library.

"You have visited before?" asked Tallis.

"Yeah, about two hundred years ago. It's thriving – and not just the planet, there's a booming economy in the asteroid belt. You should feel right at home Aiyana."

She peered at the globe. Two thirds of the surface was covered by sea, with most of the landmass concentrated in the northern hemisphere.

"Sakyamuni liked positioning the supply dumps at landmarks that would be easy to find."

"Roger that. I've already got a list of potential sites. Here's my favorite."

The image zoomed in to a lonely island in the southern ocean.

"The locals call it Lanzor – it's an extinct volcano like Kaimana. It's cold and dry, not a lot of vegetation, no extreme weather. And according to the ship no-one lives there, so there's a good chance the cache will be intact."

"All of which may have occurred to Tabarak and his little friends." Carson sighed.

"I tried to send him off in the wrong direction – remember I told him we had already explored Orpheus and found nothing – but who knows whether he took the bait. Our best weapon is speed: get in, grab the supply modules, and get out before he arrives."

"Well, the buggy is repaired and good to go. Hey ship, when do we get there?"

"Forty-seven hours and thirteen minutes."

"We had better get lots of rest," Carson said. "Oh God, I hope this one is easy."

"How are you feeling?" Aiyana asked the buggy.

"Good, the replacement battery is working fine and I love my new landing gear, but my chassis is still out of kilter."

Carson laughed. "Think of it as a badge of courage."

"Thanks, I'll file that under inexplicable cultural references."

Two days had passed; the ship had announced their arrival at the Orpheus system and launched the periscope. There was no time to waste and they were already in the final stages of preparation for the inward journey.

"Are you going to do any reconnaissance first?" Aiyana asked Carson.

"Hell no, this is one place that I'm familiar with. Imagine – when I last visited I spent weeks grubbing around for antiques and all the time I was within a few thousand kilometers of fabulous treasure."

"We'll make up for it this time," she said pulling on her new clothes.

During the long voyage Tallis had upgraded the ship's fabrication facilities, and now that Aiyana had gotten used to the idea of not walking around naked she never had anything to wear.

"How are our little spies?" Carson asked the ship.

"We're already deploying."

After the encounter with the minefield in the hinterlands of Falk they were determined not to imperil the starship again. Tallis had modified her survey fleet to create a posse of outriders that could patrol a million-kilometer sphere of surrounding space. The craft were unarmed but as her tug had demonstrated, even a tiny vessel travelling at relativistic speed could pack a mighty punch.

"No-one is going to sneak up on *me* again," said the ship.

"We will miss your smell nest-mates," Tallis said.

She was staying onboard to maintain the defenses.

"So will we," Carson said pulling a face at Aiyana. "Come on, let's get going."

He was climbing into the buggy when the ship came on the communications channel.

"Sorry to break up the party but you had better come back inside. I've just downloaded the welcome package and it's not good news."

They hurried into the bowels of the starship. As they entered the main cabin they were greeted by a new image of Orpheus. Unlike the picture of a verdant world stored in the library this one was dominated by two massive ice caps.

"Oh God!" Carson yelled. "What's that?"

The ship replied with just two words: *ice age.*

It started fifty years ago the package explained, when Orpheus's parent star revealed itself to be one of a new class of super long-term variables.

"I've heard of them," said Carson. "The trouble is they can only be detected using an incredibly long baseline – the cycles last tens of thousands of years. It wasn't until the sixth millennium that anyone even realized they existed."

Initially the inhabitants hoped that the reduction in solar output would be minor, but after two decades of dropping temperatures and increasing glaciation they were forced to confront the inevitable. Five years of political and social uproar culminated in the bitter decision to abandon the planet. Now thirty million souls and a planet-worth of infrastructure were moving to the asteroid belt.

"Can you imagine the chaos down there? Well my dear, unpack those summer outfits, we'd better run up some cold weather gear. And we should take the portable camp, we may have to rely on our own resources."

The reloaded buggy came to a halt ten thousand kilometers above Orpheus.

"So where do we land?" Aiyana said.

They scanned the magnified image of the northern hemisphere that had been overlaid with a map from the ship's library. Many of the principal cities had disappeared beneath the ice but further to the south the capital, Alarcos, still existed although it had a strange chewed-over appearance.

Carson opened a traffic control channel.

"Who the hell are you?" asked a voice. Protocol had obviously been abandoned.

"Commonwealth mail carrier. Can you give me landing coordinates? I gather things are pretty confused."

"Now there's an understatement. Find the Imperial Palace – it's in the center of Alarcos – and put down at the staging area about a kilometer to the east. You can't miss it."

"Thanks, is the Post Office still functioning?"

"You are joking, aren't you? Just land and ask around – someone should be able to take the delivery. Over and out"

The staging area was located in what had been the Royal Park. The lawn where vacationers had once picnicked was now a brown expanse of permafrost dotted with spacecraft, ground vehicles, piles of supplies, and pre-fabricated buildings. Carson found a cluster of parked craft and settled the buggy beside them.

"Oh God!" Aiyana yelled as the biting air flooded through the hatch.

They turned up the heating in their suits and jumped out. Workers and machines swarmed everywhere, but like Tallis's nest the mayhem had purpose.

"I think the site offices are over there" Carson said.

He had hooked into the local net but most of it was unresponsive or hopelessly out of date. They were going to have to rely on more primitive techniques to find their way about.

As they crunched through the frozen grass the ground rumbled and they were engulfed by a massive shadow. They looked up: the largest transport Carson had ever seen was flying over their heads. The evacuation was going full tilt.

Eventually they found themselves at sprawling prefabricated building. The interior was a single huge space filled with people and equipment. After several misdirections they located a small woman crouched over a cluster of displays. She appeared as if she had not slept in days but perked up the moment Carson introduced himself.

"Mail!" she said, "this could be good news. You have it on you? Excellent!"

He handed over the silvery package.

"Good afternoon, Postmistress Salima" the package said.

She inserted it into her consol and examined the display.

"This is a great yield – we haven't had mail in months – no starships from New Earth, you understand. Why the hell would they want to come here?"

"Did I hear you got a mail carrier?" shouted a voice behind them.

A woman in a black flight suit strode up to Aiyana. She held up her right hand.

"Have we been waiting for you!" she said. "I'm Caelin, this operation's lift boss."

"Aiyana, glad to meet you, but the mailman is over there."

"Welcome to Orpheus, or what's left of it," she said touching palms, and then went over to introduce herself to Carson.

"Do you have something for the Imperial Treasurer?" she asked.

"Sorry, I have no idea what I'm carrying."

Caelin snorted and turned her attention to the postmistress.

"Is there anything?"

There was a pause while Salima scanned the mail.

"Yes, two financial transmissions."

"Great! How much?"

"I can't tell. We need the Treasurer to open them."

"Rasul, get over here," Caelin bellowed across the room.

A bleary-eyed man scampered through the maze. Following Salima's directions he placed his hand on the consol's command plate. He immediately became agitated.

"This is fantastic! A grant of four billion from the Commonwealth Emergency Fund and one point three billion from Architectural Heritage Appeal."

He gave the postmistress a hug then turned to Carson and Aiyana. "You couldn't have come at a better time."

Caelin smiled and ran a hand through her cropped black hair. The good news had put her into a better mood.

"Say, I haven't eaten anything since dawn, why don't I take our visitors to the commissary." With that she strode off.

The commissary was a large tent-like structure some sixty meters across and thirty high at its conical apex. The entire structure was composed of thousands of linked transparent pieces like the windows of Lilly Cathedral, except these were obviously flexible and, Carson suspected, their color was programmable. He was right: the panes dimmed as pale sunlight emerged from behind a bank of clouds.

Rasul joined them at one of the trestle tables. The food was plentiful and loaded with calories – everyone was expending a lot of energy. Even as she ate Caelin's expression frequently went blank as she checked incoming messages.

"So what does a lift boss do?" Aiyana asked her.

"Lift things," she laughed. "Very large things. You've arrived at a good time, tomorrow is the granddaddy of all projects."

She nodded out of the window. Carson stared but all he could see was the ornamental turrets of the Imperial Palace.

Seeing his confusion Caelin added, "that's it, that's what we're lifting."

"The Palace?" Carson squeaked.

The Palace, Rasul explained, was considered to be one of the greatest examples of gothic architecture in the Commonwealth. Upon learning that it was to be abandoned to the glaciers, the Heritage Fund had launched a major appeal to raise the money to preserve it.

"We went ahead on the promise of a minimum of five hundred million Ecus, but we were getting nervous until you arrived."

Caelin's team had spent the last year strengthening the ancient structure and cutting it free of the bedrock. Now it stood on a ten-meter thick table of granite reinforced with a lattice of monomolecular girders. The underside was embedded with oversized push drives.

"The Palace is balanced on just stone twelve pillars. Tomorrow morning we explosively cut them, and then up she goes."

"Goes where?"

"Diotima, in the asteroid belt," Caelin said. "They're building an environmental dome to house it. Fortunately not my problem – I just get the damn stuff off the planet."

"What drives are you using, Wartsila-Sulzers?" Aiyana asked.

"Exactly right – twelve core engines. You've done some pushing?"

"Have I! I spent thirty years shunting asteroids for a living."

Caelin spun round to face her. "Hey, you could be really useful tomorrow. I need as many people as possible monitoring the drives during the lift."

She turned to Carson.

"How about you?"

"Sorry, flying a buggy is the limit of my experience."

"Carson owns a starship," Aiyana said.

"Does he now?" said Caelin, visibly unimpressed.

She stood up.

"Got to get to work. See you at zero dark five tomorrow morning." She walked out the commissary.

"How much is the evacuation of the planet costing?" Carson asked Rasul.

The Treasurer laughed. "How much have you got? We've passed four hundred billion and we're still spending. About third of that has been covered by donations from neighboring systems. It would be nice to think they were motivated purely by altruism, but in reality they're terrified of the idea of thirty million refugees."

"And the rest?"

"Debt mostly. We'll be paying off the loans for the next two hundred years, but we'll survive."

They said goodbye to Rasul and trudged to the buggy. As they walked Carson was alarmed to see that Aiyana was crying.

"These poor people, losing their home world just like we all did eight thousand years ago."

Rasul cautioned them that accommodation at the operations center was primitive and suggested that they camp out in one of the abandoned commercial buildings surrounding the city center.

"Just take your pick, if it's empty, move in."

They ended up in the atrium of Cancelli Developments, a company that had once offered homes to the discriminating wealthy. As they walked in a young woman wearing a wildly inappropriate summer dress stepped out in front of them.

"Welcome to Cancelli," she said, "builders of Citrus Realm, Orpheus's finest private metropolis."

"Someone forgot to turn the power off," Aiyana said as she walked through her.

At least it was warm and dry, and they set up camp amid a forest of three-dimensional images of luxury houses. Carson, wary of another ambush, brought the buggy inside as well.

"This is perfect, no-one will ever spot us in the middle of this mess."

"So what's the plan?" Aiyana asked him as they settled down to eat in the courtyard of a ghostly mansion.

Carson spread his hands.

"Not much of one, really. We'll hang around for the show tomorrow morning, then as soon as we can head south to check out Lanzor."

"Do you think we'll still be able to find the cache?"

"Good question – the modules may be buried under the snow. If so, I'm hoping they have enough of a radar signature to show up against the bedrock."

"Oh God, imagine coming all this way for nothing."

"Imagine."

The following day, an hour before dawn, they set out from the Cancelli building on the scooter, leaving the buggy hidden inside. By the time they arrived at the operations center it was boiling with activity. The liftoff was to be controlled by the center's automated intelligence, but most of the pre-launch preparations were overseen by humans.

One end of the giant room had been cleared and was now occupied by a live image of the Palace standing in ornate isolation. The area surrounding the projection was reserved for visitors, although in truth it was a corral to keep them from interfering with the real work. More people were arriving every minute – uniformed dignitaries, media reporters, anxious preservationists, boisterous construction workers, historians, government officials – everyone was coming to see the big show.

They found Caelin by a set of huge windows overlooking the lift site. She glowed with the synthetic perkiness of a person who had taken a lot of stimulants.

"Good to see you. Aiyana, take the console on my right. Focus on Number Eight Drive – it has a tendency to overheat and I don't trust our system's calibration."

Caelin threw herself into a large chair; she peeled off her shoes and placed both feet on interface plates, then slapped her hands on two more. Immediately she was surrounded by a hemisphere of images. This was one plugged-in woman.

"What can I do?" said Carson.

"Go over to the visitors' pen and keep them away from me" she said. Seeing his expression she added "believe me, if you can do that you are really helping."

Carson shrugged and wandered over to the corral. By now at least two hundred visitors had appeared. One group stood out: an impeccably dressed man stood surrounded by a knot of people who seemed more interested in him than the event. He was listening intently to the Operations Center manager as she pointed at the Palace's image.

"Welcome back," said a voice behind him. Carson turned round to see Rasul. "I trust you found somewhere to camp."

"Yeah, thanks. You're not working?"

The Treasurer grinned.

"No counting filthy lucre on lift day. I've been press-ganged into helping with the Important Personage." He rolled his eyes. "The King is making a morale-boosting visit."

"Two minutes to lift," an announcer said.

Everyone began to gather round the giant image of the Palace. Carson glanced over to where Caelin was seated. She and Aiyana were as motionless as statues as they absorbed the data pouring in through their interfaces.

"How many lifts have you guys made?" he asked Rasul.

"Hundreds planet-wide, virtually all of them large industrial facilities – it doesn't make sense to move smaller structures. But this is no factory; parts of the imperial compound are over two thousand years old – it's like trying to transport a billion eggshells and hoping none of them break."

"Ten seconds to severance."

They watched an ancillary display that showed the underside of the Palace. The bedrock had been carved away so that entire structure now sat on a huge slab of granite, which in turn was supported by a matrix of columns, each circled by a thick red band of high explosives.

"Zero!"

The columns disappeared in a billow of rock dust that was quickly suppressed by inertial dampeners. As the clouds cleared they saw that each pillar had been cut. The Palace was now floating on air, supported by the giant push drives.

"Verifying structural integrity."

"In other words," said Rasul, "making sure the explosions didn't knock any bits off."

"Initiating ascent."

No-one in the room breathed as the Palace crept upwards. Through the windows the carved vertical edge of the support table came into view as the structure rose above the surrounding ground.

"Looking grea–" Carson began to say.

"Emergency systems halt."

Silence turned into a worried murmur as everyone searched around seeking an explanation. Carson earned his keep by politely blocking the path of two media reporters trying to invade the business end of the room to find out what had happened. They need not have bothered; one of the displays zoomed in to the edge of the channel that had been cut around the Palace. A superconducting cable stretched taut between the floating granite table and a massive portable Higgs engine located on the adjacent ground. The mobile recorder moved in closer. The cable had sheared as planned but somehow it had managed to wrap itself around one of the stanchions anchoring the engine to the bedrock.

The statue of Caelin came to life.

"Get a cutting crew out there," she bellowed.

But Aiyana was already moving.

"I'm on it boss!" she yelled as she ran across the floor.

"Honey, leave it to the crew," Carson shouted after her. If there was one thing he had learned in his long life it was never get too close to very large moving objects, especially when they were under non-human control. But it was no use; Aiyana was disappearing through the door. Carson swore and sprinted after her. By the time he got outside she was straddling the scooter.

"Come on," she cried, thinking that he wanted to join in the fun.

Carson climbed on behind her.

"Darling," he shouted in her ear as they zipped towards the Palace, "that cable has a monomolecular sheath – you don't have anything that could possibly cut it."

"Oh yes I do," she yelled over her shoulder.

They landed by the Higgs engine. Directly in front of them the edge of the granite table trembled five meters above the surrounding ground. Normally push drives were as silent as hunting birds, but the giant Wartsila-Sulzers engines howled. Carson winced at the thought of the titanic forces surrounding them.

Aiyana was fiddling with something she had pulled out from her flight suit; it was Renshu's plasma gun. A bolt of energy shot out from the weapon and splashed against the permafrost. They both jumped.

"Well that works, I'm setting it to maximum."

Carson realized there was no stopping her. His best plan was to help Aiyana cut the damn cable as quickly as possible and get the hell out. She knelt over the stanchion where the five centimeter-thick cable was trapped. Shielding her face with one arm she pointed the flaring handgun.

It actually seemed to be working. The black sheath glowed white, melted, and began to evaporate. By the time the gun flamed out only a centimeter-wide strip was left. Aiyana tossed the weapon aside, picked up a rock, and started pounding at the last scrap of super-strong material. Carson grabbed another and joined in. The final carbon threads began to fray, though it was due more to the enormous tension than their efforts.

"Any moment now," Aiyana said panting.

Carson ran his eyes along the cable.

"We've got to get out of the way!"

"Huh?"

As the last strands began to break Carson leapt forward and grabbed Aiyana. They both crashed to the ground as the cable snapped and whiplashed over their prone bodies. They struggled to their feet the Palace renewed its ascent.

The vertical face of the granite table crept upwards in front of them, the roar of the Wartsila-Sulzers increasing as they cleared the surrounding trench. Now they could see the hewn underside studded with broken columns and the giant drives flickering with blue Cherenkov radiation.

Push drives work by shoving against the very fabric of the universe, reaching down to the smallest of scales where gravity becomes a repulsive force. Normally, the only manifestation of their functioning is the generation of thrust, but here in the face of so much power it was different. For one brief moment Carson felt his mind turn inside out as the electrons in his brain tried to join the dance with the compactified dimensions. Then it was over as the rough-hewn table rose up into the sky.

They turned at the sound of a hatch banging open and saw three suited figures unloading a tool that would, no doubt, have sliced the cable in seconds. Seeing that they were too late the cutting crew stopped and joined them in watching the ascent. All of them stared in silence until the ragged outline disappeared into the clouds.

A small cheer went up when they got back to the operations complex but the center of attention was the main display; the three-dimensional image was continuing to track the Palace as it rose into the upper atmosphere. In the background they could see the curve of the world and above it, the deep black of space. Sunlight danced off the gabled roofs and highlighted a confection of columns, cornices, piazzas, turrets, pillars, and statues. Amazingly, the Imperial pennants still flapped in the near vacuum.

"Nice touch," someone explained, "built-in actuators".

A shoal of craft spiraled down from the mesosphere like the corps de ballet greeting the principal dancer.

"System integration with interplanetary escort... preparing for handover... transfer of control completed."

The whole room erupted with cheering.

Caelin leapt up from her consol.

"That's a wrap. Terrific job everyone."

She strode through the crowd shaking hands. Finally she got across the room.

"Our hero!" she said to Aiyana and seizing her by the scruff of the neck kissed her hard on the mouth.

She slapped Carson on the back.

"Good work! One whole hero is definitely better than two halves."

"Thanks," he said, "although Aiyana, darling, you should have left it to the professionals."

"Oh spank me!" she cried.

Caelin raised an eyebrow and exchanged a smile with Carson.

Rasul pushed through the crowd.

"Hey you three, come on over. The King wants to meet you."

Gustav the Eighth, surrounded by a cloud of courtiers, was the picture of calm civility. He was a tall, pale man, and apart from his immaculate clothes the only unusual thing about him were the ghosts of old dueling scars on both cheeks.

Caelin was introduced first.

"Senior Operative Caelin," he said, "we are delighted to meet you. Congratulations on your splendid effort."

"Thank you sir," she replied, giving him a crisp handshake and assuming parade rest.

"It was an honor to work on lifting the Palace. A couple of last minute glitches but otherwise a smooth project."

"Ah yes, the cable. Engineer Aiyana, thank you for your quick initiative. We were thrilled!"

Aiyana simpered. Gustav turned to Carson.

"And Commonwealth Mail Carrier Carson, we understand you made a timely delivery of funding from New Earth."

"I'm glad to have helped sir but to be honest we had no idea any of this was happening until we arrived."

"Yes, it has all been so sudden. Still, we are all united in our efforts. Orpheus must and will survive."

He turned to Caelin.

"We trust you will take a pause in your work to celebrate."

"Absolutely sir."

She raised her voice to the general crowd.

"First round's on me, everyone!"

The King also spoke up.

"We must invoke royal precedence. Today's festivities will be financed by the Imperial Privy Purse."

That invoked the second biggest cheer of the day. Workstations were thrown into automatic and soon everyone was pouring out of the operations center.

"And we think we will join you," Gustav added.

A courtier leaned in.

"Sir, you have a meeting with the Prime Minister in thirty minutes."

"Then you should not delay in notifying her that we will be late," the King replied without turning his head.

The group stepped outside. As they crossed the frigid ground Carson darted off to where the scooter was parked and came trotting back with four bottles.

"I thought we'd be celebrating today so I packed these."

He handed one bottle to the Gustav.

"Good grief, Wurlington Brown! Our grandfather used to drink this. We never expected to see it again."

As they entered the commissary a cluster of panes overhead transmuted themselves into an image of the Royal Seal.

"We hosted countless garden parties in this tent," the king said. "Now it serves a more practical function, as do we all."

They sat down at a large table where they were joined by some of the local bigwigs. Carson popped open two bottles of the venerable beer and poured a round.

"This takes one back," Gustav said. "When we were a boy our grandfather would let us have a taste from his goblet. What a unique flavor!"

"It puts hair on your chest," Aiyana chimed in, invoking a splutter from Caelin.

"Alas, the royal cellar is much depleted," Gustav said. "We sold most of the classic vintages to help raise money for the lift."

The King's comment aroused the dealer in Carson.

"I imagine that the Imperial household must have acquired some fascinating pieces over the centuries."

"Indeed – many of our ancestors were connoisseurs of the fine arts. The Palace was a veritable treasure house but now most of the artifacts reside in the Huan Federation as collateral on loans."

"Oh God, you had to hock everything?" Aiyana shouted.

The King laughed.

"That would be a concise way of describing our predicament. We understand our collection is to be housed in a splendid new wing of the Federation Museum of Art. That is fitting, as we may finally have to sell."

"In addition to being a mailman sir, I collect antiques, and I would advise you to be very cautious in any transactions."

In other words they'll rob you blind Carson added to himself.

"I would be happy to send you a list of dealers on New Earth who can be trusted to help you get a fair price, should it come to a sale."

"That would be helpful. At least the Huan people created a thorough catalog. Perhaps you would like to see it."

Gustav raised his hand and a courtier magically appeared holding a recorder that he placed in front the monarch. The King touched the device and a three dimensional image of the Palace materialized on the table; the viewpoint zoomed inside to a spacious room filled with artwork and antiques.

Carson spotted a small device in the corner.

"That's a Manning diamond laminator – over three thousand years old but as far as I can see still in excellent condition."

"Indeed it is," said the King. "As a boy, we played a game with our brother of laminating the most unlikely objects. We once stole the toast from the breakfast table and the next morning my grandfather sat down a rack of diamond-encrusted slices."

"May I?"

Gustav nodded and Carson placed his hand on the recorder. Information about the laminator flowed through his palm.

"This item is seriously undervalued. The estimate says five hundred thousand Ecus, but a working model should go for three times that. In fact, Manning Industries still exists; they have a museum of their equipment at their headquarters on New Mars. I bet they would pay at least two million to add it to their collection."

"Good grief! To think of all those hours we spent playing with the thing. It makes one wonder whether any of our old toys could be valuable."

Carson scanned the recorder.

"I can't find any mention of them…"

"Oh, we have countless boxes of toys in the royal storage rooms. The Huan people never bothered to catalog them."

Carson leant forward, trying not to drool on the table.

"Sir, antique toys are terribly fashionable. Frankly, your collection could be worth a great deal of money. I strongly advise you to hire an independent evaluator."

He turned his attention to the image of the Palace. The viewpoint swooped to a large ornate room lined with paintings.

"This is the Hall of Ancestors," Gustav said.

Fascinated, Carson studied the pictures. He half expected to find another message from Samuelson, neatly framed and backlit, hanging on the wall, but all he saw was a procession of stern portraits. He stopped in front of a painting of an elaborately dressed man who carried a noticeable resemblance to the King.

"The catalog entry says *'Portrait of Gustav IV, artist unknown. Estimated value thirty thousand Ecus.'* In reality this work is by Vanuka."

"Really? How can you be sure?"

"Trust me, sir: the composition, the use of color, the way light models the subject, I'm sure. But you can confirm it. Vanuka liked to work the pigment with his fingers and any good forensic system should be able to extract enough genetic material to give a positive identification. He specialized in still life so this portrait is very rare. I'd estimate its value to be at least thirty million."

"Good gracious! My dear Carson, would you by any chance be interested in the position of Curator of the Royal Collection?"

"Sir, you have no idea how much I would love that job, although right now I have other priorities. But if you give me a copy of the catalog I'd be happy to check as much as possible before I leave."

"You are most kind." Gustav held up his right hand. "Here is our private address. Send us your findings." They touched palms. "So if we may inquire, what is keeping you so busy?"

Carson glanced around. Caelin had long since excused herself and had gone to join the crew's revelry; Aiyana too had wandered off the moment the catalog appeared. Meantime Rasul was deep in conversation at the other end of the table. He moved closer to the King.

"When I was last on New Earth I did some research that suggested that a cache of colonial era artifacts may be located somewhere on Orpheus. I plan to conduct a search."

"Good luck, but we fear your treasure may be buried under the glaciers. Best to return in a hundred years."

"The ice age will be over that quickly?"

"It will be if we can help it." Gustav looked down the table. "Everyone seems to have deserted us. Treasurer Rasul, can you describe the Reclamation Project for our visitor?"

Rasul moved over to join them, and went on to describe the strategy to reverse the effects of the temperature drop. The reduction of the sun's output was bottoming out he explained, but it would remain at that level for several thousand years.

"So we have to warm up Orpheus artificially."

The plan was to create a series of artificial volcanoes by blowing holes in the planet's crust. Initially the volcanic dust in the atmosphere would lower the temperature even further, but once settled it would decrease the reflectivity of the snowpack and hence aid the absorption of heat.

"But the principal benefit will come from the volcanic release of stupendous quantities of carbon dioxide gas, creating what the ancients called a *greenhouse effect.*"

"Sounds kind of tricky," said Carson. "Suppose you get too much and you end up like Old Earth?"

"I know, that's one reason we wanted to evacuate first. Still, we've already done a proof of concept. Last year we created our first artificial volcano, although we played safe by using a remote island in the southern ocean as a test site."

A small black hole materialized in Carson's stomach.

"Where was that?" he croaked.

"You will never have heard of it, a place called Lanzor. It was perfect – it is, or was, an extinct volcano so it required less explosive force. And oh did it work! The whole island is spewing lava and ash."

Carson sighed to himself, perhaps one day things would be easy. *Oh well*, he thought, *if the cache has been destroyed at least it stops Juro getting hold of it.* And it was not as if they were returning home empty handed.

A courtier leaned in and whispered to Gustav. The King nodded.

"The Prime Minister is becoming anxious. We are afraid that we should depart."

Everyone stood up.

"Will you be leaving the planet now that the Palace has gone?" Carson asked.

"Not yet, we intend to be the last person to leave Orpheus, and the first to return."

Without appearing to do so the King had raised his voice so that people in the vicinity heard his words. Carson saw many of them smile and nod. There's something to be said for hereditary monarchy, he mused, Gustav really was a born leader.

He made his farewells and went to search out Aiyana. Finally he found her standing at the bar.

"Where's Caelin?"

"Asleep in her cabin, she's been working non-stop for days."

As they trudged to the scooter Carson recounted Lanzor's fiery demise.

"Let's check it out tomorrow, but I'm note hopeful."

Aiyana climbed stiffly onto the scooter.

"Ouch!" she yelled as she sat down.

"Are you all right honey?"

"Oh, me? Sure, why wouldn't I be? Hey come on, let's get to the camp before it gets any colder."

Carson smiled to himself but said nothing as they zipped through the frigid night air.

"Well there it is."

They were in the buggy looking down at the island of Lanzor from an altitude of ten thousand meters. Directly in front of them a three kilometer-wide column of smoke and ash rose into the stratosphere. As the little craft flew lower they could see rivers of larva flowing down the outer slopes of the crater while explosions continued to spew fresh volleys of rock into the sky.

"Let's go," Carson said. "Nothing has survived down there."

They flew back in silence, both of them staring out at the empty ocean.

Eventually Aiyana said, "is it worth checking out the other locations?"

Carson shook his head.

"Rasul supplied me with up-to-date satellite imagery. All the other potential sites are under the ice. As the King said: *return in a hundred years.*"

The deserted metropolis came into view. The Palace had been replaced by a raw gash in the earth. Piece by piece the city was being eaten away.

"Aren't you worried about Tabarak finding us again?" Aiyana asked as they spiraled down to the abandoned office block where they had made their camp.

"Not so much. He got lucky on Falk, there was just one point of entry – the consulate – so it was easy to locate us; in this system we could be anywhere. And things may be chaotic but it's still a technically advanced society – he can't throw his weight around as he did last time.

"Besides," he added warming to the subject, "he may not come here at all. Remember I told him that we'd already visited Orpheus and didn't find anything. He probably didn't believe me but once he sees the ice caps he may decide I was telling the truth. If that happens he'll bust out of here and head straight for Mirama."

The buggy flew directly into the huge office atrium. Carson and Aiyana climbed out and began packing up the camp.

"Welcome back," said the image of the woman in the improbable summer dress. "We are so pleased to have you visit us again."

"It's kind of sad" Aiyana said. "All these systems humming away trying to sell property that's underneath a glacier."

"I tried to cheer them up while you were out yesterday," said the buggy. "I told them I represented a wealthy client who wanted a custom-built home. We spec'd out a beautiful villa, and you should see the garage I designed for myself."

They finished breaking camp and were soon heading into space.

"Did I tell you that Caelin asked me to stay in the Orpheus system?" Aiyana said.

"Why am I not surprised?"

"Don't be silly. She told me that with all the new immigrants there's a huge building boom going on in the Belt. She's thinking of starting her own company and my expertise would be useful. We'd go prospecting – nickel-iron asteroids, that sort of thing. It could be fun, searching for treasure out there in the void."

They both stared at each other as they realized what she had just said. Carson laughed out loud.

"If I get any more stupid I'm putting the portable stove in charge."

"I'll see if I can raise her," Aiyana said as she opened a channel.

"Aiyana! You've changed your mind."

"Sorry Caelin, no, but I do have a question for you. Where can we lease really powerful phase-array radar? The type that could be used to locate small objects in cometary orbit."

THE ARRAY

"You Aiyana?"

"No, I'm Carson."

"The contract says Aiyana."

Carson sighed and opened a private channel.

"Honey, come and talk this dumb machine."

They were back on the ship. Two days earlier, on Caelin's advice, they had interrupted their return journey to stop at Diotima in the Belt to arrange the lease of deep scanning radar. The asteroid was an elliptical chunk of rock one hundred and fifty kilometers long.

"What's that on the far end?" Carson asked Aiyana as the buggy approached the planetoid. "It almost seems like a polar cap."

"It is – standard way of storing water. At one time it was probably a Kuiper Belt object; I bet they just jammed it on the pointed end to stop it drifting away."

Aiyana was enjoying herself. This was her natural element and for once she was the expert.

It was clear that Diotima had been heavily developed; less than half the surface still showed the original raw rock and many of the large craters had been enclosed by transparent domes.

"Hey, that's where the Palace is going, though Caelin said it will be weeks before it arrives – they daren't move it too quickly."

Instead of landing on the outer surface they headed to the south pole where they found a huge circular opening capped by a shimmering blue inertial field. As the little craft pushed through the restraining membrane it announced that they were in a pressured oxygen-nitrogen environment. They had entered a kilometer-wide tunnel hewn from the axis of the little world. Running perfectly straight, it converged to a vanishing point in the remote distance.

The interior was an endless series of concentric rings interspersed with circles of pure white light that illuminated the whole interior. Everywhere the surface seethed with people and vehicles. Each ring appeared to have a separate function. Immediately next to the opening giant docks unloaded freight while further down were storage facilities, repair shops, production plants, administration buildings, and even some recreation areas. Every few seconds a transport emerged from one of the countless side-tunnels, shot down the bore and disappeared into another opening.

The buggy landed on a quay labeled *Vertical Ascent Shaft 48A.* As they clambered out a local field gently pushed them to the ground so that they were standing upright on the tunnel's surface with their heads pointing towards the axis.

"This feels kind of weird," Aiyana said, "I suppose that this close to the center real gravity is too weak to have any effect."

They walked over to a twenty meter-wide side-tunnel, which from their orientation appeared as a large hole in the floor of the quay. Without a moment's hesitation Aiyana walked off the edge. Carson followed her and squawked as they were immediately flipped upside down. Now the shaft towered above their heads.

"Kamal Prospecting," Aiyana said and they were shot vertically up.

As they travelled the view flashed between bare rock face and synthetic caverns, some of them huge; it seemed that the entire planetoid was a three-dimensional maze. At one point they found themselves going past layer after layer of green fields that stretched into the distance.

"Vertically farming," Aiyana explained. "Ground-up asteroid rock makes a pretty good growing medium."

"Why not just synthesize all the food?" Carson asked.

She pulled a face. "Would you eat the portable stove's cooking your entire life?"

Their ascent finally slowed to a stop. The peristaltic field pushed them into the entrance of a large plaza where they gently settled to the polished floor – this far from the axis the gravitational pull was enough to be serviceable. Fifty meters above them Carson could make out a ceiling of hewn rock studded with lights and conduits.

"Can you see where it is?" he asked as he checked out the shops and offices surrounding the open space.

Aiyana flexed her knees and jumped thirty meters into the air.

"Over there!" she yelled, pointing as she gradually descended.

Carson grinned – ultra-low gravity was going to take some getting used to. A cheerful man wearing a helmetless environment suit bounced over to meet them as they entered.

"I'm Mudil, welcome to Kamal Prospecting. Caelin tells me you want to rent an array."

For the next hour Carson took a back seat and let Mudil and Aiyana put together the specifications for a system that could, in theory, find something as small as the storage units left by the Yongding in the vastness of space.

"The radar arrays are modular," Aiyana told him, "so in theory they can assemble one as big as we like."

A long technical discussion ensued that Carson could not follow. Finally, the design was agreed and he joined the conversation.

"How much?"

"Bad time to be leasing, we have lots of demand..."

"So how much?"

"Twenty-five thousand a day."

"Ouch, ouch, ouch!"

"That's with a four day minimum, twenty percent in advance."

Carson groaned and began bargaining. Mudil would not budge on the price but did finally agree to throw in a free fifth day.

"It will be ready in forty-eight hours," he said. "All I need now is the deposit and the rendezvous coordinates."

"The irony is," Carson said to Aiyana as they returned down the shaft, "we're carrying cargo worth untold billions and I'm getting worked up about a lousy hundred thousand."

"I just wish there was some way I could help but I left Mita with nothing."

He kissed her.

"I know, not even the clothes on your back."

But there was a way for Aiyana to improve his mood. Once they were in the buggy and heading to the ship she persuaded Carson to show her the Huan inventory of the Palace. Within minutes he was pointing out all the treasures that the Museum had missed and ended up spending the entire journey annotating the catalog.

Carson continued to work on the inventory for the next two days while Aiyana, Tallis, and the ship formulated the optimum search strategy for the array. Eventually he forced himself to stop, packaged up the results, and sent off his findings to the King's private address.

"He should be happy, I reckon I've found him at least another two hundred million, and I haven't even seen his toy collection."

"Nest-mates, my outriders have identified a large spacecraft approaching."

"Large?"

"Very large indeed."

The array had arrived.

"Now that's what I call a piece of hardware!" exalted Aiyana as she examined the image floating in the center of the cabin.

Tallis had not exaggerated – the array was twice the size of the ship. It consisted of ten obsidian squares, each twenty meters across, joined together in a straight line. Behind the squares was a collection of push drives, Higgs engines, superconducting cable, logic arrays, and all the attendant paraphernalia required to make the deep space radar work.

"So you Aiyana? I need some identification."

She placed her right hand in a console's green circle and shot her genome across the vacuum.

"Okay, so what's the job?"

"Not so fast, first I want to see your specifications and maintenance data."

Aiyana studied the information as it flowed in.

"Why are only nine units calibrated?"

"Tenth is a spare."

"And if you have a systems failure you will need it. I want it properly calibrated in the next hour or I'm flushing you straight down the gravity well."

"Alright lady, no need to give me a hard time."

"Damned if I'm taking attitude from a machine," she muttered to Carson.

Thirty minutes later the array was fully functional. Aiyana told it about the storage modules.

"We're expecting to find maybe twenty to thirty of them, almost certainly linked together."

"Got any images?"

No, Aiyana explained, we can do better than that. She and Tallis had devised a dry run for the array. The day before the buggy had taken one of the empty units that they had found on Mirama and deposited it in the empty void. Now she challenged the array to find it.

They watched fascinated as the giant machine slid apart, separating into its ten primary components. One, the spare, remained behind while the other nine shot off, each powered by its own push drive. Eventually they halted in a three by three formation, forming a square thirty thousand kilometers wide. Then, working in precise synchronization, the array began searching the sky with an eye the size of a planet.

"Multiple baseline interferometry, that's how it gets the incredible resolution." Aiyana said.

"That's great, but what worries me is that the array's signal is like a huge beacon saying *'Hey Tabarak, here we are!'* I just hope he's been and gone."

"Perhaps he's prospecting as well."

"Not a chance. All their equipment and expertize is with Shin. I'm certain his orders are simply to steal whatever we found." *And to kill us* Carson added to himself.

Tallis and had been thinking along similar lines. She announced that she was deploying a second set of outriders so that they could follow the search while maintaining vigilance around the ship.

"Found it," the array said. The unmistakable image of the target module floated in the cabin.

"Whoopee!" Aiyana yelled. "We're in business."

The strategy was straightforward: simply sweep out a circle with a five billion kilometer radius around Orpheus's sun. The array estimated that its resolution could detect the modules within a hundred million kilometers of its location, so it was effectively searching a toroid two hundred million kilometers thick.

"I'll feed you hits up to twice that distance," it said, "but some are going to be false positives."

Circumnavigating a thirty-one billion kilometer circle in five days required travelling at a quarter of the speed of light. The array had never performed a search at such high velocity and it needed the ship's help to calculate the Fourier analysis for the incoming signals.

"It's big but it's not very bright," the ship said.

The first hit occurred within hours and Carson and Aiyana stayed glued to the displays as Tallis's fleet rushed off the check the find. Eventually an image appeared of an odd collection of rocks floating in the void.

Carson was livid.

"I mean, what the hell are they doing this far out?"

The search went on. After the initial fiasco the array agreed to send the raw data along with its analysis of the hits. This enabled the ship to run its own confirmation before sending in the fleet.

At the end of the day the ship jumped forward six billion kilometers to keep pace with the hunt. The second day passed without incident. On the third day the array scored a hit at the very limits of its search envelope. The ship's algorithms were unable to settle the matter and Tallis sent out of her craft. After six hours of flight they found a garbage dump, presumably tossed out by a passing vessel.

"Goddam vandals! I'm going to bed."

Carson drifted away, muttering to himself.

Four hours later, while they were in the depths of sleep, rosy light suffused the cabin. Gentle chimes sounded. It was the ship's standard way of waking up the crew.

"What the… what time is it?"

"It's the middle of the night. Sorry to wake you guys but I think we've found it."

By the time they were dressed the ship had coffee brewing in the galley. Tallis, who never slept, had already re-directed her fleet.

"We are very hopeful that it is the storage modules nest-mates. The radar image is a near-perfect match!"

"Are you both properly awake yet?" the ship asked.

"Sure, why?"

"Because there's more to the story. I can't be certain at this distance but it appears as if another ship is already there."

"Oh God, the bastards have beaten us to it."

It was seven hours later. They were floating in the main cabin examining an image sent by a member of Tallis's fleet. The tiny vessel had come to a halt two hundred kilometers from its target, recorded the scene, then scuttled back beyond detection range before transmitting its finding. The array picked up the faint signal – they were two light hours away – and relayed it to the ship.

There was no doubt – it was the storage modules left in orbit by the Yongding eight thousand years ago – but beside them floated another spacecraft.

"That's an interplanetary shuttle, so where's Tabarak's starship?"

Carson had a bright idea.

"Hey, array, you must be able to spot an interstellar vessel from a hell of a distance. Do you see anything?"

The huge machine was over a billion kilometers away and it took an infuriatingly long time for the reply to come through.

"Right, a starship's shell will show up clear across the solar system. I'll know more later but so far I can tell you there's nothing within a light hour."

Tabarak appeared to be acting as cautiously as they were. Carson told the ship to move closer.

"The array makes a great lookout. At least we'll see them coming."

Tallis's vessel went in for a second time. Nothing appeared to have changed.

"I don't like this. Why aren't they loading the modules? Is it a trap?"

There was nothing to do but get closer still. Eventually they rendezvoused with the array twenty million kilometers away from the orbiting storage modules. The ship kept its shell of charged black holes just below maximum spin level, ready for a getaway at a moment's notice.

Tallis directed one of her tiny spacecraft to get really close. As it approached the mystery deepened.

"That doesn't look like any clan Aniko ship that I've ever seen," Aiyana said.

Their spy was now within a kilometer of the modules but there was still no sign of it having been spotted. Carson leaned forward and stared at the image.

"Oh God," he whispered, "It's a wreck."

As Tallis's craft moved in they could see that the mystery vessel had been breached, its interior gaping open to the vacuum of space.

"The destruction is not a new event," Tallis said. "The temperature of the vessel is just four degrees Kelvin; it has achieved thermal equilibrium with surrounding space."

Carson could wait no longer. "Let's suit-up and check it out for ourselves."

They climbed into the buggy and slipped cautiously along the ship's axis. With the shell's space-time maelstrom close to critical and any deviation in their trajectory would be catastrophic.

The little vessel emerged into the open vacuum. Seen from a distance of five billion kilometers Orpheus's sun was no more than a splinter of blue-white light floating among the stars. The modules and the wrecked spacecraft lay directly ahead. At two hundred meters they clambered out of the cabin and floated forward, Tallis's fleet surrounding them like a cloud of hornets.

Only the sound of their breathing broke the silence of the desolate scene. Carson counted thirty-two linked storage modules silhouetted against the glow of the Milky Way. He amped-up his vision. Most of the modules appeared to be in perfect condition, although the last unit in the string, the one nearest the mysterious spacecraft, had been caught in the cataclysm.

The doomed vessel was a stubby ovoid about fifteen meters long. Attached to its sides was an assortment of drilling tools, grapplers, and sampling equipment – all the paraphernalia of a prospector. As they drew closer they could make out a comet-shaped logo on the side; beneath it were the words *Lopez Cometary Resources.*

They entered the craft through the meter-wide split in its hull. Aiyana turned on her suit lights and promptly let out a scream – she was facing the mummified body of a woman, her dead eyes staring blankly at the stars. The miner was still clutching a coffee mug; death must have been instantaneous.

Carson peered at the corpse. It was riddled with small puncture wounds.

"Had to be some kind of meteor strike," he said. "It burst the hull open and sprayed the crew with fragments."

He turned to Aiyana and took her arm with his gloved hand.

"She died straight away. Probably never knew what happened."

"But every ship protects itself against strikes. They would have been an inertial field, close-range radar, rapid-fire defenses – how could a meteor have gotten through?"

"Tallis's tug managed to destroy the observation platform. I guess it's just a matter of speed. Come on, we'd better look around."

They found two more crew, both men, neither wearing an environment suit. One appeared to have been asleep in his bunk, the other slumped over a consol. Carson overcame his misgivings and cut a sample of hair from one of the bodies.

"We'll carbon-date it when we get to the ship; that will give us an accurate timeline," he said; judging from the state of the bodies the wreck was not a recent event.

They slipped outside the stricken spacecraft and examined the storage modules. None had been forced open, reinforcing Carson's hunch that the meteor struck soon after the miners arrived on the scene. Only the unit closest to the ship had been caught in the blast. Half of the casing had been blown away spewing the contents – assuming there had been any – across the heavens.

Tallis recorded the scene with her high-definition cameras and then they set about checking the modules' contents. As before, gamma rays were used to image each unit's interior without the necessity of forcing it open. All but two resolved to be crammed with supplies – an overwhelming amount of treasure. They should have been elated but the stricken vessel cast a pall over the discovery.

The buggy started ferrying the containers to the ship, but to Aiyana's surprise Carson left eight full modules tethered to the miners' spacecraft.

"I'm sending the location to the King's private address," he told her. "Prices for high-end antiques are notoriously difficult to estimate, but I'll guarantee that the contents of those eight will pay off Orpheus's debts with enough left over to finance the reclamation of the planet."

She gave him a clumsy hug in her environment suit.

"Darling, that's so kind!"

Eventually all the transported modules were stowed on the outside of the ship's hull. They had been in a vacuum at close to absolute zero for eight thousand years, Carson explained; the last thing he wanted to do was warm them up in an oxygen-rich atmosphere.

When they returned to the ship Tallis asked to examine the miner's hair sample. Carson took it to the conservatory and sat down on the grass.

Two workers crawled onto his hand and played their feelers over the strands.

"This tastes old. We would estimate five hundred standard years. The man had not bathed for several days and he ate a meal of synthetic lamb a few hours before dying."

"Good God! You can work out all that from hair that's spent centuries in a vacuum?" Carson shook his head in amazement and thought about Tallis's blind world where every object told its story through taste and smell. No wonder it had taken the human race so long to learn how to communicate with the tiny creatures.

He went into the main cabin and ran the sample through carbon dating.

"Tallis was spot on: the miners died five hundred and twenty years ago. Tabarak had nothing to do with this."

Carson composed a message to the King telling him of the storage modules and their discovery of the ancient tragedy. He suggested that instead of privately selling the treasure trove Orpheus should offer the Huan Federation a swap: the modules and their contents in exchange for debt forgiveness, the return of the royal collection, and a substantial cash payment.

"I my opinion sir, this is a better option than the open market: the Federation will house the artifacts in its new museum for the enjoyment of all its citizens. They have been itching to get their hands on an Old Earth collection and you will garner the goodwill of one of the most powerful alliances in the galaxy."

"Won't the New Earth Archivists be mad?" Aiyana asked.

"Oh please, the poor things. Now they're only getting thirty-three modules stuffed with priceless treasure."

He completed his message and sent it over to the array.

"Can you shoot this down to Orpheus?"

"So now I'm a mailman? Yeah, sure. Also, I got one for you."

Carson winced. It was the invoice from Kamal Prospecting, but instead of a demand for payment the statement showed a zero balance. It was accompanied by a message bearing the seal of the Keeper of the Imperial Privy Purse.

"I am commanded by his majesty to inform you that in recognition of your services in cataloging the Palace's household, your expenses will be met out of royal funds. His Highness wishes to offer you his gracious goodwill for your ongoing journey."

"That guy Gustav is one class act."

It was time to send the array on its way. Aiyana formally signed off on the contact and they watched the huge system re-assemble itself into a single entity.

"Here's my card," it said. "Give me a call if you do any more prospecting."

And with that the machine shot sunward, down the gravity well.

"So when are you guys going to read it?" the ship asked.

"The letter from the King? We just did."

"No, I mean this."

A ghostly shape appeared in the cabin: the gamma ray image of the first empty module. Affixed to the inside surface was a faint rectangle. It was another message from Samuelson.

The leader of the Techs began as before.

The fact that you are reading this message proves that the people of New Earth have succeeded in building another starship...

Further on, it began to differ from the earlier messages:

We have taken little from this supply dump, having replenished ourselves at Mirama and Falk. I doubt you are interested in what remains, except perhaps as curios.

However, the contents of the last unit are totally different. The module contains a complete copy of the Bi Sheng Repository that is in orbit around Saturn's largest moon, Titan. It was created to ensure that a permanent record of the human race's greatest intellectual achievements would survive even when Earth itself ceased to exist. In retrospect it was a far-sighted decision.

The Repository was designed to last more than a billion years and I pray that it has survived the Melt, but the fate of the original need not concern you for it is represented here in its entirety. It contains Earth's greatest storehouses of knowledge and art: the National Libraries of Greater China and India, the Library of the New Congress; the British Museum; the Bibliotheque Universel of the United States of Europe, and many others.

We have taken our own copy of the unit's contents and have left the module for you, our brothers and sisters.

The message ended like the other two:

Perhaps in the far future our descendants will meet again. Until that day, I wish you well.

November 30, 2148

After he finished reading the ancient message Carson drifted around the cabin for a long time, staring at nothing in particular. Finally he caught Aiyana's gaze and managed a weak smile.

"Good God, the whole insane venture finally makes sense. No wonder Juro was willing to do anything to get at the Yongding's treasure."

He retrieved the sole existent image of the ancient starship, so familiar and so strange. *How little we knew* he thought.

"It's something totally unique, isn't it? I mean, there's almost nothing left of Old Earth's culture."

"Just the Book and the stuff Teng captured in his recordings. And now this – it's like discovering a gold nugget the size of a star."

It was obvious how the old man would cash in, Carson said. Unlike the antiques, which would have to be dribbled onto the market for decades to maintain their sky-high prices, the Repository could instantaneously be turned into a stupendous amount of money.

"Can you imagine? Every school, every museum, every library in the galaxy would pay a fortune for a copy. Media companies could slice and dice the contents and sell it to the public. How much would you be willing to pay for the story of Old Earth – ten Ecus, a hundred, a thousand? Now multiply that by a trillion."

"And then," Carson added, "he would use all that money to finance his crazy rebellion."

"I don't understand – why didn't the New Earth colonists have their own copy? I've never even heard of the Bi Sheng Repository. Did you know it existed?"

Carson shook his head.

"No, and neither does anyone else. This has come out of nowhere."

Aiyana sighed. "But it was in the module that was destroyed by the meteor strike. Perhaps it's just as well, at least Juro will never steal it."

"Yeah, maybe," said Carson and again fell silent.

By now he was convinced that Sakyamuni had talked about the Repository on the third tape, the one Juro had never let him hear. Would the old man stop at anything to retrieve such a prize?

Aiyana decided to leave him alone and spent the following hours preparing for the long return voyage to New Earth. In the meantime Carson told the ship to activate the Alcubierre Drive and jump to another location in the Orpheus system. He did not explain why until they sat down for a meal at the galley table.

"Honey," he began, taking her hands, "do you think you and Caelin could make a go of it? Prospecting in the asteroid belt, I mean. Tallis could join you as well."

"What, are you dumping me?" she shouted.

He grinned, leant across the table, and kissed her.

"No my darling, I'm trying to keep you alive." He lowered his eyes and added almost inaudibly, "I'm going to recover the Repository."

"But it's destroyed..." Aiyana began to say, her voice trailing off as she realized what he meant.

"You would go to Old Earth?" she whispered.

"Back to the solar system at least. I wouldn't have to get any closer than Saturn."

"But the Melt..."

"I doubt that it ever spread to the outer solar system, the temperature is too low. But that's just part of the problem." He looked her in the eye again. "Going there is a capital offense. It has to be – imagine if someone went there and got contaminated – the Melt would get out."

"So if you go and the Commonwealth finds out they will annihilate your personality?"

Carson nodded.

"Aiyana, I know it's a crazy risk but I can't begin to describe what it would mean to recover the Repository. The human race is like an orphan who knows nothing about its parents or where it comes from. We are a unique species in the galaxy, maybe in the whole damn universe, yet we don't know our own story."

"I am over eight hundred years old," he said, blinking away tears. "I've had a wonderful life, and now I think I have found something worth dying for."

Aiyana circled the table and took him in her arms.

"And what was my life like before I met you? No Mister Mailman, we're doing this together."

"How about you Tallis?" she cried.

"What a wonderful path we are following. Let us enter the dark secret places of the forest together."

"Not that anyone's asking," said the ship, "but I'm in as well."

That broke the tension. They laughed, hugged, and kissed.

"There is an incredible amount to think about," Aiyana said.

"Ain't that the truth" said Carson. "Job one is inventing the greatest fake provenance in the history of antiquing. We will need a convincing story about how we found the Repository."

"I can't believe we're going to Sol. Imagine – we'll be the first people in eight thousand years to see Old Earth."

Carson smiled and marveled at Aiyana's spirit, but it was difficult to hide his sense of dread. Nanotech devices reproduced at extraordinary speed – many times a second according to the archives. How many generations was that since the destruction of the Earth? Could the Melt have evolved, and if so what had it become?

And there was another thing. The module holding a copy of the Repository had orbited Orpheus undisturbed for thousands of years, only to be destroyed the moment it was discovered. He shuddered and thought of his vision in Lilly Cathedral.

Something was coming.

Sol

AIYANA SAT AT THE GALLEY TABLE DABBING HER EYES. CARSON, SEATED OPPOSITE, reached out, squeezed her hand, and poured two glasses of brandy. Aiyana gulped hers down and started crying again.

They had been listening to the voices of the last human beings trapped in the solar system. Captured by the colonists on New Earth eight thousand years ago, Carson did not know the recordings existed until he gained full access to the Archives. The Commonwealth had decided that they were too distressing to be released to the general public.

The basic story of the Melt was learnt by every child. Simple nanotechnology had been in use on Earth for over a century, but the glittering prize was a self-reproducing nanotech device. Just as a tree grows from a tiny seed, an invisibly small nanobot could, in theory, make enough copies of itself to build a house, a power plant, an entire city using nothing but atoms as raw material. Unlimited wealth beckoned.

But somewhere in the western section of the Asian landmass – a region called Europe – an experiment had got out of control. Instead of building a precise, controlled structure, a nanotech device had begun endlessly reproducing itself using the atoms of whatever material was around – its container, the laboratory, and the bodies of the researcher workers.

Such a disaster had long been anticipated, and all self-replicating nanobots had a failsafe that halted production after a limited number of generations. Whether the safety mechanism had been sidestepped or the system had somehow mutated would never be known. Regardless of the cause, the result was immediate and devastating. Within days a two kilometer-wide area had been transformed into a seething, formless sludge of furiously reproducing nanomachines. A desperate attempt to sterilize the site was made using a primitive explosive device called a *nuclear bomb*.

At first the drastic act appeared to have succeeded but the explosion blasted a few surviving nanobots, smaller than bacteria, into the stratospheric winds of the upper atmosphere. Within weeks outbreaks were occurring around the globe. Horribly, living tissue with its abundant atoms of nitrogen, carbon, and oxygen proved to be an ideal source of raw material for the microscopic machines. Recklessly, *nuclear bombs* were used again, each time stopping the immediate infection while ultimately spreading it still further.

In the final act the Melt accelerated and began spreading across the face of the entire Earth. This was the moment when Adhiambo Cissokho, watching from the Chu Jung Orbital Facility, had crammed every willing human being into the Yongding and fled the system.

"That's where the official story ends," said Carson. "What's rarely mentioned is the fate of the people living off-planet. There were thousands in orbit, and small colonies on the Moon and Mars, plus some research stations in the outer solar system."

The orbiting sites were the first to go. By now most of the landmass below had been transformed into a featureless sea as the Melt, having destroyed all life, began to eat the earth itself. Somehow spores reached up into the vacuum, possibly propelled by the *nuclear bombs*. More explosions occurred in orbit as power systems became unstable, scattering the nano-devices still further.

Forty-six days later the Moon succumbed. The absence of carbon in the crust initially slowed the spread but again the Melt adapted and within weeks Earth's satellite was once more a dead world.

Mars took much longer to die. Fearful that they would share the Moon's fate the colonists desperately sent out messages for help. They knew it would be ten years before their radio signals reached the Eridani system but hoped that the Yongding had returned to the edge of the solar system and would hear their cries.

For three years they begged for rescue, then the moment they dreaded arrived.

'Oh God, the observation satellites are showing something strange on Mons Olympus..."

'The Melt is spreading across the Tharsis plateau. Why don't you hear us, why don't you come?'

'Please please save us. There are more than three hundred people stranded here, twenty-two children. Please don't let us die, please...'

But, terrified that the plague would be carried to New Earth, the Yongding never returned.

The last survivors in the solar system were six scientists living in a research station on Callisto, the outermost of Jupiter's giant moons. The Melt never reached them but their lonely outpost was not meant to be self-sustaining and finally the supplies run out. Having witnessed the fate of the Martian colony they had no illusions about being rescued, but for five years, true to their calling, they continued to dispatch their observations.

They sent out one last message:

'All the food has gone. We are disabling the fusion reactor's safety mechanisms and then we will trigger it to go critical. It will be over in milliseconds. This is a matter of no importance. Thirteen billion people have already died – what do another six matter?'

'The Melt appears to have stopped in the inner planets and we pray that it never spreads beyond the solar system. We hope with all our hearts that the people who fled in the Yongding have survived and that the human race continues. Even so, you were right not to return. Learn from this terrible tragedy, never let it happen again.'

"We did learn, didn't we?" Aiyana said to Carson as he poured another round. "I mean the Covenant has protected us all these years..."

"Yes honey, we learned. It's easy for people like Juro to sneer and say that we've been too cautious, but God knows what might have happened if we'd started experimenting again. The Melt is the ultimate anti-life, the exact opposite of a harmonious ecosystem. It's like an ancient disease called *cancer* but a trillion times worse."

"Do you think the Techs kept developing nanotechnology?"

"Yeah, I guess so," Carson said rubbing his face. "Hopefully they learned too, at least to be incredibly cautious. Or maybe they didn't, and there's another planet thousands of light years away that's just a big blob of nanomachines."

He cast around for something to take Aiyana's mind off the recordings.

"Hey Tallis, how's our fake Repository?"

"We have made excellent progress nest-mates. Come and experience it for yourselves."

"Great idea."

"Oh God, that's perfect!" Aiyana cried.

They were standing in Tallis's improvised workroom. In front of them was one of the empty storage modules plucked from cometary orbit. It was so well preserved they had been able to power it up and open it without forcing an entry. Now the interior contained row after row of dense black arrays. As they watched twelve of Tallis's workers crawled up the sides and inserted another cuboid unit.

"This is what we think the module holding the Repository was like," Carson said.

"We found traces of the memory medium on the inside surface of the container struck by the meteor," Tallis explained.

"Interestingly, it's a nano-device." Seeing Aiyana's alarm Carson added, "don't worry, there's no self-replication involved. Tallis was able to duplicate it using standard manufacturing techniques."

"It is a ferrous nanoparticle shuttle."

"Oh that explains everything!" Aiyana said.

Carson laughed.

"Sorry, too much jargon. The basic component is an incredibly tiny particle of iron – no more than a few dozen atoms – that's magnetically pushed to and fro along a hollow carbon nanotube. It stores binary numbers: one end of the tube signifies zero, the other end one."

"You're kidding!"

"I know what you mean. It's one of those crazy ancient machines that actually worked, like *rocket engines*, and physically it's extraordinarily stable; as Samuelson said, it was built to last a billion years."

"So when we find the real Repository we'll transfer the data to our fake and say we found it in orbit around Orpheus"

"Roger that, just practice saying it with a straight face."

"YOU ARE ENTERING AN ABSOLUTE EXCLUSION ZONE!"

"DO NOT APPROACH! YOUR VESSEL WILL BE DESTROYED"

"UNDER AUTHORITY OF THE COMMONWEALTH SECURITY CODE THE PENALTY FOR PENETRATING THE SOLAR SYSTEM IS TOTAL PERSONALITY RECONSTRUCTION"

"I don't think they want us to come any closer," Aiyana said with a smile.

They had stopped for a navigation fix half a light year from Sol. The moment the ship launched its periscope it picked up a tsunami of warnings beamed from the monitoring stations that surrounded the solar system.

"It's nothing personal," said Carson, "those messages are transmitted on an endless loop; they have no idea we're here. The main purpose of the outposts is not so much to prevent people getting in, but to make damn sure nothing gets out."

"The theoretical limit to the spread of the Melt is the Heliopause," the ship said

A translucent raindrop shape encompassing a schematic of the solar system materialized in the cabin, the Sun glowing at its center.

"It's the boundary where the pressure from the interstellar medium matches the outward pressure of the solar wind, so even the lightest particle can go no further."

"We're approaching the leading edge," Carson said. "Thank God it exists, otherwise the Melt might have drifted all the way to New Earth."

"But all the time we're inside we could encounter a nanobot and get infected"

"Yeah, ain't that a lovely thought?"

"If you say so darling," said Aiyana. "But the Melt didn't spread beyond Mars. You said it was too cold in the outer system."

"So it's thought. Nano machines use ratchet turbines to extract energy from the random movement of molecules. So lower temperatures mean less power for the little critters."

"I'm getting worried by how much you know about this stuff."

"Believe me honey, it wasn't easy. As long as the Covenant exists they'll never be a manual called *'Build Your Own Nano Device.'* Me and the ship had to puzzle it out. I just pray we got it right."

"I've got our position," the ship said. "We can go any time you like."

Aiyana floated up behind Carson, circled her arms around his waist and rested her chin on his shoulder. She stared at the glowing image of the Heliopause.

"Next time we stop we'll be inside" she whispered.

"What happened to the buggy?" Carson yelled. "It looks like it's caught some ghastly ancient disease."

It was twelve hours later. The ship had announced their arrival in the solar system and everyone was waiting for shell spin-down so that the periscope could be launched. In the interim they had gone to the shuttle bay to see how Aiyana and Tallis had tackled the problem of recovering the Repository without getting infected

"So what are all those black spots?"

"They're uni-directional inertial field generators."

"And you complain about my jargon!"

"Each generator creates a field that pushes outward, away from the buggy, like a clean room maintaining a higher atmospheric pressure than its surroundings. Any nanobot floating in the vicinity will simply get shoved out of the way without touching."

"Very smart, and we need to be fast; the longer we stay the greater the chance of contamination."

"Periscope launching in three minutes," said the ship.

They hurried to the control room.

"Oh my God!" they shouted in unison as they floated in.

On the main display was an image of Saturn. They were three million kilometers away and slightly above the equatorial plane. From their vantage point the planet appeared as a gigantic yellow crescent bifurcated by its ring system.

"The rings seem so *solid*," Aiyana said. "I feel I could just grab them and send them skimming across space."

"Yeah, pretty amazing, and right our own back yard."

"Where is it?" Aiyana asked the ship.

"Where's what?"

"You know."

The view panned away from Saturn until the flare of the solar corona appeared at the edge of the display, then it zoomed forward. A brown dot materialized out the void. Aiyana floated forward and gently touched the screen. Carson followed her and laid his hand on hers. The birthplace of the human race glowed between their fingers.

"Poor thing, it used to be blue."

"I've deployed the interferometer; want to take a closer look?" The ship said.

A fuzzy circle replaced the image on the display.

"Hold on a moment."

Both of them cried out as the Earth snapped into focus. The image resembled a topographic map where everything – oceans, atmosphere, rivers and forests – had been stripped away to reveal the shape of the bare rock. The harsh outlines of mountains and mid-ocean ridges scarred the surface. The picture moved in closer and panned across a large continent.

"You can even see the remains of a city," the ship said as the image paused at the eastern edge of the landmass.

It was right: the faint outlines of streets ran between shapeless mounds. Deprived of most of its atmosphere, the world's mummified face would stare into space for a billion years.

Sobbing, Aiyana buried her face in her hands.

"Turn it off," Carson said.

They floated through the darkened cabin in silence.

"Are the nanobots still alive – I mean active?" Aiyana finally said.

"Damn good point – what does a self-replicating system do when there's nothing but copies of itself around?"

"Cannibalism is my guess," said the ship.

Carson pictured what would happen to a naïve traveller landing on the surface. He would be consumed within seconds. The horror of the Melt reached across eight thousand years.

"Come on," he said. "Let's find that Repository and go home."

"It would help if we knew what it looked like," said Aiyana.

They were examining an image of Titan. Mimicking its parent, the satellite appeared as an orange crescent glowing in the distant sunlight. Behind it, the impossible grooved plain of Saturn's rings curved to infinity.

"There can't be much in orbit around it – maybe the hulks of a few research satellites, possibly some small asteroids – and I reckon they did something to make it stand out."

"Well let's get going!"

"Honey," Carson said, "please don't get upset but I'm going out alone."

Aiyana tried to say something but Carson pressed on.

"The ship reckons we're safe in here protected by the shell. But suppose the worst happens out there and I get infected by the Melt. At least you and Tallis will be able to take everything we've found to New Earth."

"I thought we were in this together..."

"We are darling, but it's senseless to risk both our lives."

Before Aiyana could object Carson hurried off to the docking bay, pulling on his environment suit as he moved through the ship. Five minutes later he emerged from the shell's pole. To his right Saturn floated in surreal magnificence. Directly ahead Sol was a tiny blinding disk.

"Let's see how easy they made this," Carson said as the buggy accelerated towards Titan. He leaned forward as the image of the giant moon grew on the globular display. The Book offered just a hint of what lay under the opaque atmosphere, saying that the satellite was the only other body apart from Earth that had lakes and seas. But seas of what? The temperatures of the outer solar system ruled out water; perhaps it was methane.

He stared longingly Saturn's rings, a quarter of a million kilometers wide and no thicker than a sheet of pack ice. *God, I wish I had time to explore it all properly.*

Carson opened a channel to Aiyana.

"Hey, I think I just worked out why they left the Repository here. If you were a visitor to the solar system wouldn't you want to check out Saturn? And once you were in the vicinity you would say *'What is that wacky moon?'* and check out Titan. Then bam!"

"Very smart darling, so is the radar picking anything up?"

"Not so far," said the buggy.

Eventually it was a visual identification. At first it appeared to be a twinkling star, but that was an impossibility in the vacuum of space. As the buggy got closer it began picking up a faint radio signal.

"It's a large string of binary numbers, repeated every two seconds. Maybe the ship can puzzle it out," the buggy said.

The ship had no trouble decoding the message.

"It's a two-dimensional array. Here's a schematic."

A line drawing of the Saturn system appeared on the buggy's display. Titan was highlighted with a surrounding circle.

"Pretty smart diagram, although Tallis wouldn't have made much sense of it."

Carson guessed that the signal had originally been much stronger and designed to entice visitors into the solar system. The fact that it was still transmitting after eight thousand years was a tribute to the builders.

The buggy's display zoomed in on the twinkling object that was now only a few kilometers away. It could have been a seed designed to float away on the breeze. At its center was a red sphere from which sprouted a dozen long, thin solar arrays. Sunlight glanced off the shining surfaces as it tumbled through space. As he drew closer Carson could see that many of the arrays had deteriorated over the millennia, reducing power to the transmitter.

He came to a halt fifty meters away and sent an image to Aiyana.

"That explains the weak signal. Do you guys have any suggestions how to get at that red ball in the middle? That has to be the Repository, but I don't want to get clobbered by those sails."

"Sorry, all we can think of is that you're going to have to go out there and cut them away."

Carson swore to himself. Well at least he had put on his environment suit. He rooted around in the buggy's tool kit and pulled out a suitable tool, then, jamming on his helmet, he told the little vessel to open the hatch. For five seconds he poised like a diver waiting for an opening in the spinning arrays, then he leapt. He slammed into the red ball and desperately clung on while the universe whirled about him.

"Well I'm here," he said once he regained his breath.

"Say again..." Aiyana's voice was buried in static.

"I said I'm on the ball," Carson bellowed.

"Great! I think we're getting interference from a solar flare. I can hardly hear you."

Her voice vanished into a sea of white noise. Carson cursed and turned his attention to the solar arrays. He positioned the tool at the base of the nearest triangle and began cutting. The ancient material quickly dissolved and within moments the sail was floating away into space. Excellent! He moved on to the next one.

Back in the ship Aiyana threw up her hands in frustration. All communication with Carson had been overwhelmed by the storm.

"Don't worry," said the ship. "All he has to do is cut away the solar cells and maneuver the Repository onto the buggy. He'll be fine."

The ship was right but she was still relieved when she finally heard his voice.

"Aiyana, I'm approaching the ship now."

"Wow, terrific! That was a lot faster than we estimated. Have you finished the safety scan already?"

Tallis had built a horde of minute robots to crawl over the Repository searching for dormant nano devices. Aiyana assumed that after his excursion Carson had also submitted himself for examination.

"Yes, of course I have. I'm docking now."

A minute later he floated into the main cabin. Aiyana twisted round to greet him but before she could speak Tallis's voice came over a private channel.

"Aiyana, something does not smell right!"

The next moment the center of Carson's chest exploded as a plasma bolt drilled through his heart. Aiyana screamed as his convulsed body slammed into the cabin wall. The world turned red and she found herself paralyzed, drifting across the cabin. Through her blurred vision she saw Tabarak with another figure floating besides him.

"Don't worry my dear it was a clone, but it served its purpose" said Juro.

INVASION

CARSON FRETTED AS THE TALLIS'S ROBOTS CRAWLED OVER HIS ENVIRONMENT SUIT. Each was fitted with a minute scanning electron microscope; it was not foolproof, but if a dormant nanobot had attached itself to him – or more likely the Repository – there was an excellent chance they would be able to find and destroy it.

How long was this going to take? It had been two hours since he had last heard from Aiyana. Solar storms could last days but it surprised him that this one had blacked out communication so far from the Sun. He stared at the red sphere that was now attached to the buggy. Good God what a prize! In six days they would be returning in triumph to New Earth.

"Surface examination completed; zero foreign entities found" the robots finally announced. They scampered to their miniature hangar as Carson clambered into the buggy. Thirty minutes later he was approaching the ship.

Damn, he thought. *How the hell am I going to identify myself to the ship with all this interference?* The buggy edged towards the north pole of the shell. But the shimmering inertial field that normally capped the entrance was absent. The ship must have anticipated the problem and left the access open. *Thank God for intelligent machines!* Carson peeled off his environment suit as the buggy slid down the pole to its dock.

"I've got it!" he shouted pulling his way through the entrance hatch.

As he floated into the ship he caught a glimpse of two figures, then there was a flash and he spiraled into blackness.

"He's regaining consciousness."

Carson's eyes jerked open. He was tied to a supporting strut in the main cabin; two meters away Aiyana was bound to another column. In front of them floated Juro and Tabarak, both wearing helmetless environment suits. Crumpled in the corner was another man, apparently dead. It took Carson several seconds to realize that it was himself.

Juro drifted towards him.

"My dear boy, you may be a wonderfully predictable fool but you are also a most resourceful fool. The moment Tabarak informed me that Orpheus was covered in ice I knew that you would come to the solar system with some way of locating the Repository. All I had to do was await your arrival. And here you are with the treasure. Well done!"

Carson squinted at him; somehow he looked different.

"You're younger..."

The roots of Juro's hair were black and his skin had a healthier sheen. His voice too was firmer and he was moving with more confidence.

"Correct, the role of senior elder is no longer required and I will need my full vigor for what lies ahead."

"What a fascinating collection you have." He turned to Tabarak, his tone becoming sharper. "Turn off the radio interference and check that no-one else is aboard."

The big man consulted a portable scanner.

"I'm registering another biomass."

Pulling out a handgun he shot off through the hatch. Juro floated over to admire the Gandrian tapestry.

"Are you okay honey?" Carson asked Aiyana. She nodded but she appeared terrified. *That makes two of us.*

"Carson" said ship, "I am so sorry. They had your genome, your voice..."

"Yes," said Juro over his shoulder. "I thought the clone would be useful. And ship, I know you have been fitted with higher functionality, but if you try anything clever be aware that I will immediately kill your owner and his companion."

Tabarak came into the cabin.

"It's nothing," he sneered, "just some kind of ridiculous flower garden."

"How delightful," Juro chortled. He floated over to face Carson. "What a unique vessel! I wish I had more time to enjoy it but it is time to get down to business. While you were unconscious we examined the Repository. It contains a dense carbon array, no doubt an ancient data storage mechanism. How exactly does it work?"

"I have no idea – I only just found the damn thing."

"True, but we also found one of the Yongding's storage lockers packed with an identical material. You have gained prior knowledge. A most resourceful fool!"

"You don't need me, your technicians can work it out."

"Of course, but time is... pressing."

That news cheered Carson.

"Someone's on to you, aren't they? Did Kalidas come to his senses?"

Juro waved a hand.

"They will be too late. Besides, Kalidas is no longer with us. An unfortunate accident; he tripped and was knocked out in his clean room. Sadly he suffocated in the helium atmosphere – it was days before his body was discovered."

"So you're starting to tidy up, and that means less commission to pay. Will it be enough to buy your revolution against the Covenant?"

"My dear Carson are you really so stupid? Do you still believe this is about money?"

Tabarak was beginning to look agitated but Juro pressed on.

"Think about the contents of the Repository. It contains the totality of Old Earth's intellectual wealth including every textbook, every research paper, patents, dissertations, records of scientific conferences – the accumulated technical wisdom of the twenty-second century. Most of it primitive by our standards, but what did ancient man know that we do not?"

"Oh my God, you're dabbling with nanotechnology!"

"Precisely! The knowledge in the Repository will give us a tremendous boost. Instead of decades of trial and error, I am confident that we will be constructing self-replicating devices within months."

"You're mad to risk it, you've seen what the Melt did to the Earth."

Juro sighed, the teacher once again disappointed by his dimwitted student.

"Exactly, you idiot! Nanobots are the ultimate *weapon.* That is why my rejection of the Covenant will succeed when all others failed. We will establish a new order at Mita under my leadership. Any system that tries to interfere will face annihilation. In case anyone doubts me I shall use the Melt to set an example. New Earth is the obvious candidate."

"You would murder a billion people to set an *example*?"

"Why not? There are a millions of other planets in the galaxy."

But it would not stop there thought Carson. If New Earth were infected it would create the greatest stampede in history. Every starship in the system would flee, and inevitably some would carry the Melt with them. Then other systems would succumb and again everyone would run spreading the contagion still further. Eventually the entire galaxy would be nothing but a dead mass of nanobots.

"Juro..." Tabarak began.

"I know, we must press on. Carson, the details of the Repository's storage mechanism."

Carson glared at him. He would rather die than aid this lunatic.

"I'm sure your vessel's intelligence has the information."

"Go to hell," said the ship.

Juro took out a small handgun.

"Listen to me you insolent machine. You will tell me now or I will blow your owner's head off."

"Absolute override silence!" Carson shouted.

The ship could not speak again until he rescinded the command.

"Did you have to?" Juro sighed. "I hoped this would not be necessary"

He turned to Tabarak. The big man passed him a disposable breathing mask. Inserted into the base were two black cylinders. Carson's stomach lurched. It was a synthetic serotonin dispenser like the one the bar girl had demonstrated on Kaimana. She used it to create sexual excitement but this one had another purpose – to turn ordinary people into sadists.

"You're not using?" Juro asked Tabarak.

The big man laughed.

"No need"

Juro held the mask to his face, took three deep breaths, and tossed it aside.

"Ah, that's better. You found something suitable?"

Tabarak waved a small cylinder – it was Carson's antique soldering iron. He drifted towards Aiyana.

"Start with him," said Juro, "women are more resistant to pain."

"You're right," said Tabarak with a smile, "that's why she will be more fun!"

With that he tore open Aiyana's flight suit.

"Fuck you!" she screamed.

Juro chuckled. "Your command of Ancient English is exemplary my dear. Carry on Tabarak."

"Stop it," Carson shouted. "Call him off, you win."

Juro held up his hand. Tabarak gave him a sour look and retreated.

"If I tell you, do you swear that you will spare her?"

"You have my word."

Carson had zero faith in the promise but now he was playing for time. Behind Juro and Tabarak two black ribbons had appeared on the cabin's floor. Tallis was coming to do battle.

"It's a ferrous nanoparticle shuttle."

"And that means…"

Carson explained the technical details as slowly as possible as the advancing army crept into the room. Driven by the predatory instincts of the jungle the charge was led by scouts laying down scent trails for the others to follow. The flanks of the war columns were guarded by soldiers waving daggered mandibles while at the core countless thousands of workers followed. They were the smallest members of the nest and most could not expect to return, but on they marched. The nest would survive.

Juro was speaking again. "Thank you, that will save me several weeks."

"Incidentally, when I find that insect friend of yours I have a special surprise. I have obtained a specimen of *Myrmecophaga tridactyla*, commonly known as the giant anteater. I shall enjoy a glass of brandy while I watch her being eaten alive."

Carson was barely listening – by now the advancing phalanxes were in the center of the cabin. But the little creatures remained firmly anchored to the floor; they had no way of navigating zero gravity. He was frantically thinking of how he could help when miraculously the ants began to rise into the air. He held his breath; the ship was lifting them with an inertial field.

Juro turned to Tabarak.

"I believe we can spare some time for amusement." He nodded towards Aiyana. "Do what you like with the woman."

Grinning, the big man pulled out the soldering iron and reached for her body.

"Despoilers of the nest!"

"What the –"

As the two men turned round the ship hurled two balls of black fury in their faces. Screaming, they frenziedly slapped at the swarm as it invaded mouths, eyes, ears, and nostrils, stinging and biting everything it touched. Tabarak wrenched out his handgun as if he could somehow shoot his attackers. A beam of plasma scorched blindly across the cabin filling the air with the stench of ozone.

While the struggle continued a thin column of ants climbed to where Carson was tied. Within thirty seconds they had chewed through his bonds. Could Tallis finish them off? He had to make sure. He braced against the strut then launched himself toward Tabarak. As he charged the big man convulsed with pain, his flailing arm sending Carson crashing into a wall. Something whizzed past; it was the soldering iron. He plucked it out of the air, turned the setting to maximum, and again rushed Tabarak.

But as he struck the big man succumbed; no human being could withstand that amount of venom injected into its system. He thrashed like a fish on a hook then with a last terrible gurgle hung limply in the cabin. Unseeing eyes stared out of his swollen red face.

Carson ricocheted off the body screaming. During their collision dozens of Tallis's soldiers had embedded themselves in his hands, jaws biting in murderous frenzy. Still shouting with pain he desperately looked around. Where the hell was Juro?

The old man was not dead yet. Despite the agony he had managed to pull out a brandy flask. Now he was squirting fluid over his skin killing hundreds of ants. Carson flung himself off the wall. The two men smashed together and spun clawing through the cabin. As they struck the bulkhead Carson grabbed Juro's throat and smashed his head against the diamond-hard composite.

Juro kneed him in the groin.

"Tabarak!" he shouted. "Kill the bastard."

The next moment he saw his inert henchman.

"Do I have to do everything myself?"

He kicked off towards the drifting body, reaching out for the handgun. For once the old man had miscalculated. He had planned to snatch the weapon, spin round, and finish Carson for good. Instead he rammed Tabarak full on. There was an explosion of light as the weapon fired. Juro went limp, impaled on a spike of pure energy.

Carson finally stopped retching and cautiously approached the grisly scene. Juro and Tabarak floated in front of him, embraced in death.

"He should have spent more time in zero gee," Aiyana said.

He spun round.

"Oh my God, are you okay?"

Carson pushed over to the strut where Aiyana was secured and untied her. They held one another as Tallis's soldiers wandered through the carnage killing injured ants and carting the tiny corpses to the nest.

"You guys had better clean up too," said the ship.

"Hey," said Carson, "how come you can talk?"

"Oh please, I hacked that 'absolute override' nonsense decades ago."

Carson's laugh became louder and louder until it turned into sobbing. Aiyana hugged him for a while then towed him through the ship to the bedroom. She left him tucked in with a shot of tranquilizer. The ordeal had left her bone-achingly tired but there was still work to be done. Returning to the main cabin she put on her environment suit. After a quick survey she began hauling bodies through the airlock.

Finally Aiyana had all three corpses collected on the outside of the ship's hull. She paused while she caught her breath then lifted Tabarak's body. A kick to the groin launched it upwards. The big man's corpse rose into the vacuum, pulled by the gravitational attraction of the shell. At ten meters it began to accelerate and then in an intense flash vanished, every atom sucked into the micro black holes.

Juro went next. Finally she picked up the body of Carson's clone. Cradling his head in her arm she straightened his hair and wiped away a trickle of blood from his mouth. *Poor thing, he probably existed for only a few hours, just long enough to get Juro into the ship.* She straightened up and pushed the corpse into the void.

"Tallis, are you okay?" she asked as she re-entered the cabin.

"We are functioning, but we must attend to laying eggs to replace those that were lost"

"I'm so glad – you saved our lives."

"We saved all our lives, we are of one nest."

"I reckon you're right, may the nest always prosper."

She shook herself into alertness.

"Hey ship, can you think of any reason why we shouldn't get the hell out of here?"

"Sooner the better"

"Let's do it. Set of a course for New Earth"

Aiyana returned to the bedroom. Carson lay on the bed curled into a fetal ball. She pulled off her environment suit, climbed in beside him and snuggled against his back. Within minutes she too was asleep.

No-one spoke much the next day as they absorbed the trauma of Juro's invasion. Tallis's queen laid an enormous number of eggs that were carried off by workers to newly constructed nurseries. Meanwhile Carson, Aiyana, and the ship focused on the task of communicating with the Repository, glad to be immersed in the clean, logical world of physics. Fortunately its builders, eager to share the bounty of Earth's knowledge, had engraved the sphere with diagrams showing how to build an interface. After ten hours labor they triumphed.

"I can talk to it!" the ship announced.

The next vital step was a data dump.

"There's not much by modern standards – about a yottabyte – but I'm limited to the Repository's bandwidth. Once I've got a copy I can start sorting out the contents."

But Carson could not wait and he launched himself at the raw data as it flowed into the ship's memory. Most of it made no sense but occasionally he hit gold. That evening he appeared in the galley doorway.

But, soft! what light through yonder window breaks?
It is the east, and Juliet is the sun.
Arise, fair sun, and kill the envious moon,
Who is already sick and pale with grief,
That thou her maid art far more fair than she

"Oh that's beautiful! Did you make it up?"

"I wish, it was written by an Ancient called William Shakespeare. It's the screenplay for an entertainment called *Romeo and Juliet*."

"Is it funny?"

"Er, no, but let me tell you about this other one he wrote…"

The following morning began with a long shower.

"I love showering together," said Carson as Aiyana soaped his back.

"It saves water, and we rub each other, and…"

"I know darling, I know."

Eventually they emerged.

"Don't get dressed," Aiyana said. "Tallis has something planned for us in the Conservatory and I think it's best if we're not wearing clothes."

They were soon stretched out on the small patch of grass.

"Did you know that thousands of years ago people had patches of hair growing out of their bodies? And in the most unlikely places…"

"Do you mind? I haven't eaten breakfast."

Hundreds of Tallis's workers appeared around them.

"We must perform the ceremony of the joining."

Carson's eyes widened. As far as he knew only two other human beings had ever formally become members of a Callidus nest.

"You're right to do this naked," he said to Aiyana. "It's a bit like getting baptized."

He pulled over the branch of a rose tree and jammed a thorn into his thumb. Aiyana did the same then they laid their hands on the grass. Tallis's workers clambered over their skin and drank their blood. Soldiers followed them, each carry a tiny drop of pink gel that they deposited on their palms.

"Our turn," said Carson and they licked up the royal jelly.

"From this day forward we are one."

"We will always answer the call of the nest," they intoned.

"Excellent! We must celebrate by sipping jasmine nectar."

"Good idea Tallis, but we have our own nectar," Carson said.

He dived off, returning with two tall glasses and a grime-covered bottle.

"Have you ever heard of this stuff?" he asked Aiyana. "It's called *champagne* – it was made on Old Earth in a region of the USE called *France* but it was forgotten until Andouille founded New Bordeaux."

"Oh my God that's good!" Aiyana shouted as she took sip. "Where did you get it?"

"A farewell present from Gustav."

He raised his glass in a toast. "Here's to your queen Tallis – sorry, here's to *our* queen – and to all noble royalty!"

They drank as workers swarmed over the jasmine flowers.

In his eagerness to make an appropriate gesture Carson had forgotten about the consequences of early morning imbibing. Inevitably, the alcohol seized their libidos.

"Not here darling, you'll squash your nest-mates."

"Goodbye my beautiful giant grubs," Tallis called as they stumbled out of the Conservatory.

"Farewell, you six-legged sexpot!" Aiyana shouted back.

"This is getting too damn weird," Carson muttered as they crashed into the bedroom.

Three hours later they made a second attempt to start their day. While they had slept the ship had finished transferring the Repository and was busy organizing what it had found.

"It does have its own indexes but the metadata is passive – no active intelligence at all – so I'm building my own cognitive layers."

"How many books are there?"

"About a billion."

Carson clutched his head. Just one book, The Book, had survived the flight from Earth; it was the Archives most hallowed possession. Now there were a *billion*. The enormity of their find was just sinking in.

"That's just a small part; most of the data is other media. There are sound recordings, images, entertainments, and the like, but it takes more decoding."

As the ship revealed more and more Carson and Aiyana found they could not sleep. Later that evening they watched a production of *Romeo and Juliet*, both of them snuffling as the story unfolded.

"It was supposedly in three dimensions," the ship said, "but it was so primitive I rendered it as a flat image."

After that they viewed a celebration of the animal life of Earth; even at the end the planet had an extraordinary diversity of living creatures. The audio component was in an unknown language so they accompanied the show with the music of a singer called Umm Kulthum, *the Nightingale of the Nile.* Looking at the images of the long dead world and listening to the strange, hypnotic music was even sadder than the Shakespeare *play*. To cheer themselves up they watched a bawdy comedy called *Lysistrata*. It was written in another dead language but had been translated into Mandarin.

"Goodness!" Aiyana said, "I didn't know the Ancients were so rude."

"Yeah, and it's really, really old. The commentary says it was written in *Ancient Greece* two thousand years before the Melt. I don't think they even had nuclear fusion back then. My God, there is so much to learn. In a decade's time they'll be entire institutions dedicated to sorting through this stuff."

"Carson's College, catering to wealthy and impressionable young women."

"Sounds perfect to me. Come on, I think I can finally fall asleep."

Treasure continued to pour from the Repository. The Ancients had invented an ingenious method for storing copies of Earth's great paintings.

"They created a model of the surface," Aiyana explained. "Each data point – they took about billion per square centimeter – records not just the color and luminance but also its position in three dimensions, so brush-strokes can be reproduced."

Later that day she and Tallis modified a fabricator to recreate one of the millions of stored images.

"Isn't it beautiful? It's called *Woman with a Parasol* by an artist named Claude Monet."

Carson shook his head in wonder; the picture could have been painted yesterday. *How could we have lived without all this? And we came so close to losing it all.*

By now only two days remained before their arrival at New Earth. Tallis reverse-engineered the Repository's interface to create a way of loading its contents into their fake ancient data store.

"I hate to do it, but we will have to destroy the original before we arrive. We need a rock-solid alibi."

Another worry was the fate of Juro's starship. Carson assumed he had kept it at the edge of the solar system, waiting for them to arrive like a spider in its web.

"Suppose there were other crew aboard?" Aiyana asked.

"Yeah, I thought about that, but it wasn't Juro's style. This was a super-secret operation. Besides, if there were, once they realize the boss isn't returning they'll take off for the other side of the galaxy."

"And think about this," Carson said warming to the idea, "if any of New Earth's systems detected us entering the solar system they'll investigate and find Juro's abandoned starship. Case closed!"

The thought cheered him up. Either way he suspected that the uproar generated by the contents of the Repository would be so great it would be months before anyone took an interest in how it had been found; by that time the trail would be cold. *We're actually going to get away with this.*

He was reading the *Arabian Nights* when the ship pinged him.

"Some of the sensors in the shuttle bay are failing – maybe Juro damaged them with his fake buggy. Could you check it out?"

Carson pulled on his environment suit and pushed through the exterior hatch. The bay was little more than a tubular fold in the hull; one end opened to the vacuum while at the other the buggy nestled in its dock.

Nothing seemed out of order. He slid passed the little vessel and floated to the rear of the enclosure. The rear wall had a brown smear. What the hell was that? He moved closer. It seemed to be some kind of corrosion, but hull composite never corroded.

Then, as he watched, the stain spread. Small pieces flaked off, drifted to other areas of the hull, and began growing anew. Carson backed away, his mouth open with horror. It was the Melt.

THE ANGEL

CARSON STUMBLED THROUGH THE HATCH RIPPING OFF HIS ENVIRONMENT SUIT.

"Destroy it completely," he shouted stuffing it into an incinerator. "It's the goddam Melt! It must have been Juro; the madman didn't protect his shuttle."

"We will have to jettison part of the hull," the ship said. "Carson, locate the main connectors and..."

It was too late. On the outside where the temperature was just a few degrees above absolute zero the rogue nanobots could only reproduce at a snail's rate – they drew their power from the energy of the surrounding environment. But a few must have attached themselves to his environment suit and followed him into the main cabin. As he watched the contamination spread across the wall, structures crumbling wherever it touched.

Aiyana rushed into the cabin.

"What is it?"

"Get out!" Carson screamed. "We have to abandon the ship."

But they could not, the logical part of his brain told him. The Melt started in the shuttle bay. By now the buggy would be inoperative. Besides, where could they go in the depths of interstellar space?

He screamed again. A stain had appeared on the leg of Aiyana's flight suit. It grew as he watched. He pushed towards her then found his breath

297

seizing up. For a moment his vision blurred; when he refocused he discovered that he could no longer move. Helpless, he revolved through the cabin, finally colliding with the wall. All he could do was watch the ship dissolve around him. Aiyana floated two meters away. She too appeared paralyzed.

"**What is happening? My workers are dying!**" Tallis wailed.

"It is the Melt," the ship said calmly. "We believe it entered with Juro."

Well at least one of us isn't panicking he thought. *Not that it will do any good.*

Carson knew that he was a dead man – the Melt had undoubtedly entered his body. How long would it take? At least there was no pain. *The one mercy* it was called; as nerve-endings dissolved all feeling ceased.

He tried to look at Aiyana but he could not move his head. *Poor thing, to die so young.* After so long a life he could hardly complain, but to lose her, to lose Tallis and the ship... His vision began to blur again, filling the cabin with pearly light.

And the Repository. He felt like a vandal. For eight thousand years it had waited for someone to come, and then he arrived and within days the story of old Earth was annihilated.

But worse would follow. Eventually the Melt would consume the whole ship. Once the giant superconducting magnets that controlled the shell were destroyed the micro black holes would fly off into space, dropping a ball of nanobots into normal space-time just as the ship entered the Eridani system.

Juro had got his wish, or rather the Melt had, for Carson now had little doubt about who was in control. The old man's insane scheme to use nanotechnology as a weapon, his reckless flight to Sol; Juro thought he was the puppet master but in reality he was the puppet. Somehow the Melt had pulled the strings across the light years, and now it was free of its prison, free to eat a million worlds.

The light in the cabin continued to grow brighter. Carson squinted, a shape was appearing, coalescing into the form of a human being. *It's got into my brain. This is an hallucination; we are travelling at superluminal speed, nothing could have entered the ship.*

Now the shape was quite solid. It appeared to be a humanoid – a tall, pale woman, long red hair rippling around her shoulders as if she were underwater. She was naked, but in a strangely sexless way, like a statue;

And she was singing.

Più docile io sono, e dico di sì.
Ah, tutti contenti saremo così.

Carson recognized the music; it was from an entertainment called *The Marriage of Figaro* that he had found in the Repository just the day before.

I am kinder: I will say Yes.
Then let us all be happy.

The song came at the end of the *opera*, a moment of peace when all conflict had been resolved, and it was possibly the most divine thing he had ever heard. The light intensified as the angelic figure raised her arms.

"Blessings to you dear ship, loyal servant," she said.

Now the light was so intense it hurt his eyes.

"Great Queen, save us from the horror!" It was Tallis's voice.

The light dimmed. The Angel opened her hands. Countless intense points of light burst from the upturned palms like a blizzard caught in searchlights. One floated by Carson's face. It was a perfect miniature of the humanoid, no taller than a centimeter. It spun about and took off in the direction of the Conservatory.

"Blessings to you dear Tallis, tireless mother."

What language was she speaking? The voice was high-pitched and musical, and although the words were understandable, they slipped and slided in his mind.

"Carson," said the ship, "something extraordinary is happening."

No kidding, said some part of his dying brain. *It can't be long now,* he thought, the Melt would be burrowing into the bowels of the vessel. The life-support systems would fail very soon, although they would be dead before that happened.

As gracefully as any amoeba, the Angel slid into two.

"Blessings to you, brave, strong Aiyana," said one of the figures as she floated towards her.

The other approached Carson. The closer it got the less human it appeared. The skin was the surface of a star; beneath its glowing surface was energy, complexity, and power.

He could see every detail of the flowing hair, somehow the strands had *meaning*, as delicate and precise as polynomial equations.

"Blessings to you dear Carson, may your search never end."

Now the face was only centimeters away from his. Carson peered into the eyes and saw that they were not eyes – they were worlds. It was the Earth of ten thousand years ago, a nourishing blue sphere overflowing with life; if he looked closely enough he would see every creature on the planet.

Looking at the face that was not a face he knew that everything could be understood; he could join the Angel in *Anandatandava*, the blissful dance, the dance of life, the dance of all that is possible.

Carson summoned the last of his strength.

"Are you God?" he whispered.

The Angel smiled and for a moment became more human.

"God is love," she said, and kissed him.

Unable to see, Carson felt himself rushing upwards.

"There are gifts," said the Angel's voice, and then everything was silent.

Salt water rushed into his mouth as a wave broke over his head. Carson choked, spat, and started swimming. He pulled himself up and tried to look above the waves, squinting against sunlight broken into a million shards. The water was turbulent but deliciously warm; overhead was a thin smear of cirrus clouds tracking across an azure sky. He was naked, alone in an ocean.

What the hell?

Spinning round he could see a dark landmass on the horizon, too distant to reveal any detail, but fifty meters away was an immensely reassuring sight: the buggy bobbing on its floatation tanks. Was he really alone? He lurched upwards again slapping seawater from his face.

"Hey, over here!"

Aiyana no more than ten meters away. Carson let out a whoop and splashed through the waves to where she was swimming. They clutched each other, his mouth finding hers, and kissed for what seemed a lifetime treading water in the unknown sea. He knew if he lived for another thousand years he would never be happier than that moment, holding her secure and safe in his arms.

"What happened? Where are we?" she said.

"No idea – I think Juro slipped us some kind of hallucinogenic drug. I got this crazy idea that the ship was invaded by the Melt and some sort of angelic figure appeared."

"Me too!"

He frowned. Shared hallucinations? This was getting really weird.

"Are we on New Earth?" Aiyana asked.

"I don't think so, the sun doesn't seem right and I'm not getting any traffic on the Net."

"Let's ask the buggy."

But before they could return to the little vessel a streamlined craft sliced through the sky above them, losing altitude as it executed a wide turn. Finally it settled into the water nearby, the hatch peeling open to reveal a solitary figure.

"How did I know it would be you two?"

It was Officer Asima wearing her official black birthday suit. Carson jerked his head round and looked again at the island on the horizon; no wonder there was something familiar about it. They were on Kaimana. And it had stopped raining.

"People are simply calling it The Miracle," said Asima.

They were huddled inside the security craft's cabin, Carson and Aiyana wrapped in blankets from the emergency kit.

"Twenty-seven days ago Mita's output increased by two percent in the course of an hour. It was just enough to burn off the cloud layer. But a clear atmosphere loses more heat to outer space so the surface temperature has stayed the same. It's an extraordinary balancing act."

"And now you appear," she added, "this must be the month for miracles."

"Yeah, how did you find us?"

"Instinct – I received two simultaneous reports – one said a starship had mysteriously appeared in orbit around the planet and the other that there was an unknown shuttlecraft in the ocean. It just had to be you guys, strange things just happen around you."

Carson was beginning to think she was right. Starships do not go into orbit. Accelerating something as massive as a shell in regular space-time required titanic quantities of energy.

"We have a hell of a lot to talk about but first I must get to my buggy."

"Alright," Asima said cautiously, "but you are staying..."

"I promise. We've had more than enough dramatic exits."

The security officer maneuvered her vehicle next to the little craft so that Carson could jump through the open hatch. Inside he found two folded flight suits. Had they taken them off before going for a swim?

"When did we leave?" he asked.

"I have no idea. Sorry Carson, I seem to have had a complete systems failure; I booted up about twenty minutes ago. I'm running diagnostics right now."

He opened a channel to the ship but it was equally ignorant.

"Same for me –unprecedented systems loss – last thing I remember is we were en route to New Earth. But that was only six hours ago – how did we get here so fast?"

Carson blinked. *"Strange things just happen around you..."*

"But everything is okay, you're not physically compromised?"

"No damage, all my systems, the cargo – everything is fine – just this weird gap."

Tallis was still onboard in the Conservatory; she seemed reluctant to discuss the events before the blackout.

"The pupa has hatched," was all she would say.

He wanted to talk more but it would have to wait until there was no security officer hovering a few meters away.

"Return to the ship," he told the buggy. "I'll be in contact."

He grabbed the flight suits and leapt into Asima's hovering craft. The Security vessel lifted off and arced towards the distant island. Even from afar they could see the impact of the radical weather shift. The people of Kaimana were discovering the pleasures of seaside living and the beaches were dotted with picnickers, children playing, and sunbathers stretched out on the black sand.

"The biggest problem has been fresh water supplies," said Asima. "Until last month all the water we'd ever need just dropped out the sky. Now we're scrambling to build desalination plants."

"Is it permanent – the change to the sun I mean?" Aiyana asked.

"Who knows? We have a horde of astrophysicists trying to work out what happened, but so far Mita appears completely stable."

They flew into the interior through a circular gap in the shield that covered the crater.

"We had to open it up to prevent overheating. I suppose eventually we will remove it altogether."

Asima called ahead and reserved a suite at the Caldera View, the hotel where they had stayed what seemed a thousand years ago.

"Let's meet in the Commissioner's Office in the morning."

Carson and Aiyana exchanged glances. Seeing their expressions, Asima laughed.

"Relax, Zhou is in detention along with half her senior command. I'm Acting Commissioner."

"That's a hell of a promotion!"

"Not really – I'm sorry but I have not been completely honest with you. In truth I am an agent with the Commonwealth Security Special

Investigations Unit. Ten years ago we were asked by the Mitan government to check into allegations of corruption in their security force. I've been working undercover ever since."

Carson leaned forward.

"So if you knew Zhou was a crook why the hell did you tell her where we were really going?"

"We had to flush out the conspirators, and we did try to rescue you! You escaped from the Clan Aniko mansion just hours before we were due to raid it. We tried to locate you at the other systems but you always seemed to be one step ahead of us."

"Thanks! We nearly got killed!"

But Carson could not stay mad; he had a vision of the security agent chasing them like a worried mother following a pair of unruly children. And in the end what did it matter? He, Tallis, and Aiyana were alive and safe with a ship full of treasure.

Zhou's adjudication had not taken place Asima told them, but she would probably end up with a new personality – she was a key figure in the plot to take over Mita. Their plan was to precipitate a crisis as an excuse for declaring martial law. That would open a path for the creation of an emergency government with Juro at its head.

"What about Shin?"

Asima laughed.

"He hasn't stopped talking since we arrested him; it was his testimony that enabled us to roll up the conspiracy so quickly. Juro kept him out of the really dirty stuff – that's what Tabarak was for – so he'll get away with therapy and a few decades of community service."

The security vessel landed in front of the hotel.

"There's one question I have to ask before tomorrow," Asima said as they got up to leave. "Did you have another encounter with Juro after you left New Earth? He's disappeared."

"Juro's dead, Tabarak shot him" Carson replied using his best deadpan face. *Well technically it was true.*

Asima grimaced.

"I wondered how long it would take those two to fall out. And Tabarak?"

"Dead too," said Carson, adding in a moment of inspiration: "it was quite a fight."

"Tell me all about it tomorrow" Asima shouted as they climbed out her vehicle.

Just as soon as I finish making it up.

"So what are we going to tell…" Aiyana started saying as they walked into their suite.

"Not now darling!" Carson practically shouted.

He rolled his eyes around the room. Mitan Security had done a thorough job of bugging them once and he was not sure if the new regime had any more scruples.

Following a long afternoon of lovemaking and napping they treated themselves to an extravagant dinner in one of the hotel's restaurants. After all, they reasoned, Asima was picking up the tab and weren't they owed something? The sun had set by the time they stepped out to the sidewalk to enjoy the fresh air.

"Can you take us to the outside of the crater?" Carson asked a waiting taxi.

"No problem," the vehicle said. "You're the sixth fare today who's wanted to go to the beach."

"You from out of town?" it asked as they ascended into the night.

Carson grinned; like most Mitan tourists they were still wearing clothes. Without the camouflage of a birthday suit even Aiyana was reluctant to walk around naked.

"Thought so, I expect we'll be getting a lot more visitors with the new weather."

The taxi was right. Kaimana had done pretty well as a tourist destination with just diamond coral as an attraction. Now it was an island paradise. Carson stared down at the glowing city ringing the caldera. Within a few years parks, resorts, and vacation villas would cover the outer flanks. With a shudder he pictured Mita if Juro's coup had succeeded, its people crushed by a dictatorship hell-bent on declaring war with the rest of the galaxy.

"We want to find somewhere very private," he told the taxi.

"So did the last five," the machine said with a leer in its voice; beach sex was obviously the latest craze. It dropped them at an isolated cove on the western side of the island. Carson told it to return in an hour.

"I get it, just a quickie," the taxi said and shot upwards.

"Good choice." Aiyana said looking around – black cliffs surrounded them on three sides. "I can't imagine being spied on here."

"So what *are* we going to tell Asima?"

Carson had already plotted a believable story: Juro and Tabarak had hijacked them in cometary orbit around Orpheus where they found the Repository. Aiyana was tied and blindfolded when the fight broke out and had no idea what happened.

"Trust me – it's far safer if there is just one witness – no awkward contradictions. Let me do the lying, God knows I've had the practice."

"That will work, but what about the clan Aniko ship, wouldn't it still be in the Orpheus system?"

"It disappeared afterwards, presumably its crew decided to run."

"Say, you *are* good at this!"

Creating an alibi for Juro's disappearance was the easy part. The real puzzle was what had *really* happened.

"I would say it was all a hallucination if we weren't here on Kaimana. Somehow we travelled across thirteen light years more or less instantaneously. That's just not possible."

"And even more impossible," Carson added with a laugh, "is the Angel entering the ship and reversing the Melt. We were moving at seven hundred times the speed of light in an enclosed space-time continuum and yet something got in. I mean..."

He gave up with a shrug.

One of Kaimana's miniature moons was setting over the ocean, painting a line of silver across the water to the darkened beach. Aiyana tilted up her face to the glittering arch of the Milky Way. The atmosphere, washed by endless rain, was as translucent as quartz glass.

"Impossible for us, but what about something else?"

"Aliens?"

She shook her head.

"I can't imagine aliens being that interested in the human race's squabbles, but someone else might."

A sea breeze raised lines of goose bumps across Carson's flesh.

"The Techs?"

What would human beings be like after eight thousand years of uninhibited technological evolution; would they be human at all? Neither of them could imagine.

"Now we've seen them once, perhaps they'll visit again" Aiyana said with a small laugh.

Perhaps the Techs had been there all along, Carson thought, choosing only to intervene when the Melt threated to escape. Looking up at the sky he felt like a small boy in a very large universe.

"So many worlds..." he murmured.

On the ride to the hotel they talked about the reception they would receive on New Earth. They agreed that the Repository should be released into the data commons where it could be freely accessed by everyone, but the artifacts were a different matter.

"I'm going to ask the Archives for a finder's fee of six hundred million but I'll settle for three. That's a hundred million each for you, me, and Tallis."

"Oh good gracious!" Aiyana cried, trying to imagine so much money.

But that was just the start Carson said.

"We have another asset, one that is undisputedly our own. When this story breaks you and I will become very famous indeed, so the moment we hit New Earth we should hire the best agent we can find. The media distribution fees for our story will be colossal."

As the taxi dropped them outside the Caldera View Aiyana announced that she was spending the night with her old friend Papina.

"Huh? You're not coming back to the hotel?"

She looked at him askance.

"You never thought about me having friends, did you?"

Carson smiled.

"I guess not, we didn't exactly meet socially. Anyhow, you will be coming back in the morning?"

"Of course, we have to meet with Asima."

He did a slow shuffle on the sidewalk.

"I mean, I'd hate to lose you after all we've been through," he said, taking a sudden interest in his shoes. "I was hoping that you and I could, well..."

She took his face in her hands.

"Look at me Carson."

Still his eyes eluded her.

"*Look at me!*"

Carson stared into the wide almond eyes.

"You, yes *you* Mister Mailman saved my life. My soul was dying out there in the asteroid belt chasing rocks for a living. Do you really think I would abandon you now?"

"We saved each other."

Aiyana laughed.

"True enough! We damn near got killed a dozen times."

She stepped forward and gave him a long kiss. For a moment she stood holding his hands and smiling, then spun away and walked off down the boulevard. Carson stood watching to see whether she would glance back. Finally he sighed and headed into the hotel.

A small package was waiting on the coffee table in the suite. It was an envelope, just like the ones used to distribute mail on Falk, except this one bore no address. Puzzled, he pulled it open; inside was a white piece of paper with a green circle outlined at its center. He turned it over but the other side was blank. The function seemed obvious, although he had no idea how anyone could put a genome decoder into something so insubstantial.

He put the paper on the table and placed the tip of his right index finger in the center. Immediately the words *'One last journey'* formed and vanished again. Oh dear, was this some kind of hotel promotion?

There was no time for speculation. The outline transformed itself into a solid black spot that spread to the edges of the paper and kept on growing. In an instant it filled half the room. Carson yelped and leapt back. It was too late; the circle rushed forward and engulfed him.

"Unidentified starships, this is Commonwealth Security. Do not change orbit, identify yourselves immediately!"

He was on the ship. A cacophony of voices filled the cabin.

"This is Coastguard Command. Prepare to be boarded. Do not alter your course."

"Coastguard Command, we are launching eight squadrons."

"For God's sake man you are on an open channel. Activate encryption!"

"Hey ship," Carson yelled above the din "where the hell are we?"

"We are in circular orbit two thousand kilometers above New Earth, at an inclination of twenty degrees to the equator."

"Did I black out again? What happened? How did we get here?"

"You tell me. Thirty-eight seconds ago I was in orbit around Kaimana."

"Oh hell! There hasn't been a starship this close to New Earth in eight thousand years. They must be going crazy down there."

"This is United Media. Who are you? Where are you from? Let us tell your story."

"United Media, this is an emergency channel!"

"With respect, Coastguard Command, New Earth Security should be handling this incident."

"How are you doing Tallis?" Carson shouted.

"The Great Queen has spread her wings again."

"I think you're right, nest-mate."

"How many news feeds have got the story?" he asked the ship.

"Over two thousand at the last count, but it's growing exponentially."

Carson shook his head.

"I told Aiyana we'd be famous but this tops everything. By now everyone on New Earth must be watching."

He turned his attention to the pandemonium.

"We are prepared to make you a very attractive offer for an exclusive –"

"So help me United Media, if you don't get off this channel..."

"Coastguard, I repeat, Security should be –"

"Special tactics team locked and loaded."

"Encryption you idiot!"

A new voice came on-line.

"This is Jing-Wei, Chief of Staff to the First Secretary. I am taking over this operation as of now. United Media, shut up or face the consequences. Security and Coastguard, I want immediate integration with your systems. First order of business is the armada of unauthorized vessels heading towards the starships; under the power of Section Two of the Commonwealth Emergency Code you will override their pilots. Stop them and establish a security perimeter of three hundred kilometers. Absolutely no-one approaches any closer without my authority."

"I must protest..."

"Don't waste my time Coastguard Command, Admiral Sanjay has been fully briefed."

Carson grinned, he had met Jing-Wei once; she was a woman who took no prisoners.

Her voice returned.

"Unidentified ships – if you can hear me – please, our concern is for your safety and that of the general population. Do not attempt to maneuver. I will be in touch again momentarily."

The clamor subsided.

"Is this going to happen often?" the ship asked.

"God knows – wait, I don't think so. I received a message saying that there would be one last journey..."

"Starships, this Jing-Wei. We will be approaching each of you in unarmed civilian craft. We will not attempt to board without your permission. Again, we wish you no harm."

"Hey, what does she mean – *starships*?" said Carson. "Did some other poor devil get caught up in this?"

There was a pause.

"She's right," said the ship, "there's a large vessel one hundred kilometers up orbit from us. It seems to be inactive – no lights or identification – that's no surprise, I went into total security mode myself as soon as the jump happened."

"Can you get a visual?"

"Sort of, we're still on the night side, should be hitting the solar terminator any time now."

A darkened image appeared on the main display. What the hell was that? He was still trying to puzzle it out when the vessel burst into light as it crested the edge of the world. *What the...* For three seconds Carson stared at the display refusing to believe what he saw. Finally he shouted in astonishment; on the planet below a billion voices echoed his cry. Every human being in the galaxy would recognize the spacecraft that spun in the warm sunlight.

The Yongding had come home.

PROLOG AS EPILOG

ADHIAMBO CISSOKHO ACKNOWLEDGED THE WAVES OF THE COLONISTS AS SHE TRUDGED *through the settlement. She pulled her fur cloak around her small body. Was it her imagination or was this planet actually getting colder? She lifted her head and took in a deep breath of the pure air. A flock of meta-birds were heading home through the pale evening sky, their iridescent wings catching the last rays of sunlight. Cold or not it was a beautiful world.*

The buildings around her were a strange mix of prefabricated dwellings and homespun cabins. She much preferred the colony's own attempts at housing. The low roofs and wooden verandahs reminded her of her grandfather's home in Botswana and the countless afternoons she dozed in his rocking chair listening to the cattle bells, her schoolpad slipping from her lap. Well, that was all gone now, this was all they had.

New Earth! What an unimaginative name. Still, it had been chosen by a vote of the community. Best to let them have their way, at least in the little things. And the youngsters, bless them, were calling the moon Adhiambo.

What a joy it was to see the new generation, born under a new sun; but there would have to be so many more if they were to survive. Every fertile woman in the colony had taken an oath to bear at least six children. Cissokho bowed her head; their spirit was humbling.

Aaron Samuelson was waiting for her in the Assembly Hall. Constructed entirely of native trees it was the largest structure the colonists had built, capable of holding the entire community. The meeting was not due to start for another hour and they were alone. She smiled up at him as he bent down and kissed her cheek.

He had come from a caucus of the Technical Alliance and one glance of his face told her what had been decided.

"You are not going ratify the Covenant."

He nodded.

Cissokho looked into his eyes.

"Then you must go your own way."

"Do we have to? We agree with much of what you propose, if only you would –"

"No, we've discussed this a thousand times. It has to be complete and unanimous."

Samuelson sighed.

"Then I suppose we go. The southern continent is probably our best choice."

Her face became hard.

"You cannot stay on this planet."

"What? You want us to settle on New Mars?"

"No, you must find another system, as far away as possible. And," she added, "you must not come back."

Cissokho reached into her collar and pulled a silver chain over her head. Attached to it was a slim black logic stick. She put it into Samuelson's hand.

"This is the launch key for the Yongding. Take both shuttles, we will have no further use for them."

"You can't!" he spluttered. "You'll be stranded. What about the other supply dumps, the copy of the Repository?"

"Being marooned will prevent schism; by the time this society is capable of building a new starship the mold will have been set. You can have the supplies, take them all, we have enough, and as for the Repository, we are well rid of it. I intend this colony to become a singularity, the seed of a new life free of Earth's insane history."

Her voice became gentle again. "Aaron, these terrible events have given the human race the chance of a new beginning."

She reached up and touched his cheek.

"We will each build a better world. You and I will be Adam and Eve. Is it not fitting? We are both children of Africa, like the first ones."

She lowered her hand.

"But this time there will be two Edens."

"But to take the Yongding, the supplies..."

"We will survive, I promise you."

She closed his fingers around the launch key.

"Go now, leave tonight, the colony will awake to find you gone."

"We will never forget you," he said, tears running down his face. "And one day we will return."

Cissokho patted his hand and murmured like a mother comforting a fretting child. Then, saying no more, she turned and walked out of the Assembly Hall. For all her feelings of shame she knew she had done what was necessary; the community would believe that the Techs had stolen the starship and she would not correct them. Their anger would unite them around the adoption of the Covenant.

It had begun to snow and the chill made her wince. After a moment she straightened her back; it was important to set an example.

Samuelson stood at the entrance and watched her until she disappeared amongst the spiraling flakes. They never met again.

Made in the USA
San Bernardino, CA
09 February 2015